THE PENGUIN CLASSICS

FOUNDER EDITOR (1944–64): E. V. RIEU

EDITOR: *Betty Radice*

CARLO GOLDONI was born in Venice in 1707 and died in Paris in 1793; he was survived by his devoted wife, Nicoletta, whom he had married in 1736 in romantic circumstances. Until his marriage he led an adventurous, philandering life, writing unsuccessful tragedies, tragi-comedies and operatic libretti. It was not until he had failed to settle down as a lawyer and begun to write scenarios for a troupe of *commedia dell' arte* actors in Venice that he found the means to express his genius. He was a prolific writer, and with his comedies he reformed the Italian theatre. However, his great success was resented by rival playwrights, and after a particularly vicious public quarrel in 1762 he went to Paris to direct the Comedie Italienne; but there he was not so successful. When he was granted a royal pension he began writing in French his long and extremely interesting memoirs. The pension was stopped in 1792 and, when parliament was finally persuaded to renew it, Goldoni had died the day before.

FREDERICK DAVIES has translated twelve plays by Goldoni. Several of these have been presented throughout the United Kingdom, in most of the Commonwealth countries, and in the U.S.A. He visited Venice almost every year during the past fifteen years and his translations of Goldoni's plays have been included in an exhibition at Goldoni's house in Venice. He was recently elected to a Fellow Commonership at Churchill College, Cambridge, where he translated Goldoni's *Memoirs*.

Frederick Davies has also translated a number of plays by Molière and Labiche, and has written two novels for children.

Goldoni
FOUR COMEDIES

Translated and Introduced by
FREDERICK DAVIES

PENGUIN BOOKS

Penguin Books Ltd, Harmondsworth, Middlesex, England
Penguin Books, 625 Madison Avenue, New York, New York 10022, U.S.A.
Penguin Books Australia Ltd, Ringwood, Victoria, Australia
Penguin Books Canada Ltd, 2801 John Street, Markham, Ontario, Canada L3R 1B4
Penguin Books (N.Z.) Ltd, 182–190 Wairau Road, Auckland 10, New Zealand

—

Published in Penguin Books 1968
Reprinted 1982

—

—

Made and printed in Singapore by
Richard Clay (S.E.Asia) Pte Limited
Set in Monotype Garamond

Contents

Introduction

UNTIL recently Carlo Goldoni has been known outside Italy chiefly as the reformer of the *commedia dell'arte* and as the author of *The Servant of Two Masters*. The latter is one of his earliest plays and reveals little of his later achievements. While the former has tended to obscure his true stature as the first naturalistic playwright in the history of the drama.

The exact origins of the *commedia dell'arte* are unknown. Sometimes known as the Comedy of Masks or the Improvised Comedy, it flourished throughout Italy, chiefly in Venice and Naples, from the early Renaissance until the end of the seventeenth century. From Venice it spread all over Europe. By 1570 the Austrian and Bavarian Courts had their companies of resident *commedia dell'arte* actors. In 1577 a company settled in London, introducing to Shakespeare the clowns and fools he was to employ in his own plays. And in 1577 Henry III of France assembled in Paris the most famous of all the *commedia dell'arte* companies, the Gelosi. By 1645 this company was established in the Hotel du Petit Bourbon where Molière came to study acting under the *commedia dell'arte* actor, Tiberio Fiorilli. Molière learnt from the Italians how to construct his plays and how to perform them. Moreover he borrowed freely from them, using the *commedia dell'arte* types in his own plays.

In Italy however the *commedia dell'arte* continued to be regarded with supercilious scorn by the literary academies of critics and poetasters. To them it was merely something at which the common people roared with laughter. Yet this was the great strength of the *commedia dell'arte*. For in order to earn their living the *commedia dell'arte* actors had to become highly professional actors. *Commedia dell'arte* means professional comedy, artisan comedy, trade comedy. It was the name given it contemptuously by the academic actors of the Erudite comedy.

Commedia dell'arte was improvised. No written plays were used and the actors had no parts to learn off by heart. A short scenario was hung up in the Green Room. The actors checked their entrances and exits from this and then ran on the stage and extemporized. This was possible because the plots and the characters were conventional and familiar to the audiences. The characters in every play were the same, and the same actor played the same part in every play. The actors were usually masked and movement and gesture were stylised. The extemporized dialogue was interspersed with stock passages of repartee introduced to fit recurrent situations, the reaction of the audience or the inspiration of the moment. It was all vital, acrobatic and superbly theatrical.

By the end of the seventeenth century the masked characters had become fixed at four in number. There was Pantalone, the doddering old Venetian merchant in his red hose and long black cloak, good-hearted and shrewd. On his head is a skull cap. He has a pointed beard and long moustaches peep from under his mask. Pantalone is the first old man of the *commedia dell'arte*: a bachelor sometimes, more often a widower with an only daughter on whom he dotes. In his decadence he has become the senile shuffling fool of the Christmas pantomime, but to do him justice his name should be written 'Plant the Lion'. For he is the descendant of the Venetian citizens who once planted the lioned banner of St Mark throughout the Mediterranean.

The second masked character, and the second old man of the *commedia dell'arte*, is the Doctor in his wide-brimmed black hat, white collar and black academic gown. He is descended from the Doctors-of-law of Bologna University. He makes a vast parade of learning yet never speaks without uttering some pompous absurdity. He often has an only son named Lelio.

The third and fourth masks are the two 'zanni'. They are the two servants Arlecchino and Brighella. They both hail from Bergamo, hence their name 'zanni' which is a Bergamo dialect corruption of Giovanni or John: hence the English term 'silly John' or 'Zany'. Arlecchino is sprightly, nimble and ingenuous, forever being tricked by his roguish colleague Brighella. Arlecchino wears the tight-fitting suit of a country servant whose rags and tatters have been conventionalized into variegated triangles of red, green and yellow.

These four masked characters always spoke in Venetian dialect. The remaining characters did not wear masks and usually spoke in Italian, and usually were two pairs of young lovers, Florindo and Lelio, and Rosina and Rosaura.

By the end of the seventeenth century the *commedia dell'arte* was beginning to lose its vitality. The masked characters became rigid and stereotyped, their humour lost its Rabelaisian quality and became obscene. The man who was to give it its death-blow and cast its elements into a new mould had already been born.

Carlo Goldoni was born in Venice, in a four-storeyed palazzo at the corner of the Via Ca' Cent' Anni, on 25 February 1707. His grandfather had squandered the family fortune and his father had to earn his living as a physician, spending much of his son's childhood away from Venice attending to his practice in Perugia.

When he was eleven, Goldoni wrote a comedy which a lawyer-friend of the family refused to believe was the boy's own work. His mother sent it to his father in Perugia and it so pleased him that he had the young Carlo brought to Perugia and placed in the Jesuit school there.

Two years later his father moved to Chioggia near Venice and had Carlo put to school at Rimini. There at the age of fourteen he met some strolling players and found that they were moving on to Chioggia. He stowed away in their boat with twelve actors and actresses, a prompter, a stage-carpenter, a property man, four maids, two wet-nurses, children of all ages, dogs, cats, monkeys, parrots, pigeons and a pet lamb. From his account of this initiation into the bohemian life of the theatre, not the least of the attractions were the young actresses. From an early age Goldoni was unable to resist a pretty face.

From Chioggia his father sent him to the ecclesiastical college at Pavia from which he was expelled within a year for writing a dramatic satire on the college. For the next fifteen years he was continually on the move, constantly at the mercy of his rash escapades. At the age of twenty-five he managed at last to gain his law degree at Venice only to find that his face was too jovial to attract clients. He fled to Milan to avoid his creditors. War forced him back to Verona where in desperation he joined a group of strolling players and began to provide them with scenarios for their *commedia dell'arte* performances. For two years he wandered with them from town to town through northern Italy. Then, when he was twenty-nine years of age, they arrived in Genoa, where he saw a pretty girl sitting on the balcony of her house.

He immediately sought out her father, took him to a café, invited him to the theatre that evening, and by next day had arranged to marry his daughter. The night of his marriage he caught smallpox. In his autobiography he writes: 'Luckily it was not a dangerous attack and I did not become uglier than I was before.' He and his wife, 'the good Nicoletta' as he always refers to her, returned to Venice and for the next seven years he endeavoured to earn his living as a lawyer. Clients again were not numerous and in his spare time he wrote scenarios for a company of *commedia dell'arte* actors resident in Venice under the management of a man named Imer.

In 1743, at the age of thirty-six, Goldoni left Venice and set out with his wife for Tuscany, in order so he says to learn Tuscan. He settled in Pisa and set up practice there as a lawyer. Four years went by. It seemed there was to be no more writing of scenarios. And there probably would not have been but for a strange visitor who was shown into Lawyer Goldoni's study one day in 1747.

Goldoni describes the scene vividly in his autobiography. The strange visitor is enormously fat and tall. He has come on business. Doubtless, thinks Goldoni, some shopkeeper wanting to consult him on a legal matter. The fat stranger seats himself and rolling about in his chair and pulling extraordinarily funny faces explains that he has come from Venice with his pockets full of gold to offer the Lawyer Goldoni employment: employment as comic dramatist, full-time, to the Medebac company in Venice. He himself is Cesare d'Arbes, Pantalone to the Medebac company. Will the Lawyer Goldoni name his terms? The Lawyer Goldoni declines. He has made the law his profession. Pantalone d'Arbes presses. Lawyer Goldoni remains unmoved. Pantalone d'Arbes begs. He explains that the play Goldoni wrote for the Imer company has proved very successful. Goldoni becomes interested – for that play *The Clever Woman*, was the first scenario into which he had written all the dialogue for all the actors: the first play ever completely written down in entirety for a company of *commedia dell'arte* players. Pantalone d'Arbes continues to supplicate. He pleads, his face making the most comic grimaces. Lawyer Goldoni still protests, but his protests become feebler and feebler. The funny grimaces of the Pantalone become too much for him: he smiles, he laughs, he roars with laughter. Pantalone d'Arbes seizes his opportunity, takes out a handful of gold coins and throws them on the table in front of Goldoni. Carlo Goldoni is lost for ever to the legal profession. He promises to return to Venice if his wife is agreeable. D'Arbes promises that his company will hire the Sant'Angelo Theatre and place at Goldoni's disposal the best company of *commedia dell'arte* actors in Venice.

The next year Goldoni returned to Venice, giving up at the age of forty a most secure living for the most precarious one he could possibly have found. From 1748, when he returned to Venice, until 1762, when he left Venice for Paris, he wrote nearly two hundred plays. They were written at such speed that some were failures and many do not stand the test of time. But they include all his masterpieces.

From the age of fifteen, when he had discovered for himself the national dramas of England and France in the library at Pavia, Goldoni's ambition had been to reform the decadent *commedia dell'arte* and replace it by an Italian theatre that would rival that of England and France. He had begun by writing into his scenarios the dialogue to be spoken by the non-masked characters. Next he tried to persuade the masked characters to allow him to write their dialogue for them –

dialogue in which they would not be able to use their obscene jokes. They refused. Their whole technique was based on movement and on their lightning speed of extemporized repartee. Goldoni accepted defeat. But before he left Venice for Pisa to devote himself to his profession as a lawyer, he gave to the Imer company the first play in which he had written all the dialogue. He never saw its first performance – indeed apparently never knew it had been performed. It was this play that brought Cesare d'Arbes to Pisa to persuade Goldoni to return to Venice to embark on his career as a full-time dramatist.

Now he had an indispensable ally in Cesare d'Arbes. For d'Arbes agreed to act his part of Pantalone *unmasked* in Goldoni's next play. Unfortunately this play, *Elegant Anthony*, was a complete failure and although d'Arbes and the other masked characters agreed to learn their lines in the next play, they insisted on wearing their masks. This play, *The Prudent Man*, was a success. But Goldoni now refused to be defeated. He had observed that in real life Cesare d'Arbes displayed two opposing characteristics: he was both a shrewd man of the world and yet also possessed the childlike temperament of the born buffoon. So, determined to make d'Arbes act with his face unmasked, Goldoni seized on these two characteristics and wrote especially for d'Arbes a play which is one of his masterpieces. This play, *The Venetian Twins*, was a comedy of mistaken identities, in which d'Arbes was to act the parts of both the twins, one clever, witty and self-assured, the other timid, shy and foolish. D'Arbes must have realized he was being given the chance of a lifetime. *The Venetian Twins* was the most successful play ever performed in Venice up to that time. And it was the play which first set Goldoni's critics and rivals yelping at his heels.

The masked actors knew which side their bread was buttered and *The Venetian Twins* was the death-blow to the *commedia dell'arte*. Goldoni could now write what plays he pleased for them. He took on an average eight days to write a play. One of his masterpieces, *The Superior Residence*, he wrote in three days and nights. This play was one of those with which he made his clean break from the characters of the *commedia dell'arte*. The stock characters, Pantalone, the Doctor, Arlecchino and Brighella disappeared and in their place the people of Venice saw themselves appearing on the stage. Goldoni's naturalistic comedies of everyday life set all Venice aching with laughter. In his autobiography he makes the short and modest statement:

'There is a considerable number of Venetian plays in my collection and perhaps it is these that do me greatest honour.'

But with success came the jealousy of the critics and the academic dramatists. The attacks became malevolent and malicious and finally drove him broken-hearted from Venice. The most vicious came from his fellow-dramatist, Carlo Gozzi, but it was not until 1760 that they became virulent. This was caused by the great Voltaire himself coming unsolicited to the support of Goldoni. But though his support made Goldoni an international figure, it caused Gozzi to whet his knife for the kill, and in 1762, Goldoni left Venice. He had decided to accept an invitation from the King of France to write plays for the King's company of Italian actors in Paris. He took with him his wife, the good Nicoletta, and his little nephew, then ten years of age. He was fifty-five. He was to live for another thirty-one years but he never saw his beloved Venice again.

In Paris, Goldoni found the Italian actors uncooperative and lacking the technical skill of the Venetians. They demanded scenarios and not written plays. As a result, in Paris he wrote only one play that can be included among his masterpieces: *The Fan*. He learnt French and began writing plays in that language. One of these, *The Beneficent Bear*, achieved Goldoni's lifelong ambition: to see a play of his own acclaimed as a triumph on the same stage where Molière's plays had triumphed, that of the *Comédie française*.

Three years after he had come to Paris, Goldoni went completely blind in both eyes. He gradually recovered the sight in his right eye, but from then until his death he had lost entirely the use of his left. He was given employment for a

time as tutor at Versailles to the French princesses. Then he
was given a pension by the King and returned to Paris, to the
Rue St Sauveur, where he remained until his death. Though
he made many friends in Paris, including Rousseau, Diderot
and Voltaire, he is singularly reticent about them in his
autobiography.

In 1789 the Bastille fell. The King's civil pension list was
suspended. In August 1792, Goldoni fell ill. Friends made
efforts to relieve his poverty. He died on 6 February 1793,
eighteen days after Louis XVI, who had brought him to
Paris, died on the guillotine. The very next day, Goldoni's
friend Chénier, the brother of the poet, unaware of Goldoni's
death, stood up in the National Convention and moved that
Goldoni's pension be restored to him. The Convention
immediately agreed that the annual pension of 4000 livres
paid Goldoni by the King since 1768 should be continued and
paid to him out of the National Treasury. Two days later,
after learning of his death, the Convention immediately
granted an annuity of 1500 livres to his widow. Then on 17
February the Convention ordered the *Comédie française*, which
had been renamed *Le Théâtre de la Nation*, to give a performance of *The Beneficent Bear* for the benefit of Goldoni's family.

The consideration shown by these regicides to a foreigner
who had been receiving a pension for twenty-four years from
the King they had just executed is completely remarkable:
until one knows his plays and realizes the charm and goodness
of the man. For in his plays can be read such passages as:

'I have often heard it said that the world would be more beautiful
if it had not been spoiled by men, who for the sake of pride, have
upset the beautiful order of Nature. Nature, that common mother,
regards us all as equal. And the day will come when one pudding
will again be made of both great and small.'

Goldoni wrote that in his play *Pamela Nubile* forty years before
the fall of the Bastille and twelve years before Rousseau wrote
The Social Contract. It is a wonder that such radical sentiments
never landed him in a Venetian gaol.

Usually, however, he kept such seditious sentiments to

himself and one will look in vain for political comment in his plays. Nor will one find deep insight into human nature. What one does find is a prolific invention and a keenness of observation which very few dramatists have possessed. Moreover, his plays have one quality possessed by no other dramatist: their great charm, which springs from Goldoni's own happy and vivacious nature.

He excels in his portrayal of young women involved in the sex war. His best studies of men are confined to the elderly. Goldoni's old men are drawn in depth by means of intuitively selected details which reveal the idiosyncrasies of men for whom sex, though still potent, has become a source of surly benignity. The same intuitive selection of feminine traits, combined with a minutely careful observation of feminine talk, mannerisms and reactions, is revealed in his young women in search of husbands. They are playing a game according to rules which nobody has taught them. Theirs is the instinctive involvement in the battle for which nature has formed them. Rosaura, the artful young widow, and Mirandolina, the still more artful young innkeeper, flaunt their sex like a banner to attract admirers. They then proceed to probe with ruthless realism until they have stripped their admirers of all spurious romanticism so that by the end of the play all their admirers have been shown themselves as they really are in the eyes of the woman they have dared to admire.

Above all else, however, Goldoni's plays are orchestrated movement and for that reason they need to be seen in performance in order to realize the full enjoyment they offer. From the moment the curtain sweeps back at the beginning of a play by Carlo Goldoni, one feels that sense of happiness which comes too rarely in the modern theatre. For all that Goldoni offers is simple enjoyment.

The Venetian Twins

I DUE GEMELLI VENEZIANI

The Venetian Twins

The Venetian Twins was first performed in Venice in 1748 and was the first play in which *commedia dell'arte* actors went on the stage without their masks and triumphed. With this play the most fickle and yet most conservative audience in Italy gave its consent to the final disappearance of the old Comedy of Masks and to the building-up by Goldoni of a national comedy.

Goldoni wrote the play especially for Cesare d'Arbes, a Protean actor, in order to give him the opportunity to act two disparate rôles in the same evening. The dramatic possibilities of using twin brothers, here so alike in appearance but so different in spirit and temperament, had caught the imagination of Plautus and Shakespeare before Goldoni. Anouilh, following Goldoni, gave them to one and the same actor. Feydeau attempted a similar situation, though not with twins, in his *A Flea in Her Ear*.

During the last ten years the Genoese City Theatre has taken this play to nearly all the capital cities of Europe. When it brought the play to Paris, *The Times* special correspondent in Paris wrote:

'Rarely has the stage of Sarah Bernhardt bristled with so much fun and high spirits, such vivacity and sheer comic bravura, or such histrionic elegance and invention.'

Characters

DOCTOR BALANZONI, a Bolognese lawyer resident in Verona

ROSAURA, believed to be his daughter, later discovered to be the sister of the twins

PANCRAZIO, a friend of BALANZONI, and his guest during the action of the play

ZANETTO, the foolish twin

TONINO, the witty twin

LELIO, the DOCTOR BALANZONI'S nephew

BEATRICE, in love with TONINO

FLORINDO, a friend of TONINO

BRIGHELLA
COLOMBINA } servants in the house of BALANZONI

TIBURZIO, a jeweller

BARGELLO, the chief constable of Verona

SERVANTS and GUARDS

The action takes place in Verona.

Act One

❧ SCENE I ❧

Rosaura's room.

ROSAURA *and* COLOMBINA *are both trying to comb their hair in front of the mirror on the dressing table.*

ROSAURA: It seems to me, polite Signorina Colombina, it should be your duty to finish your mistress's hair before arranging your own.

COLOMBINA: My duty? Signorina, for two hours I've been standing curling your hair, frizzling your hair, fluffing your hair. But you're never satisfied. And you keep pushing your fingers into your hair just to annoy me. So that I don't know what I've done and what I haven't.

ROSAURA: How dare you! You've deliberately left my hair all anyhow simply to waste time on your own.

COLOMBINA: I like that! I suppose I haven't hair on my head the same as you?

ROSAURA: Maybe! But I'm the mistress and you're the servant.

COLOMBINA: Thanks very much. There's no need to keep rubbing it in.

ROSAURA: That's enough. Finish my hair. The gentleman I'm to become engaged to will be here any minute. And here I am in this state.

COLOMBINA: The gentleman *I'm* to become engaged to will be here any minute also, and I want to look *my* best.

ROSAURA: Are you daring to compare yourself with me, you impudent little hussy?

COLOMBINA: Don't you speak to me like that, signorina, or – or you'll regret it.

ROSAURA: Why, you insolent thing! Get up! Get up or I'll get a stick to you!

COLOMBINA [*rising*]: What's that? A stick! To me?

ROSAURA: Answering back to your mistress! You little wretch! I shall tell my father!

COLOMBINA: What a mistress! And what a father! Oh, yes, signorina, he and I understand each other all right.

ROSAURA: And what's that supposed to mean, you little beast?

COLOMBINA: Stop calling me names. You provoke me any more and I'll tell everything – see?

ROSAURA: Go on, then. Let's hear, you liar!

COLOMBINA: Oh, you'll hear plenty. I've kept quiet long enough. Now I've had enough of keeping quiet.

[*The* DOCTOR *enters.*]

DOCTOR: What's this noise about? What's happened? What's the matter?

ROSAURA: Father, give that woman a good scolding! She's insulted me, ill-treated me, behaved most disrespectfully.

DOCTOR [*to* COLOMBINA]: Is this how you treat my daughter?

COLOMBINA: Take care, signore. My mother told me everything. You understand?

DOCTOR [*to himself*]: The foolish woman! If she were still alive, I'd flay her! [*aside to* COLOMBINA] Colombina, for the love of heaven, say nothing. Keep quiet and I will see you don't lose by it.

COLOMBINA [*aside to the* DOCTOR]: All right, I'll keep quiet. And let myself be insulted.

ROSAURA: Well, father . . .

DOCTOR: Oh, come now, my dear, you must make haste. Your future husband, Signor Zanetto Bisognosi, son of the famous Venetian Pantalone, will be arriving any time now. Though actually he was brought up, I believe, at Bergamo by his uncle Stefanello, one of the richest merchants in Lombardy.

COLOMBINA: Remember I'm to be married as well. To his servant. You promised.

DOCTOR [*aside to* COLOMBINA]: Yes, yes! I'll arrange it. Anything you want. Only keep quiet.

COLOMBINA: Yes, you'll do well to shut my mouth by marrying me off.

DOCTOR: Oh, Rosaura, have you seen Signor Pancrazio lately?

ROSAURA: Oh, yes! I see him quite often.

DOCTOR: Ah, what a fine gentleman he is!

ROSAURA: Yes, indeed. And he gives me such good advice.

DOCTOR: So long as I live he may look on my house as his home.

ROSAURA: Oh, I'm sure you couldn't do better. He is indeed such a great help to us.

COLOMBINA: If you ask me, I think he's a complete scoundrel.

DOCTOR: Hold your tongue! How can you say such a thing! What possible reason could you have?

COLOMBINA: I've got my reasons all right.

[BRIGHELLA *enters.*]

BRIGHELLA: Signore, signore, Signor Zanetto has arrived. From Bergamo. He's just got off his horse and he's at the door speaking to someone who travelled with him.

DOCTOR: Praise be to heaven! Daughter, I'll go myself to welcome him and bring him to you immediately. [*Exit*]

ROSAURA: Oh, do tell me, Brighella. What is he like? Is he handsome? Is he elegant?

BRIGHELLA: Well, I'll tell you, signorina. As for handsome, he's not too bad: he's young, and he'll get by. But – well, from what I've just seen of him, I think he must be a bit simple in the head. Didn't even know how to get off his horse. In looks he's the spitting image of his brother, Tonino. *He* lives in Venice and I used to see him sometimes when I worked there. But though this one's the image of him in looks, he's nothing like him in any other way. His brother's a real gentleman – polished as you might say. But this one – you'd think he was some country bumpkin. Scared of his own shadow, if you ask me.

ROSAURA: This report does not please me much.

COLOMBINA [*to* BRIGHELLA]: There should be a certain Arlecchino with Signor Zanetto. His servant. Has he come?

BRIGHELLA: No, not yet. He's expected later with his master's luggage.

COLOMBINA: I'm sorry. I'm curious to see him.

BRIGHELLA: Yes, and I know why. He's the one who's to possess your charms, isn't he?

COLOMBINA: Jealousy won't get you anywhere. [*Exit*]

ROSAURA: Tell me, Brighella, how did you know this family in Venice? And why was Signor Zanetto brought up at Bergamo?

BRIGHELLA: I was servant to a rich merchant in Venice who was a great friend of the late Signor Pantalone dei Bisognosi, these twins' father. Besides these twins Signor Pantalone had a daughter, and he sent her to Bergamo, where he'd already sent Signor Zanetto – to his brother Stefanello who was rich and had no children. I heard say that this daughter disappeared, that she never arrived at Bergamo. Got lost on the journey and was never heard of again. That's about all I know. Except that as regards their position and authority, the Bisognosi family is one of the most important among the merchants of Venice.

ROSAURA: That's all right, then. But I'm sorry Signor Zanetto is not as elegant as his brother.

BRIGHELLA: Here he is now with the master. Have a good look and you'll see I was right. [*Exit*]

[*The* DOCTOR *and* ZANETTO *enter.*]

ROSAURA [*to herself*]: I like his face. Perhaps he's not such a fool after all.

DOCTOR: Come! Come on! Come on in! That's right. Come right in and make yourself at home. Daughter, this is Signor Zanetto.

ZANETTO: My bride-to-be, my respects to you.

ROSAURA: Signore, I am your most humble servant.

ZANETTO [*to himself*]: Oh, she's the servant! A good-looking girl. [*to the* DOCTOR] Tell me, father-in-law, the bride – where is she?

DOCTOR: But she's here. This is my daughter. This is the bride.

ZANETTO: But she said she was the servant!

DOCTOR: Oh, no, signore! She said, 'I am your most humble servant.' As a compliment, as a formality.

ZANETTO: I understand. A bad beginning!

DOCTOR: For what reason?

ZANETTO: Because in my marriage I don't want any lies, any formalities.

ROSAURA [*aside*]: He is a little foolish, but he certainly doesn't displease me.

DOCTOR: Oh, come now, don't give the matter another thought.

ROSAURA: Signor Zanetto, rest assured that I am sincere, that I do not know how to simulate, and that I have every respect and esteem for you.

ZANETTO: All things I don't give a fig for.

ROSAURA: Perhaps my way of expressing myself does not please you?

ZANETTO: Just as you please, signorina.

ROSAURA: My looks? Perhaps they are not to your liking?

ZANETTO: Oh, stop beating about the bush. I've come to Verona to marry you. All I'm waiting for is Arlecchino to arrive with my clothes, jewels and money.

ROSAURA: Very well. I *am* your intended wife, am I?

ZANETTO: So why all this chit-chat? Take my hand and get it over with.

ROSAURA [*to herself*]: What strange behaviour!

DOCTOR: But, my dear son-in-law, is it your wish to be married in this boorish way? Say something to your bride-to-be. Speak to her a little gracefully, a little lovingly!

ZANETTO [*to the* DOCTOR]: You are right. [*to* ROSAURA] I'm yours, all yours. I'm pleased by that beautiful face you've got. I would like to . . . [*to the* DOCTOR] Do me a favour, will you, father-in-law?

DOCTOR: Of course, what is it?

ZANETTO: G-Get out of here. You're making me shy!

DOCTOR: Certainly. I shall wait upon you. You will find me most complaisant. [*aside to* ROSAURA] Be wise, daughter. He's a little foolish but he's got money. [*to* ZANETTO] With your permission, son-in-law. [*aside to* ROSAURA] Don't look a gift horse in the mouth. [*Exit*]

ZANETTO [*to* ROSAURA]: So! We are husband and wife!

ROSAURA: I hope we are to be.

ZANETTO: And we stand here like a couple of dummies?

ROSAURA: What would you like to do?

ZANETTO: That's a good one! Husband and wife!

ROSAURA: I repeat – I hope we are to be husband and wife. But the marriage ceremony has not yet been performed.

ZANETTO: No? What d'you expect to get out of a marriage ceremony?

ROSAURA: I expect a lot of ceremonies and solemnities.

ZANETTO: Let's speak plainly. Do you accept me as your husband?

ROSAURA: Yes, signore, I accept you.

ZANETTO: And I accept you as my wife. So what need's there for any ceremony? This is the most beautiful ceremony in the world.

ROSAURA: You put it very nicely. But that's not the way we do things here.

ZANETTO: It's not? Then I will go back to Bergamo. To the mountains where I grew up. There we just fall in love. That's all there is to it. Two words and we're married. That's all the ceremony there, between a man and his wife.

ROSAURA: I repeat that here we expect certain solemnities.

ZANETTO: How long do these solemnities take?

ROSAURA: At least two days.

ZANETTO: And you think I'll wait that long!

ROSAURA: You are in a great hurry.

ZANETTO: It's either now or never.

ROSAURA: But this is an insult to me!

ZANETTO:Is it an insult to want to consummate our marriage? D'you know how many girls would give anything to be insulted in such a way?

ROSAURA:But good heavens! Can't you wait one day?

ZANETTO:Tell me, dearest one. These solemnities and these ceremonies, can't they wait till after the marriage? Let us consummate the thing, and afterwards we can go on having these ceremonies for a whole year and I won't complain.

ROSAURA:Ah, Signor Zanetto, I think you're amusing yourself a little at my expense!

ZANETTO:Of course I want to amuse myself. But *in* marriage.

ROSAURA:Well, in due time you can.

ZANETTO:The proverb says, there's no time like the present. Don't keep me in suspense. [*He approaches her and tries to take her hand.*]

ROSAURA:But this is an impertinence!

ZANETTO:Look here, that's enough of that!

ROSAURA:I've warned you, take your time!

ZANETTO:Exactly! I'll take my time – now!

[*He embraces her and she gives him a slap across the face.*]

ROSAURA:Presumption!

[*He stands astonished and speechless. He touches his cheek, looks* ROSAURA *full in the face, makes the motion of the slap, and runs silently out.*]

ROSAURA:Heavens, what an indecent person! What an improper young man! Who would have thought it? At first sight he seemed such a fool. It shows how appearances can deceive! We women should never be left alone with men. There's always some danger to be faced. Good Signor Pancrazio has told me that so often. But here he is. Ah, it is easy to see in *his* face, the goodness of his heart.

[PANCRAZIO *enters.*]

PANCRAZIO:Heaven keep you, my child! What is the matter that I perceive you so perturbed?

ROSAURA: Oh, Signor Pancrazio, if you knew what has just happened to me!

PANCRAZIO: Worse still! Worse than ever! Reveal all to me freely. Naturally, you can trust me completely.

ROSAURA: I will tell you, Signore. You know, of course, that my father has decided that I am to marry a Venetian.

PANCRAZIO [to himself]: Would that I didn't!

ROSAURA: What you may not know is that this Venetian has arrived here today from Bergamo.

PANCRAZIO [to himself]: May he break his neck!

ROSAURA: And what you certainly do not know is that the man's a fool, a presumptuous fool.

PANCRAZIO: Presumption is only to be expected from foolish people.

ROSAURA: My father insisted on my speaking with him.

PANCRAZIO: Bad!

ROSAURA: Then he actually left me all alone with him.

PANCRAZIO: Still worse!

ROSAURA: And then this fellow . . .

PANCRAZIO: Yes, yes, I can imagine!

ROSAURA: . . . in the most indecent words . . .

PANCRAZIO: Smooth and glib, no doubt?

ROSAURA: Yes, Signore.

PANCRAZIO: Then – he attempted some immodesty?

ROSAURA: Exactly.

PANCRAZIO: Continue! What took place?

ROSAURA: He offended me so much that I slapped his face.

PANCRAZIO: Oh, what a good, what a wise, what an exemplary girl you are! Worthy to be inscribed in the scroll of the heroines of our century! Words are insufficient to praise your soul's prudent resolution. Thus should all such insolent persons be treated! Thus should all who show disrespect to the fair sex be humiliated! Oh, heroic hand! Oh, illustrious and glorious hand! On this hand, which deserves the applause of the whole world, allow me with reverence and admiration to imprint a kiss. [He takes her hand and kisses it with smooth tenderness.]

ROSAURA:It merits your approval, then? The way I showed
my resentment?

PANCRAZIO:Can you doubt it? Ah, and what a way! Nowadays to find a girl who will give a man a slap out of modesty
is a miracle! You must continue. You must go on slapping
them in the face. Accustom yourself to despising these
young scoundrels from whom you can only hope to receive
bad examples, infidelity and ill-usage. And if ever your heart
decides to love, look for an object worthy of your love.

ROSAURA:But where must I look?

PANCRAZIO:Ah, Rosaura, I am unable at present to say
more. But I think of you, and of your well-being, more than
you believe. Enough! You will come to realize it is so.

ROSAURA:Signor Pancrazio, I am convinced of your kindness. You are so concerned with anything to the advantage
of our family, not to hope for even more distinguished
favours from you. For that reason, I must be sincere with
you. Signor Zanetto does not displease me. And, well, if he
were not so impudent, perhaps . . . perhaps . . .

PANCRAZIO:Fie! Fie! Do not say what you will regret! Do
not tarnish your heroic and virtuous deed with such vile
sentiments. Shame on you. Shun all the more such an
abominable object. The man who does not know how to be
modest, shows he has not the right to care for you. Your
merit makes you worthy of another, a more noble object.
Do not ever again pronounce that name in my hearing.

ROSAURA:You are right, Signor Pancrazio. Forgive my
weakness. I will go and tell my father I do not want such a
man.

PANCRAZIO:Bravo! Now I praise you. I will add my
reasons to yours.

ROSAURA:Thank you. Do not desert me. [*to herself*] What a
good man, what a wise man he is! How fortunate for my
father to have him in the house! How fortunate for me to
have his advice! [*Exit*]

PANCRAZIO [*alone*]:If I don't obtain Rosaura by false virtue
and pretended prudence, I can't hope to, that's certain. *I
haven't got youth, good looks and money. But I've found

a way by which I may be able to achieve my designs. Nowadays he who knows how to pretend, knows how to better himself. And to be wise, it is enough to seem so. [*Exit*]

⦃ SCENE 2 ⦄

A Street. On one side is the DOCTOR'S *house, and on the other is an Inn with the sign: 'The Two Towers'.*

[BEATRICE *and her* SERVANT *enter with* FLORINDO.]

BEATRICE: Signor Florindo, I must return to Venice!

FLORINDO: But – why such a sudden decision?

BEATRICE: For six days I've been waiting for Signor Tonino. To go on to Milan with him. And there's still no sign of him. I fear he has changed his mind, or else some accident has kept him in Venice. I simply must go and find out for myself.

FLORINDO: Pardon me, but isn't that very imprudent? To go back to Venice whence you've just fled on Signor Tonino's advice? If your relatives find you, you will be lost.

BEATRICE: Venice is a large place. I'll arrive by night, and in a way that nobody will recognize me.

FLORINDO: No, Signorina Beatrice. You know I cannot allow you to go. Signor Tonino sent you to me. He entrusted you to my protection. It's my duty to restrain you. I am under an obligation to look after you. My friendship for Signor Tonino demands nothing less. [*to himself*] As does my love for you.

BEATRICE: You must not blame yourself, if in spite of your determination, I find a way of going. I know where the coach leaves from, and with my servant's help I would be able to return to Venice, since it was with him I came to Verona.

FLORINDO: Oh, that would be the greatest mistake. Didn't you tell me yourself that this person named Lelio persisted in molesting you on the journey? And haven't I seen him myself here in Verona always hanging around you? In such a way that several times I've almost had to give him a good hiding? If you attempt to leave, and he manages to find out, you will expose yourself to some form of assault.

BEATRICE: A respectable lady does not fear such things.

FLORINDO: But a lady, however respectable, travelling alone with only a servant, always gives a bad impression and invites insult.

BEATRICE: Nevertheless, I am determined to go.

FLORINDO: Wait at least a couple of days.

BEATRICE: My heart tells me I have lost my Tonino.

FLORINDO: Heaven forbid such a thing! But if it should be so, what good will it be returning to Venice?

BEATRICE: What good will there be staying in Verona?

FLORINDO: Here, perhaps, you may find somebody who is convinced of your worth, somebody who would take the place of your dear Tonino.

BEATRICE: That will never be. I am Tonino's or no one's.

FLORINDO [to himself]: Still, if she stays here and if her fiancé doesn't turn up, little by little I could hope to win her.

BEATRICE [to herself]: When he least expects it, I will fly from his protection.

FLORINDO: Here comes that affected dandy, Lelio. He's forever running after you. Heaven knows what might happen if I were not with you.

[LELIO enters.]

LELIO [to BEATRICE]: Most beautiful Venetian, I have heard from the post driver that you are yearning to return to your native city. If that is so, make use of me. I will give you a coach, horses, grooms, servants, money as much as you desire, if you will but grant me the pleasure of accompanying you.

BEATRICE [to herself]: What presumption!

FLORINDO: Signore, permit me to ask by what right you offer the Signorina Beatrice such things when you see she is in my company?

LELIO: What's it to me if she is in your company? Must I stand in awe of you? Who are you anyway? Her brother? Some relative? Or some fortune-hunter?

FLORINDO: Sir, I'm astounded! At you and at your most unpleasant manner. I am a gentleman. I am, moreover, under an obligation to look after this lady.

LELIO: Well, friend, then you're in a difficult situation.

FLORINDO: And why?

LELIO: Because it needs more of a man than you are to look after a lady.

FLORINDO: I'm well able to deal with you, and anybody else like you.

LELIO: Oh, come now, friend, let's keep to the point. [to BEATRICE] Isn't there anything I can let you have? Do you not need any money, clothes, protection? What d'you say?

FLORINDO: You're making me lose my patience.

LELIO: Really? You *appear* to be quite a good-natured fellow. [to BEATRICE] Signorina Beatrice, give me your hand and let me be of service to you.

BEATRICE: *You* appear to be quite the most insolent person I've ever met!

LELIO: Faint heart never won fair lady! What good are a lot of useless compliments? Come, let us go. [*He tries to take her hand and she draws back.*]

FLORINDO [*giving him a push*]: I told you to remember your manners.

LELIO: This to me? To me, you rash fool? To me, whom nobody has ever dared give an insolent glance, without paying with his blood for his presumption? D'you not know who I am? I am the Marquis Lelio, Lord of Monte Fresco, Count of Fonte Chiara, Magistrate of Selva Ombrosa. I own more estates than you've hairs in that badly combed wig. And more money than you'll ever see in your life.

FLORINDO: And more mad ideas than there are sands in the sea! Or stars in the sky! [*to himself*] As if everybody doesn't know him. Calls himself Count, Marquis, when he's only the nephew of Doctor Balanzoni.

LELIO: Either the lady comes with me, or you will fall – victim of my anger.

FLORINDO: This lady is under my protection, and if necessary I will reply with my sword.

LELIO: Poor young man! I am sorry for you. You want to die? Is that it?

BEATRICE [*softly to* FLORINDO]: Signor Florindo! Don't endanger yourself with such a fellow.

FLORINDO [*to* BEATRICE]: Do not worry. I'll bring him down a peg or two.

LELIO: Hold on to life! You are young. Hold on to life, and leave this lady to me. The world is full of women. You have only one life.

FLORINDO: I value honour more than life. Are you going or d'you prefer the sword? [*He draws his sword.*]

LELIO: Pff! You are not my equal. You're not of the nobility. I do not fight with such as you.

FLORINDO: Nobility or not, this is the way to treat cowards like you. [*Gives him a blow with the flat of his sword.*]

LELIO [*drawing his sword*]: This to me! Gods of my ancient house assist me in this contest to the death!

FLORINDO: Now we'll see what your fine words are worth! [*They fight.*]

BEATRICE: Oh, dear! This is no place for me if there's going to be some tragedy. I'll go into this Inn here.

[*While they continue fighting,* BEATRICE *goes into the Inn, followed by her servant.*]

FLORINDO [*falls*]: Oh! I fell! I slipped!

LELIO [*holding his sword to his chest*]: Foolish fellow, you are vanquished!

FLORINDO: I slipped. It was an accident.

LELIO: No! My nobility defeats you! Die . . .

[TONINO *enters, sword in hand, in defence of* FLORINDO.]

TONINO [*to* LELIO]: Stop! Stop! When an adversary is on the ground you should lower your sword.

LELIO: What concern is that of yours?

TONINO: It's of concern to me because I'm a man of honour, and I cannot allow such outrageous conduct.

FLORINDO: It can't be . . . Signor Tonino . . . Dear friend . . . [*He rises.*]

TONINO [*aside to* FLORINDO]: Ssh! I *am* your friend and in time to save your life, but do not mention my name. [*to* LELIO, *who no longer looks so confident*] Courage, Signor bully, and apply yourself to me.

LELIO [*to himself*]: This fellow's spoilt everything. [*to* TONINO] But – who are you?

TONINO: A Venetian – with enough courage not to fear you nor ten of your sort.

LELIO: But I've nothing against you! I don't understand. Why d'you want to fight me?

TONINO: Because I've something against you, and I insist on fighting.

LELIO: Don't be a fool – what can you have against me?

TONINO: You have insulted my friend and that's as good as insulting me. In Venice we value friendship dearer than life and I would be unworthy of the name of Venetian if I did not follow the example of my brave fellow-citizens, who are the soul of honour.

LELIO: But how have *I* insulted this – great friend of yours?

TONINO: D'you call it nothing to threaten a man on the ground? D'you call it nothing to tell him he is to die, when he's stretched out flat on the ground? Come! Raise your sword!

FLORINDO [*to* TONINO]: No, dear friend, don't endanger yourself for me.

TONINO: Please! It's a trifle. To fight this puffed-up windbag is as easy as drinking a fresh egg.

LELIO: I've stood about enough of your impertinence. You have questioned my honour. And shamed the honour of my ancestors.

TONINO: That's true. What will grandmamma say? Rock-a-bye baby? What will daddy say about his great big cowardly son?

LELIO: Ah! I swear to heaven!

TONINO: Ah! I swear to – earth!

LELIO: Here I am! [*puts himself on guard opposite* TONINO.]

TONINO: Bravo! Take courage! [*They fight and* TONINO *disarms* LELIO.]

LELIO: What confounded luck! I'm unarmed!

TONINO: You're disarmed, and that's enough for me. You see how it's done? I don't kill you. I don't say 'Die'. It's enough for my honour to have beaten you. It is enough for me to keep your sword in memory of this victory. The blade, that is. I'll let you take the scabbard, so you can sell it to pay the surgeon to bleed you to get over the fright you've had.

LELIO: No more! I will have my revenge!

TONINO: I'm ready! Any time. Whenever you wish.

LELIO: You will see! You will see! [*Exit*]

TONINO: Go, indeed. 'Tis enough for your glory
    To boast that you fought against me.

FLORINDO: My dear friend, how very much I'm obliged to you.

TONINO: It was nothing. Beatrice! Where is she?

FLORINDO: Beatrice! [*aside*] I'd best dissemble. [*to* TONINO] Who is this Beatrice?

TONINO: Why, the girl I helped to escape from Venice and who I sent to you here. The girl I asked you to look after until I arrived.

FLORINDO: Friend, I have seen nobody.

TONINO: What! You're joking?

FLORINDO: I mean it; I've not seen this woman you speak of. I would have been only too glad to be of service to you.

TONINO: I see. Ah, well, the more fool me. And I thought I'd found a faithful woman at last. For two years we've been engaged. But her father didn't like me. Because he's got it into his head that I'm a wastrel, just because I like to make merry a bit with my friends, and because I'm a bit of a jack-of-all-trades and master of none. So when I saw there was no chance of getting his consent, I persuaded her to elope. Without hesitating, she packed her things and came here with a faithful servant of hers. I stayed on in Venice

for a while so as not to arouse suspicion. But some grand
foreign gentleman who also aspired to her hand sought me
out suspecting that I had arranged her disappearance. One
word led to another, with the result that I gave him a slap
on the face he won't forget for a long time. Half Venice
was buzzing about it and he determined to trap me in any
way he could. So without even stopping to get any money
or clothes I had to leave Venice and come here. Expecting
to find my dear Beatrice. But it appears she has made a
fool of me. So that's that. One word more, friend: don't
call me Tonino during the few hours I'll be here. I don't
want to be recognized.

FLORINDO: How shall I call you then?

TONINO: Call me Zanetto.

FLORINDO: Why Zanetto?

TONINO: Because I've a brother in Bergamo who's called
that and he's very like me in looks. People will think I am
he, and in that way I'll avoid any danger.

FLORINDO: This brother of yours, is he still in Bergamo?

TONINO: I believe so, but I'm not sure. We've never been on
friendly terms. He's far wealthier than I am, but I like to
have a good time more than he does. Indeed, I've heard he's
getting married, yet I don't know where or who to. He's
the world's biggest ass. It'll be a lucky woman who pleases
him!

FLORINDO: My house is at your disposal, friend, if you care
to honour it.

TONINO: I shouldn't want to inconvenience you. . . .

FLORINDO: Well, to tell you the truth, though it would give
me great pleasure, my father's rather a boor and doesn't
like seeing people.

TONINO: Think nothing of it, my dear fellow. I'll put up at
this Inn.

FLORINDO: I'm extremely sorry. Really, if you'd rather . . .

TONINO: Tonino Bisognosi has never forced himself upon
his friends. He gives. He does not take. Come to Venice
and see how you will be treated. We Venetians welcome
strangers with open arms. We pride ourselves on treating

strangers in such a way that everybody speaks well of
Venice. I am obliged to you: I know you mean well; but
the good mother does not say 'Would you like?' – she says
'Take!'.

FLORINDO: My dear friend, do come. Give me this pleasure.

TONINO: Take it that I may come. If I am able, I'll force
myself to. I am Tonino, and that is sufficient. My life, my
heart's blood, is for my country first and then for my
friends. Your servant, sir. [*Exit*]

FLORINDO [*to himself*]: Yes, I deserve his reproaches and I
should be full of humiliation, but my love for Beatrice
hardens my heart. For if I brought him into my house, that
would reveal my deception. What's important to me is that
Tonino leaves, and Beatrice stays with me. Then I'll
explain everything to her and perhaps she will not look
unfavourably upon me. I will go and find her. I'll persuade
her to stay in hiding today and tomorrow. As for her
servant, I'll send him away from Verona. I'll do anything to
get hold of this rare beauty. Even though I know I'm
betraying honour and friendship. But my great love for
Beatrice leaves me no alternative. I owe Tonino my life, and
I'm prepared to sacrifice mine for him. Yes, I'm prepared to
do everything, except deprive myself of Beatrice. [*Exit*]

[ZANETTO *enters, looking dejected and serious. Without
speaking he touches his cheek where he was slapped.* LELIO
enters.]

LELIO [*to* ZANETTO, *believing him to be* TONINO]: So, you are
alone. Now we'll see who's the better man of the two.

ZANETTO: Your humble servant.

LELIO: Less ceremony and more action. Get your hand to it.

ZANETTO: My hand? Here's my hand.

LELIO: Don't play the fool with me. Get your hand to your
sword.

ZANETTO: To my sword?

LELIO: Yes! Your sword!

ZANETTO: Why?

LELIO: Because my courage has been put in doubt.

ZANETTO: What country are you from, sir?

LELIO: I'm from Rome. Why?

ZANETTO: Because I don't understand a word you're saying.

LELIO: Well, if you don't understand me, you'll understand the meaning of this sword. [*He draws his sword.*]

ZANETTO [*yelling at the top of his voice*]: Help, everybody! Help! He wants to murder me!

LELIO: Enough of that! D'you think you can go on making a fool of me? I've seen you can handle a sword, but Mars himself would have to yield to me, unless Jove disarmed me with his own hand. Come! To the test!

ZANETTO [*to himself*]: First a slap on the face and now a sword in the stomach. I'm in for trouble everywhere.

LELIO: Bestir yourself, do you hear? Take your stand.

[LELIO *gives him a slight tap with the flat of his sword.*]

ZANETTO: Ow!

LELIO: Defend yourself, or I pierce your heart. [*He makes to strike him.*]

[FLORINDO *enters sword in hand.*]

FLORINDO: Here am I. To defend my friend. Turn your sword on me.

LELIO [*to* FLORINDO, *referring to* ZANETTO *whom he thinks is* TONINO]: This fellow's nothing but a contemptible coward.

ZANETTO [*to* FLORINDO]: Yes! He's speaking the truth, signore!

FLORINDO [*to* LELIO]: You're a liar. He's a brave man.

ZANETTO [*to himself*]: This gentleman doesn't know me very well.

LELIO: Then why won't he risk fighting me?

ZANETTO [*to himself*]: Because he's scared stiff.

FLORINDO: Because he doesn't condescend to fight with such as you.

ZANETTO [*to himself*]: This is another madman!

FLORINDO [*to* LELIO]: But never mind that. You can have me to fight with.

LELIO: Here I am. I don't fear you nor a hundred like you. [*They fight.*]

ZANETTO: At him! Polish him off! Riddle him with holes!

FLORINDO [*as* LELIO *falls*]: Behold how the proud are humbled.

LELIO: Cruel Fate! The enemy of courage!

FLORINDO: Your life is in my hands.

ZANETTO: Well done! Go on, kill him! Stick your sword in his stomach.

FLORINDO: That would not be the action of a gentleman.

ZANETTO: He wanted to rip my guts out. Was that the action of a gentleman?

FLORINDO: But the other time, when he was threatening to kill me, you yourself didn't deal severely with him once he had fallen?

ZANETTO: Are you mad? Get on with it. Finish him off!

FLORINDO: No. [*to* LELIO] Live, and be grateful to me for your life.

LELIO: You are a worthy opponent. But that fellow's a craven poltroon, a white-livered cur. [*Exit*]

ZANETTO [*calling after* LELIO]: And you're right. Absolutely right!

FLORINDO: But, my dear friend, why did you act so differently this time? Do you feel faint? Why this freakish pretence?

ZANETTO: Sir, believe me, I was not pretending. I've never been so scared in my life. If you hadn't come along he was going to murder me! On the spot. Just like that!

FLORINDO: I rejoice to have saved your life.

ZANETTO: Bless you for that. Allow me to kiss the hand that saved me.

FLORINDO: But I only did what you did for me. You saved my life and now I have saved yours.

ZANETTO: I saved your life?

FLORINDO: Yes, the first time – when you defended me against Lelio.

ZANETTO: I don't remember.

FLORINDO: Ah, people like you forget the good they do out

of modesty. Friend, I advise you to leave Verona. Because I fear you are recognized.

ZANETTO: Yes, that's what I thought. That *he* thought he knew me.

FLORINDO: And if they recognize you, be on your guard.

ZANETTO: This goes from bad to worse!

FLORINDO: You think it's a little thing to give somebody a slap on the face?

ZANETTO: To *be* given one, you mean.

FLORINDO: Oh? You mean it was you who was given the slap on the face?

ZANETTO: Yes, sir. But . . . what did you think? . . . That *I* had given somebody a slap on the face?

FLORINDO: That is what I understood.

ZANETTO: No, no! It was I, it was I who was given the slap!

FLORINDO: And the woman who was involved? You've never seen her again?

ZANETTO: No, sir, I have not.

FLORINDO [*to himself*]: I've not been able to find Beatrice either.

ZANETTO: Nor do I care whether I ever see her, either.

FLORINDO: You couldn't do better. Don't give her another thought. Follow my advice; return home again.

ZANETTO: That's just what I was saying to myself.

FLORINDO: Is there any way I can help you?

ZANETTO: You have done more than enough, signore. With your permission I will go.

FLORINDO: Then good-bye.

ZANETTO: I bid you a humble and grateful farewell.

FLORINDO [*to himself, as he goes*]: He's turning into a fool. Love plays cruel tricks on people. [*Exit*]

ZANETTO [*to himself*]: Yes, I'd have been in real trouble if that gentleman hadn't come along. I do believe everybody knows by now that Rosaura gave me a slap on the face. But I mustn't lose my head. That young man wishes me well. He advised me to go away. All the same, Rosaura pleases me, and if she would be my wife I'd be very happy. It's a nuisance Arlecchino hasn't come yet with my money and

my clothes. Then I could give her a present, and that might
please her.

[PANCRAZIO *enters.*]

PANCRAZIO [*to himself*]: Here's that good-for-nothing
Zanetto. Always hanging around this house. Simply won't
take himself away.

ZANETTO [*to himself*]: She gave me a slap: therefore she
doesn't like me. But my mother used to give me slaps and
she loved me. And she never really hurt me much. Oh, I am
a silly-billy. I didn't mean to upset her. Yes, that's what I'll
do; I'll go at once and ask her to forgive me. [*He goes
towards the Doctor's house.*]

PANCRAZIO: You! Young man! Where are you going?

ZANETTO: I'm going to see my sweetheart.

PANCRAZIO: She who slapped your face for you?

ZANETTO: Certainly. The very same.

PANCRAZIO: And you are going resolved to be reconciled
with her and to marry her?

ZANETTO: Excellent! You've guessed it.

PANCRAZIO: You like that young lady?

ZANETTO: Very much.

PANCRAZIO: You are in love with her?

ZANETTO: Madly.

PANCRAZIO: You want to marry her very much?

ZANETTO: Heaven knows how much.

PANCRAZIO: Poor young man, I'm very sorry for you!

ZANETTO: What's that?

PANCRAZIO: You are on the edge of a precipice.

ZANETTO: I am? Why?

PANCRAZIO: You don't really want to get married?

ZANETTO: Yes, sir.

PANCRAZIO: You poor unhappy young man, you are ruined.

ZANETTO: I am? Why?

PANCRAZIO: Believe me when I say that I, whose only
interest is to help my neighbour, feel it is my fraternal duty
to warn you of the enormous folly you are about to
commit.

ZANETTO: But how?

PANCRAZIO: Do you know what marriage is?

ZANETTO: Marriage . . . yes, sir . . . it is like, when you mean to say . . . well, simply . . . husband and wife.

PANCRAZIO: Ah, if you really knew the meaning of marriage, the meaning of wife, you would not speak so lightly.

ZANETTO: Now just you look here! What is it you're trying to say?

PANCRAZIO: Marriage means a chain which binds a man fast like a slave to the galleys.

ZANETTO: Marriage?

PANCRAZIO: Marriage.

ZANETTO: You don't say! Really?

PANCRAZIO: Marriage is a weight that makes your days wearisome and your nights sleepless. It weighs down your spirit, it weighs down your body, it weighs down your purse, and it weighs down your mind.

ZANETTO: Good heavens – but that's terrible!

PANCRAZIO: And the woman, who seemed so beautiful and kind, you'd never believe what she really is.

ZANETTO: Oh, my dear sir, what is she?

PANCRAZIO: The woman is an enchanting siren who allures only to deceive, who loves only to ensnare.

ZANETTO: The woman?

PANCRAZIO: The woman.

ZANETTO: You don't say!

PANCRAZIO: Those eyes, so brilliant, are two flames of fire which little by little scorch you and reduce you to ashes.

ZANETTO: Her eyes . . . two flames of fire. . . .

PANCRAZIO: Her mouth is a vase full of venom which slowly insinuates its poison through your ears to your heart – and kills you!

ZANETTO: Her mouth . . . a vase of venom. . . .

PANCRAZIO: Her cheeks, so lovely and full of colour, are witches' spells, enchanting potions.

ZANETTO: Her cheeks . . . witches' spells. . . .

PANCRAZIO: When a woman comes after you, always remember she is a fury coming to tear you to pieces.

ZANETTO: A fury . . . t-tear me to pieces!

PANCRAZIO: And when a woman comes to embrace you, she is a demon come to drag you down to hell.

ZANETTO: Keep her away from me!

PANCRAZIO: Go, think it over, and think well.

ZANETTO: I've been and thought.

PANCRAZIO: No more women?

ZANETTO: No more women.

PANCRAZIO: No more marriage?

ZANETTO: No more marriage.

PANCRAZIO: How you will bless me for my advice.

ZANETTO: Heaven sent you to me!

PANCRAZIO: Go then. Be wise, and heaven bless you.

ZANETTO: You have been more than a father to me!

PANCRAZIO: So, you may kiss my hand.

ZANETTO: Oh beloved one! Oh blessed one!

PANCRAZIO: Women. . . .

ZANETTO: Ugh!

PANCRAZIO: Marriage. . . .

ZANETTO: Ach!

PANCRAZIO: Never more. . . .

ZANETTO: Never more.

PANCRAZIO: Certain?

ZANETTO: Absolutely!

PANCRAZIO: Well done! Excellent! Excellent! [*Exit*]

ZANETTO [*alone*]: Drat it! A fine thing I'd have done if I hadn't met that gentleman. Marriage . . . a heavy weight here . . . a heavy weight there . . . a weight on your purse . . . a weight on your mind. . . . Women . . . sirens, witches, devils. . . . Ugh, what a cursed mess.

[BEATRICE *enters with her servant.*]

BEATRICE [*to* ZANETTO, *believing him to be* TONINO]: Oh, what happiness! Here is my love! Here is my sweetheart! But when did you arrive?

ZANETTO: Away with you! Keep your distance!

BEATRICE: But why! Aren't I your fiancée? Haven't you come here to arrange our wedding?

ZANETTO: That's it! The chains ... like a galley-slave! It's no use, my good woman. I know everything.

BEATRICE: What chains? Who's talking about chains? Don't you remember your promises?

ZANETTO: Promises? What promises?

BEATRICE: Of marriage.

ZANETTO: Of course, marriage! The weight on the purse and the weight on the mind!

BEATRICE: Stop it and look at me. Don't play jokes on me or I'll die.

ZANETTO [*to himself*]: Now we'll see the flames from those eyes.

BEATRICE: Perhaps you doubt me? Hear me, and I will dispel all your doubts.

ZANETTO: Shut your mouth! Shut that box of venom. I don't want it to creep in and poison my heart.

BEATRICE: Woe is me! Is it you who is speaking? I blush with shame for you.

ZANETTO: Let me look ... if her cheeks go red I'll know she is a witch.

BEATRICE: I am a desperate woman. Listen to me, for pity's sake! [*She goes towards* ZANETTO.]

ZANETTO [*retreating before her*]: Keep away, you fury. I know you come to tear me to pieces.

BEATRICE: Oh heavens! What have I done to deserve this? [*She goes towards him again.*]

ZANETTO: Away, you devil, that wants to drag me down to hell! [*Exit*]

BEATRICE [*alone*]: Can I have heard such things – and not be dead? My dear Tonino – oh, let me think what can have happened to him. He's either mad, or he's heard some evil talk about me. Oh, miserable me, what shall I do? I'll follow him at a distance, and I'll seize any means of discovering the truth. Oh, Cupid, god of love, you who to my misfortune made me leave home, parents and friends, help me through the dangers in which I find myself; if you wish for recompense, take my life rather than let me live disdained by my beloved Tonino.

Act Two

⩗ SCENE I ⩘

A Street. On one side the Doctor's house; on the other is an Inn with the sign: 'The Two Towers'.

[ARLECCHINO *enters, dressed for a journey, with a porter who is carrying a trunk and a cloak.*]

ARLECCHINO: So here we are at last. In the beautiful city of Verona – where it's possible to be in love with somebody I've never seen. Where I'm to marry a woman I've never met.

PORTER: Can't we hurry? I've other jobs to do. And I've to go and buy myself some bread.

ARLECCHINO: The trouble is I've no idea where that booby of a master of mine is lodging. Tell me, old chap, have you heard of a Signor Zanetto Bisognosi?

PORTER: No, I don't know him. Never heard of him.

ARLECCHINO: He's my master. He's come from Bergamo to Verona to get married. He's to have the lady, and I've to have her maid. To keep the money in the family. He came on here before me. I've just arrived with his things but I don't know where he's lodged nor how to find him.

PORTER: Well, Verona's a big place. You're going to have trouble finding him.

ARLECCHINO: Thanks. You're very helpful. Ssh! If this isn't him now! Come over here. I'll play a joke on him. To see if he recognizes me.

PORTER: You shouldn't play jokes on your master.

ARLECCHINO: Oh, he and I are friends. Come on, and watch me have a bit of fun.

PORTER: Well, don't take long about it. I haven't any time to waste.

ARLECCHINO: Go on! I've paid you well, haven't I?

[TONINO *enters.*]

TONINO: It's strange that I can learn nothing about Beatrice. Is it possible she's left me in the lurch, been false to me?

[ARLECCHINO, *wrapped in the cloak, passes in front of* TONINO *whom he thinks is* ZANETTO, *with an affected walk.*]

TONINO [*to himself*]: What's all this about? What does this fellow want with me?

[ARLECCHINO *turns and passes again in front of* TONINO, *this time with a rough and threatening air.*]

TONINO [*to himself*]: Perhaps it's an assassin sent to Verona by that man whose face I slapped?

[*As he passes in front of* TONINO *again,* ARLECCHINO *stamps his feet.*]

TONINO: What is it, sir? What d'you want? Who are you?

ARLECCHINO [*to himself, laughing*]: Oh, what a fool! He doesn't know me!

TONINO: D'you hear me? What is it you want with me?

[ARLECCHINO *runs towards* TONINO, *and as he reaches him swerves away from him.*]

TONINO [*drawing his sword*]: We'll see what this fine cock looks like without his feathers.

ARLECCHINO [*quickly throwing aside the cloak*]: Stop! Stop! Put up your sword. Don't you recognize me?

TONINO: Who are you? I don't know you.

ARLECCHINO: What! You don't know me?

TONINO: No, sir. I do not know you.

ARLECCHINO [*to himself*]: This city air must've affected his mind.

TONINO: Will you tell me who you are? What d'you want?

ARLECCHINO [*laughing*]: I know! You've been drinking!

TONINO: Less familiarity. Or I'll slice your legs for you.

ARLECCHINO: Then you do know me?

TONINO: No, sir, I do not know you.

ARLECCHINO: Now you'll know me. Here, take these things. Well, d'you know me now? [*He gives him a little box full of jewels.*]

TONINO [*to himself*]: What beautiful jewels! What is all this?

ARLECCHINO: So? D'you know me?

TONINO: No, sir. I do not know you.

ARLECCHINO: No? We'll try again. Here's the money. Now d'you know me? [*He gives him a purse full of money.*]

TONINO [*to himself*]: A purse full of money? [*to* ARLECCHINO] No, sir, I don't know you.

ARLECCHINO: Oh, damn and blast it! So you don't know me? Well, there's the trunk as well. And if you don't know me now – to hell with you.

TONINO: Even with this trunk I still don't know you.

ARLECCHINO: Are you mad, or drunk?

TONINO: It's you who must be mad or drunk. These jewels and this money – none of these things are mine. Take them and give them to whom they belong.

ARLECCHINO: It's you they belong to. These are all your things. The jewels, the money, the trunk, they're what you ordered me to bring you here. And that's what I've done. To the letter. So where are you lodging?

TONINO: At that Inn.

ARLECCHINO: Shall I take the trunk in?

TONINO: Do what you like with it.

ARLECCHINO: But you don't know me?

TONINO: I don't know you.

ARLECCHINO: Pah! Confounded idiot! I'm going into the Inn. I'm putting the trunk in your bedroom. Go and have a good sleep. And when the effects of the drink have worn off you'll know me.

[ARLECCHINO *picks up the trunk and the cloak and goes into the Inn.*]

TONINO [*alone*]: This is a fine how-d'you-do. A box of jewels, a purse full of money: this could have been a fine haul for someone. But as a man of honour and a gentleman, I don't pocket other people's things. That fellow's a madman. Heaven knows how he got hold of this purse and jewel-casket. But if I don't hold on to them, he'll give them to some scoundrel. I'd better look after them both, and if I can find out who has lost them I can restore them honourably.

[COLOMBINA *comes out of the Doctor's house.*]

COLOMBINA: Your servant, Signor Zanetto.

TONINO: Oh . . . oh, yes? You want me?

COLOMBINA: Yes, sir. You are Signor Zanetto Bisognosi, are you not?

TONINO: Yes, that is I, at your service. [*to himself*] All the better if she takes me for Zanetto.

COLOMBINA: If you please, sir, my mistress would like to speak with you.

TONINO [*to himself*]: I understand: the usual adventures of a stranger. [*to* COLOMBINA] Willingly. As I am not expecting anybody else, I will join you.

COLOMBINA: Oh, what beautiful jewels the Signor Zanetto has!

TONINO [*to himself*]: Ah, now I understand. Somebody's seen the jewels from that balcony. And she's been sent as an ambassador.

COLOMBINA: They are indeed! I suppose they're for the Signorina Rosaura.

TONINO: She is your mistress?

COLOMBINA: My mistress, signore.

TONINO [*to himself*]: She thinks it's I who own the jewels; but this time she's made a mistake. Still I may as well amuse myself. [*to* COLOMBINA] You could be right: it depends on whether they suit her.

COLOMBINA: In that case I'm sure they will. She's such a beautiful young lady.

TONINO [*to himself*]: Bravo! She's doing well for a procuress! [*to* COLOMBINA] But tell me, how do I have to pay?

COLOMBINA: In what connexion?

TONINO: Concerning the money.

COLOMBINA: What money?

TONINO [*to himself*]: Ah, it's the jewels that are the attraction. [*to* COLOMBINA] So she's rich, your mistress?

COLOMBINA: Well, she's a Doctor's daughter.

TONINO: A Doctor's daughter!

COLOMBINA: Oh, yes. Didn't you know that?

TONINO: But isn't there any danger of the Doctor saying something if he sees me in the house?

COLOMBINA: He also wants you to come. In fact it was really he who told me to come and ask you in.

TONINO [*to himself*]: Good heavens, the whole family are in it. All tarred with the same brush. I don't want to land myself in trouble. [*to* COLOMBINA] Listen, my girl, tell your mistress I'll come another time.

COLOMBINA: No, no, signore, she wants you to come at once. And you are such a fine gentleman, don't give up trying to please her.

TONINO: All right, but just let me go into the Inn there and put this box away and then I'll come.

COLOMBINA: Oh, how beautiful they are! Really you ought to bring these jewels with you if you want to please her.

TONINO [*to himself*]: Just as I said. It's the jewels they want. But this time I'm playing safe. They're not mine. And I'd best be cautious. Anyway I know how to look after myself.

[*The* DOCTOR *comes out of the house.*]

COLOMBINA: Here is Signor Zanetto, master. I'm tired out trying to persuade him to come into the house, but he doesn't want to.

DOCTOR: Come along now, Signor Zanetto, come into the house. My daughter is waiting for you.

TONINO [*to himself*]: I'd never've believed it!

DOCTOR: This reluctance of yours is an obvious insult to the dear girl.

TONINO [*to himself*]: It's getting better and better.

DOCTOR: Surely you don't want her to come out into the street, do you?

TONINO: Shame on you! I will come in.

DOCTOR: Excellent, excellent! Come then.

TONINO: You're sure I have your permission?

DOCTOR: Sir, you are welcome at any time, night or day.

TONINO: Open house? At any time?

DOCTOR: For Signor Zanetto the door is thrown wide open.

TONINO: For me only?

DOCTOR: For you only.

TONINO: For nobody else at all?

DOCTOR: Well – certain friends of the house, of course.

TONINO: Oh, naturally, of course. All right, I'll come.

DOCTOR: Yes, you really must.

TONINO: And I can come and go? Just as I please?

DOCTOR: Just as you please.

TONINO: Take off my clothes and make myself at home?

DOCTOR: Certainly.

TONINO: Have something to eat?

DOCTOR: Need you ask?

TONINO: I understand. After you, signore. [*He goes towards the door of the house.*]

DOCTOR: Signor Zanetto, one word, if you please.

TONINO [*to himself*]: He's wanting a tip. Now we'll see. [*to the* DOCTOR] At your command.

DOCTOR: Forgive the liberty, but what beautiful thing have you in that little box?

TONINO [*to himself*]: Ah hah! The gentleman has seen the jewels. [*to the* DOCTOR] Oh, certain trifles. Some bits of jewellery.

DOCTOR: Good, good. My daughter will be very pleased.

TONINO [*to himself*]: What a scandalous Doctor! [*to the* DOCTOR] Enough. If she will be sensible, they will be hers. [*to himself*] They certainly won't.

[TONINO *goes into the Doctor's house.*]

COLOMBINA: It seems to me that this Signor Zanetto isn't very much in love with the Signorina Rosaura.

DOCTOR: Why?

COLOMBINA: Didn't you see how difficult it was to get him to go into the house? I could see how things were. It makes me sick.

DOCTOR: On the other hand, I sympathize with him. Do you know what Rosaura did to him?

COLOMBINA: Well, what did she do?

DOCTOR: She gave him a slap on the face, a real hard one.

COLOMBINA: What for?

DOCTOR: I believe because he wanted to hold her hand a little.

COLOMBINA: Then the Signorina Rosaura was quite right. And if you'll pardon my saying, you should certainly not have sent him in to her while she's all alone.

DOCTOR: Oh, she's not on her own. Signor Pancrazio's there. He'll see nothing's amiss.

COLOMBINA: Huh! May the devil take your Signor Pancrazio.

DOCTOR: What's he done to you, to speak like this about him?

COLOMBINA: Oh, I can't bear the sight of him. Pious old humbug. And then to go and . . .

DOCTOR: Well? Go and what?

COLOMBINA: Oh, nothing. He said certain things to me.

DOCTOR: What did he say? Come on, speak up.

COLOMBINA: And he likes putting things in his pocket. Downright stealing, I call it.

DOCTOR: Hold your tongue, you wicked slanderer. Don't you dare to say such things about such an honest and honourable man. Give him the obedience and respect you would give to me. He is a respectable upright man and you are nothing but a malicious tittle-tattler. [*Exit*]

COLOMBINA: My master can say what he likes, but I'll take my oath that Signor Pancrazio is nothing but a hypocrite and up to no good.

[ARLECCHINO *comes out of the Inn.*]

ARLECCHINO: Where the devil's that lunatic got to? I've been waiting an hour and there's no sign of him.

COLOMBINA [*to herself*]: What an elegant little fellow!

ARLECCHINO [*to himself*]: I'll ask this girl if she's seen him.

[*to* COLOMBINA] Tell me, beautiful maiden, are you acquainted with a certain Signor Zanetto Bisognosi?

COLOMBINA: Certainly I know him.

ARLECCHINO: You've actually seen him? Here?

COLOMBINA: Of course.

ARLECCHINO: Then will you be so kind as to tell me where he's gone?

COLOMBINA: He's gone into that house.

ARLECCHINO: But who lives there?

COLOMBINA: The Signorina Rosaura, his fiancée.

ARLECCHINO: You know the Signorina Rosaura?

COLOMBINA: Very well.

ARLECCHINO: And her maid, you know her?

COLOMBINA: If it's her you want, I am she.

ARLECCHINO: What? You . . . the Signorina . . . Colombina?

COLOMBINA: I am Colombina.

ARLECCHINO: And . . . d'you know who I am?

COLOMBINA: I've no idea.

ARLECCHINO: Arlecchino Battochio.

COLOMBINA: You . . . Arlecchino?

ARLECCHINO: Me.

COLOMBINA: My husband.

ARLECCHINO: My bride!

COLOMBINA: But you're nice!

ARLECCHINO: And you're pretty!

COLOMBINA: What a lovely surprise!

ARLECCHINO: What a relief!

COLOMBINA: When did you arrive?

ARLECCHINO: One thing at a time. Let's go into the house and we'll talk there.

COLOMBINA: No, wait outside a moment. I must have a word with my mistress first. Before I take you into the house. I don't know if she'd like that.

ARLECCHINO: But I must also have a word with my master.

COLOMBINA: Stay there. I'll be back immediately.

ARLECCHINO: Yes, of course, my beautiful one! I just really couldn't be happier.

COLOMBINA: Oh, go away with you. You're poking fun at me.

ARLECCHINO: I'll make an honest girl of you.

COLOMBINA: You will love me?

ARLECCHINO: Yes. Stop prolonging the agony. Go on in.

COLOMBINA: I'm going. I'm going. [*to herself*] He's really charming.

[COLOMBINA *goes into the Doctor's house.*]

ARLECCHINO [*alone*]: Fortune, I thank you! She's beautiful! The loveliest girl I've seen for years. But what a risk I was taking! She might have had a squint and no teeth. But this girl – why, she's a real beauty and no doubt. Arlecchino, your luck's in!

COLOMBINA [*calling from the doorway of the house*]: Arlecchino, come on in. My mistress is delighted.

ARLECCHINO: I come, my beloved, I come.

[*He is about to go in the house when* ZANETTO *enters opposite and recognizes him from his back.*]

ZANETTO [*calling to him*]: Oy, there! Arlecchino. Arlecchino!

ARLECCHINO [*turning round*]: Signore!

ZANETTO: And about time.

ARLECCHINO: What d'you mean?

ZANETTO: You're here?

ARLECCHINO: *You* are – there?

ZANETTO: Of course I am.

ARLECCHINO: You're not in the house?

ZANETTO: What house?

ARLECCHINO: Here. In your lady friend's house. [*He points to* ROSAURA'S *house.*]

ZANETTO: Don't be silly. Of course I'm not.

ARLECCHINO [*to himself*]: So he's still trying to be funny.

ZANETTO: Where are all my things?

ARLECCHINO: Oh, that's excellent! In the Inn, I suppose.

ZANETTO: Where?

ARLECCHINO: Damned idiot! There, in 'The Two Towers'.

ZANETTO: Everything's there?

ARLECCHINO: Everything.

ZANETTO: The money and the jewels?

ARLECCHINO [*to himself*]: Now he's losing his memory. [*to* ZANETTO] The money and the jewels.

ZANETTO: Let us go and see.

ARLECCHINO: All right.

ZANETTO: Have you the key?

ARLECCHINO: Of what?

ZANETTO: Of the room.

ARLECCHINO: Me? No!

ZANETTO: You've left the money and the jewels like that?

ARLECCHINO: What d'you mean – like that?

ZANETTO: Where *are* they?

ARLECCHINO: Oh, this is excellent!

ZANETTO: Stop this nonsense!

ARLECCHINO: But I gave *you* the money and the jewels.

ZANETTO: You haven't given me anything at all yet.

ARLECCHINO [*to himself*]: I do believe he *is* mad.

ZANETTO: Where are my uncle's jewels? You did bring them?

ARLECCHINO: Of course I brought them.

ZANETTO: Then where are they?

ARLECCHINO: Look, old fellow, let us go inside, shall we? Because I'll lose patience with you in a moment!

ZANETTO: There's no need to fly into a temper. They're sure to be in my room.

ARLECCHINO: Yes, they're sure to be in your room.

ZANETTO: I'll go and see. What a helpless nincompoop you are!

[*He goes into the Inn.*]

ARLECCHINO: Go and see, then! You – bad-tempered lunatic!

[*He follows* ZANETTO *into the Inn.*]

COLOMBINA [*coming to the door of the Doctor's house again*]: Arlecchino, where are you? Oh, this is perfect! He's gone off somewhere. Shows how much *his* love means. But where can he have gone to? Ah, well, if he wants to, he'll come back. And if he doesn't, a girl like me doesn't have to go looking for a husband. [*She goes back into the house.*]

⟨ SCENE 2 ⟩

A room in the DOCTOR'S *house, with table and chairs.*

[TONINO *is seated, alone.*]

TONINO: I've been kept waiting about in here for over an hour, and not a sign of the lady. They must either take me for a fool or think that the longer I'm kept waiting the more I'll be willing to pay. Well, they certainly can't know who they're dealing with! Tonino Bisognosi, citizen of Venice! That's more than enough for anyone! Bestir yourselves and make up your mind! Ho, there! Where is everybody?

[BRIGHELLA *enters.*]

BRIGHELLA: At your service, signore. Do you want something?

TONINO: And who might you be?

BRIGHELLA: The house servant.

TONINO [*to himself*]: Like hell you are. I'm being made a fool of. [*to* BRIGHELLA] Then tell me, friend, is your mistress going to be obliging, or do I go?

BRIGHELLA: I'll fetch her at once. Yes, I'm an old house servant here now. *But* I was once a good servant of the Bisognosi family.

TONINO: What? You know me then?

BRIGHELLA: I knew your brother. A real high-spirited young lad, he was.

TONINO: Where did you know him?

BRIGHELLA: In Venice.

TONINO: You knew him when he was a boy?

BRIGHELLA: And after he'd grown up. But here comes my lady.

TONINO: No, tell me quickly – when did you know him in Venice, after he'd grown up?

BRIGHELLA: I'm sorry. I must go. We will talk later. Your servant. [*Exit*]

TONINO: What the devil was the fellow talking about? I don't remember ever seeing him in Venice.

[ROSAURA *enters*.]

ROSAURA: Your servant, Signor Zanetto. I am sorry to have kept you waiting.

TONINO: Oh, nothing surprises me, mistress. [*to himself*] What a figure! What a face!

ROSAURA [*to herself*]: He looks at me strangely. He must still be angry about that slap I gave him.

TONINO [*to himself*]: I stay in Verona! No going away now!

ROSAURA: Pardon me if I have inconvenienced you.

TONINO: Not at all, mistress. On the contrary, I can call myself fortunate that you should consider me worthy of the honour of your company.

ROSAURA [*to herself*]: It's not like him to be so full of compliments. I could almost believe he's laughing at me. I'd best fall in with his mood.

TONINO [*to himself*]: She *looks* the most modest young lady.

ROSAURA: Oh, it was my father who obliged me to have you brought into the house.

TONINO: And, if your father had not insisted, you would not have called me?

ROSAURA: I most certainly would not have been so presumptuous.

TONINO: So you do not think much of me yourself?

ROSAURA: On the contrary I have the most high regard for you.

TONINO: You are most kind. Can I hope for evidence of your high regard?

ROSAURA: You may hope for every evidence, if such is my father's wish.

TONINO [*to himself*]: Poor child! She makes me sorry for her. Her father must keep her locked up here and she has no will of her own. [*to* ROSAURA] Pardon me, but I am not sure whether you understand me. How are we to – conduct ourselves?

ROSAURA: With regard to what?

TONINO: With regard to – reciprocating our affection?

ROSAURA: You must speak to my father about that.

TONINO: Ah, it's he who arranges it all?

ROSAURA: But, of course.

TONINO [*to himself*]: Oh, what a pernicious Doctor! [*to* ROSAURA] But suppose he comes in, while we are . . . alone. We would not be able to . . .

ROSAURA: Able to what?

TONINO: To amuse ourselves a little.

ROSAURA: You are thinking of the slap on the face.

TONINO [*to himself*]: Not again! Does everyone know about the slap I gave that man in Venice! [*to* ROSAURA] Oh, such trifles aren't worth remembering.

ROSAURA: I cannot forget about it.

TONINO: But why should it trouble you?

ROSAURA: It troubles me that you should be so imprudent.

TONINO: But, my dear girl, in such circumstances one has to do something.

ROSAURA: Under such circumstances it is advisable to have prudence.

TONINO: I don't know what to say. Yes, you are right. I will not behave so again. Now that I know you love me.

ROSAURA: What makes you so sure of that?

TONINO [*sighing*]: Ah!

ROSAURA: Why do you sigh?

TONINO: Because I fear you say that to everybody.

ROSAURA: What d'you mean? To everybody? I'm surprised at you!

TONINO: Forgive me.

ROSAURA: What reason could you have to say such a thing?

TONINO: Very well! Here I am, only arrived in Verona today. Do you really think I believe you can have fallen in love with me so suddenly?

ROSAURA: Nevertheless, the moment I saw you, my heart was yours, all yours.

TONINO [*to himself*]: Is it possible? Take care, Tonino, put not your trust in women.

ROSAURA: And you, Signor Zanetto, do you love me?

TONINO: You are so beautiful, gentle and gracious, I would need be made of stone not to love you.

ROSAURA: What sign do you give me of your love?

TONINO [*to himself*]: Ah! What sign does she want: caresses or money? [*to* ROSAURA] Anything. You have only to command.

ROSAURA: But it is for you to demonstrate your affection.

TONINO [*to himself*]: I understand. This will put her to the test. [*to* ROSAURA] If I may be so bold, I have here some little jewels. May I say that they are at your service. [*He opens the box and lets her see the jewels.*]

ROSAURA: Oh, they are beautiful! You mean they're for me?

TONINO: If you wish, they will be yours.

ROSAURA: I accept with joy such a precious gift. And I will always cherish them as the first token of your love.

TONINO: Say no more. We will talk of them later. [*to himself*] What exquisite diffidence! She didn't need much persuading!

ROSAURA: But tell me, is there no other way in which you wish to assure me of your devotion?

TONINO [*to himself*]: She can't wait to get the lot. [*to* ROSAURA] Well, I have some money here. You can have that as well if you wish.

ROSAURA: No, no, you can give that to my father. I don't have anything to do with money.

TONINO [*to himself*]: Oh, this is excellent! The daughter does the dirty work while the father holds the bank. [*to* ROSAURA] Please do as you wish.

ROSAURA: But you do not seem willing to give me what I ask?

TONINO: The devil! Is it my shirt you want? Here, take it!

ROSAURA: I don't want your shirt. Nor your coat. I want you.

TONINO: Me? Here I am! The whole lot of me is yours.

ROSAURA: Then we can do it today.

TONINO: Now! Right away, if you wish!

ROSAURA: I am ready.

TONINO: I'm more than ready.

ROSAURA: Will you give me your hand?*

TONINO: Hand, feet, and anything else you want.

ROSAURA: Let us call two witnesses.*

TONINO: What the devil! What d'you want two witnesses for?

ROSAURA: So they will be present.

TONINO: Present at what?

ROSAURA: At our wedding.

TONINO: Wedding! Here, hold on a minute!

ROSAURA: But you said you were ready?

TONINO: I'm ready, yes. But what's the hurry for a wedding . . .?

ROSAURA: Go away! Go away! I see you've been making fun of me!

TONINO [to himself]: She doesn't displease me and perhaps in time I might even go so far as marriage. But what certainly doesn't please me is this facility at inviting people into the house.

ROSAURA: You are too changeable, Signor Zanetto.

TONINO: Changeable? That's not true. I'm the epitome of constancy and fidelity. But this sort of thing, as you will know better than I, needs to be done with a little give and take. It needs thinking about. Such an important decision mustn't be made hastily.

ROSAURA: And yet you say you are not changeable. One minute you want it done at once with no ceremony or formality. The next minute you're looking for excuses and wanting to think it over.

TONINO: Well, if I have to make a decision here and now . . . I'd say . . . No, I don't want you to get angry.

ROSAURA: Will you please speak plainly.

TONINO: Suppose you were to favour me with . . .

ROSAURA: Don't hope for any favours before the wedding.

TONINO: None at all?

ROSAURA: Absolutely none.

---

*Apart from the priest's blessing which would be given later, the holding of hands was a common way of performing a marriage in Venice in the eighteenth century – granted that both parties had given their free consent and that there were at least two witnesses.

TONINO: But . . . the jewels?

ROSAURA: If that was your intention in giving me them, keep them. I don't want them.

TONINO: To refuse them so virtuously makes you deserve them more than ever. You are a most honest young lady and it's a shame you have such a wicked father.

ROSAURA: How is my father wicked?

TONINO: Well, d'you think it's nothing to introduce a man unscrupulously into his house and put his daughter in danger of ruining herself?

ROSAURA: But he did that because you are my fiancé.

TONINO: Good heavens, but that's not true. We've never even spoken of such a thing.

ROSAURA: But didn't you arrange it by letter?

TONINO: No, Signorina, most certainly not. He's very cleverly deceived you. He's a wicked man. He knows I've a little money and so he entices me in here and tries to use your beauty to make a dishonest profit.

ROSAURA: Signor Zanetto, it is you who are saying a very wicked thing!

TONINO: Unfortunately, I'm speaking the truth. But listen, you are so beautiful and so honest you deserve a better life than this. Don't be downhearted. Take courage. If you love me, perhaps you may soon be my wife.

ROSAURA: No, I am very upset. D'you think, if I had not thought you were my fiancé, I would have spoken as I have done to you? If my father has deceived me, then may Heaven forgive him. But if it is you who are playing a joke on me, then it is too cruel of you. Reflect on that, and remember, in either case, that I love you – with the most honest and the most honourable love in the world. [*Exit*]

TONINO [*alone*]: Was there ever a more modest daughter and a more wicked father? Marriage? Tonino, make up your mind. When it's done, it's done, and there'll be no going back. But there's Beatrice. I made her a promise and she ran away from home on my account. But where is she? Where has she gone? Who knows whether it was for me or for

somebody else that she left home? She's certainly not come
here. Nobody's seen anything of her. It is possible that she's
deceived me. I know too well how fickle women are.

[BRIGHELLA *enters*.]

BRIGHELLA: Is there anything I can do for you, signore?
TONINO: No, friend. I am going.
BRIGHELLA: So soon?
TONINO: Why should I stay?
BRIGHELLA: Aren't you having dinner with the Doctor?
TONINO: No, thank you. And you can tell your master the
    Doctor he ought to be ashamed of himself.
BRIGHELLA: What way's that to speak?
TONINO: I think you understand quite well.
BRIGHELLA: I don't know what you're talking about. He's
    ordered me to see you have everything you want. Won't
    you take your coat off?
TONINO: No, old fellow, I will not. But so that you won't
    think I'm wanting to do you out of your tip, keep this half
    ducat.
BRIGHELLA: That's very kind of you, signore. Ah, yes, the
    Bisognosi family was always most generous. The signore
    your brother in Venice, he was always most liberal too.
TONINO [*to himself*]: He keeps on about this brother of mine in
    Venice. [*to* BRIGHELLA] But when did you know my
    brother in Venice?
BRIGHELLA: It will be about two years ago.
TONINO: Two years? Surely not?
BRIGHELLA: Yes, signore, because I was in Venice. . . .

[PANCRAZIO *enters*.]

PANCRAZIO: Brighella, go to your mistress. She has need of
    you.
BRIGHELLA: I go at once.
TONINO [*to* BRIGHELLA]: Finish what you were saying about
    Venice, old fellow.
PANCRAZIO: Pardon me but he must go. Hurry up! Be
    quick!

BRIGHELLA: Until later, most illustrious Signor Zanetto! [*Exit*]

TONINO [*to himself*]: Damn this interruption. That fellow has me puzzled.

PANCRAZIO: I'm delighted to see you, Signor Zanetto.

TONINO: My compliments, signore.

PANCRAZIO: Ah, I am sorry for you. From your face it would seem that you have paid little heed to my advice.

TONINO: On the contrary, I listen willingly to any gentleman such as yourself.

PANCRAZIO: And then go your own way, eh?

TONINO: Why should you say that?

PANCRAZIO: Perhaps I am wrong. But I see you in this house and that makes me doubtful.

TONINO [*to himself*]: Ah, now we may find out something. [*to* PANCRAZIO] In this houseful of wicked people, you mean?

PANCRAZIO: Ah, unfortunately, yes!

TONINO: People who are out to get all they can?

PANCRAZIO: And in what a way!

TONINO: This Doctor, he is indeed a most wicked man.

PANCRAZIO: You've seen through him at once.

TONINO: But the girl? What is she like?

PANCRAZIO: Never believe a word she says. She's thoroughly deceitful.

TONINO: With such an appealing little face?

PANCRAZIO: Ah, my friend, it is those who seem most modest who have the most to conceal.

TONINO: You realize what you are saying?

PANCRAZIO: I realize it only too well.

TONINO: Then what are *you* doing in the house of such wicked people?

PANCRAZIO: I labour to show them the error of their ways. In vain, alas! My good seed falls on stony ground. There is nothing to be done.

TONINO: I fear you are right.

PANCRAZIO: They go from bad to worse.

TONINO: And yet I can't help liking that young girl.

PANCRAZIO: Take care. She could melt a heart of stone. I pity the poor young man who finds favour with her.

TONINO: She would like me to consider marriage. . . .

PANCRAZIO: Marriage! Oh, what a horrible, disgusting word that is!

TONINO: Marriage a horrible word? Why, it's the most beautiful word you can find in any language.

PANCRAZIO: But don't you remember? Marriage is a weight, a weight that makes your days wearisome and your nights sleepless. It weighs down your spirit, weighs down your body, weighs down your purse and weighs down your mind.

TONINO: Don't talk nonsense! Weighs down your spirit? Rubbish! A loving wife consoles the heart and lifts up the spirit. Happy is the man whom fortune blesses with the love of a good wife. Weighs down your body? More rubbish! A wife looks after the house and the servants, and relieves her husband of all such troubles and worries. Weighs down your purse? Rubbish again. A wife helps a man to control his natural inclination to spend money unreasonably. Weighs down your mind? Absolute rubbish! If the wife's honest then there's no danger of being cuckolded. If she's not honest, there's nothing that a good beating won't cure. Take it from me, marriage is a good thing for good people and a bad thing for bad people. These lines by a Venetian poet put it in a nutshell:

> When marrying it's best to be prudent:
> To know how to give and take;
> Some should never a marriage make:
> They are the old, the mad and the impotent.

PANCRAZIO [to himself]: This fellow's not the fool I took him for. [to TONINO] But surely you remember – a woman is an enchanting siren who allures only to deceive, who loves only to ensnare?

TONINO: Pardon me, that's nothing but a pack of lies. All women are not alike. There are good ones and bad ones. The same as men. Women, enchanting sirens? Rubbish.

We see a woman, we follow her, we are enchanted. Whose fault is that? Ours, of course. If a woman twists us round her little finger, it's our own fault for running after her. No wonder women obtain such power over us. Our weakness flatters their pride.

PANCRAZIO [to himself]: This fellow's too good for me! [to TONINO] Signor Zanetto, I don't know what to say. If you love the Signorina Rosaura, marry her. But think well, first.

TONINO: I haven't said I love her. I was defending marriage but I didn't say *I* wanted to get married. I was defending woman but I didn't say *I* loved Rosaura. I don't know what she's like. She seems one thing and then another. And you've made me more suspicious. So I shan't do anything.

PANCRAZIO: You could not do better. I praise your decision. You are a man of great sensibility.

TONINO: And since you are a man of such good intentions yourself I would like to ask a favour of you, in confidence.

PANCRAZIO: You may speak freely. I know how to keep a secret.

TONINO: You see this box of jewels?

PANCRAZIO: Jewels, are they?

TONINO: Yes, signore.

PANCRAZIO: Let me see! [he examines them] Ah, yes! Beautiful! Oh, very beautiful!

TONINO: These jewels were given me, against my will, by a poor mad fellow in a shabby coat. I don't know who he was, but his master apparently is staying at the Inn here. As I shall be going away, I was thinking of entrusting them to you so that you might restore them to his master.

PANCRAZIO: I admire your thoughtfulness. You are indeed an honourable man.

TONINO: Any man of honour could do no less.

PANCRAZIO: But, suppose, after some time . . . and after having searched with all diligence, I should not be able to find their owner, how would you wish me to dispose of them?

TONINO: Uphold marriage with them! Give them as dowries to young brides.

PANCRAZIO: Ah, you are very good-hearted.

TONINO: We people of rank must accept our responsibilities. How many poor wretches live on charity? Charity is often given from selfish motives, it's true. But also from good-heartedness. That's what I'm like. For my friends I'd ruin myself. And for the ladies, I'd even take the shirt from my back. [*Exit*]

PANCRAZIO: This time charity begins at home. I'll use this fool to my own advantage. If Rosaura would like these jewels she will have to buy them with a lot of money that's nothing to her but will mean a very great deal to me. [*Exit*]

≺ SCENE 3 ≻

As in Act Two, Scene 1: a Street: on one side the Doctor's house and on the other an Inn bearing the sign 'The Two Towers'.

[ARLECCHINO *comes out of the Inn followed by* ZANETTO.]

ARLECCHINO: I'm amazed at you. I'm an honest man, and I tell you I gave you the jewels and the money.

ZANETTO [*from the doorway*]: That's not true at all. You're a little thief. I've had nothing from you.

ARLECCHINO: May that lie stick in your throat – and in your belly.

ZANETTO [*coming out*]: I say you're a thief and I want my jewels.

ARLECCHINO: And I'm telling you I gave you the jewels.

ZANETTO: Dog! Traitor! My jewels, my money and my clothes!

ARLECCHINO: You're stark staring mad – that's what's the matter with you.

ZANETTO: You've robbed me, d'you hear? Robbed me!

ARLECCHINO: Keep away! Or I'll throw this stone!

[BARGELLO, *accompanied by guards, enters.*]

BARGELLO: What's all this noise? Who is the thief? Who has been robbed?

ZANETTO: That's him! My servant! He was bringing me a box of jewels and some money from Bergamo and he's stolen the lot.

ARLECCHINO: It's not true! I'm an honest man, I am!

BARGELLO: If you are innocent you will be soon allowed out of prison.

ARLECCHINO: Prison!

BARGELLO: Now don't make any trouble.

ARLECCHINO: Damnation! And all through you, you silly fool, you big ignorant booby. If I ever come out again I'll make you pay for this! [*Exit with the guards who lead him off.*]

BARGELLO: Signore, if you're sure this fellow really is the thief, you must lodge a complaint and you will be given justice. In the meantime, I will make my report and institute criminal proceedings. If you have any evidence, bring it with you and produce it to the Clerk of the Court. [*Exit*]

ZANETTO: What was he talking about? All I want are my jewels. The jewels which my uncle left me. Which he brought from Venice when I went to live in Bergamo.

[BEATRICE *enters.*]

BEATRICE: Oh my beloved, have pity on me.

ZANETTO [*to himself*]: Those eyes of fire! That mouth full of poison!

BEATRICE: Don't go. Listen to me, for just one moment. I ask only one thing. Here I am at your feet. Let my tears move you to pity me. [*She kneels before him.*]

ZANETTO [*holding out one hand towards* BEATRICE'S *eyes*]: I don't feel them burning me. They're certainly not two flames of fire.

BEATRICE: If you will only listen to me you will be glad of it.

ZANETTO [*to himself*]: That little mouth is so beautiful. I wouldn't mind being poisoned by it.

BEATRICE: For your sake I have risked my life and my honour.

ZANETTO: For me?

BEATRICE: Yes, for you, whom I love more than life itself, for you, who are never out of my thoughts.

ZANETTO: You mean – *you* love me?

BEATRICE: Yes, I love you, I adore you, you are my whole life.

ZANETTO [*to himself*]: If she's a devil, she's a most beautiful devil!

BEATRICE: I cannot bear to suffer any longer. Tell me, oh, tell me that you love me.

ZANETTO [*to himself*]: This is more like it! Without any ceremonies and solemnities.

BEATRICE: Come, relieve me of my misery.

ZANETTO: I'm willing, signorina. What d'you want me to do.

BEATRICE: Give me your hand.*

ZANETTO: Both if you like. [*He touches her hand.*] Oh, my! Oh, what a hand! Oh, so soft! Oh, it's like silk!

[FLORINDO *enters and stands on one side.*]

FLORINDO [*to himself*]: What do I see? Tonino has found Beatrice! I must find a way to put things right.

BEATRICE: And here's one person who can serve as a witness.*

ZANETTO: This gentleman would be suitable?

BEATRICE: Oh, yes! Signor Florindo, at last I have succeeded in finding my fiancé. He is ready to give me his hand and we would like you to be a witness.

ZANETTO: Yes, signore, a witness.

FLORINDO: That is something I always do most unwillingly. But when it's between friends, one must do all one can. [*to* ZANETTO] But first, be good enough to favour me with a word?

ZANETTO: Willingly. [*to* BEATRICE *with a deep bow*] Don't go away. I shan't be a moment.

FLORINDO [*taking* ZANETTO *aside and pointing to the Doctor's house*] Tell me, friend, haven't you just been in that house?

ZANETTO: Yes, signore.

FLORINDO: For what purpose, may I ask?

*See footnote on p. 61.

ZANETTO: To get engaged to be married to the Doctor's daughter.

FLORINDO: And now you want to marry the Signorina Beatrice?

ZANETTO: Yes, signore.

FLORINDO: But if you have pledged your word to the Signorina Rosaura?

ZANETTO: Oh, well, I can marry both. That doesn't matter. [*to* BEATRICE] I'm ready now.

FLORINDO: You must be joking!

ZANETTO: I'm not! D'you think I'm not capable of taking six of them on in marriage?

FLORINDO: But good heavens, this isn't Turkey! You know as well as I that you can't marry more than one.

ZANETTO: Well, I'll marry this one. [*to* BEATRICE] Come on!

FLORINDO: But you can't even do that!

ZANETTO: Why not?

FLORINDO: Because you've promised the Doctor's daughter. You've given her your word. And if you break your word, they'll put you in prison and it'll cost you a lot of money.

ZANETTO [*to himself*]: This is a fine how-d'you-do! [*to* BEATRICE] It's all off.

BEATRICE: What did you say?

ZANETTO: I'm taking back my hand.

BEATRICE: But I don't understand.

ZANETTO: Understand or not, it's all over. Finished.

BEATRICE: How can you do this to me?

ZANETTO: I'm sorry. I've never been to prison. And I don't want to.

BEATRICE: But why should you go to prison?

ZANETTO: I can't marry two of you. There's that Doctor's daughter. I promised her. So I'd be put in prison. Good-bye. [*Exit*]

BEATRICE: Oh unhappy me! My Tonino has gone mad. He speaks so strangely that I hardly know him.

FLORINDO: Signorina Beatrice, allow me to explain. He has fallen in love with the Signorina Rosaura, the daughter of the Doctor Balanzoni, and has promised to marry her. So, torn between love and remorse, his mind has become affected and he has become nearly insane.

BEATRICE: Oh, no, no! This cannot be true!

FLORINDO: Only too true, unfortunately. You must be blind if you do not see from his way of speaking that it is so.

BEATRICE: Yes, I said I hardly knew him.

FLORINDO: What will you do now?

BEATRICE: If Tonino abandons me, I shall die.

[LELIO *enters.*]

FLORINDO: If Tonino abandons you, here is Florindo ready to serve you.

LELIO: If Tonino abandons you, here is one ready to avenge you.

FLORINDO: In me you would find a faithful lover.

LELIO: With me you would find unbelievable happiness.

FLORINDO: I am of noble birth.

LELIO: Illustrious blood runs in my veins.

FLORINDO: I am not short of money.

LELIO: Among my possessions are gold mines.

FLORINDO: I think you do not find my face displeasing.

LELIO: You see in me the most handsome man in the world.

FLORINDO: Signorina Beatrice, pay no heed to this self-inflated buffoon.

LELIO: Don't listen to this effeminate prig who hasn't got a penny to his name.

FLORINDO: If you want me, I am yours.

LELIO: If you wish it, you can be mine.

[TONINO *enters and stands aside, watching.*]

TONINO [*to himself*]: What! Beatrice . . . here . . . and with two men. . . .

FLORINDO: Speak, my beloved.

TONINO [*as above*]: My beloved!

LELIO: Open those lips, my beautiful one.

TONINO [*as above*]: My beautiful one! What is this?

FLORINDO: If Tonino has deserted you, he is a traitor.

LELIO: If Tonino has abandoned you, he's an ungrateful swine!

TONINO [*advancing on them*]: Tonino is no traitor! Tonino, by heavens, is no swine! Tonino has not abandoned Beatrice. [*to* FLORINDO] And as for you, you two-faced hypocrite, you false friend, you miserable bag of wind . . .

FLORINDO: But the Signorina Rosaura . . .

TONINO: What Signorina Rosaura? Hold your tongue, you empty dolt. You disclose my name! You tell everyone all about me! From now on do not dare to mention my name again. And don't ever dare come near me unless you want your belly riddled full of holes.

LELIO: May I say . . .

TONINO: No, you may not say, you thick-skinned heap of bluff. I disarmed you once. Next time I'll cut your heart out. [*he takes* BEATRICE'S *hand*] This lady is mine, and that's enough for both of you.

BEATRICE: So now you declare I am yours. . . .

TONINO [*to* BEATRICE]: Hush, we must talk privately. Come with me. [*to* FLORINDO *and* LELIO, *as he leads* BEATRICE *off*] Lily-livered lap-dogs! Mealy-mouthed braggarts! Canting humbugs! Windbags! [*Exit*]

FLORINDO: My name is not Florindo if I do not revenge myself!

LELIO: No one dare call me Lelio again if I do not massacre that insolent fool!

FLORINDO: Friend, he made fools of us both.

LELIO: Let us unite for vengeance.

FLORINDO: Let us think what to do.

LELIO: I am so furious I could . . .

FLORINDO: Let us both attack him sword in hand.

LELIO: No, let us fire pistols into his back.

FLORINDO: That would be treacherous.

LELIO: The end justifies the means. So long as he dies, I care not how! [*Exit*]

FLORINDO [*alone*]: No, Signor Lelio, your fine heroic words will not kill anybody. It is best I seek my revenge alone. Beatrice will be mine! Or Tonino will fall, pierced by this sword! [*Exit, flourishing his sword.*]

Act Three

A Street: on one side the Doctor's house and on the other an Inn with the sign 'The Two Towers'.

[PANCRAZIO *comes out of the Doctor's house just as* TIBURZIO, *the jeweller, comes out of the Inn.*]

PANCRAZIO: Ah, I was just coming to look for you, Signor Tiburzio. If I had not found you here, I was coming to your shop.

TIBURZIO: Signor Pancrazio, I am yours to command. How can I serve you?

PANCRAZIO: I will tell you. I have some jewels to sell. They belonged to a good-hearted widow who left me them to dispose of as dowries for young girls. Would you, with your usual sincerity, tell me their value?

TIBURZIO: Most willingly. I am always ready to be of service to you. Have you them with you?

PANCRAZIO: Here they are. Examine them carefully. [*He takes out the little box and opens it.*]

[*The* CHIEF CONSTABLE *and the* GUARDS *enter and stand watching the jewels at a distance.*]

TIBURZIO: Signor Pancrazio, these jewels are very valuable. It is impossible to estimate how valuable off-hand. Bring them to my shop and I will examine them there.

PANCRAZIO: I will indeed. Some of them are a little dirty. Do you have any secret process for cleaning them?

TIBURZIO: As a matter of fact I have. A very rare powder. I don't tell people about it because it contains a very dangerous poison.

PANCRAZIO: Still you can make an exception of me. You

cannot doubt that I would abuse your confidence. You know who I am. . . .

TIBURZIO: I know you to be an honest man and I will help you. By good fortune I have a little box of the powder with me. Here it is. Take it and use it. You will find it makes the jewels clean and shining. And if you decide to sell them I may perhaps be able to get you a good price for them.

PANCRAZIO: I will see you do not lose by it. Meanwhile I am much obliged to you. I shall wait upon you tomorrow.

TIBURZIO: I shall always be ready to serve you. [*Exit*]

PANCRAZIO [*to himself, looking at the jewels*]: Beautiful! True, the settings are old-fashioned, and the diamonds are very dirty. Ah, but some of this powder will make them sparkle again.

BARGELLO [*to himself*]: That little box of jewels is exactly like the one Arlecchino described.

PANCRAZIO [*to himself*]: And of course – with such a beautiful present I may hope to gain the favours of my dear Rosaura.

BARGELLO: One moment, if you please, signore.

PANCRAZIO: What is it? What d'you want?

BARGELLO: Those jewels.

PANCRAZIO: For what reason?

BARGELLO: Because they are stolen property.

PANCRAZIO: How dare you! I am an honest citizen.

BARGELLO: In that case, signore, you won't mind telling me who you got them from?

PANCRAZIO: From Signor Zanetto Bisognosi.

BARGELLO: Well, well! And Signor Zanetto Bisognosi says his jewels have been stolen. As they are in your possession consider yourself as under suspicion of having stolen them.

PANCRAZIO: Ridiculous! A man in my position!

BARGELLO: Be thankful I'm not arresting you here and now. As it is, I will take the jewels to the Chancellery and if you're innocent you can come and prove it.

PANCRAZIO: I? To the Chancellery! To the law courts! But everybody knows *me*! Everybody knows I'm the soul of honour!

[ZANETTO *enters.*]

Ah! Here's Signor Zanetto himself! Tell them how you came by these jewels.

ZANETTO: Jewels? My jewels?

BARGELLO: Signor Zanetto, do you recognize these jewels?

ZANETTO: Yes, yes! These are the jewels my uncle left me. Of course I recognize them. They're mine.

PANCRAZIO: There you are! He recognizes them! They were his uncle's. They were his.

BARGELLO [*to* ZANETTO]: And you gave them to Signor Pancrazio?

PANCRAZIO: Yes, yes, he gave them to me. [*to* ZANETTO]: That's right, isn't it?

ZANETTO: I never gave you anything!

PANCRAZIO: What d'you mean: you've never given me anything? I'm surprised at you!

ZANETTO: And I'm surprised at you. These are mine!

PANCRAZIO: Heavens above, man! D'you want to lose me my reputation?

ZANETTO: You can lose what you like; I don't know what you're talking about. [*to the guard holding the box*] Give me my jewels, young man.

PANCRAZIO: Are you out of your mind? There, in the Doctor's house, in the Signorina Rosaura's room, you gave me them! And you know why!

ZANETTO: Oh, what a liar! You tell lies, lies, lies. All lies. You tell me also women have eyes of fire. It is not true.

PANCRAZIO: Signor Bargello, this man must be mad! Give me those jewels.

BARGELLO: Mad or not, the jewels are going to the Chancellery. It will be up to you to prove who gave you them. [*to the Guards*] Go and release Arlecchino and bring him in custody to the Chancellery. [*The Guards go out.*]

PANCRAZIO: I'll find witnesses! Immediately! I'll bring the Doctor, Brighella, Signorina Rosaura, Colombina! I'll bring everybody from the Doctor's house. I'll go now! Wait for me! I'll come with you. Oh, my reputation! My reputation! My reputation! [*He runs into the Doctor's house.*]

ZANETTO: All I want are my jewels. Give them to me. Or I will become ill with worry.

BARGELLO: Come along to the Chancellor. If he says I can give you them, then I'll give you them.

ZANETTO: But what's it to do with the Chancellor?

BARGELLO: You can't have them without his permission, and that's that.

ZANETTO: But suppose he says no?

BARGELLO: Then you can't have them.

ZANETTO: What will you do with them?

BARGELLO: Whatever the Chancellor orders.

ZANETTO: You mean I might lose them?

BARGELLO: No might about it. You would.

ZANETTO: Well! It would've been better to let that old man keep them. At least he took some risk and trouble to steal them.

BARGELLO: Are you accusing the Chancellor of stealing them now?

ZANETTO: All I know is they're mine and through him I might lose them. I don't see any difference between stealing and keeping.

BARGELLO: I think you'd better find yourself a good lawyer.

ZANETTO: What do I want with a lawyer?

BARGELLO: So that *he* can explain to the Chancellor just why *you* think these jewels are yours.

ZANETTO: But what need's there for a lawyer to do that? He couldn't know better than I do, that those jewels are mine.

BARGELLO: Maybe. But *you* won't be believed.

ZANETTO: Me . . . no? A lawyer . . . yes? Lies are believed? But the truth no?

BARGELLO: Nothing of the sort! It's simply that lawyers know how to put a case better than their clients.

ZANETTO: But doesn't a lawyer have to be paid?

BARGELLO: Of course. You pay him his fee.

ZANETTO: And the Chancellor?

BARGELLO: He also requires his fee.

ZANETTO: And you? You get nothing?

BARGELLO: Of course I have to be paid. And all my men.

ZANETTO: So between the Chancellor, the lawyer, and you and your guards, it's good-bye to all my jewels.

BARGELLO: But that's how these things are done. Everybody has to get what's due to them.

ZANETTO: You mean everybody except me? Good! Fine! That makes me very happy! I go back to my mountains. No Chancellors there! No lawyers! No guards! There, what's mine's mine. There, people don't try to fleece me while pretending they're doing me a service. Divide the jewels between yourself and the others, and if there's anything left for me, let me know so that I can thank you from the bottom of my heart. Well, come on, you lot of thieves, what are you waiting for? Rob me of my shirt as well and finish me off while you're at it. It's all the same to the sheep whether the wolf eats her or the butcher cuts her throat. It's all the same to me whether I'm ruined by thieves or by your fine gentlemen. [*Exit*]

BARGELLO: That fellow *must* be mad. Or else he's asking for trouble. No matter. We guards have thick skins. We have to. To put up with insinuations of that sort. [*Exit*]

[TONINO *enters*.]

TONINO [*alone*]: So *that's* all that friendship means nowadays. When Florindo was in Venice, I treated him like a brother. I take him into my confidence and send him the woman who means everything to me. And he betrays me! It's beyond my understanding. How can a man behave like that? If I were capable of such iniquity, I'd fear the very earth would open and swallow me up.

[LELIO *enters*.]

LELIO [*to himself*]: There he is, my fortunate rival. Let's see what a little flattery can do.

TONINO [*to himself*]: At least I can settle accounts with this fellow.

LELIO: I bow before the exalted, before the noblest of all the most celebrated heroes of Venice.

TONINO: Your servant, you loud-mouthed proclaimer of your own importance.

LELIO: I beg your pardon if, with the tedious articulation of my pronunciation, I dare to offend the tympanum of your ear.

TONINO: Regurgitate the trumpet of your eloquence, lest I touch not only its tympanum but also its drum.

LELIO: I must make known to you that I am overcome with the most delirious madness.

TONINO: I suspected it from the first.

LELIO: Love's poisoned arrows have pierced my impenetrable heart.

TONINO: And your brain as well, I'd say.

LELIO: Ah, Signor Zanetto, you who are of the family Bisognosi, deny not your aid to one who has need of you.

TONINO: *You* have need of *me*? For what?

LELIO: I am burning with love.

TONINO: Well, if it's sympathy you want . . .

LELIO: You alone can heal me of my wounds.

TONINO: Where was it you said you came from?

LELIO: I come from a city where misfortune reigns. I was born under an unlucky star and raised among desperadoes and reckless men.

TONINO: You mean you've escaped from a lunatic asylum?

LELIO: I will cut the thread of my labyrinthine discourse and come to the point. I love Beatrice. I desire her. I pant for her. My fate depends on you. I appeal to your immeasurable, to your more than illimitable kindness, to give her to me.

TONINO: I will cut the knot of my reply with my knife of frankness. Beatrice is mine. I will surrender all the wealth of India before I surrender the beauteous beauty of my beautiful one. [*to himself*] Damn him, he's started me doing it as well.

LELIO: You sentence me to death!

TONINO: That'll be one lunatic the less.

LELIO: Oh, horror!

TONINO: Oh – go away.

LELIO: Tyrant!

TONINO: Demented lunatic!

LELIO: If my love should change to hate, you will tremble before my fury.

TONINO: I will be like an impenetrable rock before the burning spite of your raging bestiality.

LELIO: I am going . . .

TONINO: Good.

LELIO: I am going . . .

TONINO: Hurry, then.

LELIO: I am going, sadist . . .

TONINO: Make up your mind or I'll make it up for you.

LELIO: I go! Yes, I go! But, before the sun has hidden his rays below the horizon, vengeance will be mine! [*Exit*]

TONINO: Mad! Stark, raving mad! He must have been born like it. And if he stays here he'll have me crazy too. We're all a little mad. And those who think they're not, are madder than the rest. But this fellow's the nonpareil of madmen.

[PANCRAZIO *comes out of the Doctor's house, followed by* BRIGHELLA.]

PANCRAZIO [*to* BRIGHELLA]: Come on! Hurry! To the Chancellery. You will be able to bear witness to my innocence.

BRIGHELLA: Here's Signor Zanetto. Over here.

PANCRAZIO [*to* TONINO]: Oh, how could you deny you gave me those jewels? Gave me them with your own hands?

TONINO: Signore, that is true. I did give you them.

PANCRAZIO [*to* BRIGHELLA]: D'you hear? He admits it. Go and tell the Chancellor!

TONINO: How does the Chancellor come into it?

PANCRAZIO: That was a fine thing you did! Endangering my reputation like that.

TONINO [*to himself*]: Perhaps the owner of the jewels has turned up. [*to* PANCRAZIO] Surely you didn't think they had been stolen?

PANCRAZIO: That, unfortunately, is exactly what *they* thought. And it's all your fault.

TONINO: My dear sir, I acted out of the best of intentions.

PANCRAZIO: That may be. You'd have had me thrown into prison, all the same.

[ARLECCHINO *enters*.]

ARLECCHINO: Well, they've had me thrown out, thank heaven.

TONINO: Here's the one who gave me the jewels.

ARLECCHINO: Who d'you say gave you the jewels?

TONINO: Why, you gave me them.

ARLECCHINO: And the money?

TONINO: Yes, the money as well.

ARLECCHINO: And yet you've been saying I didn't? What sort of trick's that to play on anyone?

TONINO: I've not been saying you didn't. You forced those jewels and that money on me against my will. Against my will, I took them. I'm an honest man. I don't need such things but if I did I'd rather die than get hold of them in such a way. I no longer have the jewels. I understand they are with the Chancellor. You can regain possession of them and do what you like with them. This money is not mine and I don't want it. You gave it me here. And here I restore it to you. Take your purse of money. There! I throw it at your feet to show how much I scorn money that isn't mine! [*Exit*]

ARLECCHINO [*singing*]: He's mad! Mad! Mad!

BRIGHELLA: If to throw your money away is to be mad, then he's truly a very great madman. I'll follow him just for curiosity. [*Exit*]

PANCRAZIO: I will keep this purse until Zanetto comes to his senses. Friend, come with me to the Chancellor and let us regain possession of the jewels.

ARLECCHINO: D'you know what I think? I think I want to go back to the valleys of Bergamo.

PANCRAZIO: Why?

ARLECCHINO: Because this city air makes people mad. [*Exit*]

PANCRAZIO: The air's the same there as here. Men become

mad everywhere. Mad through vanity, through ignorance, through pride, through greed. I am become mad through love, and that is a greater madness than all the others. [*Exit*]

[ZANETTO *enters.*]

ZANETTO [*alone*]: Ah, love! Love is a wonderful thing! The very moment I first saw the Signorina Rosaura, I felt myself burning all over like a roasted chicken. I can't stay here without seeing her, without speaking to her. I will go and visit her again and see if I can arrange our marriage. [*He knocks at the door of the Doctor's house.*]

ROSAURA [*appearing at the window*]: Why, Signor Zanetto!

ZANETTO: Oh, most beautiful one, will you allow me to come up to you?

ROSAURA: No, signore, my father does not wish it.

ZANETTO: But why not?

ROSAURA: Because you said he procures me as a prostitute.

ZANETTO: How can you! As if I would ever say such a thing! Aren't we to be husband and wife?

ROSAURA: And my father has shown me the letter.

ZANETTO: The letter I wrote him? Good.

ROSAURA: So you did write to him asking my hand in marriage, and yet you told me you hadn't.

ZANETTO: I didn't say marriage. I said we would do immediately what had to be done.

ROSAURA: I don't understand you. Sometimes you seem really too silly, and sometimes you seem a little too clever.

ZANETTO: Look, let me come up? Or d'you want me to get a twist in my neck?

ROSAURA: No, you can't come up here.

ZANETTO: Then you come down.

ROSAURA: That would be worse! A fine thing if I came out on the street!

ZANETTO: You want me to die then?

ROSAURA: Poor man! You will certainly die of passion.

ZANETTO: You think I won't? Without you, I'm like a fish out of water. I'm crazy. I'm delirious. If you don't help me, if you won't give me your hand, I'll drop dead before your eyes, here before your very door, burnt to death in the fire of your cruelty.

ROSAURA: What nonsense! Go on, though, let me hear what else you'd do?

ZANETTO: What else I'd do? With you up there and me down here? Ah, if you really wanted to know what else I'd do, you would come down here, or let me come up there. I'd swear to behave honourably.

ROSAURA: But can't you also behave honourably at a distance?

ZANETTO: I'm sorry, but I don't know how to do anything at a distance.

ROSAURA: But what would you do if you were nearer?

ZANETTO: I would ... I would ... No, I don't like saying it. If you don't mind, I'll sing it in a song.

ROSAURA: Yes, do! I'd love to hear it!

ZANETTO [*singing*]:

> If I were nearer
> Your beautiful face,
> I would from that little mouth
> Steal something.
>
> If I were nearer,
> My dearest love, (don't misunderstand)
> I would on that sweet breast
> Find relief.
>
> If I were nearer –
> (Oh don't misunderstand,
> But do say yes and let me
> Come upstairs!)
>
> If I were nearer –
> (Oh, now I'm blushing
> At what I'd do if I
> Were nearer!)

ROSAURA: Bravo! Well done!

ZANETTO: You liked it? Well, I'm ready, if you are?

ROSAURA: But you must explain one thing. I can't understand . . . why d'you make yourself appear to be two completely different people? Sometimes you appear stupid. At
other times you are quite witty. Sometimes you're a little
too impudent. And then at other times you're bashful and
timid. Why d'you keep changing like this?

ZANETTO: Do I? I didn't know. It must be . . . because I feel
what I didn't know that . . . I mean, for instance . . . well,
those eyes of yours . . . because, you see, if I could only . . .
yes! That's it! Signorina, that's it! Now, I've got it!

ROSAURA: There you are! That's just what I meant. Now
you're talking like a stupid fool. You don't make sense.

ZANETTO: But I do make sense to myself . . . inside myself.
But I don't know how to explain myself. Oh, do come
down here. I could explain so much better if you were down
here.

ROSAURA: Do you know what I think? About this silly way
you have of speaking sometimes? I think you're deceiving
me. That you don't really love me at all.

[BEATRICE, *accompanied by her* SERVANT, *enters and stands
listening.*]

BEATRICE [*to herself*]: Tonino speaking to a young lady? We
must listen.

ZANETTO: I love you so much that without you I seem to be
like a bird without a branch . . . like a gander without a
goose . . . like a ram without a sheep . . . like a little pig
without a little sow. Yes, my beloved darling, I love you
and I long to drown myself in the sea of your beauty, I long
to splash about like a crane in the heady depths of your
kindness, I long to jump about in the dust of your favours
. . . like . . . like . . . yes, like a donkey kicking up the dust in
some wide sandy desert.

ROSAURA [*to herself*]: He's becoming odder than ever!

BEATRICE: Why, you ungrateful, deceiving wretch! So this
is what your promises mean? Three times now you've
deceived me! Look at me, you villain! Look me in the face

if you have the heart to. No! You daren't. You haven't even the courage to face my scorn! You despicable thing! You liar! Perjurer! Why tempt me to leave my father's house? Why make me give up home and family? Why offer me your hand in marriage, if all the time your heart belonged to another? Oh, if I were told of such wickedness I would never believe it. Go away! I'll never believe another word you say. I never want to see you again! Wait! I will fetch the letter with which you tried to betray me. Yes, look at her well, you cruel savage brute, love her well, worship her beauty so much greater than mine – but never hope to find another with a love as great as Beatrice's!

[BEATRICE *turns and goes, followed by her servant. While she spoke,* ZANETTO *listened attentively without saying a word. As soon as* BEATRICE *goes he turns again to* ROSAURA.]

ZANETTO [*to* ROSAURA]: And so, to go back to what I was saying . . .

ROSAURA: Pretending to say, you mean – you hypocrite! How could you say all those things to me, when you'd already promised to marry someone else! Well, my answer's the same. No! No! No! Go and find somebody else to tell your lies to. I hate you. I despise you! Wait, wait! This will show you how much I hate you and despise you. I will go and get the letter you wrote my father asking for my hand in marriage. And you will see then how such deceivers are treated by Rosaura! [*She goes back into the house from the window*.]

ZANETTO [*alone*]: When we're married, it will be all right – I hope! This one says: 'Deceiver!' The other one says: 'Villain!' To one I'm a hypocrite, to the other I'm a savage brute. Poor Zanetto! I'm desperate; they're all against me, nobody wants me, I'll never be married. If I had a rope I'd hang myself. Or a knife, I'd cut my throat. There isn't even a canal here to drown myself in. Women! They're all jealous if I speak to any other woman but themselves. I'd do better to keep my mouth shut. Women! Don't any of them want me? I'm really not a savage brute. No, they're all the same. None of them want me. They're all against me. They're all horrible to me. Oh, curses on the fate that made me so handsome and good-looking. [*Exit*]

[ROSAURA *reappears at the window*.]

ROSAURA [*alone*]: Here it is, here's the letter! Well, would you believe it, if the worthless wretch hasn't run away. Serves me right for flattering myself he'd wait. The shame and confusion were too much for him. But I'll have him found. And then we'll see whether I know how to revenge myself.

[TONINO *enters*.]

But here he is back again. You shameless beast, how dare you come near me again! Go away, I'm not paying any attention to you. Here's your letter. There! Torn to bits. Scattered to the winds. And I wish I could do the same to that shameless heart of yours. [*She tears the letter up, throws it into the street and goes back into the house*.]

[TONINO *has been looking up at the window without speaking. Now he picks up the pieces of the letter from the ground.* BEATRICE *enters with a letter in her hand, accompanied by her servant*.]

BEATRICE: Here it is! I've found it at last, you villain. Here's your letter, you cruel brute. And there! That's how I treat it. [*She tears the letter into bits and throws the pieces on the ground*.] If only I could tear you to pieces as well, you nest of vipers. [*She goes, with her servant*.]

[TONINO *now picks up the pieces of this letter, and piecing them together, compares contents and handwriting*.]

TONINO [*alone*]: What is all this? Two of them tearing up their letters and throwing them in my face? I've never written to Rosaura and I've certainly never been unfaithful to Beatrice. They've either both gone mad or else there's something very strange going on. Let's see if I can make out what's in the letters. [*He joins together the pieces of* BEATRICE'S *letter on the ground.*] 'I promise . . . to the Signorina Beatrice etcetera, etcetera. I, Tonino Bisognosi'. Well, this one's mine, all right. Let's see the other one. [*Reads*] 'With this further letter . . . you may rest assured . . . a marriage between the virtuous . . . young lady . . . the Signorina Rosaura Balanzoni . . . and the Signor Zanetto Bisognosi . . .' But this is a forgery! I'm not Zanetto. When was this written? [*Reads*] 'Bergamo, January the fourteenth, 1746.' From Bergamo? Just what is all this? Where's the signature? [*Reads*] 'Zanetto Bisognosi.' Certainly everybody here believes I'm Zanetto, but nobody has the right to pretend they're me by signing themselves Zanetto. It's not my handwriting. Could this Zanetto be my brother who lives in Bergamo? It could be. Yes, he could be here in Verona without my knowing it. That servant Brighella who kept speaking about my brother in Venice made me wonder whether he suspected I really wasn't Zanetto. This might be the explanation of all these extraordinary happenings. Who knows? It could be. Though it would really be too good to be true. How can I find out? That servant in the house there, he'll know. I'll sound him without revealing myself. Damn it though, that means I'll have to behave myself. This will need tactful handling. Ho there! Anybody at home?

[*He knocks on the door of the Doctor's house,* BRIGHELLA *opens it.*]

BRIGHELLA: Your servant, signore. Was it you who knocked?

TONINO: Yes, indeed. It was I.

BRIGHELLA: I'm sorry but it is not possible to come in at the moment.

TONINO: No? Why not?

BRIGHELLA: My mistress is having a fit of the vapours and the master's in a bad temper. I advise you to go away quickly because if they see you here there's likely to be trouble.

TONINO: But what've I done?

BRIGHELLA: I don't know. I hear them complaining about you but I've no idea why.

TONINO: Tell me, friend, you knew my brother in Venice?

BRIGHELLA: Certainly I knew him.

TONINO: Does he look like me?

BRIGHELLA: You're alike as two peas in a pod. Anyone could see at a glance that you were twins.

TONINO: And it's two years since you saw him?

BRIGHELLA: Two years about.

TONINO: My brother . . .

BRIGHELLA: Yes, signore? You mean Signor Tonino?

TONINO: And I, who do you think I am?

BRIGHELLA: That's a good one! Why, you're Signor Zanetto.

TONINO: Who comes from?

BRIGHELLA: From Bergamo. To marry the Signorina Rosaura.

TONINO: Bravo, I see you know all. You're an honest fellow. [*to himself*] And now I see all.

BRIGHELLA: Forgive my curiosity, your honour, but did you ever hear anything of your sister?

TONINO: Never. So you also know that she was lost?

BRIGHELLA: Certainly. How many times your dear father told me all about it.

TONINO: Ah, yes. He never got over it. He had sent her to Bergamo and she disappeared on the way. Nobody knows how.

BRIGHELLA: What could you do? One dowry the less. Well, if there's nothing more I can do for you I'd better go into the house. If I'm seen speaking to you, *I'll* be in trouble as well. Good-bye. [*He goes back into the house.*]

TONINO [*alone*]: Many thanks, friend. And they talk about coincidences. Who would have believed it! My brother here in Verona and neither of us seen the other. Yet one of us is taken for the other and a thousand mistakes follow all in one day. Now I understand that business over the jewels and the money. That Arlecchino must be my brother's servant and he thought he was giving them to him. If I'd known they were my brother's I certainly wouldn't have returned them. What wouldn't I give to see this brother of mine! Yes, I'll search around until I find him.

[COLOMBINA *enters*.]

COLOMBINA: You should hear how that Rosaura's carrying on! Can't find things bad enough to say about the Signor Zanetto. She makes me sick. I just can't put up with her.

TONINO: What is it, lass? What are you so upset about?

COLOMBINA: Well, if you only knew, signore, it's all because of you.

TONINO: Because of me?

COLOMBINA: Yes. The cheek of her. Just because she thinks she's a fine lady, she thinks she can say what she likes about everybody.

TONINO: You mean she's been saying things about me?

COLOMBINA: You should have heard her! And all just because I took your part and spoke up in your defence, she went for me like a wild cat. The little beast. Oh, I'd pity her if it wasn't that I know who she really is.

TONINO: But – isn't she the Doctor's daughter?

COLOMBINA: She's an orphan, that's what she is. A foundling, devil take her. She was found in the street by a pilgrim.

TONINO: I don't understand. Why does the Doctor say she's his daughter, then?

COLOMBINA: Because he's an old rogue. He wants to make a fortune out of arranging a rich marriage for her.

TONINO [*to himself*]: I said that Doctor was up to no good. [*to* COLOMBINA] Then the Signorina Rosaura doesn't know she isn't his daughter?

COLOMBINA: No, and never will.

TONINO: How long has she passed as the Doctor's daughter?

COLOMBINA: Ever since she was a baby.

TONINO: How old is she now?

COLOMBINA: She thinks she's twenty-one, but that's just what she's been told.

TONINO: She can't be much more. Tell me, this pilgrim – where was he coming from?

COLOMBINA: From Venice.

TONINO: And where did he find this baby?

COLOMBINA: They say it was near Caldiero, between Vicenza and Verona.

TONINO: The baby was dressed in baby's clothes?

COLOMBINA: Yes, of course.

TONINO: Have you seen these baby clothes?

COLOMBINA: The Doctor told me he'd kept them, but I've never seen them.

TONINO: Could she have been this pilgrim's child? Did he say she had any name?

COLOMBINA: No, she wasn't his. He'd found her on the road, where four bandits had killed and robbed some travellers, and left this baby alive by accident. He didn't even know her name. It was the Doctor who called her Rosaura.

TONINO [*to himself*]: This is wonderful! She must be my sister Flaminia who disappeared when my poor mother was assassinated on the road bringing her to Bergamo.

COLOMBINA [*to herself*]: What the devil's he saying to himself?

TONINO: Do you know if there was a medallion, with two little portraits, among this baby's clothes?

COLOMBINA: I seem to have heard mention of that . . . but why are you asking me so many questions?

TONINO: That will be all. [*to himself*] There's no doubt about it. It *is* my sister. Heaven, I thank you! What incredible luck. Two brothers and a sister! All here! All together! It's like the climax of a comedy.

COLOMBINA [*to herself*]: It looks as if she's turned out to be some rich man's daughter. [*to* TONINO] Signore, if ever the Signorina Rosaura finds out she's somebody important, please don't tell her I said anything bad about her.

TONINO: Don't worry. I know you girls can't help gossiping about your mistresses. You'd rather live on bread and water than do without your little grumble now and then. [*Exit*]

COLOMBINA [*alone*]: There I go, talking too much again. Harming myself and doing a bit of good to Rosaura, by the look of it. That Signor Zanetto asks too many questions. And just so he can cause more trouble I expect.

[PANCRAZIO *and the* DOCTOR *come out of the house.*]

DOCTOR: Colombina, what are you doing on the street?

COLOMBINA: I came out to see if the man was coming with the vegetables.

DOCTOR: Well, get inside quickly.

COLOMBINA: Have you seen Signor Zanetto?

DOCTOR: Into the house, you little gossip!

COLOMBINA: Bad-tempered old thing! [*She goes into the house.*]

DOCTOR: Signor Pancrazio, to you who are the dearest friend I have, I confide my complete determination that the marriage between my daughter Rosaura and the Signor Zanetto Bisognosi will take place, despite all that has happened.

PANCRAZIO: But how can you? If she has torn up his letters in his face and doesn't want him?

DOCTOR: She did that out of jealousy. Things have advanced so far that it is not possible to abandon the marriage without offence to my personal dignity. All Verona is talking about it, and then, between ourselves, Signor Zanetto is very rich and at the expense of a small dowry I can secure a fortune for my daughter.

PANCRAZIO: So that's what it is. Avarice. You would sacrifice that poor innocent child for money.

DOCTOR: My mind is made up. Your advice, which I have always valued and esteemed, will not cause me to alter a decision which I consider just, honourable and to the dignity of my house.

PANCRAZIO: Think it over. Take your time.

DOCTOR: You yourself have told me often: 'Time and tide wait for no man'. Go immediately and find Signor Zanetto. I want them married before night falls. Dear friend, oblige me, and return quickly. [*He goes back into his house.*]

PANCRAZIO [*alone*]: Behold the downfall of all my hopes. The Doctor means to force her upon that Venetian. And I, poor unfortunate, what shall I do? If I dared to make my passion known I would lose all my good reputation, I would lose my only source of income. If she marries this fellow, she will go with him to Bergamo and I'll never see her again. Ah, that must never be! There is nothing I will not stoop to do in order to prevent that. I will take off my mask and be known as I really am, rather than lose Rosaura whom I love above all the things of this world.

[ZANETTO *enters*.]

ZANETTO: Signor Pancrazio, I am in despair.

PANCRAZIO: Death can be your only comfort then.

ZANETTO: I'm bursting to get married but nobody'll have me. All the women, they scold me! They scorn me! They tell me to go away as if . . . as if I were a dog, an animal, a donkey! Signor Pancrazio, I'm in despair. I can't go on.

PANCRAZIO: There you are! If you'd only followed my advice, you wouldn't be in such misery now.

ZANETTO: Don't you be cross with me! Yes, you're right. I did so want to have nothing to do with women. But I can't. Something seems to force me to run after them, just like a whirlwind forces the water up into the air.

PANCRAZIO: But you are not made for marriage.

ZANETTO: Why aren't I?

PANCRAZIO: I know you're not and that's enough. If you get married you'll be the most miserable and unhappy man on earth.

ZANETTO: Then what can I do?

PANCRAZIO: Leave the women alone.

ZANETTO: But if I can't?

PANCRAZIO: Follow my advice. Leave this city immediately, go back to the country and try your fortune there.

ZANETTO: But it will be the same there. The women of Bergamo make fun of me and scorn me.

PANCRAZIO: Then what else can you do?

ZANETTO: I do not know. I'm in despair.

PANCRAZIO: If I were you, do you know what I'd do?

ZANETTO: What would you do?

PANCRAZIO: I would let death take me from myself.

ZANETTO: Death? Dear signore, is there no other remedy – beside death?

PANCRAZIO: What other remedy is strong enough to cure your illness?

ZANETTO: Look, you are such a wise man, do not you know of any secret remedy that would drive away this cursed desire I have to get married?

PANCRAZIO: Ah, yes. I do indeed. [*to himself*] I've got him! [*to* ZANETTO] I feel so much pity for you that I will deprive myself of a little of a very rare and precious treasure which I alone possess and which I guard with the greatest secrecy. I have the very thing you need. I carry it always with me in case of an emergency. I also in my youth felt tormented like yourself, and woe was me if I didn't have this powder in this little box with me. With this powder I have freed myself many times from the powerful urges of lust, and, repeating the larger dose every five years, I have lived free from all the pains of love to the very age at which you now see me. One pinch of this powder will free you from all torments. If you drink it in some wine, you will find yourself looking on women with indifference; nay, more, you will find yourself scorning them and revenging yourself upon them for their disdain. They, on the contrary, will begin to run after you. But you, cured by the virtue of this miraculous powder, will make them pay a dear price for the insults with which until now they have dared to scorn you.

ZANETTO: Oh, if only that could be so! Oh, that I may taste it! For the love of heaven, Signor Pancrazio, for charity's sake give me a little of that powder!

PANCRAZIO: But . . . to deprive me of this powder . . . which cost so much. . . .

ZANETTO: I will give you as much money as you wish.

PANCRAZIO: Mmm . . . no. To show you that I am not motivated by any personal interest and that when I can, I give most willingly to those near me, I will make you a present of a pinch of this powder. You will drink it in some wine and you will instantly be restored to health. At first, though, you will certainly feel some disturbance in your stomach and it may seem to you that you are going to die. But the disturbance will pass away, and you will find yourself another man. You will be happy, and you will bless Pancrazio.

ZANETTO: Thank you, signore. Bless you, signore. Give it me. Don't let me suffer any longer.

PANCRAZIO [*to himself*]: Tiburzio's poison is just the thing to rid me of this stupid rival. [*to* ZANETTO] This is the powder. But you need some wine. [*He shows him the box.*]

ZANETTO: I will go home and drink it.

PANCRAZIO [*to himself*]: He might change his mind. [*to* ZANETTO] No, no, wait. I will fetch you some. [*to himself as he goes into the Doctor's house*] I'm sorry for him but, to remove this obstacle to my love, he must be deprived of life.

ZANETTO [*alone*]: I certainly can't go on living like this. Whenever I see a woman, I feel myself burning from head to toe. And they all mock me, they all scorn me. May they all break their necks! Ah, but now *they* will come to *me*! They'll come running after *me*! And me, neither more nor less, firm as a rock. We'll be quits. I can't wait to get my revenge on that bitch Rosaura. He's coming. Have you brought the wine?

PANCRAZIO [*coming out of the house carrying a glass of wine*]: Here it is. Put the powder into it.

ZANETTO: Like this? [*He puts the powder into the glass of wine.*]

PANCRAZIO: Bravo! Now drink. But take care to tell no one that I have given you the secret.

ZANETTO: Do not fear.

PANCRAZIO: Take courage.

ZANETTO: I am ready. Firm as a rock.

PANCRAZIO: And if it hurts, you will endure it?

ZANETTO: I will endure all.

PANCRAZIO: Then I will leave you. Otherwise people might suspect and you know how they would plague me if they knew what I had given you.

ZANETTO: You are right.

PANCRAZIO: Oh, how we will laugh at these women!

ZANETTO:All running after me! And me not giving a damn!

PANCRAZIO:Ruthless! Cruel as a lion!

ZANETTO:Will they burst into tears?

PANCRAZIO:Indeed they will!

ZANETTO:And me cool as a cucumber?

PANCRAZIO:Not caring a straw.

ZANETTO:I drink.

PANCRAZIO:Be brave!

ZANETTO:Good health! [*He drinks half the glass of wine.*]

PANCRAZIO [*to himself as he goes*]: The deed is done! [*Exit*]

ZANETTO [*alone, drinking the wine sip by sip*]: Ugh, what vile stuff! Ugh, what a poisonous drink! My stomach's burning! It's on fire. I'm drinking no more of that. [*He puts the glass on the ground.*] Oh! I'm dying! I'm dying! No, I can't be. It's only the powder doing its work. If I want to have all the women desperately in love with me, I must endure it. Signor Pancrazio told me that. But . . . oh . . . oh! I'm really ill! I'm done for . . . I shouldn't have drunk it, I'll drink no more of it . . . oh! some water . . . water . . . water. I can't see any more . . . the ground's shaking under my feet . . . my legs are giving way . . . oh, my heart . . . oh, my heart. Courage, be brave, Zanetto; all the women will be running after you . . . and you . . . you will laugh at them . . . oh, how it will serve them right! I can't stand . . . I'm falling . . . I'm dying . . . [*He falls to the ground.*]

[COLOMBINA *comes out of the house, and, seeing* ZANETTO *on the ground, runs up to him.*]

COLOMBINA:What is it? Signor Zanetto! What's the matter? What's happened?

ZANETTO [*to himself*]: There, d'you see . . . it's true . . . the women are running after me.

COLOMBINA:What on earth! He's foaming at the mouth. He's been taken ill. Oh, the poor man. I'll call help. *I* can't do anything. [*She runs back into the house.*]

ZANETTO [*alone*]: See . . . she's fallen in love with me . . . she's in despair . . . and I take no notice . . . but . . . oh! I feel faint . . . I'm pegging out . . . I'm kicking the bucket . . . Help! . . . Help!

[FLORINDO *enters*.]

FLORINDO: What? Tonino on the ground? Now's my chance to revenge myself.

ZANETTO: Another woman running after me . . . [*He tries to turn himself*.]

FLORINDO [*to himself*]: You'd think he was dying.

ZANETTO: I'm murdered . . . I'm murdered . . .

FLORINDO [*to himself*]: He really is dying. [*to* ZANETTO] What's wrong with you?

ZANETTO: I'm murdered. . . .

FLORINDO: How? Who did it? [*to himself*] Although my rival, this is pitiful.

ZANETTO: I drank . . . yes . . . the women . . . Signor Pancrazio . . . oh! . . . I'm poisoned . . . I'm murdered . . . but no . . . Away with you, you women . . . don't give a damn, you see . . . oh! [*He dies*.]

FLORINDO: The poor fellow's dead! Who can have murdered him? How has he died? What's this? A wine glass? [*He picks up the glass and looks at the wine still in it*.] And the wine's all cloudy! The poor wretch has been poisoned! [*He puts the glass back on the ground*.]

[COLOMBINA *comes out of the house followed by the* DOCTOR *and* BRIGHELLA.]

COLOMBINA [*to the* DOCTOR *as they come out of the house*]: Come quickly, signore, and help this poor young man.

DOCTOR: Brighella, go fetch a surgeon at once.

FLORINDO: That will be no use. Signor Zanetto is dead.

DOCTOR: Dead?

BRIGHELLA: He's dead, the poor fellow?

COLOMBINA: Poor Signor Zanetto dead?

[ROSAURA *comes out of the house*.]

ROSAURA: Forgive me, father, for coming into the street. Did I hear you say Signor Zanetto is dead? It can't be true?

DOCTOR: Only too true, alas. There he lies, the poor man.

[BEATRICE *and her* SERVANT *enter.*]

BEATRICE: Oh, no, it can't be. Dead? My beloved dead?

[ARLECCHINO *enters.*]

ARLECCHINO: What's the matter? Is Signor Zanetto having a sleep?

BRIGHELLA: More than a sleep. The poor unfortunate man's dead.

ARLECCHINO: Oh, if it's like that, then I'm off back to Bergamo.

DOCTOR: Let us take him into the Inn. It is not right to leave him lying in the middle of the street.

ROSAURA: Oh, my heart is overcome with grief.

COLOMBINA: Poor girl. You're a widow before you're married. [*to herself*] They're all so vexed I could almost be glad.

DOCTOR: Brighella, have him brought into the Inn. [*He points to* ZANETTO.]

BRIGHELLA: Come on, Arlecchino, give me a hand. [*to Beatrice's* SERVANT] You, young man, you can help as well.

BEATRICE: Miserable Beatrice! What will become of me?

FLORINDO [*softly, to* BEATRICE]: If your Tonino's dead, is there no hope for me?

BEATRICE: I shall hate you forever.

ARLECCHINO: Carry him gently, comrade. Even if he is dead, there's no need to break his neck.

[ARLECCHINO *and the* SERVANT *carry the dead* ZANETTO *into the Inn.*]

ROSAURA: My heart is breaking.

BEATRICE: What evil villain could have done this?

DOCTOR: Yes, how did he come to die like this?

FLORINDO: It is quite obvious to me that he was poisoned.

DOCTOR: But – by whom?

FLORINDO: I don't know, but I've good reasons to believe that is how he died.

ROSAURA: Oh, pray search for any clues! So that it will be possible to avenge the death of this unhappy young man.

[TONINO enters.]

TONINO: So there you are, Signorina Beatrice!

DOCTOR [*terrified*]: How's this?

BRIGHELLA [*fearfully*]: The ghost of Signor Zanetto!

ROSAURA: He's not dead!

BEATRICE: He's alive!

[*They all make gestures of bewilderment, glancing at one another fearfully.* ARLECCHINO *comes out of the Inn with the* SERVANT. *He sees* TONINO, *whom he believes to be* ZANETTO, *and is terrified.*]

ARLECCHINO: Oh, my poor heart, what's that I see?

TONINO: But what's the matter? What's wrong? Why such confusion, such amazement?

DOCTOR: Signor Zanetto, you are alive?

TONINO: By Heaven's grace.

DOCTOR: But weren't you just lying there on the ground like somebody dead?

TONINO: Of course not. I've just come.

BRIGHELLA: Here, what's going on?

ARLECCHINO: Wait, wait. [*He runs into the Inn and comes out again immediately*.] This is too much! He's half dead and half alive! I'm off! Good-bye all! Good-bye! [*Exit*]

BRIGHELLA: What's he talking about? [BRIGHELLA *runs into the Inn and comes out immediately*.] It's not possible! One inside – dead, one outside – alive!

DOCTOR: Let me see. [*The* DOCTOR *runs into the Inn and comes out immediately*.] Signor Zanetto, just inside – there is another Signor Zanetto!

TONINO: Quietly, quietly, signore. Everything will be explained. Allow me to go in there myself. I will come out again immediately. [*He goes into the Inn*.]

ROSAURA: Thank heaven Zanetto is alive.

BEATRICE: Though faithless to me, I am glad he is alive.

TONINO [*coming out of the Inn, surprised and sad*]: So be it! I have seen him – too late. I have known him – much too late. He who is in there and who is dead is Zanetto, my brother.

DOCTOR: Then who are you?

TONINO: I am Tonino Bisognosi, brother of the unfortunate Zanetto.

ROSAURA: What did you say?

DOCTOR: What nonsense is this?

BEATRICE [*to* TONINO]: So you are my fiancé?

TONINO: Yes, indeed I am. But you? Why did you tear up my letter? Why did you treat me so?

BEATRICE: But why did you give me up for another? Why did you make love to the Signorina Rosaura before my very eyes?

TONINO: Not at all, my lass, not at all. The likeness between me and my brother has caused a lot of fantastic things. But I am yours and you are mine. That is certain.

ROSAURA: But, Signor Zanetto, what about the promise you made me?

TONINO: We two could never marry. And, after all, I am not Zanetto.

DOCTOR: Zanetto, Tonino, whichever you are, if you're not too proud to be related to me by marriage, you could still marry my daughter. [*to himself*] This one will be richer still, because he'll inherit the other's money.

TONINO: Very well. I am ready to marry your daughter.

DOCTOR: Give her your hand then!

TONINO: But where is your daughter?

DOCTOR: She's here!

TONINO: Oh, now, come! I'm surprised at you. This is not your daughter.

DOCTOR: What? What was that you said?

TONINO: You see, I know all. I know about the pilgrim. I know about everything.

DOCTOR [*to* COLOMBINA]: You gossiping little villain!

TONINO: Tell me, signore, that medallion you found among the baby's clothes, you have it still?

DOCTOR [*to himself*]: He even knows about the medallion. [*to* TONINO] A medallion with two portraits?

TONINO: Exactly. With two portraits.

DOCTOR: There you are. Examine it. Is that it?

TONINO: Yes, indeed, this is it. [*to himself*] My father had it
made when we twins were born.

DOCTOR: Since all is discovered, I confess Rosaura to be, not
my daughter, but an unknown baby found by a pilgrim
between Vicenza and Verona. The pilgrim told me he
found her on the ground, abandoned and alone after four
bandits had robbed and killed those who had custody of
her. I begged him to leave her with me. He agreed. And
from that time I have treated her as if she were my own
daughter.

TONINO: This is Flaminia, my sister. Going from Venice to
Bergamo, my poor mother, wishing to see her son Zanetto
and to leave this little daughter also in the care of my uncle
Stefano, was attacked by bandits. My mother and all who
were travelling with her were killed. This young girl,
thanks to her tender age, they left alive.

ROSAURA: Now I understand the love I had for you. It was
the love of a sister for her brother.

TONINO: And for that same reason did I love you.

FLORINDO [*to himself*]: Now all my hope for Beatrice has
gone.

TONINO [*to* ROSAURA]: Now I see why I misunderstood
about the letter and about the kindness you did me. [*to the*
DOCTOR] And I am afraid I misjudged the poor Doctor
here.

DOCTOR: Ah, you have ruined me!

TONINO: But how?

DOCTOR: I received an inheritance from my brother of thirty
thousand ducats on condition it was used for the upbringing
and education of my only child, a baby called Rosaura. The
baby died and I would have lost the inheritance because the
will stipulated that in the event of her death all the money
must go to my nephew. Having lost my daughter but not
wishing to lose such a rich inheritance, I decided to sub-
stitute another child for the dead Rosaura. An opportunity
was at hand with the arrival of this abandoned child. With

the help of the nurse, Colombina's mother, the substitution succeeded. But now it is still not too late for my nephew to dispossess me of the inheritance.

TONINO: But who is this nephew?

DOCTOR: A certain Lelio.

TONINO: D'you mean that thick-skinned gentleman who calls himself a Count and a Marquis?

DOCTOR: Yes, that's the one.

TONINO: Here he is coming. Do not worry. Leave this to me.

[LELIO *enters.*]

LELIO: Stop where you are! All of you. You see before you a desperate man.

TONINO: It's no use, Signor Lelio. What's done, is done. Beatrice is to be my wife.

LELIO: I will confound hell itself! I will convulse the entire universe!

TONINO: But why?

LELIO: Because I am frantic with despair.

TONINO: There could be a remedy.

LELIO: Such as what?

TONINO: Marriage with the Signorina Rosaura. Fifteen thousand ducats dowry. And another fifteen thousand on the Doctor's death.

LELIO: Thirty thousand ducats dowry? The idea is not displeasing to me.

TONINO: And the girl? Do you find her pleasing?

LELIO: Who wouldn't find her pleasing? Thirty thousand ducats reveal a most rare beauty.

TONINO: Then we need say no more. It will be arranged. But not in the street here. Let us go into the house and we will settle everything. Beatrice is mine, Rosaura will be Signor Lelio's. [*to* ROSAURA] You are happy?

ROSAURA: I will always do the will of – my father.

DOCTOR: Thank you, my child. You have saved my life. Dear Signor Tonino, I am obliged to you. Let us go in immediately and make all the arrangements.

TONINO: So everyone is happy.

FLORINDO: I cannot be while overcome with grief that I should have betrayed our friendship.

TONINO: What you tried to do was the most unworthy action any man could possibly do. You should indeed feel ashamed. Yet, I am sorry for you. You acted so through love, and now you regret it. Because of that I shall be glad to have you as a friend again.

FLORINDO: I accept your generous kindness. I swear that in future you will find me your most faithful friend.

[PANCRAZIO *enters*.]

PANCRAZIO [*to himself*]: What do I see? Zanetto not dead? Hasn't he taken the poison? What a fool I was to think he would!

DOCTOR: Signor Pancrazio, come quickly. We have some most wonderful news.

PANCRAZIO [*softly, to the* DOCTOR]: If you would kindly excuse me a moment, Signore. [*he calls* TONINO *aside*] Tell me, did you drink?

TONINO: Drink? Are you suggesting I am drunk?

PANCRAZIO: No, no. Did you drink what I gave you?

TONINO [*to himself*]: This needs looking into. [*to* PANCRAZIO] No, I haven't drunk it yet.

PANCRAZIO: But the women who torment you? How are you going to endure them?

TONINO: But how can I stop them?

PANCRAZIO: As soon as you've drunk, you'll be free.

TONINO: What is it I've to drink?

PANCRAZIO: The powder, you fool! The powder I gave you. What have you done with the glass of wine and the powder?

TONINO [*to himself*]: A glass of wine and some powder? I understand. [*to* PANCRAZIO, *loudly so that all can hear*] You lying-tongued scoundrel, you cunning humbug, you damned hypocrite! It was you! It was you who murdered my brother! Yes, he did drink it. And so through you, he's dead. I am not Zanetto. I am Tonino. We were twins, identical twins. Tell me, you assassin, why did you kill him? Why did you murder him?

PANCRAZIO: I'm surprised at you! I know nothing about it. I don't even know what you're talking about. A person such as I am is incapable of such an iniquity.

TONINO: Then why did you ask me if I'd drunk it? If I wanted to be free from women?

PANCRAZIO: What I meant was . . . if you were drinking . . . that is to say, for the wedding . . . for the wedding.

TONINO: Yes, all confused now, aren't you? You infamous villain, you murdered my brother!

PANCRAZIO: Oh, heavens, must I listen to such things and still live?

DOCTOR: Signor Pancrazio is an honourable man – I will testify to that.

FLORINDO: I found near the dying Zanetto a glass and the wine in it was all cloudy.

COLOMBINA: And only a little while ago Signor Pancrazio came into the house and took a wine glass when he thought nobody was looking.

FLORINDO [*picking up the glass which is still on the ground*]: We'll soon see if it's the same.

TONINO: You hear? If you did kill him, you will pay for it. And the jewels, what have you done with them?

PANCRAZIO: They are still in the hands of the Chancellor.

TONINO: Good, then those can be recovered.

FLORINDO [*holding out the glass*]: This is the wine with which Zanetto was poisoned.

COLOMBINA: And this is the wine glass which Signor Pancrazio took from the house.

TONINO: Is it true?

PANCRAZIO: It is true.

TONINO: You poisoned him then?

PANCRAZIO: That is *not* true. I am a gentleman. Give me that glass and I'll prove my innocence.

FLORINDO: Take it then.

PANCRAZIO: See, I will drink it myself.

DOCTOR: I said so. Signor Pancrazio is not capable of committing such an iniquity.

TONINO [*to himself*]: If he drinks, it can't be poisoned.

COLOMBINA: It may at least poison this scoundrel.

TONINO: By Heaven, look at his eyes! They're rolling horribly. He's killed himself!

PANCRAZIO [*having drunk is feeling the effects of the poison*]: Friends, I am dying and there is no remedy. Now that I am near death, I will reveal all. I loved the Signorina Rosaura and I was not able to bear that she should become the wife of another. I poisoned that unfortunate man to free myself of a rival. Alas, I cannot go on. I am dying, and I am dying as wickedly as I lived. All my goodness was a pretence, a sham. Be warned by my example. Put little trust in those who affect an excessive perfection, for there is not a more wicked man than he who pretends to be good, and is not. [*Exit, staggering.*]

COLOMBINA: I always said he was a scoundrel.

TONINO: He's robbed the hangman of his fee. Oh, my poor brother, how I grieve for you. My dear sister, it consoles me to have found you, but I mourn the death of poor Zanetto.

ROSAURA: I mourn also. But we must patiently endure our sorrow.

DOCTOR: Come now, let us go into the house.

TONINO: If it pleases you, I will bring my bride.

LELIO: And I also will come in with my goddess.

DOCTOR: Come all and be witnesses of the arrangements that have to be made. [*to himself*] That's what matters to me.

TONINO: I myself will return to Venice to arrange the legal estate of my brother, and as soon as that is in order I will return. If he had lived, there is something my brother would have done willingly. But as he is dead, I will go myself to Caldiero and bring those four bandits to justice. With all my heart I thank the good fortune which has given me, in one day, both a sister and a bride – despite all the mishaps that have resulted from so many people mistaking the identities of – the Venetian twins.

The Artful Widow

LA VEDOVA SCALTRA

The Artful Widow

GOLDONI followed *The Venetian Twins* in 1748 with *The Artful Widow* and achieved an even greater triumph. It had an even longer run, has been acclaimed ever since as an authentic masterpiece, and is today one of the most popular of Goldoni's plays in Italy.

Both plays reveal to a high degree the musical quality of Goldoni's dialogue. In them he is as near to Metastasio as he is to Molière. The melody and rhythm of the language is such that it would seem easily converted into a duet, a trio, or a quartet. *The Artful Widow* was in fact made into an opera by Wolf-Ferrari.

In Italy in recent years it is being pointed out that the linguistic problem is central to any critical appreciation of Goldoni's achievement. The lack of realistic dialogue in *The Artful Widow* appears in no way to lessen the impact of the play as a realistic comedy. It is now being realized that Goldoni, in order to achieve comic effects, began by using the characters speaking cultivated Italian almost contrapuntally against the characters speaking the Venetian dialect. This, of course, is one of the greatest problems in translating Goldoni.

Goldoni finally developed his linguistic craftsmanship to such perfection that when he came to write such masterpieces as *The Superior Residence* and *The Chioggian Brawls** he was able to dispense with cultivated Italian and achieve his high comic effects in the Venetian dialect only.

*Published by Heinemann under the title: *It Happened in Venice*.

Characters

ROSAURA, Widow of Stefanello dei Bisognosi and
  daughter of DOCTOR LOMBARDI
ELEONORA, her Sister
PANTALONE DEI BISOGNOSI, Brother-in-law of
  ROSAURA and in love with ELEONORA
DOCTOR LOMBARDI, Father of ROSAURA and
  ELEONORA
MILORD RUNEBIF, an English Gentleman
MONSIEUR LEBLEU, a French Gentleman
DON ALVARO DI CASTIGLIA, a Spanish Gentleman
THE CONTE DI BOSCO NERO, an Italian Gentleman
MARIONETTE, ROSAURA's French Maidservant
ARLECCHINO, a Waiter at the Inn
BIRIF, Servant to MILORD
FOLETTO, Servant to the CONTE
SERVANTS to PANTALONE
A COFFEE-SHOP PROPRIETOR and his WAITERS

*The action takes place in Venice at an Inn, in Rosaura's
  Room, in a Coffee-shop, and in the Street.*

Act One

*The room of an Inn. A large round table prepared for a meal.
Various bottles of wine and spirits. Two small round tables with
table cloths. Candlesticks with candles burning.*

[MILORD RUNEBIF, MONSIEUR LEBLEU, DON ALVARO
and the CONTE DI BOSCO NERO *are seated at the large table
with glasses full of wine in their hands. Led by* MONSIEUR
LEBLEU *they are all heartily singing a French song. When the
song finishes*:]

MONSIEUR: Three cheers for the bottle that cheers! Hip –
hip –

ALL: Hurray!

MONSIEUR: Hip – hip –

ALL: Hurray!

MONSIEUR: Hip – hip –

ALL: Hurray!

CONTE: Our landlord deserves to be congratulated. That
was an excellent supper.

MONSIEUR: It was tolerably good. You Italians do not know
how to eat like the French.

CONTE: We have French cooks.

MONSIEUR: Yes, but when they come to Italy, they forget how
to cook. Ah, you should see how we eat in Paris! There
eating is an art!

MILORD: You Frenchmen have a bee in your bonnet about
Paris. You think it's the only place in the world. I'm as good
an Englishman as the next chap, but you never hear me
talking about London.

DON: Yes, I laugh when I hear Paris praised. Madrid is the
finest city in the world.

CONTE: No, signori, the truth is every country is as good as another if you have money in your pocket and happiness in your heart.

MONSIEUR: Hear, hear! Long live happiness! After a good supper what we need is a beautiful young lady to talk to. It's nearly dawn so there's no point in going to bed now. What did you think of that beautiful young widow we had the honour of meeting at the ball last night?

MILORD: Very nice girl. Respectable.

DON: She had a soulfulness that ravished my heart.

MONSIEUR: I thought at first she was French. She had all the vivaciousness of a French girl.

CONTE: The Signora Rosaura is indeed a lady of exquisite taste, honoured and respected by all. [aside] And adored by me.

MONSIEUR [pouring wine for all]: Come! Let us drink to the Signora Rosaura.

DON: To the Signora Rosaura!

MILORD ⎱
CONTE ⎰ : To the Signora Rosaura!

[MONSIEUR LEBLEU *begins singing the same French song and all join in.* ARLECCHINO *enters and stands listening with admiration. When the song ends he approaches the table, fills a glass with wine, sings the same song himself, drinks, and goes.*]

CONTE: Bravo! He's a real Italian, that waiter! I like his spirit.

DON: Such foolery amuses you? In Spain a waiter would get a good beating for such impertinence.

MONSIEUR: And in France he would make his fortune. There we appreciate such high spirits.

MILORD: Yes, you value high spirits more than common sense.

MONSIEUR: Do not change the subject. That widow has stolen my heart.

DON: And mine – already I sigh for her!

CONTE: My advice is – forget about her.

MONSIEUR: Why?

CONTE: Because the Signora Rosaura has sworn herself the
enemy of love. She disdains all men and is incapable of
tenderness. [*aside*] Except to me.

MONSIEUR: Aha! Like that, is she? Then let her be more
savage than a wild beast, a true Frenchman such as I, will
know how to tame her. When I speak to her some of our
sweet-nothings, designed for the enchantment of women, I
swear you will see her sighing and begging for mercy.

DON: She would be the first woman ever to reject the advances
of Don Alvaro di Castiglia. Men of rank like myself are
born with one great privilege: we know how to handle the
fair sex.

CONTE: Neither French skill nor Spanish diplomacy will be of
any avail. I know what I'm talking about. Believe me, I
know her.

MONSIEUR: This very night I saw her regarding me closely.
My eyes have already pierced her heart. And then when I
gave her my hand on leaving, she spoke so sweetly to me.
It was a miracle I did not fall prostrate at her feet.

DON: I do not like boasting about my success with the ladies.
If I did you would not be so confident.

CONTE [*aside*]: I begin to burn with jealousy.

MONSIEUR: Her brother-in-law, Signor Pantalone, is a good
friend of mine. He will be only too pleased to take me to
call on her.

DON: Her father, Doctor Lombardi, is one of my dependents.
He will take *me* to her.

CONTE [*aside*]: Not if I can help it.

MILORD [*getting up and calling*]: Ho, there!

[ARLECCHINO *enters.*]

ARLECCHINO: You called, Illustrious?

MILORD: Come here. [*He takes him aside.*]

[*The others remain at the table talking among themselves.*]

ARLECCHINO: I am here.

MILORD: D'you know Madam Rosaura? The sister-in-law of
Pantalone dei Bisognosi?

ARLECCHINO: The widow? Yes, I know her.

MILORD: Take this ring. Give it to Madam Rosaura. Tell her Lord Runebif sent it. Tell her this is the ring that took her fancy last night. And tell her I'll come and visit her this morning. To drink a cup of chocolate with her.

ARLECCHINO: But, signore, I'd better tell you . . .

MILORD: Take it. And here are six zecchini for you.

ARLECCHINO: Much obliged. But that wasn't what I meant. What I meant was that Signor Pantalone . . .

MILORD: Hurry, or I'll get my stick to you.

ARLECCHINO: If it's like that, you needn't bother. I'll do what I can – but don't blame me. [*Exit*]

[*Three other* WAITERS *enter.*]

MILORD [*to one of the waiters*]: Light me the way to my room. [*to the others at the table*] Friends, I'm off for a little rest.

[*He goes out with the waiter carrying one of the candles.*]

MONSIEUR: I think we'd all best have a sleep. [*They all rise.*]

CONTE: If we don't meet at breakfast, we will meet later for coffee.

MONSIEUR: Perhaps you will not see me.

CONTE: Have you an engagement?

MONSIEUR: I hope to be with Madame Rosaura.

CONTE: That is impossible. She never receives anybody. [*He goes out with a servant carrying a candle.*]

MONSIEUR: The Conte is annoyed! He's in love even more than we are. I wonder? Perhaps he is already receiving what we are seeking?

DON: If that is so, he will soon have cause to be jealous.

MONSIEUR: He's an Italian – so what can you expect? [*Exit with another waiter carrying a candle.*]

DON [*to himself*]: He can be as jealous as he likes. Spanish money can work miracles. [*Exit with another waiter carrying a candle.*]

⊰ SCENE 2 ⊱

Rosaura's room, with chairs.

[ROSAURA *and* MARIONETTE. MARIONETTE *wears the dress of a French maidservant.*]

ROSAURA: Tell me, dear Marionette. You were born in France and you were brought up in Paris. How do you think I would compare with your fine French ladies?

MARIONETTE: You have *joie de vivre*, signora. And that would be enough in France.

ROSAURA: Sometimes I wish I were not so high-spirited. In Italy you'll find plenty more high-spirited than I.

MARIONETTE: No, what I meant was that in Italy they like *loud* high spirits but in Paris they like *quiet* high spirits.

ROSAURA: Then the ladies there must be very boring.

MARIONETTE: Not at all. Everything appears charming when it is done gracefully.

ROSAURA: Well, tell me, do I look worn-out after being at the ball all night?

MARIONETTE: You have a natural complexion. But in France that is not sufficient. There the ladies use rouge to make themselves beautiful.

ROSAURA: I don't approve of that. I don't see any reason for it.

MARIONETTE: But when were women ever reasonable, signora? They're mad, signora, all of them. Quite mad.

ROSAURA: All right, I don't intend starting a new fashion.

MARIONETTE: You will be wise not to. It is best to do as others do. If you make yourself conspicuous you are not thought the better for it.

ROSAURA: On the contrary, I intend following the fashions more carefully. I was forced to marry a rich old man. Now that death has freed me, I intend to make the most of myself while I'm still young.

MARIONETTE: Then you must find a young man and make up for lost time.

ROSAURA: Yes, and I'm not going to waste any time about it. Signor Pantalone, my brother-in-law, treats me very well here, but it's not like living in my own house and being independent.

MARIONETTE: You'll not lack offers. You are young, you are beautiful, and what's more important, you have a good dowry.

ROSAURA: Yes, thanks to that old man, my husband.

MARIONETTE: Tell me the truth now. Have you anybody in mind?

ROSAURA: *So* soon? I've been a widow only a few months.

MARIONETTE: Ah, the young wives of old men always have somebody in mind. I remember I used to – with my first husband. He was seventy years old.

ROSAURA: Oh, you are always joking! Still, the Conte does not displease me.

MARIONETTE: He wouldn't make a bad match. But he's too jealous.

ROSAURA: That shows he really loves me.

MARIONETTE: *I* think you should look for something better. Now if you could find a Frenchman! Lucky you!

ROSAURA: Why, what advantage would there be in marrying a Frenchman?

MARIONETTE: You could have a good time without his being the least jealous. In fact, the more you did as you pleased, the more highly he'd think of you.

ROSAURA: That's a fine privilege to have.

MARIONETTE: French husbands are most considerate. Believe me. I know from experience.

ROSAURA: My sister is a long time coming.

MARIONETTE: She will be still dressing.

ROSAURA: She never knows when to stop.

MARIONETTE: Poor child! She also looks for a husband.

ROSAURA: We must find one for her as well.

MARIONETTE: If you don't, her father will let her become an old maid.

ROSAURA: That is why I keep her with me.

MARIONETTE: She is a good girl.

ROSAURA: I think my brother-in-law has his eye on her.

MARIONETTE: If I thought he would die as soon as yours did, she could do worse than marry him. But I think she'd rather have somebody young and handsome.

ROSAURA: Who is this man who has just come into my ante-room?

MARIONETTE: He's a waiter from the Inn. From the Scudo di Francia. I know him because I stayed there. He's a funny fellow. Always playing jokes.

ROSAURA: Well, he's no right to walk in here like this. Ask him what he wants.

MARIONETTE: Oh, let him come in. It will make you laugh.

[ARLECCHINO enters.]

ARLECCHINO: Will you be so kind as to allow me to enter? Ah, you do. You *are* kind. I am obliged. Most deeply obliged. At your great kindness.

ROSAURA: What politeness!

MARIONETTE: I told you. He overdoes everything. Even being polite.

ARLECCHINO: I trust I do not disturb you, but I was forced to acquire the rôle of ambassador.

ROSAURA: Speak plainly. So that I can understand you.

ARLECCHINO: Milord Runebif sends his greetings.

ROSAURA [*to* MARIONETTE]: It's that English gentleman I saw last night at the ball.

ARLECCHINO: And after you've had his greetings, he says he'll be coming to call on you this morning. Oh, yes, and he sends you this ring. To show he means what he says.

ROSAURA: I am surprised at you. And at him who has chosen you as his ambassador for such a purpose. If Milord Runebif wishes to call on me, he may. But that ring offends me. It is obvious he does not know me. Yes, tell him to come, if only to learn to know me better.

ARLECCHINO: What? You refuse a ring like this! Where did

you learn such uncivilized manners? Nowadays ladies don't do such things. Refuse gifts like this!

ROSAURA: That's enough of your back-chat. Take it back to him who sent it and tell him Rosaura has no need of his rings.

ARLECCHINO: I'm flabbergasted! I'm stupefied! No, really, I must be dreaming. A woman refuses a ring? It's a miracle! It's – not natural!

MARIONETTE: Let me see that ring, young man.

ARLECCHINO: Examine it carefully. You see, even Marionette can't get over it. No Frenchwoman would do such a thing.

MARIONETTE: But it's beautiful! It must have cost at least three hundred crowns. And you really won't keep it?

ROSAURA: Do you think any respectable woman could stoop to accept such a present?

MARIONETTE: Yes, you are right. [to ARLECCHINO] Take it back to him and tell him to come here.

ARLECCHINO: I will! I'll tell him! I'll tell all Venice a woman has refused a ring. And they'll all believe me. I don't think! [Exit]

ROSAURA: Some foreigners have a very poor opinion of Italian women. They think they've only to shower us with their gold and jewels and we're their slaves for life. For myself, if I *have* to receive a present, I'll see that whoever offers it has first to beg me to accept it and second to realize that my accepting his present will be all the reward he can hope for.

MARIONETTE: Yes, indeed, signora. That's what every woman should do, but it's not so easy. Here's that waiter back again already!

ROSAURA: And Milord with him. He certainly loses no time.

MARIONETTE: The English believe in actions not words.

ROSAURA: Yes, they're too serious for me.

MARIONETTE: And for me. Every quarter of an hour they speak ten words.

ROSAURA: Bring the Englishman in and then go and prepare some chocolate.

MARIONETTE: I'll have a chat with Arlecchino.

ROSAURA: Don't lead him on.

MARIONETTE: I know how to look after myself. I'm a Frenchwoman, remember. [*Exit*]

ROSAURA [*alone*]: If Milord hasn't wrong ideas about me, I will invite him to my dinner parties. And perhaps in time . . . but here he is.

[MARIONETTE *enters followed by* MILORD *and then goes again*.]

MILORD: Ma'am.

ROSAURA: Your servant, milord.

MILORD: Why send this ring back, eh? You seemed to like it last night.

ROSAURA: It is not possible to have everything I like.

MILORD: But one still wants what one likes.

ROSAURA: Wanting and having are two different things.

MILORD: Ma'am, with all respect, I don't like arguing.

ROSAURA: Please do sit down, won't you?

MILORD: After you.

ROSAURA: No, please, after you.

MILORD [*sitting*]: Ma'am, I said I don't like arguing.

ROSAURA: Have you rested well after your late night?

MILORD: Not much.

ROSAURA: Did you enjoy the ball?

MILORD: Very much.

ROSAURA: The ladies were very beautiful, were they not?

MILORD: Very. Very beautiful.

ROSAURA: Whom did you think the most beautiful?

MILORD: You, ma'am.

ROSAURA: Now you are joking!

MILORD: No, I mean it.

ROSAURA: Then I don't deserve it.

MILORD: You deserve everything. Yet you accept nothing.

ROSAURA: Because I don't wish to be under any obligation.

MILORD: I don't want anything from you. If you take the ring, it'll please me. And if you like it, I'll be more than satisfied.

ROSAURA: If you put it like that, I can't be so ungracious as to refuse your kindness.

MILORD: Take it.

[*He takes the ring out of his pocket and gives it to her.*]

ROSAURA: I would like to thank you, but I fear that might displease you.

MILORD: Quite, quite. No need at all.

[MARIONETTE *enters carrying two glasses of chocolate on a tray.*]

ROSAURA: Here is the chocolate.

MILORD [*taking a cup and giving it to* ROSAURA]: Ma'am.

ROSAURA [*aside*]: What a vast vocabulary! [*She drinks.*]

MILORD [*to* MARIONETTE, *as he drinks*]: You are French, Marionette?

MARIONETTE [*curtseying*]: Yes, signore.

MILORD: You must take great care of Madam.

MARIONETTE: I do all I can, signore.

[*He puts his glass back on the tray and puts a piece of money under it.*]

MARIONETTE [*aside, as she looks to see what it is*]: For me! A whole crown!

ROSAURA [*holding out her cup to* MARIONETTE]: Take it.

[*As* MARIONETTE *takes the cup she sees the ring on* ROSAURA'S *finger.*]

MARIONETTE [*aside to* ROSAURA]: I like the ring!

ROSAURA [*aside to* MARIONETTE]: Be quiet!

MARIONETTE [*to herself*]: All right, I will! [*She goes out with the tray.*]

MILORD: You're a widow, eh?

ROSAURA: I am. And if I can find a suitable match, I may be one again someday.

MILORD: I'm not the marrying sort, myself.

ROSAURA: But why not?

MILORD: Prefer my freedom.

ROSAURA: And love never bothers you?

MILORD: Only when I see a lovely woman.

ROSAURA: Then yours must be a fickle love.

MILORD: Why? Must love be forever?

ROSAURA: Constancy is the greatest virtue of a true lover.

MILORD: Constancy lasts as long as love does. And that's as long as the lover is near his beloved.

ROSAURA: I don't understand you.

MILORD: I'll explain. I love you and I'll be faithful as long as I love you. And I'll love you while I'm with you.

ROSAURA: So when you leave Venice you will forget all about me?

MILORD: What good would it be to you if I loved you in London or if I loved you in Paris? My love wouldn't be any use to you then and I'd only be making myself miserable and getting nothing out of it.

ROSAURA: And what do you expect to get out of it while you're near me?

MILORD: To see you and be seen by you.

ROSAURA: You *are* a gentleman!

MILORD: What more could a *lady* hope for?

ROSAURA: I think you're perfect.

MILORD: I am all yours.

ROSAURA: As long as you stay in Venice?

MILORD: Mm – I should think so.

ROSAURA [*aside*]: What droll humour!

MILORD [*aside*]: She pleases me more and more!

MARIONETTE [*entering*]: Signora, the Signor Conte would like to pay you a visit.

ROSAURA: The Conte di Bosco Nero?

MARIONETTE: Himself.

ROSAURA: Bring another chair and ask him to come in.

MARIONETTE: Yes, signora. [*aside, as she places a chair*] There'll be no tip for me from this jealous fellow. [*Exit*]

MILORD: Is the Conte your lover, ma'am?

ROSAURA: He would like to be.

[*The* CONTE *enters.*]

CONTE [*stiffly*]: I salute the Signora Rosaura.

ROSAURA: Good morning, Conte. Please be seated.

CONTE: I am glad to have some enjoyable conversation.

MILORD: Friend, you have come in the nick of time. This beautiful signora is bored to death with me.

CONTE: On the contrary, I'm sure you've amused her very much.

MILORD: No, you know me better than that.

ROSAURA: Marionette! [*to the others*] With your permission. [*She takes* MARIONETTE *aside and speaks softly.*] Tell my sister Eleonora to come here. And seat her near Milord. [MARIONETTE *goes out.*]

CONTE: I did not expect to find you entertaining so early.

ROSAURA: Milord has done me the favour of drinking some chocolate with me.

CONTE: Ah yes, you are generous to everybody.

ROSAURA: Conte, take care or you may offend me.

MILORD [*aside*]: This fellow's wild with jealousy.

CONTE [*ironically*]: Surely it can't be denied that Milord does not possess *all* the charming qualities desirable in a gentleman.*

MILORD [*aside*]: Damn the fellow!

[ELEONORA *enters.*]

ELEONORA: May I join you?

ROSAURA: Come in, Eleonora, come in.

MILORD [*to* ROSAURA]: Who is this lady?

ROSAURA: My sister.

ELEONORA: And your most devoted servant.

[MILORD *bows to her without speaking.*]

ROSAURA [*to* ELEONORA): Sit near Milord.

---

*This appears to be the opposite to elliptical irony – the using of *too many* words to gain an ironical effect. Goldoni rarely puts directions as to the way a line should be spoken and the fact that he does so in this case reveals a deliberate intention on his part. Personally I think he means that the Conte is indulging in what the Conte thinks is the English sense of humour – very heavy!

ELEONORA: If he permits me.

MILORD [*without looking at her*]: Honoured, I'm sure.

ELEONORA: You are English, aren't you?

MILORD [*as above*]: Yes, ma'am.

ELEONORA: Have you been long in Venice?

MILORD [*as above*]: Three months.

ELEONORA: Do you like our city?

MILORD [*as above*]: Of course.

ELEONORA: Oh, signore, why answer me so abruptly? I am Rosaura's sister.

MILORD: Excuse me, I was thinking of something. [*aside*] This one's not to my taste.

ELEONORA: I don't want to disturb your thoughts. . . .

MILORD [*rising*]: Your servant.

ROSAURA: Where are you going, Milord?

MILORD: To the Piazza.

ROSAURA: You are bored?

MILORD: A little pensive. We will meet again today. Good-bye, ma'am. Au revoir, Conte.

ROSAURA [*making as if to rise*]: Allow me at least to . . .

MILORD: No, no, I forbid it. Stay and console the poor Conte. I see he's dying to have you to himself. I also love you. But simply because I love you, I enjoy seeing you surrounded by those who adore you. That does justice to your charms and pays tribute to my choice. [*Exit*]

ELEONORA: Thank you sister, for the enjoyable conversation you forced on me. I'm much beholden to you!

ROSAURA: I'm sorry. He means well but he is a little eccentric.

ELEONORA: He'll not treat me like that again, that's certain.

CONTE: Milord means very well indeed, no doubt, but I must say I'm most upset to see myself repaid so badly.

ROSAURA: Now what are you complaining about?

CONTE: At seeing you displaying your charms to a foreigner.

ROSAURA: I like that! Do I belong to you? Have you perhaps bought me? Am I your wife? Are you daring to tell me what to do? By what right? Tell me that? With what authority? Conte, I do love you. In fact I love you more than you think. But I will never sacrifice my freedom just for that. Honest people say what they think. And a decent woman treats everybody the same. That's what I always try to do and if there's anybody I've given any privileges to, it's you. But do not abuse them. Or I will treat you again like I do all the others. And perhaps even forbid you my house. [*Exit*]

ELEONORA: That's put you in your place, Signor Conte. But it's your own fault. This cursed jealousy exasperates us poor women. My sister would do better to ignore it. As for me, if I ever have a jealous husband, I'd feel like making him die of desperation. [*Exit*]

CONTE: How can one not be jealous? I love a beautiful woman and I find her sitting beside another man. Oh, yes, it's all very well to treat everybody the same. I don't deny it. Civility is a fine thing. But what begins with civility can end with affection. Meanwhile I fall in love more and more. To hell with whoever invented morning cups of chocolate! [*Exit*]

≮ SCENE 3 ≯

The Street outside Rosaura's house.

[*The* DOCTOR *and* PANTALONE *enter.*]

PANTALONE: That's how it is, my dear friend and relative. My brother Stefanello has died and left no children. So to prevent our family disappearing I have decided to get married.

DOCTOR: Not a bad idea. As long as you succeed in begetting a son.

PANTALONE: I'm getting old, I know. But as a young man I never over-indulged myself, so I hope to be capable of something in my old age.

DOCTOR: Who is it to be? Have you everything cut and dried?

PANTALONE: My brother married Rosaura and I fancy Eleonora. In this way your two daughters would be in my house. Looking at it from that angle, you can't refuse me.

DOCTOR: I couldn't wish anything better. And I thank you for honouring me and my daughters. As long as Eleonora is willing, take her with my blessing.

PANTALONE: To tell you the truth, since she's been staying in my house with her sister, she's seemed to have been eyeing me favourably and I'm hoping she'll accept me.

DOCTOR: If you like, I'll speak to Eleonora myself. You have a word with Rosaura, and between the three of us, everything should work out all right. But now, my friend, I have some business to attend to. We will meet again before this evening. [*Exit*]

PANTALONE: To tell the truth, if I hadn't that girl there in the house all the time, I'd never have thought of getting married. I've taken such a fancy to her I can't live without her.

[MONSIEUR LEBLEU *enters.*]

MONSIEUR: Ah, Monsieur Pantalone, your servant, monsieur.

PANTALONE: Your most humble servant, mongsoor Leblo.

MONSIEUR: You value yourself very highly.

PANTALONE: Why do you say that?

MONSIEUR: Because you seem to find little enjoyment in the company of your friends.

PANTALONE: Ah, an old man can't stay up all night like he used to. I still like to enjoy myself but I have to be careful. As for the ladies, I've had to beat a retreat.

MONSIEUR: Perhaps. But I still would not like to have you as my rival for the love of a beautiful woman. You may be old but you do not look it.

PANTALONE: Yes, I have always looked after myself.

MONSIEUR: May you have many more years before you, Monsieur Pantalone dei Bisognosi. I have a bottle of twelve-year-old Burgundy. It would bring a corpse to life. Won't you join me?

PANTALONE: Why not? I'm always ready for a bottle.

MONSIEUR: And how is your Cyprus wine? I once drank a very good bottle of that in your house.

PANTALONE: I have a new barrel that's almost perfect. It's ready to be decanted into flasks.

MONSIEUR: Excellent. We must taste it.

PANTALONE: Whenever you wish.

MONSIEUR: Why not now? There's no time like the present.

PANTALONE: No, now's not the best time. We'd have to pay our respects to the ladies. Let us wait until they go out and then we can do as we please.

MONSIEUR: Oh, I don't mind paying my respects to the ladies. Come, let us go in.

PANTALONE: We'd have to mind our p's and q's.

MONSIEUR: Oh, Madame Rosaura will be pleased to have the opportunity for a little chat. She is a remarkable woman. You have a wonderful sister-in-law, Signor Pantalone.

PANTALONE [*aside*]: So that's the kind of wine he wants to drink. Those two girls are in the house. No, I don't want that . . . I'd better keep him away. [*aloud*] Yes, she's a decent, respectable widow.

MONSIEUR: Friend, do me a favour. Take me in to say good morning to her.

PANTALONE: You are making a mistake. I am Pantalone dei Bisognosi, not a procurer.

MONSIEUR: You're master of your own house, aren't you? You could introduce me if you wanted to, couldn't you?

PANTALONE: I could if I wanted to, but I don't want to.

MONSIEUR: Why not?

PANTALONE: Why not? D'you think a brother-in-law has the right to tell his sister-in-law what to do?

MONSIEUR: Come, forget these details. Be a friend and I'll do the same for you.

PANTALONE: Thank you very much but I have no need of such services. I am beyond them.

MONSIEUR: Either I'm going mad or you can't be understanding me. I like the Signora Rosaura. I want to see her. I am begging you to introduce me. Does that seem to you to be asking too much?

PANTALONE: Not at all. Those who have no moral sense, don't want to understand anything.

MONSIEUR: Then I'll go in without you.

PANTALONE: Please yourself.

MONSIEUR: She is a widow. You can't order her about.

PANTALONE: You're quite right.

MONSIEUR: I would have been most obliged to you.

PANTALONE: I am not interested.

MONSIEUR: Anybody else would have been glad to do me such a favour.

PANTALONE: Well, I'm the exception.

MONSIEUR: No gentleman refuses to help a friend.

PANTALONE: In anything lawful and honest.

MONSIEUR: I am an honest man.

PANTALONE: I believe you are.

MONSIEUR: How about a dozen bottles of Burgundy? I'll send them to you.

PANTALONE: I'm astounded at such a proposition. I don't need your wine. I could drown you and fifty like you in the wine I have in my cellar. You may make this sort of offer to other men but not to Pantalone dei Bisognosi. Do you hear me? And don't think you'll drink any of my Cyprus wine in my house. Such wine is too good for the likes of you! [*Exit*]

MONSIEUR: Ha, ha, ha! That one makes me laugh. He's a good fellow but too Italian. But what's it matter to me if he won't introduce me? I've no need of him as a go-between. I'm quite capable of knocking at a door myself. [*He knocks on the door*] Anybody in?

MARIONETTE [*coming to the window*]: Who is it?

MONSIEUR: Is Madame . . .? What! Marionette?

MARIONETTE: Monsieur Lebleu!

MONSIEUR: You here?

MARIONETTE: You in Venice?

MONSIEUR: Yes. . . . Is Madame Rosaura at home?

MARIONETTE: Come in. Come in! Let's talk in comfort.

[*She closes the window and opens the door.*]

MONSIEUR [*as he enters the house*]: This is the way to do things!

⊰ SCENE 4 ⊱

Rosaura's room. ROSAURA *is seated, reading a book.*

[MARIONETTE *enters.*]

ROSAURA: What wisdom! The author of this book intended it to be liked by women. Listen [*she reads aloud*] 'The father should provide his daughter with a husband and she should provide herself with a gentleman friend. He will be her intimate confidential private secretary and obey her more than her husband. This gentleman friend will be a most useful person to the husband because he will relieve the husband of many cares and will moderate the unquiet spirit of a flighty wife.' Yes, I wish I had read this unknown author before I was married. *I* never had a gentleman friend whom I could order about more than my husband. The wife who hasn't a gentleman friend is certainly missing a great deal.

MARIONETTE: I didn't want to disturb you while you were reading.

ROSAURA: Here, you can have it. This isn't my kind of book.

MARIONETTE: I do believe you don't agree with that about a wife having a gentleman friend. Believe me it's the fashion with all the married ladies in Italy today. But never mind that now. My lady, fate is ready to reward your charms.

ROSAURA: What are you talking about?

MARIONETTE: A French gentleman is here, overwhelmed by your beauty and dying to meet you.

ROSAURA: What is this – gentleman's name?

MARIONETTE: Monsieur Lebleu.

ROSAURA: Ah, yes, I know him. He dances with great affectation. When he took my hand at the ball last night I thought he wanted to cripple me.

MARIONETTE: That's not important. He is rich, young, handsome. Not the jealous, hard-to-please sort. In one word, he's a Frenchman.

ROSAURA: And that excuses every fault, does it?

MARIONETTE: But he really is all I say. He's in the ante-room waiting permission to come in.

ROSAURA: And you let him into the house just like that?

MARIONETTE: He is my countryman.

ROSAURA: Now tell me, why should it matter to me if he's your countryman?

MARIONETTE: Don't be so particular. He'll have some rings as well.

ROSAURA: Don't be impertinent! What a thing to say!

MARIONETTE: I was only joking, my lady. If you really don't want to see him . . .

MONSIEUR [*calling from outside*]: Marionette, is Madame asleep?

MARIONETTE: No, signore, but at the moment she can't . . .

MONSIEUR [*entering*]: Oh, if she's not sleeping, I'm sure she will allow me to come in.

MARIONETTE [*to Monsieur*]: Why did you do this?

ROSAURA: Signore, here we do not behave with such audacity . . .

MONSIEUR [*kneeling*]: Behold me at your feet begging your forgiveness for my impertinence. If you have as beautiful a heart as you have so beautiful a face, you will not refuse it me.

MARIONETTE [*aside*]: Well done, Monsieur Lebleu!

ROSAURA: Please get up. You haven't done anything so terrible that you should throw yourself at the feet of somebody who does not deserve such a tender submission.

MONSIEUR [*rising*]: Ah, thank heaven! Your words fill my heart with joy.

ROSAURA [*to herself*]: Even if it is a little affected, I find this approach extremely attractive.

MONSIEUR [*aside to* MARIONETTE]: Marionette, I don't need you any more. Go and get on with your work.

MARIONETTE [*to* ROSAURA]: Can I do anything, signora?

ROSAURA: Put a chair near me here.

MARIONETTE: There you are. [*aside to* MONSIEUR] Remember the customs of our country, monsieur.

MONSIEUR [*aside to* MARIONETTE]: Yes, some nice present for you. I'll find you one.

MARIONETTE [*to herself as she goes*]: I'd rather have a crown now. A bird in the hand is worth two in the bush. [*Exit*]

MONSIEUR: Ah, madame! Heaven, which makes all good things, could not have created such beauty as yours simply to torment your lovers. Your great beauty can only be equalled by your great compassion.

ROSAURA: Since I know I am not beautiful, I cannot claim to be compassionate.

MONSIEUR: Ah, to esteem yourself so lowly, proves only your great modesty. But by heaven, if an artist had to portray Venus, he need only paint your portrait.

ROSAURA: Over-fulsome praise, monsieur, degenerates into flattery.

MONSIEUR: I tell you – I speak sincerely, from the heart, from the mind, as a gentleman, and as a Frenchman: you are the most beautiful of all the beautiful women walking this earth.

ROSAURA [*aside*]: And he can keep it up as well!

MONSIEUR: And to your natural beauty you add the beautiful art of a perfect hair-style. Who arranges your hair, madame? Our Marionette?

ROSAURA: None but herself.

MONSIEUR: I recognize the Paris fashion. Pardon me, madame, but one insolent little hair is wanting to spoil your perfection.

ROSAURA: That is not important.

MONSIEUR: Ah, but it is. It is bad. If you will allow me, I will correct it.

ROSAURA: I will call Marionette.

MONSIEUR: No, no, the honour of waiting upon you must be mine. One moment.

[*He takes from his pocket a little silver case. From this he selects a pair of scissors and cuts a hair from* ROSAURA'S *head.*

Then from the same case he selects a hair-pin and fastens it in her hair. Not satisfied, he takes out a little comb from another pocket and arranges her hair. From the silver case he takes a little packet of powder and blows some on her hair. Then from the case he takes a little knife and removes the powder from her forehead. He wipes her forehead with a handkerchief, then takes out a mirror for her to look at herself. Finally he takes out a bottle of scented water, puts some on his hands to clean them and then wipes them with the handkerchief. While doing all this he keeps up a running commentary. Then, seating himself, he says:]

MONSIEUR: Now that will stay absolutely perfect.

ROSAURA: You are obviously a connoisseur and the epitome of gallantry.

MONSIEUR: As for being a connoisseur, I do not deny that Paris holds me in some esteem. All the best French tailors correspond with me to let me know their ideas. And they never start a new fashion without my approval.

ROSAURA: It is obvious that your clothes are most unusual.

MONSIEUR [*rising and walking about*]: Do you not admire the cut of the waist? See how the two sides show off the body. It preserves the perfect symmetry. That is the reason you saw me so successful at the ball last night.

ROSAURA [*aside*]: He gets worse and worse.

MONSIEUR: But I waste time over trivialities. I forget to tell you that you please me excessively, that I love you with all my heart. And, that you should reciprocate my passion is all that I desire.

ROSAURA: Signore, that I please you is my good fortune, that you love me reveals your kindness, but to reciprocate is not in my power.

MONSIEUR: On whom are you dependent? Are you not your own mistress?

ROSAURA: A widow is open to criticism more than other women. If I favoured you, people would talk about me.

MONSIEUR: You should not worry about such people as long as you behave prudently.

ROSAURA: A prudent woman must either keep herself to herself, or else find herself a husband.

MONSIEUR: I do not accept that, but if you wish I will supply you with a husband.

ROSAURA: And who, signore, might that be?

MONSIEUR: Lebleu, who worships you. I, my darling, will give you my hand as I have given you my heart.

ROSAURA: You must give me time.

MONSIEUR: Yes, my beloved, as much time as you like. But do not leave me too long in torment. [*He goes to her to take her hand.*]

ROSAURA: Monsieur, a little more modesty, please.

MONSIEUR: Is not one little thing allowed to him who is to be your husband?

ROSAURA: You must be patient.

MONSIEUR [*attempting again to take her hand*]: But I burn for you. I cannot live without you!

ROSAURA [*aside*]: This has gone far enough! [*She rises.*]

MONSIEUR: Do not flee from me! [*He follows her*] Have pity on me!

ROSAURA: Behave more decorously, I said. You are too importunate.

MONSIEUR [*on his knees*]: Forgive me!

ROSAURA [*aside*]: He's starting again! [*aloud*] Get up and stop embarrassing me.

MONSIEUR: Madame, a weakness of the heart prevents me rising without the aid of your hand.

ROSAURA: Come then, I will help you. [*She gives him her hand and he kisses it.*]

MONSIEUR: The accomplished lover does not ignore his opportunities.

ROSAURA: Monsieur! You are too bold!

MONSIEUR: And you are too beautiful!

ROSAURA: Enough! I can no longer permit myself to enjoy your charming mannerisms.

MONSIEUR: I see it will be unwise at the moment to prolong our meeting. I will go.

ROSAURA: I shall reply to your proposal at another time.

MONSIEUR: This hand of mine is pledged for you.

ROSAURA: And I am not far from accepting it. [*aside*] I'll think well before I do.

MONSIEUR: Farewell, my queen, sovereign of my heart and of my thoughts. Ah! what beauty! What charm! What a pity it is, you were not born in Paris! [*Exit*]

ROSAURA [*alone*]: Exactly! If I had been born in Paris, I wouldn't be what I am! I am glad I live in a country where commonsense is valued more than anywhere else. Italy today teaches the world how to live. She retains all the good from foreign countries and rejects the bad. This is what makes Italy admired and loved by all the peoples of the world when they come to visit her. This Frenchman would not displease me if he were not so affected. His every word is obviously spoken for effect. The Englishman would not promise to love me after he's left this city. I fear this Frenchman would tire of loving me while he is still here.

Act Two

❦ SCENE I ❧

Rosaura's room.

[ROSAURA *and the* DOCTOR.]

ROSAURA: I thought my father had forgotten me. You never come to see me.

DOCTOR: You know I have my business to attend to, daughter. I possess no private income. I have to work.

ROSAURA: I do hope you'll let me know if you need anything.

DOCTOR: No, no. I do not wish to be a burden to you. On the contrary, by having your sister Eleonora here with you, you relieve me of a considerable worry.

ROSAURA: We must try to arrange a good marriage for her.

DOCTOR: That is why I am here. I have come to tell you that your brother-in-law, Signor Pantalone, would like to marry her.

ROSAURA: Oh, no! Not an old man like him!

DOCTOR: You married an old man yourself.

ROSAURA: Exactly. That's why she mustn't.

DOCTOR: That is enough. I will speak to her, and if she is agreeable you must not stand in her way.

ROSAURA: If she's agreeable, all right. But you must not force her against her will.

DOCTOR: And you, Rosaura? Would you not like to marry again?

ROSAURA: Why not? If a good match presented itself – who knows?

DOCTOR: I am acquainted with a Spanish gentleman who appears to have taken a great liking for you.

ROSAURA: What is his name?

DOCTOR: Don Alvaro di Castiglia.

ROSAURA: I know him. He was at the ball last night.

DOCTOR: He has asked me to introduce him to you and is at this moment awaiting permission to enter. He is a most honest and respectable gentleman. I should be very pleased if you would receive him. And his liking for you could indeed be to your advantage.

ROSAURA: If my own father introduces him, how can I refuse?

DOCTOR: My daughter, it would be well if you married again. You must not mind my saying this, but a widow frequenting dances late at night does not present a very pleasant picture. [*Exit*]

ROSAURA [*alone*]: He means well. But what conquests I must have made last night! I've enchanted them all. I didn't know I was so extraordinary. The Spaniard as well! And here he is – like all his countrymen – as serious as a problem in geometry.

[DON ALVARO *enters.*]

DON: My deepest respects to the lady Rosaura.

ROSAURA [*curtseying*]: I bid welcome to Don Alvaro di Castiglia.

DON: Your father insisted that I inflict my presence upon you. I did not wish to displease him nor rob myself of the pleasure of seeing you again.

ROSAURA: It was too bad of my father to put you to the trouble of enduring my conversation.

DON: You are a lady of exceptional merit. That recompenses me for any inconvenience I may have suffered.

ROSAURA: Please do sit down.

DON [*aside, as he seats himself*]: She's even more beautiful by day than by night.

ROSAURA [*aside, as she also seats herself*]: He quite overawes me!

DON: Will you partake of a pinch of snuff? [*He hands her his snuff-box.*]

ROSAURA: It is indeed excellent.

DON: It arrived yesterday from my mother the Duchess.

ROSAURA: It could not be better.

DON: It is yours.

ROSAURA: I will not refuse the honour of putting a little in my own snuff-box.

DON: Make use of mine.

ROSAURA: But I could not deprive you of it.

DON: Then give me yours in exchange.

ROSAURA: But mine is silver. Yours is gold.

DON: Gold! What is gold! To us gold is as mud. I value good snuff like that more than a hundred gold boxes. Please oblige me.

ROSAURA: If you insist. [*She gives him her snuff-box and keeps his*] How do you like our beloved Italy, Don Alvaro?

DON: It is beautiful, but I do not see that majestic charm which permeates every corner of Spain.

ROSAURA: And Italian ladies? What think you of them?

DON: They do not appreciate their own beauty.

ROSAURA: Why?

DON: Why? Because they are too modest. They do not know how to make the most of their charms.

ROSAURA: Would you prefer them to be proud and arrogant?

DON: I would prefer them more reserved, less exuberant.

ROSAURA: But that is the way we are made.

DON: Now, now. I was not speaking of you. You are not typically Italian. Last night you surprised me. I saw shine from your eyes a ray of brilliant majesty that filled me with veneration, with respect and with wonder. You seemed to me like one of our own ladies, who despite the subjection in which we keep them, have nevertheless the power to conquer us with one glance, with one look.

ROSAURA: Thank you for your good opinion of me. But take care you are not mistaken.

DON: A Spaniard cannot be mistaken. We know merit when we see it.

ROSAURA: Perhaps you do, but sometimes passion blinds us.

DON: No, no, it is impossible for a Spaniard to be blinded by passion. We take care first to examine carefully the object of our passion. With us beauty is not the prime consideration.

ROSAURA: Oh? What is, then?

DON: A certain constraint. A certain dignity.

ROSAURA [*aside*]: Characteristics of his own country.

DON: I do not wish to detain you overlong. What is the time?

ROSAURA: It must be nearly midday.

DON: Let us see what our old infallible says. [*He takes out his watch*] This is the most perfect English workmanship.

ROSAURA: Do they not make watches in Spain?

DON: How droll you are! Scarcely anybody works in Spain.

ROSAURA: Then how do the poor people live?

DON: In Spain there are no poor people.

ROSAURA [*aside*]: Oh, this one's perfect too!

> [*While looking at his watch* DON ALVARO *accidentally drops it on the floor.*]

DON: Go to the devil!

> [*He kicks the watch to the other side of the room.*]

ROSAURA: What *are* you doing? Such a beautiful watch?

DON: I cannot soil my hands with something that has touched the ground.

ROSAURA [*aside*]: He has a smooth answer for everything.

DON: Now what about yourself. In the half-hour you have been with me, you have not asked me for anything.

ROSAURA: I would not know what to ask, except the honour of your friendship.

DON: The friendship of a Spaniard is not easy to acquire. But you are beautiful. You bear yourself with dignity. I like you. I love you. I am all yours. Do with me as you please. [*He rises.*]

ROSAURA: Yet you wish to leave me already?

DON: I do not trust myself. I may begin to weaken.

ROSAURA [*aside*]: I'll do as his Spanish ladies do. [*aloud*] Expect only to receive haughty glances from me.

DON: Those are what I enjoy.

ROSAURA: I will make you suffer before I have pity on you.

DON: I will endure with delight.

ROSAURA: At my command you must not betray your suffering by even a sigh.

DON:It will be beautiful to die for a lady who knows how to take seriously such a serious matter.

ROSAURA:Then begin from this moment to fear me. Go!

DON:I obey you with all speed!

ROSAURA:Do not look back at me!

DON:This is sublime! What incomparable severity! I feel already the great joy in suffering the greatest pain in the world! [*He only half turns to her as he goes out with a sigh.*]

ROSAURA [*alone*]: Oh, this is the most amusing one of them all! I've never met anyone like him! He actually likes being hurt. He wants to be treated disdainfully. So now I have four suitors. And each has his merits and each his faults. The Italian is faithful but too jealous. The Englishman is worthy but fickle. The Frenchman is gallant but affected. And the Spaniard is affectionate but much too serious. And it's obvious I'll have no peace till I choose one of them. But which? I suppose it ought to be the Conte, even though he does annoy me so much sometimes with his jealous suspicions. After all he has the advantage over the others of being my fellow countryman. That's an advantage which would count anywhere in any country. [*Exit*]

⊀ SCENE 2 ⊁

A room at the Inn.

[MONSIEUR LEBLEU *and* ARLECCHINO.]

MONSIEUR:You are indeed a man of infinite jest. Why hide yourself away in an Inn like this where nobody can appreciate you?

ARLECCHINO:To tell you the truth, master, the only thing I'm really good at is eating. And there's no better place for that than at an Inn, is there?

MONSIEUR:No, friend, you underestimate yourself. There is something you are much better at. You are a born ambassador of love.

ARLECCHINO:No, you are not a good fortune-teller. I've never done any procuring.

MONSIEUR:How you change the meaning of words in Italy! What is this 'procuring'? An ambassador of love is an interpreter of the human heart, a harbinger of felicity and joy, a person esteemed by all and engaged in one of the most honourable callings in the whole world.

ARLECCHINO:An interpreter of the human heart? A harbinger of felicity and joy? In other words you mean – somebody who plays gooseberry?

MONSIEUR:I shall be the one to give your chance to shine, to show your true ability. You know Madame Rosaura, sister-in-law of Signor Pantalone dei Bisognosi?

ARLECCHINO:Yes, signore. I know her.

MONSIEUR:Are you gallant enough to present to her in my name, and ask her to accept as a gift, a most precious jewel that I will give you?

ARLECCHINO:It wouldn't be some sort of ring, would it?

MONSIEUR:Of course it's not a ring! It is a jewel beyond price.

ARLECCHINO:Because if it was a ring I wouldn't take it. All right, I'll have a go. But you won't forget the labourer is worthy of his hire, will you?

MONSIEUR:Execute the commission and you will be amply rewarded.

ARLECCHINO:Was your Excellency ever in England? Does your Excellency know the customs of the English in matters like this?

MONSIEUR:No, I have never been there, and I don't know what you're talking about.

ARLECCHINO:In England the labourer gets his reward first.

MONSIEUR:This is not England. Do as I say and have no fear.

ARLECCHINO:I'll take your word then.

MONSIEUR:One moment. I don't want you to say you are a servant at an Inn.

ARLECCHINO:What then?

MONSIEUR:You must go as my servant. As you know, I dismissed mine three days ago.

ARLECCHINO: Then I'd better wear his uniform, hadn't I?

MONSIEUR: Come into my room. I'll fit you out as a French manservant.

ARLECCHINO: A la français! Fine! Let's go. Now I'll be a real mongsoor.

MONSIEUR: Remember to act the part, at ease, debonair, brisk! Hat in hand. Constant gestures. Ceaseless chatter. Forever bowing. [ARLECCHINO *tries to do all these things at once and fails.*]

MONSIEUR: Here is the jewel you must take her. It is my own portrait which she is sure to appreciate more than all the jewels in the world. [*He gives* ARLECCHINO *a silver locket containing his portrait.*]

ARLECCHINO [*examining it*]: Oh, what a jewel! What a beautiful jewel!

MONSIEUR: And now listen carefully to the message you must give her. You must not forget one word of it.

ARLECCHINO: Don't worry. I'll repeat it word for word. Tell me.

MONSIEUR: This is what you must say: Madame, one whose entire aspiration it is to serve you with respect and humility, sends you in anticipation his portrait. Keep it as a token of the love that will be yours when fate permits him the honour to . . .

ARLECCHINO: No more, for heaven's sake! I'll not remember a word of it.

MONSIEUR: Can you read?

ARLECCHINO: A little.

MONSIEUR: Come into my room and I'll write it down on a piece of paper. Then you can learn it off by heart.

ARLECCHINO: If I have to keep on reading it until I know it by heart I'll be reading it when I die.

MONSIEUR: Come along. Don't keep me waiting. I am most anxious to know what Madame's answer will be. And your reward will depend on it as well. Take great care of the jewel I've just given you. It is worth a king's ransom. Even a princess would be glad to have it. [*Exit*]

ARLECCHINO: But not a poor man like me. [*Follows him out.*]

[*The* CONTE *enters.*]

CONTE [*alone*]: Rosaura is annoyed with me. I have offended
her with my jealous suspicions. I must find some way of
propitiating her. This letter will, I hope, obtain for me her
forgiveness and restore to me the sweet possession of her
charms. [*calls*] Ho, there! Foletto!

[FOLETTO *enters.*]

FOLETTO: Yes, Illustrious?

CONTE: Do you know the house of Signor Pantalone dei
Bisognosi?

FOLETTO: Yes, Illustrious.

CONTE: And do you know Signora Rosaura, his sister-in-law?

FOLETTO: Yes, Illustrious, I know her.

CONTE: Go to the house, then, and give her this letter.

FOLETTO: At once, Illustrious.

CONTE: Do your best to obtain a reply.

FOLETTO: Yes, Illustrious.

CONTE: And while you're there, try to see whether there's
anyone with her.

FOLETTO: Leave it to me, Illustrious.

CONTE: And remember your manners when you're there.

FOLETTO: Don't worry, Illustrious, this sort of thing is part
of a good servant's job. [*Exit*]

CONTE [*alone*]: Yes, I'll grant him that. Italian servants know
how to go about such things. They're a little familiar at
times, but what does that matter? No man's a hero to his
valet. [*Exit*]

[MILORD *enters. He walks up and down silently, then takes a
little jewel case from his pocket. He opens it, looks at the jewels,
closes it, and then calls.*]

MILORD: Birif!

[BIRIF *enters without speaking, takes off his hat and stands
waiting silently.*]

MILORD: Take these diamonds to Madam Rosaura. You know
her?

BIRIF: Yes, sir.

MILORD: Tell her I sent you because I'm not able to come myself.

BIRIF: Yes, sir.

MILORD: Bring me her reply.

BIRIF: Yes, sir. [*Exit*]

MILORD [*alone*]: A thousand ducats. No, it's not expensive enough. She's worth more. Yes, I'll do it. [*Exit*]

[ARLECCHINO, *now dressed as a French manservant, enters holding a piece of paper in his hand.*]

ARLECCHINO: This time maybe I am going to make my fortune. Anyway, he's dressed me like a Frenchman and there'll be more to follow if he's a true Frenchman himself. I'd better read the compliment again that I have to say to the Signora Rosaura, so that I'll begin to remember it.

[*He starts opening the paper when he sees the Spaniard coming.*]

DON [*entering*]: Your servant, signore.

[ARLECCHINO *looks all round, not believing that it is himself who is being spoken to.*]

ARLECCHINO: Who is it you are speaking to?

DON: Friend, I'm speaking to you.

ARLECCHINO: I am honoured.

DON: Tell me, do you know Donna Rosaura, sister-in-law of Don Pantalone?

ARLECCHINO: Yes, signore, I know her. [*aside*] The devil! They're all after that woman!

DON: Then yours must be the honour of presenting her, in my name, with a treasure.

ARLECCHINO: A treasure? Oh, think nothing of it! Certainly, I'll give it her. But you won't forget the labourer is worthy of his hire.

DON: There. [*Gives a scroll*] Simply take that paper to her and you will be amply rewarded.

ARLECCHINO: Is this the treasure?

DON: Yes, indeed. A treasure of inestimable value.

ARLECCHINO: Signore, pardon my curiosity, but how is this a treasure?

DON: That is my family-tree.

ARLECCHINO [*aside, laughing*]: A treasure to equal the Frenchman's!

DON: You will give it to the Donna Rosaura and you will say to her thus: 'Great Lady, model yourself on these glorious ancestors of your beloved Don Alvaro and be glad that yours will be the honour of becoming a lady of Spain.'

ARLECCHINO: Listen, I'll take the treasure but not all those words. It's impossible for me to remember them. You'll have to write them out for me.

DON: Yes, I will do that. Come into my room. And you may rest assured that if you bring me a favourable reply, there will be a little treasure also for you.

ARLECCHINO: It needn't be too little. [*aside*] Still I should do all right out of both of them. [*He follows* DON ALVARO *out.*]

⟪ SCENE 3 ⟫

Rosaura's room.

[THE DOCTOR *and* ELEONORA.]

DOCTOR: My daughter, a marriage with Signor Pantalone would be very advantageous for you. With all the money he has inherited from his brother, Signor Stefanello, he will be twice as rich.

ELEONORA: Dear father, to tell the truth, I have nothing against such a marriage except the disparity of our ages. I am too young and he is too old.

DOCTOR: His advanced age should not appear an obstacle to you. He is a charming man, full of good cheer and good health. And what is more important, he loves you and would treat you like a queen.

ELEONORA: Since you think it would be a good marriage for me, I cannot refuse. My only desire is to obey your wishes.

DOCTOR: Well done, daughter. Nothing could please me more. I will go at once to Signor Pantalone, in case he should change his mind. I must make your good fortune sure and certain. [*Exit*]

ELEONORA [*alone*]: It would be very nice to be rich and to be one's own mistress, but I'm not happy at the idea of marrying such an old man.

[MARIONETTE *enters.*]

Marionette, I have good news for you. I am to be married.

MARIONETTE: I am so pleased! Who is it to be?

ELEONORA: Signor Pantalone.

MARIONETTE: And you call that good news? You mean that makes you happy?

ELEONORA: Why not? He is a good match, isn't he?

MARIONETTE: Yes, for a woman of fifty. Not for a young girl like you.

ELEONORA: That's what I thought myself at first. But then when I thought how rich he is, his age didn't seem to matter.

MARIONETTE: It matters very much! Very much indeed! Ask your sister what it's like to be married to an old man. I'm not old but I've had three husbands and if I marry again it'll certainly be to a young man.

ELEONORA: If I could find one myself, I certainly wouldn't say no.

MARIONETTE: A young Frenchman, that's who you should have.

ELEONORA: Then you find me a Frenchman who would have me!

MARIONETTE: Oh, I could find you one all right.

ELEONORA: But he must be rich and handsome as well as young.

MARIONETTE: We've plenty like that in France.

ELEONORA: Must I go to France then to get married?

MARIONETTE: No, signorina, there are many Frenchmen in

Venice. In fact there's one who seems to like your sister. But she gives him little encouragement. It could be he might make a declaration to you.

ELEONORA: If he's in love with my sister he won't notice me.

MARIONETTE: Ah, but Frenchmen change easily. You could soon have him at your feet.

ELEONORA: You make him sound very fickle.

MARIONETTE: What will that matter once you're married to him?

ELEONORA: A husband's love for his wife matters, doesn't it?

MARIONETTE: I see it's little you know of such things. But never mind that now. Do you want to meet this French-man?

ELEONORA: Yes, I'll meet him willingly.

MARIONETTE: Leave it all to me then. Your sister's head over heels in love with the jealous one and has no time for any of the others. That's the worse for her and the better for you. Think of it! A Frenchman! What a happy marriage that would be for you!

ELEONORA: But I've promised my father to marry Signor Pantalone.

MARIONETTE: Tell him you've changed your mind.

ELEONORA: He'll say I'm fickle.

MARIONETTE: That will be your excuse: you are a woman.

ELEONORA: He will scold me.

MARIONETTE: Let him.

ELEONORA: He will threaten me.

MARIONETTE: Don't let him frighten you.

ELEONORA: He will try to force me.

MARIONETTE: He can't force you to marry against your will. Be firm.

ELEONORA: I'm frightened I won't be able to resist.

MARIONETTE: I'll tell your sister. We'll both support you.

ELEONORA: Dear Marionette, I will rely on you.

[ROSAURA *enters*.]

MARIONETTE: Come and rescue your dear sister, Signora Rosaura. Your father wants to marry her to your brother-in-law, Signor Pantalone. She's very upset but she hasn't the courage to disobey your father.

ELEONORA: Dear Rosaura, you will help me, won't you?

ROSAURA: Of course. I've already spoken to Signor Pantalone. He told me my father had given him cause to hope, but I made it very clear to him that a woman must have absolute freedom in her choice of a husband.

ELEONORA: Thank you, thank you. Our mother could not have done more for me.

ROSAURA: I think it will be best if you keep to your room at the moment.

ELEONORA: If father comes to plead with me, what shall I say?

ROSAURA: Tell him it's a matter you can't decide without me.

ELEONORA: He'll say he's my father.

ROSAURA: Your answer to that's simple. It is I who will be providing your dowry.

ELEONORA: That's an answer I'll give him with all the pleasure in the world. [*softly, to* MARIONETTE, *as she goes*] Marionette, don't forget the Frenchman. [*Exit*]

MARIONETTE: Her mother certainly could not have done more for her than you are doing.

ROSAURA: My sister is very dear to me. I must do all I can to make her happy.

MARIONETTE: There's somebody come into the ante-room. I'll go and see who it is. [*Exit*]

ROSAURA [*alone*]: It is a barbarous custom that allows a woman's heart to be disposed of at the cost of her happiness.

[MARIONETTE *comes back.*]

MARIONETTE: Signora, he says he's Monsieur Lebleu's servant and that he's here as Monsieur Lebleu's ambassador.

ROSAURA: Let him come in.

MARIONETTE: But d'you know who he really is? He's that waiter from the Hotel. Arlecchino! The French gentleman has made him his servant! [*Exit*]

ROSAURA [*alone*]: So the Frenchman attacks! But before I yield I'll make good use of all my defences.

MARIONETTE [*entering*]: Come in, come in, Signor Waiter from my beloved France.

[ARLECCHINO *enters making many exaggerated bows to* ROSAURA.]

ROSAURA: Bravo! Bravo! But don't tire yourself out. Do speak, if you have something to say to me on behalf of your master.

ARLECCHINO [*trying to speak in a different voice*]: Madame, I have come on behalf of my master to present you with a jewel.

ROSAURA: A jewel? For me?

ARLECCHINO: For you, Madame. But before I give it to you, or to put it better, before I present it to you, I must deliver to you a message. But for the life of me, I can't remember a word of it.

MARIONETTE: Arlecchino, you should be ashamed of yourself.

ROSAURA: If you can't remember it, how will I know what it is?

ARLECCHINO: Being a man of some wit I foresaw that little difficulty, and so did not leave it to chance. [*aside*] That was a mouthful! [*aloud*] Here is the message written down on this paper.

ROSAURA: Well done!

MARIONETTE: Bravo!

ARLECCHINO [*presenting the paper to* ROSAURA]: Here is the paper. See what it says, because between ourselves, I can't read or write.

ROSAURA: Listen, Marionette. How beautifully and gallantly our Frenchman expresses himself. [*Reads*] 'Madame, the poor memory of my new servant obliges me to add these few lines to the token of my esteem which I am sending you. I trust you will deign to accept it in the knowledge that it comes to you accompanied by all my love.'

MARIONETTE: What a beautiful French style he has!

ROSAURA [*to* ARLECCHINO]: Well? What is it that you have to present to me?

ARLECCHINO: It's a precious jewel. A French jewel. Here it is. [*He gives her the locket.*]

ROSAURA: Is this the jewel?

MARIONETTE: Well, isn't it? The portrait of a Parisian?

ROSAURA: It's certainly unusual.

ARLECCHINO: Madame, may I beg you for your reply, on which depends the happiness of my master and the interest of his servant.

ROSAURA: Certainly. Wait a moment and I will give it you. [*She goes to the table and writes.*]

MARIONETTE: Dear Arlecchino, how did you come to have this good fortune?

ARLECCHINO: Fate intended me to become a Frenchman with the help of Marionette.

MARIONETTE: If you continue like this, I really might see what I can do with you.

ARLECCHINO: I'm just beginning to realize my own capabilities. If I haven't made the most of myself till now, it was because I had not met my fate, my fortune, my destiny.

MARIONETTE: Very nicely put!

ROSAURA: Here is the brief reply you must take to Monsieur Lebleu. It is not a letter. I have not sealed it and I do not know the address.

ARLECCHINO: Would it be a favourable reply?

ROSAURA: You could say so.

ARLECCHINO: May I hope to be suitably rewarded?

ROSAURA: That depends on the generosity of him who sent you.

ARLECCHINO [*making many different kinds of bows*]: Madame, your most deeply humble servant.

MARIONETTE: You're overdoing it.

ARLECCHINO [*more bows*]: Vastly obliged, I'm sure.

MARIONETTE: That's enough!

ARLECCHINO: Your respectful servant. Good day, your Excellency. [*Exit*]

MARIONETTE: I like that little fellow!

ROSAURA: He is indeed most obliging.

MARIONETTE: And he's so full of life. Anybody would take him for a Frenchman.

ROSAURA: You remember I told you, Marionette, that Signor Pantalone is very annoyed with me because I spoke against his marrying my sister. I almost believe he would like to turn me out of his house. And I think I'd rather anticipate him in that.

MARIONETTE: You would soon be able to find a house.

ROSAURA: Yes, but it's not good for a widow to live alone.

MARIONETTE: Take your sister with you.

ROSAURA: She still needs a guardian.

MARIONETTE: Go and live in your father's house then.

ROSAURA: I wouldn't be free enough there.

MARIONETTE: Then you'd better get married.

ROSAURA: That would be the best solution.

MARIONETTE: Well, why don't you?

ROSAURA: Because I have four suitors. And they've put me in a state of utter confusion.

MARIONETTE: Choose one of them.

ROSAURA: I'm frightened of making a mistake.

MARIONETTE: Stick to the Frenchman and you won't go far wrong.

ROSAURA: I'm beginning to think he's the worst of the lot.

MARIONETTE: Well, if you don't want him, let your sister have him.

ROSAURA: I'll think about it.

MARIONETTE: Look! Now there's another servant in the ante-room!

ROSAURA: Whoever can it be? Tell him to come in.

MARIONETTE: There's no need to. He's an impudent one, this.

[FOLETTO enters.]

FOLETTO: I am your Excellency's humble servant.

ROSAURA: Who are you?

FOLETTO: I am Foletto, servant to the Illustrious Signor the Conte di Bosco Nero.

ROSAURA: And what has your master to say?

FOLETTO: The Illustrious Signor the Conte, my master, sends this letter to the Illustrious Signora Rosaura. [*He gives her the letter.*]

MARIONETTE [*as* ROSAURA *reads the letter*]: Friend, were you ever in Paris?

FOLETTO: No, signora.

MARIONETTE: Then you can't be a very good servant.

FOLETTO: Why not?

MARIONETTE: Because that's the only place to learn your calling.

FOLETTO: Nevertheless, though I've never been in Paris, I've learnt a thing or two.

MARIONETTE: Such as what?

FOLETTO: Such as when the master makes love to the mistress, the servant does the same to the maidservant.

MARIONETTE: Then you've learnt a little too much!

ROSAURA: I see. Well, you can say to your master . . .

FOLETTO: For the love of heaven, give me the answer in writing, Madame, otherwise . . .

MARIONETTE: You'll lose your tip, won't you?

FOLETTO: Just so. That's something I can't teach you, obviously.

MARIONETTE: Oh, go and talk to yourself!

ROSAURA [*going to the table*]: I will think how to reply.

FOLETTO [*to* MARIONETTE]: How many lovers have you, little Frenchwoman?

MARIONETTE: Quite enough, thank you.

FOLETTO: Do they try to get in through your window at night?

MARIONETTE: Not with me they don't.

FOLETTO: No, I shouldn't think they would. D'you think I'd get in?

MARIONETTE: What d'you think?

FOLETTO: I'll try tonight.

MARIONETTE: You beast! Heaven knows how many you've had!

FOLETTO: Naturally. On my miserable wages I couldn't lead much of a life if I hadn't four maidservants to support me.

MARIONETTE: Get out!

FOLETTO: Now, now! You will be the fifth.

ROSAURA: Here is the reply.

FOLETTO: Thank you, your Excellency. Would that be all, Excellency? Nothing for the messenger?

ROSAURA: Here you are. [*She gives him a tip.*]

FOLETTO: Much obliged to your Excellency. A long life to your Excellency. See you tonight, Frenchwoman. [*Exit, running*]

MARIONETTE [*aside*]: You try and see what you get!

ROSAURA: From the way the Conte writes, I do believe he really loves me.

MARIONETTE: It would be better if you understood the meaning of Monsieur Lebleu's present. By sending you his portrait he shows he wants to be always with you.

ROSAURA: I don't like his sending it to me and calling it a jewel.

MARIONETTE: Never mind then. I understand. You've already made up your mind it's to be the Conte. Good for you.

ROSAURA: Believe me, I'm not at all decided yet.

MARIONETTE: Oh, my goodness, here's another ambassador! What a day you're having!

ROSAURA: Who is it this time?

MARIONETTE: Can't you tell? It's an English manservant.

ROSAURA: It must be Milord's servant!

MARIONETTE [*going to the door*]: Come in.

BIRIF [*entering and making a bow*]: Madam.

MARIONETTE [*aside*]: How serious we are!

ROSAURA: What is it you want, my good man?

BIRIF: Milord Runebif has sent me because he can't come himself.

ROSAURA: Well? What for?

BIRIF: He sends this little thing. [*He gives her the jewels.*]

ROSAURA: Oh, how lovely! Look, Marionette! What beautiful jewels!

MARIONETTE [*aside, to* ROSAURA]: This is much better than the love-letter!

ROSAURA [*aside, to* MARIONETTE]: And the portrait! [*to* BIRIF] There is no message?

BIRIF: No, madam.

ROSAURA: Please thank him for me.

BIRIF: Madam. [*He bows and is about to go.*]

ROSAURA [*offering him a tip*]: Here, take this.

BIRIF: I am surprised at you, madam! [*He does not take the tip and goes.*]

MARIONETTE: An Italian would never have done that.

ROSAURA: Nor a Frenchman.

MARIONETTE: This Englishman must be very rich.

ROSAURA: And generous as well. But who on earth is this? All wrapped up in a cloak?

MARIONETTE: Oh, my goodness! It's Arlecchino! Dressed up as a Spanish manservant.

ROSAURA: But why this transformation?

MARIONETTE: Softening of the brain, I'd say.

[ARLECCHINO *enters, taking off his hat.*]

ARLECCHINO [*raising his hat*]: May heaven protect you for many years to come, Donna Rosaura.

ROSAURA: What comedy is this? How many people *are* you? And who's sent you this time?

ARLECCHINO [*raising his hat*]: Don Alvaro di Castiglia, my master.

ROSAURA: And what's *he* told you to say to me?

ARLECCHINO [*raising his hat*]: He sends to the Donna Rosaura a treasure.

MARIONETTE: Good heavens! A treasure! He must have had it sent from India!

ROSAURA: What does this treasure consist of?

ARLECCHINO: Here it is. [*He raises his hat*] Everybody bow their heads. This is the family-tree of the house of Don Alvaro, my master. [*He makes a low bow.*]

MARIONETTE: Some treasure!

ROSAURA [*taking it*]: It is not to be disdained. Is there any message?

ARLECCHINO: He said — but he said so much that I would

never never have been able to remember it all if he hadn't wisely written it down on this piece of paper. [*He gives the paper to* ROSAURA.]

ROSAURA [*going to the table*]: I will give you my reply at once.

MARIONETTE [*to* ARLECCHINO]: But tell me, what mad idea is this change of dress?

ARLECCHINO: A little more respect, if you please.

MARIONETTE: Well! You've become very high-and-mighty, haven't you?

ROSAURA: Here is the reply.

ARLECCHINO: At your service, Donna Rosaura. [*He raises his hat and puts it on again.*]

ROSAURA: Good day.

ARLECCHINO: Good-bye, Marionette. [*He walks out very sedately.*]

MARIONETTE: Well! Did you ever see anything so ridiculous? And he made such a fine Frenchman.

ROSAURA: I think he's remarkably versatile. He can adapt himself perfectly to any character.

MARIONETTE: Signora, your four suitors have all given you presents. Which seems to you to merit your favour the most? I feel sure you will say the Englishman. These jewels are very beautiful.

ROSAURA: No, Marionette. I will not prefer him to the others on account of them. Love is not to be bought with such things. And Milord does not want a wife.

MARIONETTE: Then I don't think you will have much difficulty in deciding in favour of him of the portrait.

ROSAURA: Wrong again. All those bright colours can't persuade me of *his* sincerity.

MARIONETTE: Then it must be him of the beautiful family-tree?

ROSAURA: No. Such noble rank is certainly not to be disdained, but it alone would not satisfy me.

MARIONETTE: There then, I knew it! That jealous fellow's letter takes first place!

ROSAURA: No, Marionette, you are still wrong. You see, I

know that in order to impress his beloved, a lover can pretend and dissemble.

MARIONETTE: So none of them pleases you?

ROSAURA: On the contrary, they all do.

MARIONETTE: But you can't marry all of them!

ROSAURA: One of them I will.

MARIONETTE: But which?

ROSAURA: I will decide. And when I do, it will be with my head not my heart. I am not looking for good looks, nor love, nor fidelity. I am a widow and I know the world. To choose a lover, is one thing. To choose a husband is something very different. When I choose I shall choose prudently and with both eyes open. [*Exit*]

MARIONETTE: Which means you'll do like all of us women: choose the worst. [*Exit*]

⊰ SCENE 4 ⊱

A Street.

MILORD *and the* CONTE, *walking together.*

CONTE: Milord, how long were you with Madame Rosaura?

[MILORD *walks on without replying.*]

CONTE: She is truly a remarkable lady. Worthy of the attentions of gentlemen of the highest rank. You have made an excellent choice. I confess I did have some inclination that way myself. But when I saw how things were with you, I decided to withdraw. [*aside*] He won't speak. I can't discover anything. [*aloud*] This will be an opportune moment to visit her. When I used to visit her, I took care never to lose precious moments. Oh, what the devil! Are you dumb? Can't you speak? What sort of man are you? You are so phlegmatic I can't tell whether you're happy or miserable?

MILORD: That is something you will never know.

CONTE: Praise be to heaven! You've spoken! Really, your

taciturnity is most enviable. Most Macchiavellian. We Italians should practise it more. We talk too much.

[BIRIF *enters and* MILORD *walks to one side with him.* FOLETTO *enters and the* CONTE *walks to the other side with him.*]

BIRIF [*to* MILORD]: Sir.
FOLETTO [*to* CONTE]: Illustrious.

[*The Conte signs to Foletto not to speak. Foletto gives him a letter.*]

MILORD [*aside, to* BIRIF]: Have you done it?
BIRIF [*aside, to* MILORD]: Yes, sir.
MILORD [*aside, to* BIRIF]: Was she pleased?
BIRIF [*aside, to* MILORD]: She thanks you.
MILORD [*aside, to* BIRIF]: That will be all then.

[*He gives* BIRIF *a small purse of money.* FOLETTO *observes this.* BIRIF *bows and goes. The* CONTE *signs to* FOLETTO *to go.* FOLETTO *holds out his hand for a tip. The* CONTE *deliberately ignores him.*]

FOLETTO [*aside*]: They arrange some things better in England. [*Exit*]
CONTE [*aside*]: He gave something to Milord. I'm sure it was a letter from Rosaura. [*aloud*] Congratulations, friend. Some are born lucky. Women always running after them. Letters flying back and forward. Madame Rosaura . . .
MILORD: You're mad. [*Exit*]
CONTE [*alone*]: Mad, am I? We'll see who's mad! He'll regret this! He'll face my sword for injuring me in such a way! But what has my dear Rosaura to say? Does she bid me live or die? Whichever it be, let me learn my beloved's decision. [*He opens the letter and reads slowly*] Oh, happy me! Oh, darling Rosaura! Oh, how can I ever be worthy of your love, my one and only treasure? May I dare then to hope? Are you thus challenging me to love and be faithful to you? Then I will, my beloved. I will indeed. Have no fear of that. As for you, Milord. I no longer fear you. Yes, you may well

say I was mad to think I had a rival in you. I alone possess her heart. Rosaura will be mine alone. That is my only desire, my only hope. And this letter makes me almost certain it will be so. [*Exit*]

[DON ALVARO *enters and walks up and down.*]

DON [*to himself*]: Rosaura cannot realize what is at stake! Or that Arlecchino is a useless servant! To keep me waiting like this. The suspense is unendurable! I'll give him such a beating when he comes. This is no way to treat a gentleman like me. . . . Still . . . perhaps I should remember the example of my ancestors throughout the known world. Twenty-four generations of them . . . Beginning with a king. Many princes. All renowned. Yes, this tardiness deserves my pity.

[ARLECCHINO *enters but is not seen by* DON ALVARO *who is walking the other way.*]

ARLECCHINO: Illustrious!

DON [*turning*]: What news do you bring?

ARLECCHINO: Long live our King! [*He raises his hat and* DON ALVARO *does the same.*] Donna Rosaura loves you with all her heart.

DON: I know that. What did she say about my wonderful family-tree?

ARLECCHINO: She kissed it and kissed it again and again. She fluttered her eyelashes in astonishment. She clenched her teeth in wonder.

DON: You gave her the message word for word?

ARLECCHINO: Perfectly.

DON: And her reply?

ARLECCHINO: Behold the revered handwriting of Donna Rosaura. [*He raises his hat and gives* DON ALVARO *a letter.*]

DON: Prepare for joy, my heart! [*He reads*] 'I accept with the greatest pleasure the portrait you have so kindly sent me. . . .' [*to* ARLECCHINO] What's this about a portrait?

ARLECCHINO [*aside*]: Now I've done it! I've given him the Frenchman's reply! I'll have to bluff it out.

DON: Well? Why don't you answer?

ARLECCHINO: But the family-tree of your house is the portrait of your greatness, is it not?

DON: Yes, of course. That is how I think of it myself. [*He goes on reading the letter*] 'Because I think so highly of the original. . . .' [*to* ARLECCHINO] The original? What original?

ARLECCHINO [*to* ALVARO]: Tell me, who comes first on that family-tree?

DON: A King of Castiglia.

ARLECCHINO: You see? Ah, she's an artful one, she is! She's comparing you with a King. He's the original. The origin of your house.

DON: Of course. Yes, that's exactly how I think of it myself. [*He goes on reading the letter*] 'I cannot send you mine, because I have not one.'

ARLECCHINO [*quickly*]: She hasn't a family-tree, you see.

DON: Yes, yes! That is how I understood it. [*Goes on reading*] 'I shall always cherish this precious jewel . . .' [*to* ARLECCHINO] Precious jewel?

ARLECCHINO: Yes, something very valuable. She means the family-tree.

DON: Of course, that's what I thought she meant. [*He continues reading the letter*] 'I would like to have it mounted in a circle of gold.' What the devil! My family-tree in a circle of gold?

ARLECCHINO: She means a golden frame.

DON: Of course. That's what I've intended doing myself. [*He goes on reading*] 'And wear it always on my breast.' [*to* ARLECCHINO] A frame of that size on her breast?

ARLECCHINO: But don't you understand? She means it poetically. She will carry it always in her heart.

DON: Precisely. That's what I intended her to do with it. Farewell. [*He attempts to go.*]

ARLECCHINO: Illustrious!

DON: What d'you want?

ARLECCHINO: How's your memory?

DON: Do not be insolent!

ARLECCHINO: Gentlemen who make promises should keep their word.

DON: You are right. I had forgotten. You have served me well and you deserve to be rewarded. You took a treasure to Donna Rosaura; here also is a little treasure for you. [*He gives him a folded paper.*]

ARLECCHINO: What's this?

DON: Your indentures as my servant. [*Exit*]

ARLECCHINO [*alone*]: Well, I'll be damned! That's a fine treasure, that is! What sort of joke is that to play on a poor gentleman? I'll get my revenge for this! But here's that Frenchman. He'd better not see me dressed like this. That Spaniard tricked me all right. I'll see if I can make up for it with this fellow. [*Exit*]

[MONSIEUR LEBLEU *enters looking at himself in a mirror.*]

MONSIEUR [*alone*]: This wig still does not seem to fit properly. Yes, there is a lock of hair here which does not want to stay where it should. And one side seems a little longer than the other. I really shall have to dismiss my barber and get another from Paris. They simply don't know how to make a wig here. And as for the shoemakers! They're still worse. They insist on making shoes too large, and apart from not being comfortable they're not even well-made. Oh, Paris! Paris! There is nowhere like Paris.

[ARLECCHINO *enters dressed in French clothes and making many exaggerated bows to* MONSIEUR LEBLEU.]

MONSIEUR: Bravo! Excellent! You look splendid! Have you been to Madame?

ARLECCHINO: I have. But would that I had never been!

MONSIEUR: Why do you say that?

ARLECCHINO [*with affectation*]: What beauty! What charm! What eyes! What a nose! What a mouth!

MONSIEUR [*aside*]: This fellow must have been to Paris. That's the drawback of French servants: they fall in love themselves with the object of our affections. [*aloud*] Did you present the portrait?

ARLECCHINO: I did. And she pressed it tenderly to her breast.

MONSIEUR: Ah, say no more – lest I melt with exquisite joy!

ARLECCHINO: She could not stop kissing it and looking at it.

MONSIEUR: Oh, delight! You gave her my message?

ARLECCHINO: I declaimed it and she was overcome with tears.

MONSIEUR: Bravo, Arlecchino! Did I not say you were born for such a task! [*embraces him*].

ARLECCHINO: Ah, but then, signore – then she – oh, Heaven, how can I tell you?

MONSIEUR: What happened? What happened, Arlecchino?

ARLECCHINO: Hearing your beautiful words, she fainted.

MONSIEUR: No! Ah, Arlecchino, you have made me the happiest of men! You have raised me to the seventh heaven of joy! I am beatified! But she gave you an answer?

ARLECCHINO [*aside*]: The devil! Now I think of it, that's what I gave the other one! [*aloud*] Yes, she gave it me . . . but . . .

MONSIEUR: But what?

ARLECCHINO: I've lost it.

MONSIEUR: Villain! Scoundrel! You lose a thing so precious? By heavens you deserve my sword through your chest! [*He draws his sword.*]

ARLECCHINO: No! Wait! I've found it! I've found it! [*aside*] Rather than be killed I'll give him the Spaniard's letter. [*aloud*] Here it is. Take it.

MONSIEUR: Ah, my dear Arlecchino! Thou relievest my pain! Thou restorest my joy! [*embraces him*].

ARLECCHINO [*aside*]: One minute he's for killing me. Next minute he's embracing me.

MONSIEUR: Oh, adorable little letter! Thou art balm to my wounds! As I open thee I feel my heart consumed with the most exquisite joy. Let me read thee. 'I am filled with admiration at the magnificent family-tree of your house.' [*to* ARLECCHINO] What family-tree?

ARLECCHINO [*aside*]: Here we go again. [*Aloud*] You don't understand?

MONSIEUR: No!

ARLECCHINO: I will explain. Are you not the last of your house?

MONSIEUR: Yes.

ARLECCHINO: So you ought to get married?

MONSIEUR: That is so.

ARLECCHINO: And marriage bears fruits, does it not? Children?

MONSIEUR: Certainly.

ARLECCHINO: And that which bears fruits is called a tree, is it not?

MONSIEUR: That's true.

ARLECCHINO: So you are the family-tree of your house.

MONSIEUR: Madame Rosaura is as subtle as that?

ARLECCHINO: And even more.

MONSIEUR: What a woman! What wit! What delicate innuendo! [*He goes on reading the letter*] 'And I see that you are descended from princes and kings.' [*to* ARLECCHINO] What's all this?

ARLECCHINO: A Frenchman like you with your quick wits, and you don't understand that?

MONSIEUR: I admit the truth. That I do not understand.

ARLECCHINO: Looking at your portrait, she came to this wonderful conclusion, this great and noble conclusion, that in your veins runs the blood of princes and kings.

MONSIEUR: What an excellent fellow you are! [*embraces him*] Let us continue! 'If I shall have the honour of being admitted to the scroll of your glorious ancestors . . .' [*to* ARLECCHINO] Who are these glorious ancestors?

ARLECCHINO: She means your guardian spirits who wish you well.

MONSIEUR: Ah, yes, there must be many of them. [*Goes on reading*] '. . . it will add to the glory of my own family-tree.' [*to* ARLECCHINO] And what's that mean?

ARLECCHINO: It will add to her own glory and to her father's, who is the family-tree of her house.

MONSIEUR: Well done, Arlecchino! For this you deserve the greatest possible reward!

ARLECCHINO [*aside*]: At last!

MONSIEUR: I must think what to give you that will be worthy of a task so well accomplished.

ARLECCHINO: For a similar task an Englishman gave me a purse of money.

MONSIEUR: A purse of money? Too little! You could not have done for him what you have done for me. No, you deserve an exemplary reward, some quite extraordinary recognition. I have it! Yes, a reward that will be truly commensurate with your great deserts. Here is a fragment of the most precious jewel in the world, a piece of this letter. [*He tears off a corner of Rosaura's letter, gives it to* ARLECCHINO *and goes.*]

[ARLECCHINO *overcome with astonishment stands with the piece of paper in his hand, gaping after* MONSIEUR.]

MARIONETTE [*entering*]: Monsieur Arlecchino, what are you doing?

ARLECCHINO: Thinking about the generosity of a Frenchman.

MARIONETTE: Of Monsieur Lebleu?

ARLECCHINO: The very same.

MARIONETTE: He has given you a present?

ARLECCHINO: And how!

MARIONETTE: Well, if you want to be a French manservant you must learn French customs. When the servant of the lover is given a tip, he shares it with the maid of the lady. Because it's the maidservant who sees to all the arrangements and makes sure everybody enjoys themselves.

ARLECCHINO: Of course, Marionette! Yes, you do indeed deserve the greatest possible reward!

MARIONETTE: I have certainly done all I can for your master.

ARLECCHINO: I must think what to give you that will be worthy of a task so well accomplished.

MARIONETTE: Ten scudi should pay me for the trouble I've taken on his behalf.

ARLECCHINO: Ten scudi? Too little! No, you deserve an exemplary reward, some quite extraordinary recognition. I have it! Yes, a reward that will be truly commensurate with your great deserts. Give me your hand. Here is a fragment of the most precious jewel in the world, a piece of this letter. [*He tears off a tiny piece of the corner of the letter, gives it to her and goes.*]

MARIONETTE [*alone*]: The miserable little Italian upstart! The ignorant common creature! A scrap of paper! For me? How dare he play such a joke on me! Oh, I'll get my own back on him for this! Doesn't he know who I am? I am Marionette, the daughter of the servant of the nurse of the King. I am a woman whose admirers are numberless. And if I say I want somebody given a good beating with a stick, a thousand of my admirers will tumble over themselves to avenge my honour and the honour of my country! [*Exit*]

Act Three

[*Rosaura's room*: ROSAURA *and* MARIONETTE.]

ROSAURA: Marionette, I have had a wonderful idea! And don't say your French ladies would have thought of a better one.

MARIONETTE: You know I have always said you are far more like a French lady than an Italian.

ROSAURA: Well, I am going to try an experiment on my four suitors. At the Carnival of the Masks I will disguise myself. I will meet each of them separately, and pretend to be in love with them. In this way I shall be able to test them. And to make the test even more effective, I will pretend to each of them that I am a lady from their own country. I will put on the appropriate dress and mask. I can speak each of their languages sufficiently well. Altogether I will make each of them believe I am their countrywoman. I know I will succeed, because when I was young I was very good at imitating people. And the one who resists this temptation – the one who spurns my advances – that one I shall choose.

MARIONETTE: It's not a bad idea, but I'm afraid it will end by your marrying nobody.

ROSAURA: Why?

MARIONETTE: Because it will be very difficult for any man to resist such a temptation.

ROSAURA: We shall see. Now I shall need some advice if I'm to sustain all these different parts. You can help me with the French lady.

MARIONETTE: And with the English lady. I was in London for three years. But all you need really are a few mannerisms common to each country.

ROSAURA: I shall do my best.

MARIONETTE: But what about your voice? Won't they recognize that?

ROSAURA: The mask will alter my voice completely.

[PANTALONE *enters*.]

PANTALONE: May I presume to enter?

ROSAURA: Come in, dear brother-in-law. After all, you are my landlord.

PANTALONE: My dear sister-in-law, I have come to beg your pardon if I spoke to you a little warmly this morning. We men have our little weaknesses and I trust you will try to overlook them.

ROSAURA: It is I should apologize to you, for the sharpness with which I opposed the marriage of my sister. Dear brother-in-law, if my sister refuses to consent, do you really mean to sacrifice her youth and your own peace of mind for a mere whim?

PANTALONE: If she refuses, we shall see. Though I am sure you could persuade her to accept me, if you wished. But enough of that. What I wished to say, my child, is that if in the heat of the moment I made you feel unwelcome here in my house, I am deeply sorry. I beg you not to think of leaving. For if you do, I fear you may take with you she who has become the light of my life.

ROSAURA: Signor Pantalone, I thank you for your kindness. As a further demonstration of your goodness to me, may I beg a favour from you?

PANTALONE: Of course, my child. Anything you wish.

ROSAURA: Several ladies have been kind enough to invite me to their houses. I should like to return their hospitality. Might I invite them to a little entertainment here in my room this evening?

PANTALONE: But you are the mistress of my house. I am amazed that you should ask. You have only to say what you will need – candles, refreshments – and I will have them sent to you.

ROSAURA: You put me ever more deeply in your debt.

PANTALONE: And you will put in a good word for me? If you

should have the opportunity for a little talk with Signorina Eleonora? Persuade her to be sensible?

ROSAURA: I shall do all I can most willingly. I hope you will see the results very soon.

PANTALONE: Dear sister-in-law, you fill me with hope. We old men are like little children. We like to see ourselves being made a fuss of. [*Exit*]

MARIONETTE: Your brother-in-law will die of generosity.

ROSAURA: Love makes us do strange things.

MARIONETTE: But are you really going to persuade your sister?

ROSAURA: Do you think I'm as mad as he is? I said that simply to keep him quiet.

MARIONETTE: And this party here this evening? What's that for?

ROSAURA: A pretext to invite my four suitors.

MARIONETTE: You mean to do it then?

ROSAURA: This is the opportunity. So you had best go and prepare my dresses.

MARIONETTE: Where will you find your four suitors?

ROSAURA: In the coffee-house. They are always there in the evening.

MARIONETTE: Well, all I say is – heaven help you.

ROSAURA: Those who never try their luck, never deserve to win. [*Exit*]

MARIONETTE [*alone*]: You needn't tell me! That's what we women have always been experts at. Hiding our artfulness behind a mask. [*Exit*]

❖ SCENE 2 ❖

[*The Street outside Rosaura's house.* MONSIEUR LEBLEU *enters from one side and* DON ALVARO *from the other. Each holds Rosaura's letter in his hand and is looking at it.*]

MONSIEUR [*aside*]: A family-tree? But how can I be a family-tree? It seems a most inept comparison.

DON [*aside*]: My family-tree my portrait? How can my family-tree be the same as my portrait! It sounds absurd to me.

MONSIEUR [*aside*]: She sees I am descended from princes and kings? This must be sarcasm!

DON [*aside*]: Because she thinks so highly of the original? But the founder of a family-tree is not called the original.

MONSIEUR [*aside*]: It is stretching a figure of speech, to call her father the family-tree of her house!

DON [*aside*]: She will wear my family-tree on her breast? I don't believe it!

MONSIEUR [*aside*]: Arlecchino has misunderstood it completely.

DON [*aside*]: That servant's explanation was a lot of rubbish.

[ARLECCHINO *enters and sees them both deep in thought, holding the letters in front of them. As they stand with their backs to each other, he comes between them on tiptoe and looks over their shoulders. He sees that each has the other's letter, given by him in error.*]

ARLECCHINO: By your leave, signori.

[*He quickly changes over the two letters, putting the right one into the hand of the one who should have received it. With a bow to each he goes out again. They return to reading the letter in their hand unaware of the dumb-show that has just taken place.*]

MONSIEUR [*aside, reading the letter*]: 'I accept with the greatest pleasure the portrait you have so kindly sent me, because I think so highly of the original.' [*to himself*] But now she is speaking of me!

DON [*aside, reading the letter*]: 'I am filled with admiration by the wonderful family-tree of your house.' [*to himself*] But this is more to the point!

MONSIEUR [*aside, reading the letter*]: 'I cannot send you mine, because I have not one.' [*to himself*] What does that matter?

DON [*aside, reading the letter*]: 'I see that you are descended from princes and kings.' [*to himself*] Good! That indeed is so!

MONSIEUR [*aside, reading the letter*]: 'I shall always treasure this precious jewel. I would like to have it mounted in a circle of gold and wear it always on my breast.' [*to himself*] Oh, adorable one! Oh, what a beautiful letter! [*He kisses it.*]

DON [*aside, reading the letter*]: 'If I have the honour of being admitted to the scroll of your glorious ancestors, it will add to the glory of my own family-tree.' [*to himself*] Ah, yes! It will indeed!

MONSIEUR [*aside*]: That fellow mixed everything up.

DON [*aside*]: Arlecchino distorted the entire letter.

MONSIEUR [*aside*]: I'll wager he changed it with Don Alvaro's.

DON [*aside*]: Perhaps he confused it with a letter to the Frenchman.

MONSIEUR [*turning to* DON ALVARO]: Friend, did you send your family-tree to Madame Rosaura?

DON: Did you send her your portrait?

MONSIEUR: I do not deny it.

DON: Neither do I.

MONSIEUR: I congratulate you on the esteem in which she holds your house.

DON: I am happy to know she thinks so highly of your handsome charms.

MONSIEUR: It seems that we are rivals.

DON: And therefore – enemies.

MONSIEUR: But surely the charms of Madame Rosaura are more than sufficient for both of us.

DON: Don Alvaro of Castiglia does not share the favours of his beloved with another.

MONSIEUR: What then do you intend to do?

DON: I intend that you yield her to me.

MONSIEUR: That I will never do.

DON: Then our swords must decide.

MONSIEUR: You are willing to die for a woman?

DON: Renounce her or fight!

MONSIEUR: I never refuse to fight.

DON: We will find a suitable place.

MONSIEUR: Wherever you please.

DON [*aside*]: This means I must contaminate my sword. [*Exit*]

MONSIEUR: Long live the joys of love! Long live such beauty as Rosaura's! I go to a fight I have already won!

[*He is about to follow* DON ALVARO *when he is stopped by the voice of* MARIONETTE *from the window of the house.*]

MARIONETTE: Monsieur Lebleu!

MONSIEUR: Marionette!

MARIONETTE: Would you like to meet Signorina Eleonora?

MONSIEUR: Ah! If only heaven would grant me such a boon!

MARIONETTE: I will call her to the window. [*She retires inside.*]

MONSIEUR [*alone*]: I am impatient to see her! But Don Alvaro awaits me for the duel . . . still, what does that matter? Must I forego seeing a beautiful woman to fight a duel with a madman? [ELEONORA *appears at the window.*] Behold on this balcony a new sun arises from the Orient! And with surpassing beauty! A beauty the equal of Rosaura's. And worthy to be so esteemed. Mademoiselle, behold a heart overwhelmed by your beauty and ready to consecrate all to its worship.

ELEONORA: Signore, I have not the honour of knowing you.

MONSIEUR: I am your most faithful lover.

ELEONORA: Since when?

MONSIEUR: Since the moment I saw you.

ELEONORA: You fall in love so quickly?

MONSIEUR: When confronted with such beauty as yours.

ELEONORA: I think you are making fun of me.

MONSIEUR: I swear to you – on the word of a true Frenchman – I love you with all my heart.

ELEONORA: And I – with all respect – do not believe you.

MONSIEUR: If you do not – you will see me die, here, beneath your window.

ELEONORA: Now you *are* being romantic.

MONSIEUR: You mock my love! You disdain my bitter tears! [*He pretends to weep.*]

ELEONORA: Tears, as well?

MONSIEUR: Does not the fiery heat from my burning eyes pierce and melt the icy cold of your cruelty?

ELEONORA: No, I can't feel it.

MONSIEUR: Oh, most beautiful one! Allow your door to be

opened to me that I may sigh forth my passion nearer to your heart!

ELEONORA: No! Sigh forth your passion out there! Where the air may cool your temperature.

MONSIEUR: So beautiful! And yet so cruel!

ELEONORA [*aside*]: Here comes my father! [*aloud*] I think I had best retire. [*She disappears from the window.*]

MONSIEUR: Oh, heavens! To leave me like that! Without even good-bye. How can anyone be so pitiless? Oh, what cruelty! What cruelty!

[*The* DOCTOR *has entered and been standing listening.*]

DOCTOR: Signore, who has upset you so?

MONSIEUR: By your clothes, signore, you are a Doctor. Allow me to tell you all. Hear my sad story. A young girl – a heartless young girl named Eleonora – is deaf to my entreaties, impervious to my tears. She refuses to return my love. She denies me even one shred of pity.

DOCTOR: Your Excellency – is in love with this girl?

MONSIEUR: I love her so much I exist only to be near her.

DOCTOR: How long is it you have loved her?

MONSIEUR: Since a few moments ago. I saw her for the first time but now at her window.

DOCTOR: You fall in love with astonishing speed.

MONSIEUR: We Frenchmen are ready of spirit and tender of heart. One look from a pair of beautiful eyes and we are doomed.

DOCTOR: How long does this love of yours last?

MONSIEUR: As long as the goddess of love commands it to.

DOCTOR: So if tomorrow the goddess of love commanded you to forget this girl, you would obey?

MONSIEUR: Of course.

DOCTOR: Then you can start forgetting her now.

MONSIEUR: Why?

DOCTOR: Because I won't have Eleonora trifled with.

MONSIEUR: What has Mademoiselle Eleonora to do with you?

DOCTOR: Everything. She is my daughter.

MONSIEUR: Monsieur! Most excellent Doctor! Dear friend!

Most venerable father-in-law! I beg you – I entreat you –
do not forbid me to love your daughters!

DOCTOR: What! Both of them?

MONSIEUR: Ah! They are equally lovable!

DOCTOR: What sort of love is this?

MONSIEUR: Love which recognizes the highest when it sees
it.

DOCTOR: But how is it possible to love more than one?

MONSIEUR: The flames of a Frenchman's passion could satisfy
the love of a hundred women!

DOCTOR: Then get back to France. You'll find enough
material there to feed your flames.

MONSIEUR: Ah, but your calm manner, your compassionate
look, they tell me that you pity me! Come! Order the door
to be opened!

DOCTOR: This is not my house. That, however, does not
prevent me knocking at the door.

MONSIEUR: Long live the happy father of such rare and beautiful daughters!

[*The Doctor knocks at the door and it is opened.*]

MONSIEUR: Escort me in!

DOCTOR: In this country a father does not escort lovers into
the presence of his daughters. [*He enters and closes the door.*]

MONSIEUR: Monsieur! Monsieur! Ah, well, never mind. The
father may have closed the door. But the daughters have
not yet locked it! [*Exit*]

⊰ SCENE 3 ⊱

*A Street containing a Coffee-house. Chairs and all other
accessories of such a shop.*

[*The* PROPRIETOR *of the Coffee-house, his waiters,* MILORD
and the CONTE.]

CONTE: Give me a coffee. [*They bring coffee to* MILORD *and the*
CONTE] No, no! You mustn't give coffee to Milord! He's

used to drinking chocolate with the ladies. This sort of drink wouldn't suit him.

[MILORD *shakes his head and drinks.*]

CONTE: But we really must drink a little less chocolate, Milord old chap.

[MILORD *shakes his head and drinks.*]

CONTE: You know – this silence of yours seems more animal than human.

[MILORD *looks at him sourly.*]

CONTE: The Signora Rosaura must surely have noticed these savage moods of yours.

[MILORD *rises and steps into the street.*]

CONTE: Yes, do have a breath of fresh air. It may do you good.
MILORD: You! Come over here.
CONTE: Who are you to give me orders?
MILORD: If you are a gentleman, you and I must fight.
CONTE: In that case, I am at your service. [*He rises and comes into the street.*]
MILORD: I intend to teach you not to open your mouth so much.
CONTE: I do not need you to teach me what to do.
MILORD: Look to yourself. [*He draws his sword and the* CONTE *does the same.*]
CONTE: How do we fight?
MILORD: Till one draws blood.
CONTE: Good.

[*Those in the shop rush out and try to separate them.*]

MILORD: Keep away or I'll shave your faces for you.
CONTE: Allow us to fight. This duel is only to the one who first draws blood.

[*They fight and the* CONTE *is wounded in the arm.*]

CONTE: There you are. Blood. Satisfied?

MILORD: Yes. [*He sheathes his sword.*]

CONTE: I go to have my wound attended to. [*Exit*]

MILORD [*to himself*]: This Italian jester is beginning to annoy me. If he offends me again, he'll get a wound he won't be able to attend to. Gentlemen should treat one another with respect. Such familiarity breeds contempt. But who is this masked lady wearing an English dress?

[ROSAURA *enters masked, and wearing an English dress. She curtseys like an English lady.*]

MILORD [*aside*]: She's not Italian. Only an English lady could curtsey like that.

[ROSAURA *goes nearer* MILORD *and curtseys again.*]

MILORD: Your servant, ma'am. Can I get you a coffee?

[ROSAURA *shakes her head.*]

MILORD: Some chocolate?

[ROSAURA *shakes her head.*]

MILORD: Some punch?

[ROSAURA *nods her head.*]

MILORD [*aside*]: She's English all right. [*to the* PROPRIETOR] Bring a glass of punch. [*to* ROSAURA] Who accompanies you to this country?

ROSAURA: My father.

MILORD: What's his business?

ROSAURA: The same as yours.

MILORD: You are a lady then?

ROSAURA: Yes, milord.

MILORD: Oh, I say, do sit down, won't you? [*He brings a chair and then leads her to it with his right hand.*] You know me then?

ROSAURA: Alas! Only too well!

MILORD: Good lord! You mean – you're in love with me?

ROSAURA: With all my heart.

MILORD: Where have we met?

ROSAURA: In London. [*They bring the punch and she drinks.*]

MILORD: Who are you?

ROSAURA: I cannot tell you.

MILORD: I know you?

ROSAURA: Yes.

MILORD: Was I in love with *you*?

ROSAURA: I do not know.

MILORD: Ha! Well, I am now!

ROSAURA: But you have promised yourself to another.

MILORD: Who?

ROSAURA: Madam Rosaura.

MILORD: I made her no promise.

ROSAURA: Then you are free?

MILORD: I am.

ROSAURA: And I may hope?

MILORD: You may, ma'am.

ROSAURA: That you will love me?

MILORD: Indeed you may, ma'am.

ROSAURA: That you will be mine and mine alone?

MILORD: But who are you?

ROSAURA: I cannot tell you.

MILORD: And I do not make blind dates.

ROSAURA: You will see me this evening.

MILORD: Where?

ROSAURA: At a party.

MILORD: But where?

ROSAURA: You will be told.

MILORD: Shall I have the honour of attending upon you?

ROSAURA: And Madam Rosaura?

MILORD: A lady from my own country takes precedence.

ROSAURA: I shall be wearing another dress.

MILORD: Then I may not know you.

ROSAURA: Give me something by which you will recognize me.

MILORD: This case? [*He gives her a gold case.*]

ROSAURA: That will be sufficient. [*She rises.*]

MILORD: You are going? [*He rises.*]

ROSAURA: Yes.

MILORD: I will accompany you.

ROSAURA: No. And if you are a gentleman you will not follow me.

MILORD: I obey.

ROSAURA: Good-bye, milord. [*She makes the same curtsey and goes.*]

MILORD [*to himself*]: What a pleasant surprise! An English lady here in Venice! And what a pleasant way of speaking! Precise. To the point. No superfluities. And she actually knows me. Loves me. Desires me. If she proves as beautiful as she is charming, she will deserve my entire devotion. Rosaura has many worthy qualities – but this one is a lady – and from my own country. On those two counts alone, she is to be preferred. [*Exit*]

[DON ALVARO *enters.*]

DON [*to himself*]: Monsieur Lebleu escaped me! Transported by my rage, I looked not back to see that he followed. So! If he will not face my sword, I will try my stick on him! I will search him out. I will find him! Bring me coffee!

[*The waiters fetch hi*n *coffee and biscuits.* ARLECCHINO *enters as they are serving him.*]

ARLECCHINO [*aside*]: Now's a good moment to make it up with the Spaniard. [*to* DON ALVARO] May heaven protect you always, signore.

DON: Good day, Arlecchino.

ARLECCHINO: I must speak to your Excellency about . . . you know what.

DON: About what? I do not understand you.

ARLECCHINO: About Donna Rosaura.

DON: Ah, if only I could be assured of her love!

ARLECCHINO: That's what I mean. She sent for me. She was at table – like you are now. She was trying to eat. But she wasn't getting much down her because she kept weeping and sighing. Sighing your name. The illustrious name of Don Alvaro.

DON: My darling Rosaura! Precious light of my life! Come,

thou faithful harbinger of happiness, what said she of me? Tell me all!

ARLECCHINO: Well, she'd almost reached the end of her meal. So she takes a biscuit – just like this one here. [*He picks up a biscuit from in front of* DON ALVARO *and develops an exaggerated mime.*] Then she has a sip of some dark wine – something the colour of this coffee here. [*He helps himself to the coffee and continues eating the biscuits.*] Then she says: 'Go and find Don Alvaro and tell him – I don't care a fig for him!' [*He runs off laughing.*]

DON [*alone*]: Villain! Scoundrel! Stop him! Kill him! Bring me his head! Donna Rosaura would never do such a thing! She loves me! She worships me! Oh, fury! Oh, this has filled me with such rage! Such anger!

[MONSIEUR LEBLEU *enters.*]

MONSIEUR: Do not think I was avoiding you. . . .

DON: Aah! You! You're just in time! Draw your sword!

[*He draws his.*]

MONSIEUR [*drawing his sword*]: Beautiful Rosaura, to you I consecrate this victim!

DON: Vile coward, you thought to escape me!

MONSIEUR: Liar! And this proves you so! [*They fight.*]

[ROSAURA *enters masked, and wearing the dress of a French lady. She comes between them, stopping them and saying to the Frenchman*]:

ROSAURA: Monsieur! What are you doing?

MONSIEUR: I fight for my Venetian lady, O beautiful masked one.

ROSAURA: You risk your life for an Italian lady? While we French ladies languish in despair? For shame! Condemn us not to die for want of one look from your eyes!

MONSIEUR: But if this rival challenges me, I must not refuse to fight.

ROSAURA: This rival will cease to wish you dead, if you yield his lady to him.

MONSIEUR: I? Be so base . . .?

ROSAURA: Then if you fear to yield her lest you are thought a coward, yield her at the entreaties of a French lady who sighs for love of you.

MONSIEUR: Who is this lady?

ROSAURA: Behold her at your feet. [*She kneels before him.*] Have pity on one who exists only to love you.

MONSIEUR: Arise, O precious jewel, lest you wish me to die of shame.

ROSAURA: Arise I cannot — till you assure me of your love.

MONSIEUR [*kneeling beside her*]: I do! I do! I promise, I swear to love you and be true to you always and forever.

ROSAURA: Ah! That is more than I can believe!

MONSIEUR: Believe me you must! I am yours alone, always yours, forever yours.

ROSAURA: But you fight for another!

MONSIEUR: I will leave her for you.

ROSAURA: Yield her then to your rival.

MONSIEUR: Wait here. That is soon done. [*He leaves* ROSAURA *and approaches* DON ALVARO] Friend, this French lady is dying for love of me. If she proves to be as beautiful as she is charming, then Rosaura is yours. Let us then postpone our duel for the time being.

DON: It is useless to hope to escape me again.

MONSIEUR: I am a gentleman. Either I yield Rosaura to you, or we fight it out here and now. It is permitted for a gentleman to bargain with his enemy.

DON: Do not presume to tell me what a gentleman may or may not do. I learnt that before I learnt the alphabet. However, please yourself. I agree. [*He sheathes his sword and goes back into the coffee-house.*]

MONSIEUR: Madame. It is done. I have yielded Rosaura as you commanded. And now for the pleasure of seeing your face.

ROSAURA: At the moment that is not possible.

MONSIEUR: When will it be possible?

ROSAURA: In a few hours.

MONSIEUR:But – you do know me? And it is I whom you love?

ROSAURA:Yes. It was for you I left Paris. It was for you I abandoned our beloved France and came a stranger into Italy.

MONSIEUR [*aside*]: Only a French lady could be capable of such a love! Only a Frenchman such as I could inspire it! [*to* ROSAURA] But I cannot live, if you do not allow me one glimpse of your face.

ROSAURA:That is impossible.

MONSIEUR:What prevents you?

ROSAURA:My modesty. A respectable lady does not permit herself to be seen in public without her mask.

MONSIEUR:In France we are not so particular.

ROSAURA:Here we are in Italy, and we must conform to the customs of the country.

MONSIEUR:Then let us find a more secluded place. Your face I must see, or I die!

ROSAURA:No, stay. I am going.

MONSIEUR:I shall most certainly follow you.

ROSAURA:If you dare, you will never see me again.

MONSIEUR:Did you come only to torment me?

ROSAURA:You will see me this evening. Give me something that I may show you. So that you will know me.

MONSIEUR:Here is a little bottle of scent. [*He gives her a small bottle.*]

ROSAURA:You will know me by this.

MONSIEUR:But where, O my beloved, shall I see you?

ROSAURA:You will be told.

MONSIEUR:Heaven speed these hours of anguished waiting!

ROSAURA:Heaven trust they bring you not disillusion!

MONSIEUR:Ah, madame, you are too cruel!

ROSAURA:Ah, monsieur, you have much misunderstood me! [*Exit*]

MONSIEUR [*to himself*]: I am not to follow her? I am forbidden to see her face? Whoever can she be? A French lady come all the way to Venice – for me? That is something I deserve – yet find hard to believe. Could she be amusing herself at my expense? Yet I found myself enchanted by her. I felt myself burning with love for her. But should I yield Rosaura to my rival for some unknown masked lady? I must not act too rashly. No, I must not lose Rosaura before I am certain I've acquired something better. [*He calls to* DON ALVARO *who is sitting in the coffee-house.*] Don Alvaro!

DON [*rising and coming into the street*]: What do you want?

MONSIEUR: The French lady refuses to let me see her. I am not now so certain I prefer her to Rosaura.

DON: All the same you yielded Rosaura.

MONSIEUR: But now I intend to keep her. [*He draws his sword.*]

DON [*drawing his sword*]: Love always gives the victory to Don Alvaro!.

MONSIEUR: Not this time it doesn't! [*They fight.*]

[ROSAURA *enters masked, and wearing the dress of a Spanish lady.*]

ROSAURA: Gentlemen, put up your swords!

DON [*aside*]: A Spanish lady!

MONSIEUR: Madame, your command disarms me and your beautiful eyes conquer me!

ROSAURA: I do not know you. I am speaking to Don Alvaro di Castiglia.

DON: How may I serve you?

ROSAURA: Make this Frenchman go away. I wish to speak to you.

DON [*to* MONSIEUR]: Be good enough to step on one side a moment.

MONSIEUR: Willingly. [*aside*] Thus ends the second duel. [*Exit*]

ROSAURA [*speaking gravely and haughtily*]: Don Alvaro, I am surprised at you. All Spain will be surprised at you. To disregard your noble ancestry in this way. To degrade yourself by marrying the daughter of a vile merchant. A merchant! Does not the very word fill you with disgust, you who were born in Spain? Ah, if your mother, the Duchess, knew of it she would die of shame! Don Alvaro, the royal blood in your veins, the honour of your fatherland, call you to repent. And if they are not strong enough, let me add to them my command. The command of an unknown lady, who has nevertheless the honour of knowing you and the right so to command you.

DON [*aside*]: Woe is me! I am overcome with shame. I acknowledge my fault. I confess my detested villainy. Rosaura is beautiful but she is not of the aristocracy. She deserves love but not the love of a Castigliano. [*aloud to* ROSAURA] Most noble lady – for such your manner of speaking reveals you to be – from my confused demeanour you will understand the shame in my heart. And if you, out of your goodness, will help me to amend the error of my ways. . . .

ROSAURA: You profess too quick a change of heart. You have made ridiculous the honour of Spain. A greater sign of repentance will be required.

DON: Don Alvaro, who bows only to the will of his sovereign the King, will accept any penitence you see fit to impose.

ROSAURA: To show that you are truly penitent, that you truly regret your vile and shameful deed, you must promise to love me without seeing me, and to obey me without knowing me.

DON: Ah, but this is too much. . . .

ROSAURA: It is less than you deserve! To fall in love with a merchant's daughter!

DON: You are right. Yes, I will do it.

ROSAURA: You must serve me faithfully, without the certainty of any reward.

DON: Alas! You make me tremble!

ROSAURA: You must obey my every wish without question.

DON: Yes, I will obey. [*aside*] None but a Spanish lady could be so noble and stern!

ROSAURA: I will follow you everywhere so that you may see whether I approve or disapprove of your conduct. I will do so without speaking to you. Give me something by which you may know me.

DON: This is my snuff-box. [*He gives her the snuff-box previously given him by* ROSAURA *herself.*]

ROSAURA: Ah! A present from some beautiful lady?

DON: I exchanged it for Rosaura's. I shall not miss it since I value it little.

ROSAURA: Now you begin to please me.

DON: Praise be to heaven!

ROSAURA: Remember then, Don Alvaro, your own dignity and my love.

DON: I will be true to my word.

ROSAURA: We shall meet again.

DON: May I not at least know who you are?

ROSAURA: When you know that, I promise you will be astonished. [*Exit*]

DON [*to himself*]: This is most certainly one of the first ladies of Spain! This is beyond doubt a princess who has fallen in love with me and is jealous for my honour. Love! Love! Thou wouldst have degraded me! But my guardian angel had sent this beautiful unknown lady to save the honour of my illustrious family! [*Exit*]

⊰ SCENE 4 ⊱

A lonely Street. Enter the CONTE *and* ARLECCHINO.

CONTE: What are you trying to say? I don't understand you.

ARLECCHINO: I am saying that the Signora Rosaura has sent me to invite the guests for the party this evening.

CONTE: What the devil are you talking about? What guests?

ARLECCHINO: I mean. . . . No, it's no use! I can't get over the joke I played on the Spaniard! It's still making me laugh so much, I don't know what I'm saying.

CONTE: You've played some joke on Don Alvaro?

ARLECCHINO: Yes, him! Himself!

CONTE: What was it?

ARLECCHINO: I pretended to bring him a message from the Signora Rosaura.

CONTE: You mean . . . Don Alvaro is on such terms with the Signora Rosaura that. . . .

ARLECCHINO: Oh, yes, he's on terms with her all right! And what terms! This evening he's even been invited to the widow's party.

CONTE: He has? And not I?

ARLECCHINO: Oh, yes, you're invited, signore. That's what I was trying to say about the message to the guests.

CONTE: Now I understand. The signora is giving a party at her house and I am invited?

ARLECCHINO: Yes, signore.

CONTE: The invitation pleases me, but I fear I will find too many rivals among the guests.

ARLECCHINO: Don't worry, signore. Such a nice lady will know how to arrange things.

[ROSAURA *enters masked, and wearing a Venetian headdress of fine silk. She walks past them ostentatiously, without speaking, giving coy looks at the* CONTE.]

CONTE: Arlecchino! Did you see the look that masked lady gave me?

ARLECCHINO: You be careful, signore. A mask can hide age as well as youth. [*Exit*]

CONTE: Can I be of service, masked lady?

[*Rosaura sighs.*]

CONTE: No, these sighs do not succeed with me. I used to be taken in by them once. But that time is past. I see through them now. Now if Monsieur Lebleu were here, you would have more luck.

ROSAURA: You insult a lady whom you do not even know?

CONTE: I beg your pardon, signora, but that mask and that dress led me to believe you were something less than a lady.

ROSAURA: Love makes one do strange things.

CONTE: Love? You are in love with me?

ROSAURA: Alas, yes.

CONTE: But I do not love you.

ROSAURA: If you knew me, you might not say so.

CONTE: If you were Venus herself, there would still be no danger of my loving you.

ROSAURA: Why not?

CONTE: Because my heart already belongs to another.

ROSAURA: To whom, if I may be allowed to ask?

CONTE: You may. She whom I adore is the Signora Rosaura Lombardi.

ROSAURA: The widow?

CONTE: The same.

ROSAURA: What poor taste you have! She is not even beautiful.

CONTE: She pleases me. And that is enough.

ROSAURA: She is not of the aristocracy.

CONTE: She is wise and gracious, and her family is one of the oldest in this city.

ROSAURA: I believe she has given promises to others.

CONTE: You may believe that: I don't. If I did, I should know how to die. But I trust her completely.

ROSAURA: You are too faithful.

CONTE: I do what is right.

ROSAURA: And I who sigh for you – I can hope for no pity?

CONTE: I told you – you can hope for nothing.

ROSAURA: But if I told you who I am, perhaps then you would not be able to help loving me?

CONTE: You are wrong. And I advise you not to unmask yourself. You will save yourself the indignity of being repulsed.

ROSAURA: Then I will leave you.

CONTE: Indeed you must.

ROSAURA: If only I had something to remember you by.

CONTE: Why should you want to remember someone who does not love you?

ROSAURA: Do me this one favour. Give me some souvenir.

CONTE [aside]: I understand. [aloud] If you need it, I can let you have half a ducat.

ROSAURA: I do not need your money.

CONTE: What is it you want then?

ROSAURA: This handkerchief will do. [*She takes the handkerchief from his hand and goes.*]

CONTE [*alone*]: So much the better. She could have said right away she was in love with my handkerchief. What strange people there are in the world. Even now, at this hour of the evening, the Piazza is full of these beautiful unknown ladies. This one was more discreet than most. She was satisfied with a handkerchief. Some would have taken the money. I never know how to treat them. To me the most horrible thing in the world is a grasping mercenary woman. [*Exit*]

⊰ SCENE 5 ⊱

Rosaura's room arranged for the party with tables and chairs and various lamps.

[ELEONORA *and* MARIONETTE.]

MARIONETTE: Well, what do you say? Don't you think Signor Pantalone is very nice? He does all he can for you.

ELEONORA: I have been thinking it over, and I'm not sure I want him.

MARIONETTE: What about the Frenchman then? Does he please you?

ELEONORA: I'll tell you the truth. His face pleases me, his manner delights me, his impudence fascinates me, but I don't believe a word he says.

MARIONETTE: Why not?

ELEONORA: Because he tries too much to be the great lover and says the most preposterous things.

MARIONETTE: But you would believe facts?

ELEONORA: Such facts that he mentions are quite unbelievable.

MARIONETTE: So if he asked you to marry him, you wouldn't know whether to believe him?

ELEONORA: But that's just what he won't do.

MARIONETTE: If he did, would you be happy?

ELEONORA: Of course I would.

MARIONETTE: What will you give me if I arrange it?

ELEONORA: Something very nice indeed.

MARIONETTE: Leave it to me then. And I hope you'll be satisfied.

ELEONORA: But what will my sister say? She's been thinking of marrying the Frenchman herself.

MARIONETTE: She has four to choose from and, from what I see, this one hasn't much chance.

ELEONORA: All right. I will trust you.

MARIONETTE: And I will keep my word. I've arranged more marriages than I've hairs on my head. Here's your sister. Don't say anything yet.

ELEONORA: Just as you say – mistress.

[ROSAURA *enters.*]

ROSAURA: Sister, I have been looking everywhere for you.

ELEONORA: And I was just coming to find you.

ROSAURA: Listen. It is possible that this evening I may arrange to get married again. What will you do without me?

ELEONORA: I had hoped you would arrange a marriage for me first.

ROSAURA: Do you want Signor Pantalone?

ELEONORA: Not if I can help it.

ROSAURA: Then what can I do?

MARIONETTE: Devil take it, with so many after you – can't you find one for her?

ROSAURA: Well, really! Do you think I can arrange a marriage as easily as if it were – well, a game of cards? Here they are, now!

[*The* CONTE *enters.*]

CONTE: I am most deeply honoured by your kindness, Signora.

ROSAURA: The honour is mine that you have deigned to favour me.

MARIONETTE [*aside*]: The Conte arrives first – jealous again.

ROSAURA: Do sit down, won't you?

[*She sits near the* CONTE. ELEONORA *seats herself some distance away*.]

[DON ALVARO *enters*.]

DON: My most humble respects to you, Signora Rosaura.

ROSAURA [*rising*]: Your servant, Don Alvaro.

DON: And to all present, a very good evening.

ROSAURA: Please. [*She indicates the chairs*.]

DON [*aside*]: I hope that unknown lady isn't here. [*He looks round carefully and then sits near* ELEONORA.]

MARIONETTE [*aside*]: That's worked out all right.

DON: Where have you placed my family-tree?

ROSAURA: In my room.

DON: You should have put it in here. Then all your guests could have admired it.

MARIONETTE: We'll hang it on the door in the street. Then everyone can see it.

DON [*aside*]: Impertinent Frenchwoman!

[MILORD *enters*.]

MILORD [*to* ELEONORA]: Servant, ma'am. [*to* DON ALVARO *and the* CONTE] Gentlemen.

ROSAURA [*to* MILORD]: Your most humble servant, milord. [*They all rise and salute him*.]

MILORD: Ma'am. [*He sits near the* CONTE.]

MARIONETTE [*aside*]: Ma'am! Ma'am! He can't say anything but ma'am!

ROSAURA: It is kind of Milord to favour me.

MILORD: I am the favoured one.

MARIONETTE [*aside*]: That's what he thinks.

[MONSIEUR LEBLEU *enters*.]

MONSIEUR: Madame Rosaura, your most humble servant. [*He kisses her hand*.] Mademoiselle Eleonora, I bow low before your beauty. [*He kisses her hand forcibly and she pulls it back.*] At your service, friends. Good evening, Marionette. [*They all rise and salute him.*]

MARIONETTE [*aside*]: This one at least will liven things up.

ROSAURA: Do be seated, Monsieur.

MONSIEUR: The seat appears to be taken. No matter. I will sit next to this charming young lady. [*He sits between* DON ALVARO *and* ELEONORA.] Madame Rosaura, I am astonished.

ROSAURA: At what?

MONSIEUR: I thought to see a jewel on your breast and I do not.

ROSAURA: Do you mean the locket containing your portrait?

MONSIEUR: That is to what I refer.

ROSAURA: Then now you know better.

MARIONETTE [*aside*]: He did not deserve that.

ROSAURA: Gentlemen, before we begin a more general conversation, may I have your attention? Since I have received marks of favour from all four of you, I intend first to make a short speech. By offering me the family-tree of his house, Don Alvaro honoured me. By giving me his portrait, Monsieur Lebleu enchanted me. With his splendid jewels, Milord astonished me. By his tender expressions of respect, the Conte affected me deeply. I am grateful to you all. But I cannot divide myself between you all. I can choose but one of you. The choice I am now about to make is not made capriciously, but after much thought and reflection.

Milord, an English lady has asked me to remind you that you made no promise to Madam Rosaura, that you are completely free to marry this English lady to whom you have promised your love and fidelity. She therefore sends you this case and asks me to tell you that she who returns it to you is the same that received it from you.

[*She returns the gold case to* MILORD.]

Monsieur Lebleu, an unknown French lady has asked me to remind you that you yielded Rosaura to your rival. She returns this little bottle of scent as a reminder of your promise to her. That unknown lady is she who now speaks so reproachfully to you.

[*She gives the bottle of scent to* MONSIEUR LEBLEU.]

Don Alvaro almost won me, but he also must be reminded of the unknown Spanish lady who made him realize the degradation of marrying a merchant's daughter and who ordered him to abandon this merchant's daughter and love and obey her only. Here is the widow's snuff-box that he disdained to keep.

[*She returns the snuff-box to* DON ALVARO.]

And now the Conte, who treats unknown masked ladies with such incivility, who denies the slightest favour to one who sighs for him, and who parts unwillingly with even a silly silk handkerchief. To him I say, here in the presence of his rivals, that the unknown masked lady who carried off his handkerchief, now gives him her hand* and promises to be his wife.

[*She offers the* CONTE *her hand and he takes it tenderly and affectionately.*]

CONTE: I am the luckiest man in the world! And the happiest!

MILORD: Well done, old fellow! I trust we can remain friends, what?

MARIONETTE [*aside*]: I said she'd pick the worst of the lot!

DON [*rising*]: I would not have believed that an Italian lady could behave so wickedly! To have impersonated a Spanish lady is an insult to all the ladies of my country. Such a disgraceful act impels me to depart never to return. And to punish your inordinate presumption, I shall deprive you of the honour of my protection. [*Exit*]

MONSIEUR: Madame Rosaura, I should indeed be sorrowful if in order to marry you were departing to India. But since you are marrying the Conte and so will not be leaving Italy, my sorrow is lessened by the knowledge that I shall still have the pleasure of seeing you. I shall therefore

* See footnote on p. 61.

remain as ever at your service and, with your husband's permission, will have the honour of waiting upon you.

CONTE: No, monsieur. I thank you, but the Signora Rosaura will no longer have need of your services.

MARIONETTE: Monsieur Lebleu, I am sorry to see you so cast down. And since you are my countryman I would like to do something for you. The Signora Rosaura is now engaged to be married. You could be so yourself – if you do not wish to starve while others eat!

MONSIEUR: So be it, dear Marionette! Marry me in the French way. Arrange it all for me.

MARIONETTE: Here then is your wife.

MONSIEUR: Mademoiselle! But – she does not believe a word I say! Nor is she in love with me!

MARIONETTE: How little you know her then.

MONSIEUR [to ELEONORA]: Tell me, my little treasure, is this true? What Marionette says?

ELEONORA: It is true indeed.

MONSIEUR: You would be my wife?

ELEONORA: If you think I am worthy . . .

MONSIEUR: Long live love! Long live marriage! [to ROSAURA] Signora sister-in-law, my cup of happiness is twice full! For now the Conte can no longer be jealous of me!

CONTE: You will nevertheless not live with us but find a house of your own.

MARIONETTE: Poor Signora Rosaura! Now I am sorry for you!

ROSAURA: Donkey! You don't know how happy I am!

[PANTALONE *and the* DOCTOR *enter*.]

PANTALONE: How is the party going, signori?

DOCTOR: What have you done to Don Alvaro? He came out muttering curses on all Italian ladies.

MONSIEUR: Signor Pantalone! Signor Doctor! My dear father-in-law! My venerable brother-in-law! Permit me to inform you that I am to have the honour of marrying this beautiful young lady.

PANTALONE: What's this? What's this?

DOCTOR: Without a word to me – her own father?

ROSAURA: Fate has decided it all. In one evening two marriages have been arranged. My own with the Conte di Bosco Nero and my sister's with Monsieur Lebleu. Have you anything against them?

DOCTOR: I have always left such things to you. And if you are satisfied, then I am also.

PANTALONE [aside]: I had best make a virtue of necessity. [aloud] I had myself wished to marry the Signorina Eleonora but only if that was what she wanted herself. Since it was not, I have lost nothing but a young lady who might have made me die of despair.

MONSIEUR: Bravo, Signor Pantalone!

MILORD: I couldn't have put it better myself.

ROSAURA: And so my designs are all happily concluded. A widow and a young girl have found what they lacked and without which their state was uncertain and dangerous. I confess that my methods have been artful, but my artfulness has never departed from what is honourable and just. And so I dare to hope that, even if I do not deserve to be applauded, I have at least merited your indulgence, and perhaps – your envy.

Mirandolina

LA LOCANDIERA

Mirandolina

IN this play, first performed in Venice in 1753, Goldoni shows his mastery of stage-craft and characterization more fully than in any other single play. It is Goldoni's *Much Ado About Nothing*. Mirandolina is an eighteenth-century Beatrice. Bold, coy, tender, coquettish, indifferent, as suits her plan, she brings a young eighteenth-century Benedick to her feet. But unlike Shakespeare's Beatrice, Goldoni's Mirandolina condemns him to perpetual bachelorhood for having presumed to doubt the power of her sex.

Here, in the Marquis and the Count, are two perfect examples of Goldoni's skill in creating cantankerous yet likeable old men.

Following the precedent of some modern Italian editions of this play, two very minor characters, the foreign actresses, have been omitted. The few scenes in which they appear delay the action and are not needed. Goldoni appears to have introduced them to ridicule the characters and dialogue of the old Comedy.

Characters

The MARQUIS OF FORLIPOPOLI
The COUNT OF ALBAFIORITA
FABRIZIO, a Servant at the Inn
The BARON RIPAFRATTA
MIRANDOLINA, the Mistress of the Inn
The Baron's servant

The action of the play takes place in Mirandolina's Inn at Florence.

Act One

The guests' sitting-room at the Inn.

The MARQUIS OF FORLIPOPOLI *and the* COUNT OF ALBAFIORITA.

MARQUIS: Between you and me there's quite a difference.

COUNT: At this Inn my money's as good as yours.

MARQUIS: The mistress of the Inn doesn't seem to think so. She gives me far better service.

COUNT: What makes you think that?

MARQUIS: I am the Marquis of Forlipopoli.

COUNT: And I am the Count of Albafiorita.

MARQUIS: Exactly. Counts are two a penny.

COUNT: So are Marquises with no money.

MARQUIS: That's enough! I am I! And I'm accustomed to being treated with respect!

COUNT: Yes! Everybody must treat you with respect. But *you* can treat everybody as you damn well please!

MARQUIS: I am staying at this Inn because I am in love with its mistress. Everybody knows that. And so I expect everybody to refrain from pestering a young lady who meets with my approval.

COUNT: Here we go again! Hands off Mirandolina! Just what d'you imagine keeps me here in Florence! Why d'you suppose I'm staying at this Inn?

MARQUIS: Oh, I know what you're up to. You haven't a chance.

COUNT: And you have?

MARQUIS: Yes. I have, and you haven't. I am I. My protection is what Mirandolina needs.

COUNT: What Mirandolina needs is money.

MARQUIS: I've enough of that.

COUNT: Ten ducats a day is what I spend here. *And* I give her a present every day.

MARQUIS: And *I* don't need to boast what I spend.

COUNT: Everybody's got a good idea.

MARQUIS: Oh, no, they haven't.

COUNT: Oh, yes, they have. Servants talk, my dear Marquis. Three ducats a day, isn't it, my dear Marquis?

MARQUIS: That servant Fabrizio! Can't stand him. Seems to me our hostess has a soft spot for the fellow.

COUNT: Maybe she's thinking of marrying him. Now that wouldn't be a bad idea. Her father's been dead six months and this Inn's too much for a young woman on her own. As a matter of fact, I've promised her three hundred ducats if she'll get married.

MARQUIS: If she gets married I'm the one who'll protect her and who'll . . . well, I know how to go about it!

COUNT: Look, why not let's arrange it as between friends? We'll both give her three hundred and share and share alike.

MARQUIS: What I do I don't share with others. I am I. And I don't need to boast about it. [*calling*] Ho, there! Anybody there?

COUNT [*to himself*]: There's no pride like that of a poor man!

[FABRIZIO *enters.*]

FABRIZIO [*to the Marquis*]: You called signore?

MARQUIS: Signore? Who are you calling 'signore'?

FABRIZIO: I beg your pardon.

COUNT [*to* FABRIZIO]: Tell me, how is our hostess?

FABRIZIO: Very well, Illustrious.

MARQUIS: Is she out of bed yet?

FABRIZIO: Yes, Illustrious.

MARQUIS: You stupid ass!

FABRIZIO: Why, Illustrious?

MARQUIS: Who are you calling 'Illustrious'?

FABRIZIO: It's what I called this other gentleman.

MARQUIS: Between him and me there's quite a difference.

FABRIZIO [*to himself*]: Yes, between his tips and yours.

MARQUIS: Tell your mistress to come to me. I wish to speak to her.

FABRIZIO: Very well, Excellency. Have I got it right this time?

MARQUIS: You have. And about time too. I've been staying here three months now. Dumb insolence, that's what it is.

FABRIZIO: I'm always ready to oblige, Excellency.

COUNT [*to* FABRIZIO]: Would you like to see the real difference between the Marquis and me?

MARQUIS: What are you up to now?

COUNT [*to* FABRIZIO]: Here's a zecchino for you. Now try and get one from him.

FABRIZIO [*to the* COUNT]: Thank you, Illustrious. [*to the* MARQUIS] Excellency . . .

MARQUIS: I don't throw money away like a fool. Get out!

FABRIZIO [*to the* COUNT]: Heaven bless you, Excellency. [*aside*] It's money not titles that counts with me. [*Exit*]

MARQUIS [*to the* COUNT]: That sort of thing won't get you anywhere. My rank counts more than all your money.

COUNT: What can your rank buy you?

MARQUIS: That's all you can think of! What you can buy! Oh, Mirandolina has you weighed up. You'll get nowhere with her.

COUNT: Nor will you, with only your title. You don't get anywhere without money.

MARQUIS: Money? Poof! It's rank that inspires obedience and bestows protection.

COUNT: Can rank give somebody three hundred ducats?

MARQUIS: Rank inspires respect!

COUNT: Money buys respect!

MARQUIS: You don't know what you're talking about!

COUNT: And I suppose you think you do!

[*The* BARON *enters.*]

BARON: Well, well, what a to-do! Having a quarrel – friends?

COUNT: We are arguing a rather fine point.

MARQUIS [*ironically*]: The Count presumes to argue with me over the importance of rank.

COUNT: I was not denying the importance of rank. I simply maintain it's money that makes life easier.

BARON: Actually, my dear Marquis . . .

MARQUIS: Let us talk of something else.

BARON: But what on earth started such an argument?

COUNT: Oh, something quite ridiculous.

MARQUIS: Yes, the Count makes everything ridiculous.

COUNT: His Excellency the Marquis is in love with our hostess. So am I, of course. Only more so. He thinks his rank will cause his affection to be returned. I hope to be rewarded for certain little attentions I give. A ridiculous matter to argue about, don't you agree?

MARQUIS: He refuses to realize the powerful protection my rank can give her.

COUNT [*to the* BARON]: He offers protection. I offer money.

BARON: Was there anything ever less worth arguing about! To argue over a woman! To upset yourselves over a woman! A woman? I can't believe it. Over a woman? Well, one thing's certain: that's something I'll never be in danger of arguing over. Women are by nature stupid, selfish, and dogmatic. The great tragedy of life is that they've made themselves indispensable. To put it plainly women bore me utterly, absolutely, and completely.

MARQUIS: All the same, Mirandolina is a woman quite out of the ordinary.

COUNT: For once the Marquis is right. The mistress of this Inn is the most charming woman I have ever met.

MARQUIS: Of course I'm right. If I'm in love with her she must be charming – quite out of the ordinary.

BARON: This is beginning to amuse me. How is she so out of the ordinary?

MARQUIS: She has charm. Quite natural, mind you. Bred in the bone. That's what makes her out of the ordinary. Charm.

COUNT: In other words she's pretty, speaks well, dresses neatly, and has perfect taste.

BARON: Are we talking of the same woman? I've been at this Inn three days and that's not how she's impressed me.

COUNT: Have a close look at her then.

BARON: I've seen her close enough, thank you. She's like any other woman.

MARQUIS: She is not like any other woman. Allow me to inform you, sir, I have known the finest ladies in the land. And never – never, sir – have I met one with her modesty and charm. Such a combination, sir, is something quite out of the ordinary.

COUNT: By gad, yes! I flatter myself I know how to get my way with the ladies. I know their little weaknesses. But this one's different. I've gone to the limit in presents, courtesies, attentions – and dammit I haven't even touched her hand yet.

BARON: So that's it! She's leading you both up the garden path, you poor fools. Women? They're all the same. I'd like to see her try it on me.

COUNT: Have you never been in love?

BARON: Never. And never will. Oh, some have tried their damnedest to marry me. They could have saved themselves the trouble.

MARQUIS: But, dammit, man, don't you want a son to carry on your name?

BARON: Yes, I have thought of that, quite often. But then I always remember that to have a son you need a wife.

COUNT: What will you do with your money?

BARON: Have a good time – with my friends.

MARQUIS: Bravo, Baron! Bravo! We'll help you.

COUNT: And women will get nothing of it?

BARON: Absolutely nothing. They won't fatten themselves on me.

COUNT: Here's our hostess. Now look and see if she isn't adorable.

BARON: Oh, marvellous! But give me a good hunting-dog.

MARQUIS: Well, if you don't appreciate her, I do.

BARON: You could have her even if she were as beautiful as Venus.

[MIRANDOLINA *enters.*]

MIRANDOLINA: Good morning, gentlemen. Which of you was asking for me?

MARQUIS: I was asking for you. But not in here.

MIRANDOLINA: Where do you want me, Excellency?

MARQUIS: In my room.

MIRANDOLINA: In your room? If you need anything, kindly call the waiter.

MARQUIS [*aside to the* BARON]: Charming modesty!

BARON [*aside to the* MARQUIS]: Damned impertinence!

COUNT: Dear Mirandolina, I will speak to you in public. I won't put you to the inconvenience of coming to my room. Examine these ear-rings. You like them?

MIRANDOLINA: They're quite nice.

COUNT: They are diamonds, you know.

MIRANDOLINA: Yes, I *can* tell diamonds when I see them.

COUNT: They're yours.

BARON [*aside to the* COUNT]: My dear fellow, have some sense.

MIRANDOLINA: Why do you wish to give me them?

MARQUIS [*to* MIRANDOLINA]: They're not worth having. You have others twice as beautiful.

COUNT: They are mounted in the latest fashion. Please accept them, with my love.

BARON [*aside*]: He's mad!

MIRANDOLINA: Oh no really, signore . . .

COUNT: If you don't take them, I shall be offended.

MIRANDOLINA: Well, in that case . . . since I value the friendship of my guests . . . yes, so as not to offend *you*, Count, I will take them.

BARON [*aside*]: The little devil!

COUNT [*aside to the* BARON]: What a ready wit, eh?

BARON [*aside to the* COUNT]: Too damn ready! She grabbed them without even thanking you.

MARQUIS: Truly, Count, you are surpassing yourself. To give a present to a lady in public! Out of pure vanity! Mirandolina, I really must speak with you privately. Something quite confidential. Oh, and quite honourable.

MIRANDOLINA [*to herself*]: And with nothing in it for me,

you stingy old miser. [*aloud*] If that is all, gentlemen, I will
retire.

BARON [*contemptuously*]: One moment, mistress. The linen
sheets in my room are not good enough. If you have no
better, I will provide my own.

MIRANDOLINA:I can provide better, signore. And, signore,
though I am your servant I think you could address me a
little more politely.

BARON:You take my money. Must you have compliments
thrown in as well?

COUNT [*to* MIRANDOLINA]:Be patient with him. He's the
arch-enemy of all women.

BARON:Her patience or otherwise, is a matter of complete
indifference to me.

MIRANDOLINA:Oh, poor us! What *can* we have done to you?
Why are you so cruel to us, Signor Baron?

BARON:That's enough. Don't try to be familiar with me.
Have the linen changed. I will send my servant for it.
[*changing to a more friendly tone*] My friends – we will meet
later. [*Exit*]

MIRANDOLINA:What a brute! I never saw anything like it!

COUNT:Ah, dear Mirandolina, it is not everybody who can
appreciate your charms.

MIRANDOLINA:No, truly, he has upset me very much. I shall
ask him to find lodgings elsewhere. At once!

MARQUIS:Good! And if he's awkward about it, let me know.
I'll have him out dam' quick. Make use of my protection,
my dear.

COUNT:And don't you worry about losing what he pays you.
I'll make it up. I'll pay double. [*aside*] Treble – if it would
get rid of the Marquis as well.

MIRANDOLINA:Thank you, gentlemen, thank you. I am
quite capable of turning anybody out of my Inn. As for
money, I never have an empty room for long.

[FABRIZIO *enters.*]

FABRIZIO [*to the* COUNT]:Illustrious, someone is asking for
you.

COUNT: D'you know who it is?

FABRIZIO: A jeweller, I think. [*aside to* MIRANDOLINA]
Mirandolina, don't stay in here.

COUNT: Ah, yes, of course. He has a jewel he wants to show
me. Mirandolina, those ear-rings need something to go
with them.

MIRANDOLINA: Now really, you mustn't, Signor Count . . .

COUNT: No, no, you must have the best. Money's no object
with me. I'll go and have a look at this jewel. I shan't be
a moment, Mirandolina. Until later, Marquis. [*Exit*]

MARQUIS [*aside*]: Damn and blast him and his money!

MIRANDOLINA: Really, the Signor Count goes to too much
trouble.

[*The* MARQUIS *takes a fine silk handkerchief from his pocket,
unfolds it and makes as if to dab his forehead.*]

MIRANDOLINA: What a pretty handkerchief!

MARQUIS: It is rather fine, don't you think? Yes, I have good
taste.

MIRANDOLINA: Indeed you have.

MARQUIS: It comes from London.

MIRANDOLINA: No! Really?

MARQUIS [*folding up the handkerchief carefully*]: It must be
folded properly so that it does not crease. Things of this
sort should be taken great care of. [*He offers it to* MIRAN-
DOLINA.] Take it.

MIRANDOLINA: You want me to have it put in your room?

MARQUIS: No, in yours.

MIRANDOLINA: In mine? Why?

MARQUIS: Because I'm giving it you.

MIRANDOLINA: Oh, but really, your Excellency. . . .

MARQUIS: Not a word now. It's yours.

MIRANDOLINA: But I couldn't. . . .

MARQUIS: Now don't make me angry.

MIRANDOLINA: Your Excellency knows I don't like to
offend anyone. Well . . . so that you won't be angry, I'll
accept it.

[*The* COUNT *enters.*]

MARQUIS: Ah, here's the Count. [*softly to* MIRANDOLINA] Show it to him.

MIRANDOLINA [*showing the handkerchief to the* COUNT]: Look, Count. See what a lovely present the Marquis has given me.

MARQUIS: Oh, it's nothing. A mere trifle. Put it away. I'd rather you didn't show it to people. I don't want everybody knowing what I do.

MIRANDOLINA [*aside, putting the handkerchief in her pocket*]: He doesn't want it known, but he makes me show it.

COUNT [*to* MIRANDOLINA]: If the Marquis will permit, I should like a word with you.

MARQUIS [*to* MIRANDOLINA]: That handkerchief will get all creased in your pocket like that.

MIRANDOLINA: I'll wrap it up in cotton wool. It won't get crushed then.

COUNT [*to* MIRANDOLINA]: You see this little diamond?

MIRANDOLINA: Oh, isn't that beautiful!

COUNT: How would that go with the ear-rings I gave you?

MIRANDOLINA: But it's even more beautiful than they are.

MARQUIS [*aside*]: Damn this Count, his diamonds, his money – *and* the devil that possesses him!

COUNT: Yes, it will put the finishing touch to those ear-rings. That's why I'm giving it to you.

MIRANDOLINA: But I simply can't take it.

COUNT: You'll offend me, if you don't.

MIRANDOLINA: Oh, dear, I hate to give offence. Well ... so you won't be offended, I'll take it. What do you think, Marquis? Isn't it a beautiful diamond?

MARQUIS: Of it's kind, that handkerchief is finer.

COUNT: Rather a big difference in kind, I should say.

MARQUIS: That's it! At it again! Boasting in public of what you spend.

COUNT: Oh, of course, you make your gifts in secret.

MARQUIS: I'll make you pay for this!

COUNT: Now what are you grumbling about?

MARQUIS: You know quite well. I am I! And I won't be treated in this way. Mirandolina, take great care of that handkerchief. Handkerchiefs of that quality are very rare.

Diamonds are easily come by. But not handkerchiefs like
that.

COUNT [*to* MIRANDOLINA]: You know that what I do is done
for you. My heart and all my wealth are yours. Use them as
you wish. For you are their mistress. [*Exit*]

MARQUIS: Some people have got to make a show of their
money! The big I-am! Oh, I know his type. I've seen something of the world, I have.

MIRANDOLINA: So also have I.

MARQUIS: They think women of your sort can be had at the
expense of a few gifts.

MIRANDOLINA: Oh, a few gifts never did me any harm.

MARQUIS: *I* would think it an insult to you – to give you
presents and put you under an obligation to me.

MIRANDOLINA: There is no danger of that from you, Signor
Marquis.

MARQUIS: I would never insult you in such a way.

MIRANDOLINA: I'm quite sure you wouldn't.

MARQUIS: But otherwise I am yours to command.

MIRANDOLINA: Otherwise?

MARQUIS: Try me?

MIRANDOLINA: You give me an example.

MARQUIS: Damn – you're a teasing little devil!

MIRANDOLINA: Now you're making me blush, your Excellency.

MARQUIS: To hell with 'your Excellency'! By gad, I could
make a fool of myself over you!

MIRANDOLINA: How, signore?

MARQUIS: If only I were simply a Count like that fellow.

MIRANDOLINA: Because of his money?

MARQUIS: Money? To hell with his money! No, if only I
were a fiddling little Count I'd . . .

MIRANDOLINA: Yes? What would you do?

MARQUIS: Marry you, blast it! [*Exit*]

MIRANDOLINA [*alone*]: Huh! Marry him! His Excellency
Signor the Marquis Skinflint! That would be the day! The
husbands I'd have, if I'd married all that had wanted to
marry me! They've only got to enter this Inn and they fall

in love with me and think they can marry me on the spot.
Except this Signor Baron, the ill-mannered lout! What
right's he got to think himself too high and mighty to be
civil to me? Nobody else who's ever stopped at this Inn has
ever treated me so! I certainly don't expect him to fall in
love with me at first sight – but to behave like that! That
sort of thing infuriates me. So he hates women? Doesn't
want anything to do with them? The poor fool. He hasn't
met the woman yet who knows how to set about him. But
he will. Oh, yes, he will, all right. And, who knows if he
hasn't just met her. Yes, this fellow might be exactly what
I need. I'm sick to death of men who run after me. As for
marriage – there's plenty of time for that. I want to enjoy
my freedom first. And here's a chance to really enjoy it. Yes,
I'll use every art I have to conquer this enemy of women!

[FABRIZIO *enters*.]

FABRIZIO: Hoy! Mistress!
MIRANDOLINA: What is it?
FABRIZIO: That fellow in the middle room is complaining
about his linen.
MIRANDOLINA: I know, I know. He told me. I'll see to it.
FABRIZIO: Very well. Show me what to take him.
MIRANDOLINA: No, you go along. I'll take it myself.
FABRIZIO: You want to take it him yourself?
MIRANDOLINA: Yes I, by myself.
FABRIZIO: You seem to think a lot of this fellow.
MIRANDOLINA: No more than any of the others. Get off
with you.
FABRIZIO [*to himself*]: I'd best face up to it. She's only been
leading me on. Nothing can ever come of it.
MIRANDOLINA [*to herself*]: Poor lad! He's fallen too. I want
to keep him hoping because he's so faithful.
FABRIZIO: It's always been understood I wait on the guests.
MIRANDOLINA: You're a little too off-hand with them.
FABRIZIO: And you're a little too obliging.
MIRANDOLINA: I know what I'm doing. I don't need anyone
to tell me.

FABRIZIO: All right. Find yourself another waiter then.

MIRANDOLINA: Why – Signor Fabrizio! Have you had enough of me?

FABRIZIO: May I recall to you what your father said to both of us – just before he died?

MIRANDOLINA: Yes. And when I decide to get married, I will not forget what my father said.

FABRIZIO: It's just that I'm very easily hurt. And some things I can't stand.

MIRANDOLINA: What d'you think I am? An empty-headed little flirt? I thought you knew me better than that! How d'you expect me to behave with guests who are here today and gone tomorrow? If I treat them well, that's in my own interest, for the good name of my Inn. I've no need of their presents. And if I want to make love, one's enough for me and I have him already. I know when I'm well off, and when I want to marry. . . . I shall remember my father's wishes. And those who serve me well, won't regret it. I know how to be grateful. I know he who deserves rewarding . . . but I am not known.* There, Fabrizio. Do understand me. If you can. [*Exit*]

FABRIZIO [*alone*]: It needs a cleverer man than I to understand her. One minute she wants me, the next she doesn't want me. She says she's not a flirt, yet she wants to act like

---

*This is a literal rendering of the original and it puzzled me considerably. My reading of the whole speech in which it occurs makes me feel that Goldoni's meaning is that Mirandolina is telling Fabrizio that she is not known sexually. The whole speech shows clearly that she is very upset by Fabrizio's reproaches – in fact it is the only time in the play that her defences are down. My reading therefore is that Goldoni knows she is in love with Fabrizio but she does not know it herself. This is borne out by the non-sequiturs in her speech. This speech and her soliloquy towards the end of the play when she makes up her mind to marry Fabrizio are the only speeches in the play in which Goldoni uses dotted lines . . . to convey perturbation.

Other translations of this line do not make it more comprehensible. Lady Gregory translates it as:

'I know him but he doesn't know me' [omitting Goldoni's dotted line].

And Clifford Bax translates it as:

'I appreciate true worth . . . but I am not appreciated myself'.

[Translator]

one. I don't know what to do. Best wait and see. I like her, I
want her. We'd get on well together. I'll shut one eye and
let things take their course. As she said, the guests are here
today and gone tomorrow. I'm always here. I'll get the best
of the bargain in the end. [*Exit*]

⊰ SCENE 2 ⊱

[*The Baron's room*: *the* BARON *and his* SERVANT.]

SERVANT: This letter has arrived for you, Illustrious.
BARON: Bring me my chocolate. [*The servant goes out. The*
  BARON *opens the letter and reads*] 'Siena, the first of January,
  1753' – Hm, who can it be from? Ah, Orazio Taccagni –
  'My dear friend. The tender friendship I have for you urges
  me to warn you that your return home is imperative. The
  Count Mann is dead . . .' Poor Mann! I am sorry. 'He has
  left an only daughter of marriageable age, heiress to one
  hundred and fifty thousand ducats. All your friends wish
  this fortune yours and are making arrangements. . . .' They
  needn't trouble themselves on my behalf. They know well
  enough my views on marriage. And this dear friend better
  than any of them. Yet he pesters me the most. [*He tears up
  the letter.*] What are one hundred and fifty thousand ducats
  to me? On my own I can manage on far less. If I weren't on
  my own, they wouldn't be nearly enough. A wife for me?
  I'd rather the plague.

  [*The* MARQUIS *enters.*]

MARQUIS: Friend, d'you mind if I keep you company a
  moment?
BARON: The honour is mine.
MARQUIS: Yes, you and I speak the same language. Not like
  that fool of a Count.

BARON: Allow me to differ, my dear Marquis. You should respect others, if you wish to be respected yourself.

MARQUIS: Oh, come, you know me. I'm courteous to everybody. It's just that I can't stand that fellow.

BARON: You can't stand him because he's your rival in love. You should be ashamed of yourself. A nobleman like you in love with the mistress of an inn! An experienced man of the world like you running after a woman!

MARQUIS: Baron, that woman has cast a spell on me.

BARON: Don't talk rubbish! D'you think she uses witchcraft? What you want to ask yourself is, why don't women ever cast their spell on me? I'll tell you why. Because I keep them at a distance and don't give them a chance to use their charms on me.

MARQUIS: Maybe you're right. The trouble is I've something else on my mind. The fellow who looks after my estates for me.

BARON: What's he done?

MARQUIS: Words fail me, my dear chap.

[*The Baron's* SERVANT *enters carrying a cup of chocolate.*]

BARON: That sounds bad. [*to the* SERVANT] Make another cup at once.

SERVANT: There isn't any more, Illustrious. They've run out of chocolate.

BARON: Then they'd better get some. [*to the* MARQUIS] If you would care to accept this. . . .

[*The* MARQUIS *takes the chocolate without thanks and begins to drink and talk at the same time.*]

MARQUIS: As I was saying, this bailiff of mine . . . [*he drinks*]

BARON [*aside*]: So I go without.

MARQUIS: He'd promised to send me . . . [*he drinks*] . . . twenty zecchini. . . . [*He drinks.*]

BARON [*aside*]: Here it comes.

MARQUIS: And he's not sent them. [*He drinks.*]

BARON: Oh, they may have been delayed.

MARQUIS: The point is . . . the point is . . . [*he finishes the drink*]

Take it away. [*He gives the cup to the servant who goes out.*] The point is, I'm rather in debt and I don't know what to do.

BARON: A few days is neither here nor there. . . .

MARQUIS: Being a nobleman yourself, you know what it means to keep one's word. I'm in debt, and – well – it's damned embarrassing.

BARON: I'm sorry things are so bad. [*aside*] This is going to be awkward.

MARQUIS: Would it make things difficult for yourself to help me out, only for a few days?

BARON: My dear Marquis, I would if I could, with pleasure. If I had any money, you could have it here and now. I happen to be waiting for some myself.

MARQUIS: You don't expect me to believe you haven't a penny on you?

BARON: Look for yourself. That's all I have. It doesn't come to two zecchini. [*He shows a zecchino and some small change.*]

MARQUIS: You've got a whole zecchino there.

BARON: Yes, my last one.

MARQUIS: Lend me that. It'll help. . . .

BARON: But what about me?

MARQUIS: What are you frightened of? I'll pay it back.

BARON: There's no more to say, then. Take it. [*He gives him the zecchino.*]

MARQUIS [*taking the zecchino*]: I have some urgent business to attend to, dear friend, so for the moment, many thanks. We'll see one another at dinner. [*Exit*]

BARON [*alone*]: That's good! The Marquis tries to do me out of twenty zecchini and then is glad to get away with one. Well – one's neither here nor there to me, and if he doesn't pay it back he won't dare bother me again. What does annoy me is his drinking my chocolate. The fellow's no manners. And next minute it'll be: 'I am I! I am a nobleman, I am!' Oh, yes, a most noble nobleman!

[MIRANDOLINA *enters carrying the linen sheets.*]

MIRANDOLINA [*entering with affected timidity*]: May I come in, Illustrious?

BARON [*sharply*]: What d'you want?

MIRANDOLINA [*advancing a little*]: I've brought some better linen.

BARON [*pointing to the table*]: Good. Put it there.

MIRANDOLINA: May I beg you to put yourself to the trouble of seeing whether you consider it is satisfactory?

BARON: What's it made of?

MIRANDOLINA [*advancing a little further*]: The sheets are cambric.

BARON: Cambric?

MIRANDOLINA: Yes, signore. Ten paoli a yard. You see?

BARON: But I didn't mean anything as good as that. All I want is something better than I've been given.

MIRANDOLINA: This sort of linen was made for persons of quality, for those who will appreciate it. To be quite candid, Illustrious, I've brought it only because you are you. I wouldn't think of giving it to certain other people.

BARON: 'Because you are you'! The usual flattery.

MIRANDOLINA: Have a look at this table-cloth.

BARON: But that's the finest Flanders cloth! If you wash it, it loses its quality. There's no need to dirty that on my account.

MIRANDOLINA: For a nobleman like yourself, I don't bother over such trifles. I have several of these cloths and I will reserve them for your Most Illustrious Excellency.

BARON [*aside*]: There's no denying, she's a very obliging woman.

MIRANDOLINA [*aside*]: No wonder women don't please him if he always looks so grumpy.

BARON: Give the linen to my servant, or put it down there somewhere. There was no need to go to so much trouble about it.

MIRANDOLINA: Oh, but nothing is too much trouble, when I'm serving a nobleman of such quality.

BARON: Yes, fine, that will be all then. [*aside*] Flattery, that's all it is. Women! They're all the same.

MIRANDOLINA: I'll put it in the cupboard.

BARON [*thoughtfully*]: Yes, wherever you wish.

MIRANDOLINA [*aside, as she puts the linen in the cupboard*]: He's a tough one, this! I'm not getting anywhere.

BARON [*aside*]: This is how fools get taken in; they start listening to such flatteries and end up believing them.

MIRANDOLINA [*returning without the linen*]: Now what would you like for dinner?

BARON: Anything you've got.

MIRANDOLINA: No, I must know your likes and dislikes. If there's something you'd like more than anything else, you really must tell me.

BARON: If there's anything I want, I'll tell the waiter.

MIRANDOLINA: Ah, but men don't give the attention and patience to such things as we women do. What about a nice little ragout with some special sauce?

BARON: Thank you. You may have got round the Count and the Marquis like this. But you won't with me.

MIRANDOLINA: Yes! Did you ever see such a couple of spineless nincompoops? They no sooner come to lodge at an Inn than they immediately begin to make love to the mistress of the Inn. As if I haven't other things to attend to beside listening to their nonsense. Of course, I've got to make myself pleasant, engage them in some light conversation, for the good of the house. But it does make me laugh when I see they think I'm going out of my way to flatter them.

BARON: Excellent! That's the sort of plain talk I like to hear.

MIRANDOLINA: Oh, I believe in saying what I think, straight out!

BARON: Ah, come, now, you must admit you do put it on a little with those two.

MIRANDOLINA: Me? Heaven forbid! With those two? Ask them if you like. Ask them if I've ever once given them a single sign of encouragement. Naturally I don't rebuff them. That would hardly be in my own interests. Though I'm sorely tempted to sometimes. I just can't bear these effeminate men. And d'you know what I detest just as much? Women who run after men! Oh, I know I'm not as young as I used to be. Nor got the looks I had once. But I've had my chances. It's just that I've always valued my freedom too much to get married.

BARON: Yes, indeed, that's very true. One's freedom is one's greatest treasure.

MIRANDOLINA: And so many simply throw it away like stupid fools.

BARON: I couldn't agree with you more . . . Keep your distance!

MIRANDOLINA: Are you married, Illustrious?

BARON: Me? Heaven forbid! I've no need of women.

MIRANDOLINA: Wonderful! Don't ever change! If you only knew, signore . . . but I shouldn't speak badly of my own sex.

BARON: Do you know, you're the first woman I've ever heard talk like this?

MIRANDOLINA: I'll tell you a secret. When you're the mistress of an Inn like I am – well, the things you hear! If men only knew, they've every reason to be wary of my sex. They have my sympathy.

BARON [aside]: What an unusual woman she is.

MIRANDOLINA [pretending to go]: If you will permit me, Illustrious.

BARON: Oh! . . . Must you go?

MIRANDOLINA: I don't want to seem a nuisance to you.

BARON: Not at all. You please me. You interest me.

MIRANDOLINA: There! You see, signore? This is how I'm like with the others. I chat for a few moments, I'm friendly by nature, so I make a few jokes to amuse them. Then before you know where you are, they're ready to throw themselves at my feet, imagining they're in love with me.

BARON: You can hardly help having good manners.

MIRANDOLINA [curtseying]: You're too kind, Illustrious.

BARON: And they really fall in love?

MIRANDOLINA: Isn't it absurd? To fall in love just like that, all at once.

BARON: That's something I never could understand.

MIRANDOLINA: How firm you are! How manly!

BARON: What weak effeminate beings they are!

MIRANDOLINA: There speaks a real man! Signor Baron, give me your hand!

BARON: My hand? What for?

MIRANDOLINA: Because it would be such an honour. Look, mine is quite clean.

BARON: All right.

MIRANDOLINA [*taking his hand*]: This is the first time I've had the honour of shaking hands with a real man.

BARON: Yes – well – that'll be enough.

MIRANDOLINA: What *would* have happened if I'd done that with those other two? They'd think I'd fallen madly in love with them! They'd have passed out on the spot! Oh, but I wouldn't let them be the least familiar, for all the gold in the world. They don't know how to behave. It's simply wonderful to be able to speak freely with someone like you, signore. Oh . . . signore! Please pardon my presumption. I let myself be carried away. But if there's anything at all I can do for you, order me to do it without hesitation. I'll do it more willingly than for anyone else in the world.

BARON: Why are you singling me out for your favours?

MIRANDOLINA: Oh, it's nothing to do with your wonderful qualities as a man. Nor with your rank. It's just that I feel I can behave quite naturally with you – without wondering whether you'll take advantage of me. I know you will never forget I'm your servant, and start pestering me with ridiculous attentions.

BARON [*aside*]: How the devil this one became so out of the ordinary, I simply don't understand.

MIRANDOLINA [*aside*]: He's coming to heel, bit by bit.

BARON: Look . . . if you've other things to do . . . don't let me detain you.

MIRANDOLINA: Yes, signore, I will go and look after my little household duties. It is they who are my lovers; it's they which give me joy. If there is anything you want, I'll send my servant.

BARON: Good . . . and if you can come occasionally yourself, you'll be very welcome.

MIRANDOLINA: To tell the truth I . . . I never enter the guests' rooms. But I'll come to yours sometimes.

BARON: Mine! . . . Why?

MIRANDOLINA: Because I do like you so very much, Illustrious.

BARON: You like me?

MIRANDOLINA: Yes, I like you because you're not soft and weak. You are not one of those who'd only be wanting to make love to me. [*aside*] If he isn't wanting to by tomorrow, I'll eat my hat. [*Exit*]

BARON [*alone*]: Oh, I know what I'm doing. As for women – let them keep their distance. But this one could make me fall for her more than any. Yes, she has a certain frankness about her, an openness. Quite uncommon. Yes, quite out of the ordinary. But she won't get me falling in love with her just because of that. Still – simply to amuse myself of course – I'd rather talk to this one than any other. But fall in love? Give up my freedom? No fear! I'm not such a fool. [*Exit*]

Act Two

The Baron's room. The table and chairs are set for dinner. The BARON *is walking up and down deep in a book. His* SERVANT *stands by the door.*

[FABRIZIO *enters carrying the soup.*]

FABRIZIO [*to the* SERVANT]: Tell your master, the soup is here if he's ready to be served.

SERVANT [*to* FABRIZIO]: You tell him yourself.

FABRIZIO: I don't want my head bitten off.

SERVANT: Oh, his bark is worse than his bite. It's only women servants he's rude to. He can't stand women.

FABRIZIO: Can't stand women? The poor fool. Doesn't know what's good for him. [*He puts the soup on the table and goes.*]

SERVANT: Dinner is served, Illustrious.

[*The* BARON *puts down his book and sits at the table.*]

BARON [*to the* SERVANT, *as he begins his meal*]: It's early today.

[*The* SERVANT *stands behind the Baron's chair with a plate under his arm.*]

SERVANT: This room's been served before all the others. The Count of Albafiorita was shouting that he wanted to be served first, but the mistress of the Inn said you were to be, signore.

BARON: That is good of her.

SERVANT: Oh, she's a real lady, she is, signore. I've come across all sorts but never a mistress of an Inn like her. Real considerate, that's what she is.

BARON [*turning a little towards the* SERVANT]: You like her, eh?

SERVANT: If it wasn't that I don't want to leave you, signore, I'd come here and work as a waiter for Mirandolina.

BARON: Poor fool! What good would that do you?

[*He gives the* SERVANT *his plate. The* SERVANT *hands him a clean one.*]

SERVANT: I'd follow a woman like that around like a little dog, signore. [*He goes out to fetch the next dish.*]

BARON: Good heavens, that woman puts her spell on everybody. It would be a joke if she bewitched me as well. Tomorrow I leave for Leghorn!

SERVANT [*re-entering carrying a boiled chicken and another plate*]: The mistress of the Inn says if you don't care for chicken she'll send in some pigeon.

BARON: I like anything. What's that supposed to be?

SERVANT: Oh, she particularly asked me to let her know if you liked this sauce. Because she made it with her own hands.

BARON: She's certainly out to please me. [*He tastes it*] Mm! Excellent! Tell her I like it very much indeed. And give her my thanks.

SERVANT: Yes, signore.

BARON: Now! At once.

SERVANT: Of course, signore. [*aside, as he goes out*] Incredible! A woman's pleased him at last! [*Exit*]

BARON [*alone*]: This sauce is really exquisite. I've never tasted better. [*Goes on eating.*] If this is how Mirandolina looks after her guests she'll certainly never have an empty room. Good food, good linen. And one has to admit she's quite charming. Though what I like most is her frankness, her sincerity. Yes, that's just what most women lack. Sincerity in a woman is a fine thing.

SERVANT [*re-entering*]: She thanks your Excellency for his great kindness.

BARON: Good, good.

SERVANT: And now she's making another dish with her own hands. But I don't know what it is.

BARON: She's actually making it herself?

SERVANT: Yes, signore.

BARON: Fetch me a drink!

SERVANT [*going to sideboard to fetch bottle*]: Yes, signore.

BARON: I shall have to find some way to repay her for all this. A most remarkable woman. Yes, I'll pay double. I'll show I appreciate it. And then I'll be off to Leghorn. [*The* SERVANT *pours his drink.*] Has the Count had his dinner yet?

SERVANT: Yes, he has just been served, signore.

BARON: And the Marquis? Has he been served yet?

SERVANT: He was annoyed at being kept waiting and went out. He's not back yet.

BARON [*pushing away his plate*]: Right. I'm ready.

SERVANT [*taking his plate*]: Yes, signore.

[MIRANDOLINA *enters with a dish of food in her hand.*]

MIRANDOLINA [*at the door*]: May I come in?

BARON: Who is it?

SERVANT: It's – it's your dinner, signore.

BARON [*turning round*]: Relieve the lady of that dish!

MIRANDOLINA [*putting the dish on the table*]: No, no, you must let me have the pleasure of putting it on the table with my own hands.

BARON: But you shouldn't be doing this.

MIRANDOLINA: Oh, signore, who am I? One of your fine ladies? I'm the servant of any who are kind enough to stay at my Inn.

BARON [*aside*]: What modesty!

MIRANDOLINA: To tell the truth, I wouldn't mind waiting on all my guests myself. But for certain reasons I find it best not to. You'll understand what I mean, I know. Of course, I need have no doubts about your Excellency.

BARON: Thank you. What dish is this?

MIRANDOLINA: It's a little ragout I've made with my own hands.

BARON: Ah, then it will be good. If you made it, it must be.

MIRANDOLINA: Oh, signore! Now you're being too kind. I don't really know how to do anything well. I only wish I did, so I could please such a fine gentleman as yourself.

BARON [*aside*]: Leghorn, tomorrow! [*aloud*] If you've other things to be doing, don't let me keep you.

MIRANDOLINA:Oh, there's nothing for me to do, signore. The Inn is well provided with cooks and servants. I should be glad to know if this dish is to your taste.

BARON:Certainly, I will try it. [*He tastes it.*] Wonderful! It couldn't be better. But tell me, what is it you've flavoured it with?

MIRANDOLINA:Ah, I have my secrets, signore. These hands of mine know a thing or two.

BARON [*to the* SERVANT, *violently*]: Get me another drink.

MIRANDOLINA:With that dish you should drink something good, signore.

BARON [*to the* SERVANT]:Give me some Burgundy.

MIRANDOLINA:Excellent. Burgundy's a splendid wine. In my opinion it's the best wine one can drink at dinner.

[*The* SERVANT *puts the bottle of wine and a glass on the table*.]

BARON:You are a good judge of everything.

MIRANDOLINA:Well, I don't often make a mistake.

BARON:But this time you have.

MIRANDOLINA:In what way, signore?

BARON:In thinking I deserve your special attention.

MIRANDOLINA [*sighing*]:Ah! Signore. . . .

BARON [*perturbed*]: What's the matter? What are you sighing for?

MIRANDOLINA:Oh, it's nothing, signore. It's only that I do try to please and nobody ever seems to be grateful.

BARON [*gently*]: I will not be ungrateful.

MIRANDOLINA:Oh, please don't think I meant anything. It's only that when one does one's duty, one does hope. . . .

BARON:No, no, believe me, I understand. I'm not such a clumsy lout as you may think. I won't give you cause to complain.

[*He pours some wine into the glass*]

MIRANDOLINA:But . . . signore . . . I don't understand. . . .

BARON [*raising his glass*]: Your very good health. [*He drinks.*]

MIRANDOLINA:Thank you. Thank you, signore. You are too good.

BARON: Mm! It is indeed an excellent wine, this.

MIRANDOLINA: Yes, I adore Burgundy myself.

BARON [*offering her the wine*]: Would you care for some?

MIRANDOLINA: Oh! Thank you, signore, but I had better not.

BARON: Have you dined?

MIRANDOLINA: Yes, signore.

BARON: You won't try a little wine?

MIRANDOLINA: Well, it's very kind of you.

BARON: Not at all, the pleasure is mine.

MIRANDOLINA: Then just a little. But I really don't deserve such kindness.

BARON [*to the* SERVANT]: Bring another glass.

MIRANDOLINA: No, no, if you will allow me, I will take this. [*She picks up the Baron's glass.*]

BARON: But I've used that one!

MIRANDOLINA [*laughing*]: Ah, but by drinking from this I'll know what you really think of me!

[*The* SERVANT *puts another glass in front of the* BARON.]

BARON [*aside, as he pours himself some more wine*]: The little hussy!

MIRANDOLINA: Perhaps this wine might upset me if I don't eat something with it. May I have a piece of bread?

BARON: Of course. [*giving her some bread*] There you are.

[MIRANDOLINA, *holding the glass in one hand and the bread in the other, stands awkwardly, as if not knowing what to do with herself.*]

BARON: But how clumsy of me! Won't you sit down?

MIRANDOLINA: Oh, but that would be too much, signore!

BARON: I insist! Besides we are alone. [*to the* SERVANT] Bring a chair.

SERVANT [*aside*]: He must be ill. I've never seen him like this before. [*He places a chair for* MIRANDOLINA *at the table beside the* BARON.]

MIRANDOLINA: Poor me, if the Count or the Marquis knew of this!

BARON: Why?

MIRANDOLINA: A hundred times they've tried to persuade me to eat or drink with them, but I wouldn't.

BARON: Never mind that. Make yourself comfortable.

MIRANDOLINA: I must obey you. [*She sits beside him and puts the wine and bread on the table.*]

BARON [*aside to the* SERVANT]: Don't you tell a soul about this!

SERVANT [*aside to the* BARON]: Never fear! [*to himself*] This *is* something new!

MIRANDOLINA [*raising her glass*]: To the Baron! May all his wishes come true. [*She drinks.*]

BARON: I thank you – most charming hostess.

MIRANDOLINA: And down with women!

BARON: What's that?

MIRANDOLINA: I know you can't stand the sight of women.

BARON: That's true. I never *was* able to. . . .

MIRANDOLINA: May you never change.

BARON: I . . . er . . . I wouldn't like you to . . . [*He glances at the* SERVANT.]

MIRANDOLINA: You wouldn't like me to what?

BARON: Listen. [*He leans across to her and speaks into her ear*] I wouldn't like you to make me feel differently.

MIRANDOLINA: I, signore? But how could I do that?

BARON [*to the* SERVANT]: Go and boil a couple of eggs. Bring them in when they're ready.

SERVANT: D'you want them soft- or hard-boiled?

BARON: Any way you like! Get out!

SERVANT [*aside*]: He's warming up all right. [*Exit*]

BARON: Mirandolina, you are a very attractive young lady.

MIRANDOLINA: Oh, signore, now you're making fun of me!

BARON: Listen. What I'm going to tell you is the truth, the complete truth. And it's something you should be very proud of.

MIRANDOLINA: Oh, please do tell me!

BARON: You are the very first woman I have ever enjoyed talking to.

MIRANDOLINA: Oh, I wouldn't say that's anything for me

to be especially proud of, signore. You see, signore, it takes all sorts to make a world, and when you meet somebody you've got something in common with, you seem to recognize them instinctively. It's a feeling, a sort of sympathy. D'you know, I myself've a feeling for you which I've never had for anybody else.

BARON: D'you want to rob me of my peace of mind?

MIRANDOLINA: Oh, come, signore, you're a sensible man. Be sensible. Don't give in to weakness like others do. Indeed, if I thought you might, I wouldn't come here again. Though I must confess that I too . . . feel . . . something *I've* never felt before. But *I'm* not going to make a fool of myself over any man. And certainly not over a man who hates women and who maybe's just leading me on for a bit of fun. May I have a little more Burgundy, Illustrious Signor?

BARON: What? . . . Oh, yes, of course! [*He takes her glass and pours more wine into it.*]

MIRANDOLINA [*aside*]: He's ripe for picking.

BARON [*giving her the glass of wine*]: There you are.

MIRANDOLINA: Thank you. But aren't you having any yourself?

BARON: Yes, I'll have some. [*aside*] I'd best get drunk. One devil may chase out the other. [*He pours more wine into his own glass.*]

MIRANDOLINA [*coaxingly*]: Signor Baron?

BARON: What's the matter?

MIRANDOLINA: Touch glasses! [*She touches his glass with hers*] To good friendship!

BARON [*rather despairingly*]: To good friendship.

MIRANDOLINA: To all who are in love with each other . . . frankly and sincerely. Drink!

BARON: Your health. . . .

[*The* MARQUIS *enters.*]

MARQUIS: Here I am! Whose health are we drinking to?

BARON [*discomposed*]: What d'you want, Marquis?

MARQUIS: Excuse me, old fellow. But I did give you a shout but nobody answered.

MIRANDOLINA [*making to go*]: If you will allow me. . . .

BARON [*to* MIRANDOLINA]: No don't go! [*to the* MARQUIS] Look here! I don't walk into *your* room uninvited.

MARQUIS: Do forgive me. Between friends, you know. And I thought you were alone. Delighted you're getting acquainted with our charming hostess. What d'you say now, eh? A real pearl, isn't she?

MIRANDOLINA: I came here, signore, to wait upon the Baron. A little faintness came over me and he kindly gave me a glass of Burgundy to put me right.

MARQUIS [*to the* BARON]: Is that Burgundy?

BARON: It is.

MARQUIS: Real Burgundy?

BARON: Well I'm paying enough for it.

MARQUIS: Leave it to me. Let me try it and I'll soon tell you if it's the real thing or not.

BARON [*going to the door and calling*]: Ho, there!

[*The* SERVANT *enters with the eggs.*]

BARON: A small glass for the Marquis.

MARQUIS: Needn't be small. Burgundy's not a liqueur. You can't judge it properly unless you have enough of it.

SERVANT: Here are the eggs, signore. [*He puts them on the table.*]

BARON: That will be all, then.

MARQUIS: What have you got there?

BARON: Eggs.

MARQUIS: Take 'em away. Can't stand 'em.

[*The* SERVANT *puts the eggs on the sideboard.*]

MIRANDOLINA: Marquis, if the Baron will permit, won't you taste this little ragout made with my own hands?

MARQUIS: Rather! [*to the* SERVANT] Well? What about a chair?

[*The* SERVANT *places a chair for the Marquis at the table and places a wine glass for him.*]

MARQUIS: I'll need a fork.

BARON [*to the* SERVANT]: Get him the lot.

[*The* SERVANT *lays cutlery in front of the* MARQUIS.]

MIRANDOLINA [*rising*]: I'm feeling much better now, Baron. I will go.

MARQUIS: Do me the pleasure of staying a little.

MIRANDOLINA: But, signore, I have my work to attend to. And then the Baron. . . .

MARQUIS [*to the* BARON]: D'you mind if she stays a little longer?

BARON: What do you want with her?

MARQUIS: I want you both to try a little Cyprus wine of mine. You won't find its equal anywhere. And I'd particularly like to hear Mirandolina's opinion on it.

BARON [*to* MIRANDOLINA]: Then you'd better stay. To please the Marquis.

MIRANDOLINA: The Signor Marquis must excuse me.

MARQUIS [*eating*]: You don't want to taste it?

MIRANDOLINA: Another time, your Excellency.

BARON: I said you'd better stay.

MIRANDOLINA [*to the* BARON]: Are you ordering me to?

BARON: I am asking you to.

MIRANDOLINA [*sitting again*]: I will do as you ask.

BARON [*aside*]: She really does want to please me!

MARQUIS [*eating*]: Excellent! What a superb dish! Most savoury ragout I've ever tasted.

BARON [*softly to* MIRANDOLINA]: The Marquis is jealous because you're sitting close to me.

MIRANDOLINA [*softly to the* BARON]: He doesn't mean a thing to me.

BARON [*as above*]: So you are a man-hater then?

MIRANDOLINA [*as above*]: Yes! Just like you're a woman-hater!

BARON [*as above*]: Is this how women are to have their revenge on me?

MIRANDOLINA [*as above*]: What *do* you mean, signore?

BARON [*as above*]: You artful little rogue! You know what I mean!

MARQUIS [*raising his glass of Burgundy*]: My friend, your very good health.

BARON: Well? What d'you think of it?

MARQUIS: With all respect, I think nothing of it. You shall try my Cyprus wine.

BARON: But where is it, this Cyprus wine?

MARQUIS: I have it here. I carry it with me. You'll enjoy this. This is something worth tasting. [*He takes a tiny bottle from his pocket.*]

MIRANDOLINA: From the look of that, Marquis, you're making sure we don't get drunk on your wine.

MARQUIS: On this? But this isn't to be drunk. It's to be tasted! Drop by drop! [*to the* SERVANT] Well? Where are the glasses?

[*He opens the bottle. The* SERVANT *brings some glasses.*]

MARQUIS: Eh, those are too big! Haven't you any smaller? [*He covers the bottle with his hand.*]

BARON [*to the* SERVANT]: Bring the liqueur glasses.

MIRANDOLINA: Couldn't we just have a smell of it?

MARQUIS [*smelling it*]: Beautiful! A most soothing fragrance!

[*The* SERVANT *puts three tiny glasses on the table. Very slowly and carefully the Marquis pours a little of his wine into each of the glasses. He hands one to the* BARON, *one to* MIRANDOLINA *and keeps one himself. He then carefully recorks the bottle.*

MARQUIS [*taking a sip of his wine*]: Ah! Nectar! Ambrosia! Wine of the gods!

BARON [*softly to* MIRANDOLINA]: What is this stuff?

MIRANDOLINA [*softly to the* BARON]: Dregs from bottles.

MARQUIS [*to the* BARON]: Well? What d'you say?

BARON: Good. Very fine.

MARQUIS: Ah! [*to* MIRANDOLINA] Mirandolina! You like it?

MIRANDOLINA: I, signore? I can't say what I don't think. No, I don't like it. I think it's horrible and I'm not going to pretend I like it. It may be a useful thing to be able to pretend and deceive. But the person who can deceive in one thing can deceive in another.

BARON [*aside*]: That sounds like one for me. Though I don't see why.

MARQUIS: Then you're no judge of this sort of wine, Mirandolina. I am sorry for you. You liked that handkerchief I gave you. You were able to appreciate that. But you know nothing about Cyprus wine. [*He goes on sipping from his glass.*]

MIRANDOLINA [*softly to the* BARON]: Such boasting!

BARON [*softly to* MIRANDOLINA]: Not like me.

MIRANDOLINA [*as above*]: You boast about your contempt for women.

BARON [*as above*]: And you about all the men who run after you.

MIRANDOLINA [*as above, coquettishly*]: Not all men.

BARON [*as above, with some feeling*]: Yes – all.

MARQUIS [*to the servant*]: You there! Three clean glasses. [*The servant brings three more.*]

MIRANDOLINA: No more for me.

MARQUIS: Don't worry. This isn't for you. [*He pours some Cyprus wine into the three glasses.*] Now, my man, with your master's permission, go to the Count of Albafiorita and tell him from me – loudly so everyone can hear – that I'd like him to come and try a little of my Cyprus wine.

SERVANT: Certainly, signore. [*aside*] He'll not get drunk on that. [*Exit*]

BARON: Marquis, you're really too generous.

MARQUIS: I? You should ask Mirandolina about that.

MIRANDOLINA: Oh, quite!

MARQUIS: Has the Baron seen the handkerchief?

MIRANDOLINA: No.

MARQUIS [*to the* BARON]: Get her to show it you. [*He puts his bottle of wine, of which he has used hardly any, back in his pocket.*] The flavour of this wine will stay with me all evening.

MIRANDOLINA: Mind it doesn't go to your head, Marquis.

MARQUIS [*to* MIRANDOLINA]: Ah! If you only knew what does go to my head!

MIRANDOLINA: What?

MARQUIS: Those lovely eyes of yours!

MIRANDOLINA: Is that so?

MARQUIS: Baron, I'm in love with her. Completely. Irrevocably.

BARON: Then I'm sorry for you.

MARQUIS: But *you've* never known the meaning of love. Ah, if only you had, how you would sympathize with me!

BARON: Yes – I do sympathize with you.

MARQUIS: But you've no idea how wild with jealousy it makes me. Oh, I don't mind her being here with you, of course. I know your feelings in the matter. If I didn't I wouldn't let her near you for a hundred thousand crowns.

BARON [*aside*]: This fellow's beginning to annoy me.

[*The* SERVANT *enters carrying a bottle on a tray.*]

SERVANT [*to the* MARQUIS]: The Count thanks your Excellency and sends you this bottle of Canary wine.

MARQUIS: What! He puts his dam' Canary wine on a par with my Cyprus wine! Let's see it! The fellow's mad! [*He takes the bottle, uncorks it and smells it.*] Pigwash! I can tell by the smell! [*He rises with the bottle and begins walking to the door.*]

BARON [*to the* MARQUIS]: Taste it first.

MARQUIS: Taste it? Taste this pigswill! It's a dam' insult to offer such stuff to anybody. This is the last straw. He's always trying to go one better than me. Trying to show me up. Trying to provoke me. Well, this time he's gone too far. Mirandolina, if you don't turn that Count out of this Inn, I'll . . . I'll . . . well, there'll be no telling what I won't do! That fellow's asking for it. I am I, and I'll not be insulted like this! [*He goes out taking the bottle with him.*]

BARON: That fellow's going crazy.

MIRANDOLINA: I don't know: he didn't forget to take the bottle with him.

BARON: He's mad, I tell you. And it's you've made him like that.

MIRANDOLINA: Now, really! Am I the sort to make men mad?

BARON [*feverishly*]: Yes, you are!

MIRANDOLINA [*rising*]: Signor Baron, with your permission . . .

BARON: Stay where you are!

MIRANDOLINA [*going*]: Excuse me. I make nobody go mad.

BARON [*rising but remaining near the table*]: Listen to me.

MIRANDOLINA [*going towards the door*]: Pardon me.

BARON [*commandingly*]: Stop, I tell you!

MIRANDOLINA [*turning, haughtily*]: What do you want with me?

BARON [*confused*]: Nothing . . . let us have another glass of Burgundy.

MIRANDOLINA: Well, hurry up, then. Be quick because I'm going.

BARON: Sit down.

MIRANDOLINA: Standing, standing!

BARON [*gently giving her the glass*]: Take it then.

MIRANDOLINA: I'll give you a toast before I go. A little verse my grandmother taught me.

> Wine and Love are for you and me!
> Wine in the mouth, but Love in the eyes.
> I drink the wine: but with my eyes,
> I look at you – as you look at me.

[*Exit*]

BARON: I *do* like that! Now come here and listen to me. . . . Why, the little devil, she's escaped! She's gone! And left me with a hundred devils to torment me.

SERVANT: Shall I put the fruit on the table?

BARON: The devil take you as well!

SERVANT: Yes, signore. [*Exit*]

BARON: 'I drink the wine: but with my eyes,
                I look at you – as you look at me.'

What the devil is that supposed to mean? But what else can it mean? The little villain's out to get me! And she knows how to do it, the charming little rogue she is! If I stay here she'll be twisting me round her little finger. Leghorn! I must leave for Leghorn tomorrow! And never set eyes on

her again! And she'd better not dare come back in here.
Damn all women. I swear I'll never set foot again in any
place where there's a woman! But what about tonight? If
I sleep in this house tonight who knows what mightn't
happen? Mirandolina could easily finish me off. Ruined,
that's what I'd be. [*He thinks*] Yes, I'll do it! I'll act like a
man!

   [*The* SERVANT *enters.*]

SERVANT: Signore!
BARON: Now what is it?
SERVANT: The Marquis is waiting in his room. He'd like to
speak to you.
BARON: What's that imbecile after now? He's not getting any
more money out of me, that's certain. Oh, let him wait.
When he's fed up waiting, he'll give up. Go and find that
waiter and tell him to bring my bill at once.
SERVANT [*about to go*]: Certainly.
BARON: Wait! And get the luggage ready for us to leave in
two hours.
SERVANT: You're leaving?
BARON: Yes. Bring my sword and hat and don't let the
Marquis see you.
SERVANT: But suppose he sees me getting the luggage?
BARON: Say anything. You understand me?
SERVANT: Yes, but I don't like leaving Mirandolina like this.
  [*Exit*]
BARON [*alone*]: Neither do I. The very thought of leaving her
fills me with a sadness I've never known before. But that's
all the more reason why I must go. And the sooner the
better. Women! This only shows how right I was! Even
when they try to be helpful, all they do is cause trouble!

   [FABRIZIO *enters.*]

FABRIZIO: Is it true, signore, you want your bill?
BARON: Yes. Have you brought it?
FABRIZIO: The mistress of the Inn is making it out now.
BARON: She makes out the bills?

FABRIZIO: Oh, yes, signore. She's always done that, even when her father was alive. She can do the accounts better than any clerk could.

BARON [*aside*]: What an astonishing woman she is!

FABRIZIO: But do you have to leave so suddenly?

BARON: Yes . . . urgent business matters, you understand.

FABRIZIO: You won't forget the waiter then, signore?

BARON: Bring me the bill and you'll find I know what to do.

FABRIZIO: You want it brought to you here?

BARON: Yes, in here! I'm not leaving my room for the time being.

FABRIZIO: Yes, you're wise. That old skinflint the Marquis is on the look-out for you. He's a fine one. Keeps trying to make love to the mistress. Lot of good that'll do him. Mirandolina's going to be my wife.

BARON [*savagely*]: The bill!

FABRIZIO: At once, signore. [*Exit*]

BARON [*alone*]: The whole dam' lot of them are crazy about Mirandolina! No wonder I began to fall for her myself. But I'll get away. *I'll* not become like the rest of them – fascinated by this strange power of hers.

[MIRANDOLINA *enters with the bill in her hand.*]

MIRANDOLINA [*sadly*]: Signore. . . .

BARON: What is it, Mirandolina?

MIRANDOLINA [*remaining by the door*]: Excuse me. . . .

BARON: Please do come in.

MIRANDOLINA [*sadly*]: You sent for your bill. I have brought it.

BARON: Give it to me.

MIRANDOLINA: There you are. [*She wipes her eyes with her apron as she gives it to him.*]

BARON: What's the matter? Are you crying?

MIRANDOLINA: It's nothing, signore. Some smoke must have got in my eyes.

BARON: Some . . . smoke in your eyes? Oh? . . . Well . . . Yes, well, what does the bill come to? [*He looks at it.*] Twenty paoli? For four days only twenty paoli?

MIRANDOLINA: That is your bill.

BARON: But those two special dishes you gave me today? You haven't put those down?

MIRANDOLINA: Forgive me. What I give, I do not charge for.

BARON: *You've* been giving *me* presents?

MIRANDOLINA: Please forgive me. And accept them as a token of. . . . [*She covers her face as if to hide her tears.*]

BARON: But what's the matter?

MIRANDOLINA: It . . . it may be the smoke . . . or something wrong with my eyes.

BARON: I do hope it's not through cooking those two wonderful dishes for me.

MIRANDOLINA: Oh, if it were I would suffer it . . . gladly. . . . [*She appears to be trying to prevent herself bursting into tears.*]

BARON [*aside*]: I must get away! [*aloud*] Here are two ducats. Get something with them to remember me by . . . and think of me sometimes . . . with pity. [*Without speaking,* MIRANDOLINA *collapses on to one of the chairs as if in a faint.*] Mirandolina! Oh, good heavens, she's fainted! Mirandolina! Can she really be in love with me? So quickly? But why not? Aren't I in love with her? Oh, darling Mirandolina! . . . What am I saying! I? Calling a woman 'darling'? But if she's fainted, and because of me . . . oh, how lovely you are! If only I'd something to bring you round. I've no women's things, no scents, no smelling salts. Ho, there! Is anybody there? Where is everybody? I'll go myself! Oh, my poor darling, how adorable you are! [*Exit*]

MIRANDOLINA [*sitting up*]: At last! I have him! I thought that would do it. When everything else fails, there's nothing like a good fainting fit. It always brings men to their knees. He's coming back. Here goes! [*She collapses as before.*]

BARON [*returning with a glass of water*]: Here I am! Here I am! She hasn't come to yet! Oh, how she must love me! Perhaps if I sprinkle a little water on her face. [*He throws water on her face and she begins to move.*] There, there, my darling, I am here. I will never leave you now.

[*The* SERVANT *enters carrying the sword and hat.*]

SERVANT [*to the* BARON]: Here are your sword and hat.

BARON [*to the* SERVANT]: Get out!

SERVANT: The luggage . . .

BARON: Go away, damn you!

SERVANT: Oh! . . . Mirandolina. . . .

BARON: Get out or I'll break your neck! [*The* SERVANT *goes.*] She's still unconscious! Her dear little forehead is all moist and wet. Oh, Mirandolina, dear Mirandolina! Open your eyes! Speak to me!

[*The* MARQUIS *and the* COUNT *enter.*]

MARQUIS: Baron!

COUNT: Oh, I say!

BARON [*aside, frantically*]: Damn and blast them!

MARQUIS: Mirandolina, it is I!

MIRANDOLINA [*getting up*]: Oh, dear! Oh, dear me!

MARQUIS: There! I've brought her round.

COUNT: I congratulate you, Baron.

MARQUIS: Yes, dam' quick work – for somebody who can't stand women!

BARON: What the devil d'you mean?

COUNT: So you've fallen, too?

BARON: Go to hell, the lot of you!

[*He throws the glass at them. It breaks in pieces on the floor. He then rushes furiously out of the room.*]

COUNT: The Baron's gone mad! [*He rushes out after him.*]

MARQUIS: No! That was an insult! To me! I demand satisfaction! [*He also rushes out after them.*]

MIRANDOLINA [*alone*]: Victory at last! He's on fire, in flames, burning to red-hot cinders! Now all that's left to do, to finish him off, is to make my triumph public. Everyone shall see how I have upheld the honour of my sex and taught a lesson to all such presumptuous men! [*Exit*]

Act Three

[*The same as Act One. On the table a pile of linen is waiting to be ironed.*]

MIRANDOLINA [*alone*]: I must stop amusing myself for a moment and get some work done. I'd better iron this laundry and put it away. [*She calls softly*] Oh, Fabrizio!

FABRIZIO [*entering*]: Yes, signorina?

MIRANDOLINA: Be nice to me – and bring me the hot iron.

FABRIZIO [*morosely, turning to go*]: Yes, signorina.

MIRANDOLINA: You don't mind, do you?

FABRIZIO: Not at all, signorina. I eat your bread, so I must obey you.

MIRANDOLINA [*as he is about to go*]: No, wait. Listen to me. There is no 'must' between you and me. You are not obliged to obey me in anything. You see, Fabrizio, I know what you do for me, you do most willingly . . . and as for me . . . but no more of this at the moment.

FABRIZIO: As for me, yes! For you I would carry irons all day. But I see that it's all wasted on you.

MIRANDOLINA: How d'you mean – wasted? In what way am I ungrateful?

FABRIZIO: A man's no use to you if he's poor. The nobility are more to your liking.

MIRANDOLINA: You're mad! Why, if *you* knew what *I* know! Off with you and fetch me that iron.

FABRIZIO: I know what I've seen . . . with my own eyes. . . .

MIRANDOLINA: Will you get along and stop talking nonsense. Bring me the iron.

FABRIZIO: All right, I'm going. But I'll be going for good soon. [*He goes towards the door.*]

MIRANDOLINA [*pretending to speak to herself but meaning to be heard*]: With some men, the more you love them the worse it is for you.

FABRIZIO [*stopping and turning, and speaking tenderly*]: What did you say?

MIRANDOLINA: Are you getting that iron or aren't you?

FABRIZIO: Yes, yes, I'm getting it. [*aside*] I don't understand. One minute she's leading me on. And the next giving me the cold shoulder. I just don't understand. [*Exit*]

MIRANDOLINA [*alone*]: Poor lad, he can't help doing what I ask. But it does amuse me – making men do what I want. This Baron, for instance. Yes, this dear enemy of women! Just what couldn't I make him do now, if I wanted to!

[*The Baron's* SERVANT *enters.*]

SERVANT: Signorina Mirandolina?

MIRANDOLINA: Yes, what is it, friend?

SERVANT: My master's compliments and he's sent me to see how you are.

MIRANDOLINA: Tell him I am very well.

SERVANT: He says he thinks you should drink a little of this. It's some Melissa spirits. He's sure it will do you good.

[*He gives her a small gold bottle.*]

MIRANDOLINA: But – this bottle! It's made of gold!

SERVANT: That's right, signorina, real gold. I can vouch for that.

MIRANDOLINA: How is it he didn't give me some of this before? When I had that horrible fainting spell?

SERVANT: Oh, he didn't have that bottle then.

MIRANDOLINA: How does he come to have it now?

SERVANT: Between ourselves – I'll tell you. He's just sent me out to find a goldsmith. He bought that bottle from him. Paid twenty zecchini. Then he sent me to the chemist to buy the Melissa spirits.

[MIRANDOLINA *breaks into uncontrollable laughter.*]

SERVANT: Why are you laughing?

MIRANDOLINA: Because he sends me the remedy when I'm better.

SERVANT: It will do for another time.

MIRANDOLINA: I'll drink a little, to be on the safe side. [*She drinks and then offers him the bottle back again.*] There you are. Thank him for me.

SERVANT: But the bottle is yours.

MIRANDOLINA: How mine?

SERVANT: That's why he bought it. Just for you.

MIRANDOLINA: Just . . . for me?

SERVANT: Yes. Please don't let on I told you!

MIRANDOLINA: Take the bottle back and say I'm much obliged.

SERVANT: Oh, but . . .

MIRANDOLINA: Take it back, d'you hear? I don't want it.

SERVANT: You *want* to offend him, is that it?

MIRANDOLINA: Don't talk nonsense. Just do as I say. Take it back.

SERVANT: Well, this beats everything! All right, I'll take it. [*aside*] What a woman! To refuse twenty zecchini! I'll never come across another like her. [*Exit*]

MIRANDOLINA [*alone*]: So! He's roasted, basted and done to a turn! But not for what I can get out of him. Oh, no! All I want is to make him admit that women can have power over men, without wanting to get anything out of them.

[FABRIZIO *enters, carrying the iron.*]

FABRIZIO [*distantly*]: Here is the iron.

MIRANDOLINA: Is it nice and hot?

FABRIZIO: Yes, signorina. Flaming hot. Like *me!*

MIRANDOLINA: Now what's the matter with you?

FABRIZIO: This Illustrious Baron – that's what's the matter with me. He's been sending you messages and presents! His servant's just told me.

MIRANDOLINA: Yes, *signore*, he has. He sent me a gold bottle. And I sent it back.

FABRIZIO: You sent it back?

MIRANDOLINA: Yes. Ask that servant of his, if you like.

FABRIZIO: Why did you send it back?

MIRANDOLINA: Because . . . Fabrizio . . . I can't say. . . . Look, can't we talk of something else?

FABRIZIO: Mirandolina . . . please . . . have pity on me.

MIRANDOLINA: Go away! Let me do my ironing!

FABRIZIO: I'm not in your way.

MIRANDOLINA: Well, go and heat another iron . . . and then bring it here.

FABRIZIO: Very well. But you must believe that I. . . .

MIRANDOLINA: If you say another word you'll drive me crazy!

FABRIZIO: All right – I'll keep silent. [*aside*] It's she who'll drive me crazy. Because I love her. [*Exit*]

MIRANDOLINA [*alone*]: That sorted itself out quite well. By refusing the Baron's gold bottle, I've pleased Fabrizio at any rate. [*She goes on ironing.*]

[*The* BARON *enters.*]

BARON [*aside*]: So, there she is! Oh, what the devil made me start looking for her!

MIRANDOLINA [*aside, as she sees him out of the corner of her eye and continues ironing*]: Here he is! Here he is!

BARON: Mirandolina.

MIRANDOLINA [*ironing*]: Oh, there you are, Baron! I beg your pardon, I didn't see you.

BARON: How are you?

MIRANDOLINA [*going on ironing and not looking at him*]: Very well, thank you.

BARON: You have made me very unhappy.

MIRANDOLINA [*glancing up at him for a moment*]: How, signore?

BARON: By refusing a little bottle I sent you.

MIRANDOLINA [*ironing*]: What did you *think* I'd do?

BARON: Keep it for when you might need it.

MIRANDOLINA [*ironing*]: I'm not subject to fainting spells, thank heaven. In fact I've *never* experienced before what happened to me today.

BARON: Dear Mirandolina . . . I shouldn't like to think I was the cause of it.

MIRANDOLINA [*ironing*]: Well, I'm afraid you were.

BARON [*deeply moved*]: Was I? Really?

MIRANDOLINA [*ironing away furiously*]: You made me drink that cursed Burgundy. And it upset me.

BARON [*almost speechless with mortification*]: Is that all you mean?

MIRANDOLINA [*ironing*]: Yes, that. And nothing else. I'll never set foot in your room again.

BARON [*lovingly*]: Ah, now I understand. You don't want to be seen in my *room* any more. So, that's all it is! You had me quite mystified. Yes, of course, now I understand. But come to me *now*, my darling, and you will find everything will please you.

MIRANDOLINA: This iron's getting cold. [*calling loudly*] Fabrizio! If the other iron's hot, bring it here.

BARON: Come, be nice to me now. Take this bottle.

MIRANDOLINA [*scornfully, going on ironing*]: Signor Baron, I do not accept presents.

BARON: You do from the Count.

MIRANDOLINA [*ironing*]: That's different. I have to from him so as not to offend him.

BARON: So you don't mind offending me?

MIRANDOLINA: What's it matter to you if a woman offends you? You can't stand the sight of them.

BARON: Ah, Mirandolina, that's no longer true.

MIRANDOLINA: Signor Baron, are you affected by the moon?

BARON: Affected by the moon! How can you! No, this change in me is a miracle wrought by your charm and your beauty.

[MIRANDOLINA *laughs loudly and goes on ironing.*]

BARON: You laugh?

MIRANDOLINA: Shouldn't I? You say something funny and expect me not to laugh?

BARON: You little rascal! Being funny, was I? Come, take this bottle.

MIRANDOLINA [*ironing*]: Thank you – no.

BARON: Take it or I'll lose my temper.

MIRANDOLINA [*calling loudly and emphatically*]: Fabrizio! The iron!

BARON [*angrily*]: Are you taking it or aren't you?

MIRANDOLINA [*taking the bottle and throwing it scornfully into the linen basket*]: Temper! Temper!

BARON: How dare you do that!

MIRANDOLINA [*calling loudly as before*]: Fabrizio!

[FABRIZIO *enters carrying the iron. He bridles jealously at the sight of the* BARON.]

FABRIZIO: Here I am.

MIRANDOLINA [*taking the iron*]: Have you made it nice and hot?

FABRIZIO [*frigidly*]: Yes, signorina.

MIRANDOLINA [*tenderly, to* FABRIZIO]: What is the matter? You seem upset.

FABRIZIO: It's nothing, signorina. Nothing at all.

MIRANDOLINA [*as before*]: Aren't you feeling well?

FABRIZIO: Give me the other iron. If you want it heating.

MIRANDOLINA [*as before*]: I really don't think you look at all well.

BARON: Give him the iron and let him get out of here!

MIRANDOLINA [*to the* BARON]: I think a lot of him, you understand. In fact, I don't know what I'd do without him.

BARON [*aside, in a frenzy of fury*]: I can't stand much more of this!

MIRANDOLINA [*giving the iron to* FABRIZIO]: Take it, my dear, and heat it for me.

FABRIZIO [*tenderly*]: Ah! Signorina! I would do. . . .

MIRANDOLINA [*chasing him out*]: Hurry! Hurry!

FABRIZIO [*aside, as he goes*]: What sort of a life is this! Oh, I can't stand much more of this! [*Exit*]

BARON [*to* MIRANDOLINA]: Extraordinarily kind to your waiter, aren't you?

MIRANDOLINA: And just what d'you mean by that?

BARON: Obviously you're madly in love with him.

MIRANDOLINA [*frowning*]: I – in love with a waiter? Obviously *you* don't know me very well. When I want to fall in love, I shan't throw myself away so cheaply.

BARON: Ah, you are worthy of the love of a king!

MIRANDOLINA [*ironing*]: The king of barons or the king of waiters?

BARON: I'm not joking, Mirandolina. Talk seriously!

MIRANDOLINA [*ironing*]: All right, talk. I'm listening.

BARON: Can't you stop ironing a moment?

MIRANDOLINA: I'm sorry. It's important I have this linen ready for tomorrow.

BARON: That linen's more important to you than I am?

MIRANDOLINA [*ironing*]: Certainly.

BARON: You mean that?

MIRANDOLINA [*ironing*]: Of course. This linen's some use to me. You're not.

BARON: On the contrary, I could be of far more use to you.

MIRANDOLINA: You – who can't stand the sight of women!

BARON: Will you stop tormenting me. You've had your revenge. I respect you. I respect all women like you – if there are any more. I respect you, I love you. I beg you to have pity on me.

MIRANDOLINA [*ironing hastily she knocks a cuff on to the floor*]: Yes, signore, let us take all that for granted.

BARON [*picking up the cuff and giving it her*]: You must believe me. . . .

MIRANDOLINA: Please don't trouble yourself.

BARON: You deserve to be waited on hand and foot.

[MIRANDOLINA *laughs loudly.*]

BARON: You laugh?

MIRANDOLINA: Because you are being funny again.

BARON: Mirandolina, I can't suffer any more!

MIRANDOLINA: Are you ill?

BARON: Yes, I do feel faint.

MIRANDOLINA [*throwing him his bottle contemptuously*]: Take some of your Melissa spirits then.

BARON: Stop treating me like this! I love you. I swear it. [*He tries to take her hand and she burns his with the iron*] OW!

MIRANDOLINA: I'm sorry – I didn't do that on purpose.

BARON: Never mind. It's nothing. Nothing to what you've already done to me.

MIRANDOLINA:How, signore?

BARON:My heart! You have wounded my heart!

MIRANDOLINA [*laughing*]:Fabrizio!

BARON:Stop calling that fellow!

MIRANDOLINA:But I need the other iron.

BARON:Then wait and I'll call my servant.

MIRANDOLINA [*continuing to call*]:Fabrizio!

BARON:If that fellow comes in here again, I'll crack his skull for him!

MIRANDOLINA:This is going beyond a joke! Aren't my own servants allowed to work for me now?

BARON:Call another one then. I can't stand the sight of that fellow.

MIRANDOLINA [*moving away from the table with the iron in her hand*]:You're getting a little too close, Signor Baron.

BARON:Have pity on me! I don't know what I'm doing!

MIRANDOLINA:I'll go into the kitchen. Then you'll be all right.

BARON:Oh, my beloved, don't leave me!

MIRANDOLINA [*moving further away from him*]: This is getting better and better!

BARON [*following her*]:Have pity on me!

MIRANDOLINA [*retreating before him*]:So I'm not even allowed to call whom I choose?

BARON [*following her*]: All right, I admit it. I'm jealous of him.

MIRANDOLINA [*aside, still retreating*]: Now I've only to make him sit up and beg.

BARON [*following her*]: I've never been in love like this before.

MIRANDOLINA [*retreating*]: *I've* never been ordered about like this before.

BARON [*following her*]: But I wasn't ordering you – I was . . . begging you.

MIRANDOLINA [*turning proudly*]: And what is it you're begging from me?

BARON:Love . . . compassion . . . pity.

MIRANDOLINA:This morning you couldn't bear the sight of a woman. Now you're begging for love and pity? Oh, no, it's not possible. You can't be serious! I don't believe a word of it! [*Exit*]

BARON [*alone*]: Damnation on the moment I first looked at that woman! I've fallen into the trap and I'm done for!

[*The* MARQUIS *enters.*]

MARQUIS: Baron, you have insulted me!

BARON: I'm sorry, it was an accident.

MARQUIS: I must say I'm surprised at you.

BARON: After all, the glass didn't hit you.

MARQUIS: A drop of water has stained my coat.

BARON: I repeat – I'm sorry.

MARQUIS: It was a damned impertinence.

BARON: I didn't do it on purpose. For the third time – I'm sorry.

MARQUIS: I demand satisfaction.

BARON: If you won't accept my apologies, if you require satisfaction – I am ready. I am not afraid of you.

MARQUIS [*changing his tone*]: It's just that I'm a little worried the stain may not come out.

BARON [*disdainfully*]: When a gentleman has apologized, what more can he do?

MARQUIS: Well, if you didn't do it deliberately to annoy me, let us forget about it.

BARON: I repeat I'm quite prepared to give you satisfaction.

MARQUIS: No, no, let's forget all about it.

BARON [*exploding*]: You ignorant snob!

MARQUIS: I say, that's not playing the game, what? I've got over my annoyance so what've you to be annoyed about?

BARON: You've caught me in a bad mood.

MARQUIS: I sympathize. I know what your trouble is, all right.

BARON: You mind your own business.

MARQUIS: Yes, you've got it badly, haven't you, Signor woman-hater?

BARON: What the devil are you talking about?

MARQUIS: You're in love.

BARON: Go to hell!

MARQUIS: Why try to hide it?

BARON: Keep out of my way, d'you hear? Or, by heaven, you'll be sorry. [*Exit*]

MARQUIS [*alone*]: Yes, he's in love. Ashamed of it and doesn't want anyone to know. Or perhaps he doesn't want anyone to know because he's afraid of me and what I might do to him if I thought he was my rival. It's a nuisance about this stain. These women usually have things for removing stains. [*He searches in the basket and then on the table and sees the bottle.*] What a beautiful little bottle! Is it gold or just imitation? It'll be imitation. If it was real gold it wouldn't be lying about here. If it contained eau de cologne, that might take this stain out. [*He opens it, smells it and then tastes it.*] No, it's Melissa spirits. That might do. I'll try it. I know, I'll go and ask those foreign ladies who are staying here to help me get this stain out. [*He goes out carrying the bottle in his hand.*]

[*The Baron's* SERVANT *enters and begins searching in the basket, on the table, and then all round the room.*]

SERVANT: Where the devil can that bottle have got to? [*He continues to search*] Well, I can't see the thing. I'd better go and tell Mirandolina I can't find it. [*Exit*]

[*The* MARQUIS *comes back through another door.*]

MARQUIS: These foreign ladies certainly have a way with them. Still, they seemed very pleased when I let them keep that little bottle. Just as well it wasn't real gold. If the worst comes to the worst, I can always put the matter right. Yes, if Mirandolina wants her little bottle I can always pay her for it – when I can.

[*The* SERVANT *comes back through the other door and begins searching on the table again.*]

MARQUIS [*to the* SERVANT]: What are you looking for, my man?

SERVANT: A little bottle of Melissa spirits. The Signorina

Mirandolina wants it. She says she left it here but I can't find it.

MARQUIS: A little imitation gold bottle?

SERVANT: Oh, no, signore, it was real gold.

MARQUIS: Real gold?

SERVANT [*still searching*]: Of course it was real gold. Didn't I see it bought and paid for? Twenty zecchini it cost.

MARQUIS [*aside*]: Oh, good heavens! And I've given it away as a present to those foreign ladies. [*aloud*] But how did a gold bottle like that come to be left lying about?

SERVANT [*still searching*]: She says she forgot it. But I can't find it.

MARQUIS: Oh, it couldn't possibly be real gold.

SERVANT: It was, I tell you. Perhaps your Excellency has seen it?

MARQUIS: I? I've seen nothing.

SERVANT: Well, I'll just have to tell her it's not here. It's her loss. She should have put it in her pocket. [*Exit*]

MARQUIS [*alone*]: Oh, what a calamity! I've given away a gold bottle worth twenty zecchini. And all because I thought it was imitation gold. What on earth shall I do? If I try to get the bottle back, I'll make myself look ridiculous. If Mirandolina finds out I had it, my honour will be in question. I am a nobleman. I'll simply have to pay her for it. But I've no money.

[*The* COUNT *enters.*]

COUNT: Well, Marquis, what d'you think of the great news?

MARQUIS: What news?

COUNT: That woman-hater of a Baron is in love with Mirandolina.

MARQUIS: Yes, I know. But I'm keeping my eye on him. I'll see he gets nowhere there.

COUNT: But supposing Mirandolina encourages him?

MARQUIS: Impossible. She wouldn't do such a thing to me. She knows who I am. She knows all I've done for her.

COUNT: I've done more for her than you. But it's not counting much with her. She's definitely encouraging him, paying him little attentions she's never paid us. But that's the way with women. The more you do for them, the less thanks you get. They run after those who despise them.

MARQUIS: If I thought that were true . . . but it can't be. . . .

COUNT: Why can't it?

MARQUIS: You're not comparing the Baron with me, are you?

COUNT: Well, you saw her yourself sitting at his table with him. Has she ever done that with us? He has to have the best linen. His meals have to be served first. Special dishes have to be made for him with her own hands. Oh, the servants have noticed it, all right. Fabrizio is raging with jealousy. And what about that fainting fit? Whether she put it on or not, wasn't that as plain a declaration of love as you could ask for?

MARQUIS: What! D'you mean she made that delicious ragout for him herself? And gave me rice soup and some tough old beef? You're right! It's an insult, that's what it is! An insult to me, of all people!

COUNT: And what about me? After all I've spent on her?

MARQUIS: And me! Present after present I've given her. I even gave her a glass of my precious Cyprus wine. The Baron hasn't given her a fraction of what we have.

COUNT: Well, of course, he has given her one present.

MARQUIS: What? What has he given her?

COUNT: A gold bottle – containing Melissa spirits.

MARQUIS [aside]: Oh, good heavens! [aloud] How d'you know that?

COUNT: His servant told me.

MARQUIS [aside]: Damn and blast! This will mean trouble with the Baron!

COUNT: I see now she doesn't know the meaning of gratitude. I want nothing more to do with her. I shall leave here immediately.

MARQUIS: Yes, you are quite right. You must go.

COUNT: And you – a nobleman such as you are – you should not stay. You must come with me.

MARQUIS: But . . . where could I go?

COUNT: I'll find somewhere. Let me think.

MARQUIS: Where?

COUNT: We'll go to the house of a friend of mine. It will cost us nothing there.

MARQUIS: All right. I can't refuse such a good friend as yourself.

COUNT: Let us go. Let us both be revenged upon this ungrateful woman.

MARQUIS: Yes, we'll go. [aside] But what about that bottle? I'm a gentleman not a thief.

COUNT: Do not hesitate about it, Marquis. Let us get away from here at once. Back me up and I'll see you don't suffer.

MARQUIS: Well . . . if that's how you feel . . . but in confidence, quite between ourselves . . . my bailiff is a little late sometimes sending me my remittance.

COUNT: And you owe something here?

MARQUIS: Yes – twelve zecchini.

COUNT: Twelve zecchini! You can't have paid anything for months!

MARQUIS: Well, that's how it is. . . . I owe her twelve zecchini. I can't leave without paying. Could you possibly oblige me?

COUNT: Willingly. Here you are. [He takes out his purse.] Twelve zecchini.

MARQUIS: Wait. Now I come to think of it – it's thirteen. [aside] I'd better give the Baron back his zecchino.

COUNT: Twelve, thirteen, it's all the same to me. There you are.

MARQUIS: I'll pay you back as soon as I can.

COUNT: Whenever you please. Money's nothing to me – and to be revenged on that woman I'd spend a thousand crowns.

MARQUIS: Yes, I've never met such ingratitude. After all I've spent on her, to treat me like this!

COUNT: I'll ruin this Inn for her! I've already persuaded those two actresses to leave.

MARQUIS: What two actresses?

COUNT: Those two foreigners that were staying here.

MARQUIS: You mean they weren't – ladies?

COUNT: Good heavens, no!

MARQUIS [*aside*]: My bottle! [*aloud*] Where are they lodging now?

COUNT: At an Inn near the theatre.

MARQUIS [*aside*]: I'll get that bottle back then. [*Exit*]

COUNT [*alone*]: That's got him out of here. Now for the Baron. He won't make a fool of me again. There's a way I can get him out of here as well. And I'll set about it right now. [*Exit*]

[MIRANDOLINA *enters through another of the three doors.*]

MIRANDOLINA [*to herself*]: Oh, dear, this is terrible! What on earth's come over the Baron? The devil must have got into him. If he finds me I'm done for. I'd better lock this door. [*She locks the door she came in by.*] I'm almost sorry I started all this now. It amused me at first, making him run after me. The arrogance of the fellow to despise women like that! But I've taken on more than I bargained for. The way he's going on, my life won't be safe soon. There's nobody here to defend me. Except Fabrizio. Yes, that's what I'll do. I'll tell Fabrizio I'll marry him. But I've promised and promised that so often he's giving up believing me. . . . But it *would* be the best way out of this for me to marry Fabrizio. Then I'd have somebody to protect me who wouldn't be ordering me about all the time.

[*The* BARON *is heard hammering at the door she has just locked.*]

MIRANDOLINA [*to herself*]: What a row! Whoever can it be? [*She goes closer to the door.*]

BARON [*calling, outside*]: Mirandolina!

MIRANDOLINA [*to herself*]: Talk of the devil! It's him!

BARON [*as above*]: Mirandolina! Open the door!

MIRANDOLINA [*to herself*]: Open the door? I'm not such a fool! [*aloud*] What do you want, signore?

BARON: Let me in!

MIRANDOLINA: Go to your room and wait for me. I'll come in a moment.

BARON [*as above*]: Why don't you want to let me in?

MIRANDOLINA: Some guests are arriving. Please go away. I'll be with you directly.

BARON [*going*]: All right. But if you don't come, it'll be the worse for you!

MIRANDOLINA [*to herself*]: Oh, dear, this is getting worse and worse! I'll have to do something to put matters right. Has he really gone? [*She looks through the keyhole.*] Yes, he's gone, all right. But he won't get me coming to his room. [*She goes to one of the other doors and calls*] Fabrizio! [*to herself*] Now what'll I do if Fabrizio decides to have his own back on me and won't . . . oh, there's no danger of that, if I really put myself out to win him round. [*She goes to the third door and calls*] Oh, Fabrizio?

[FABRIZIO *enters.*]

FABRIZIO: Were you calling me?

MIRANDOLINA: Come here! I've something to tell you!

FABRIZIO: I am here.

MIRANDOLINA: What d'you think of this! The Baron has suddenly decided he's madly in love with me!

FABRIZIO: I know all about that.

MIRANDOLINA: You do? You know? And yet I hadn't noticed a thing myself!

FABRIZIO: You poor innocent child! You hadn't noticed? Couldn't you see the way he was looking at you when you were doing your ironing? Couldn't you see how jealous he was of me?

MIRANDOLINA: I'm afraid I *am* a little unsuspecting. But the things he's just been saying to me, Fabrizio! Well, really! They made me blush!

FABRIZIO: It's time you listened to me. This sort of thing is bound to happen to a young woman all on her own, without a father or mother or anyone. It wouldn't happen to you if you were married.

MIRANDOLINA: Yes, I think you're right. As a matter of fact, I had been thinking the same thing.

FABRIZIO: Remember what your father said.

MIRANDOLINA: Yes, I am remembering. I am indeed.

[*The* BARON *is heard banging at the same door again.*]

MIRANDOLINA [*to* FABRIZIO]: There! Listen!
FABRIZIO [*loudly, going towards the door*]: Who is it?
BARON [*outside*]: Open this door!
MIRANDOLINA [*to* FABRIZIO]: It's him. It's the Baron!
FABRIZIO [*going to the door and calling*]: What d'you want?
MIRANDOLINA: Wait till I go.
FABRIZIO [*to* MIRANDOLINA]: What are you frightened of?
MIRANDOLINA: Dear Fabrizio, I don't know ... I ... I ...
   I'm afraid he'll force me against my will.
FABRIZIO: All right, leave this to me.

[MIRANDOLINA *goes out through one of the other doors.*]

BARON [*outside*]: Open this door! D'you hear me?
FABRIZIO: What d'you want, signore? What's all this shout-
   ing for? This is no way to behave in a respectable Inn.
BARON: Open this door! [*He is heard trying to force it.*]
FABRIZIO [*to himself*]: The devil take him! This looks like
   real trouble. [*He goes to one of the other doors and calls.*]
   Ho, there! Is there anyone about?

[*The* MARQUIS *and the* COUNT *enter by the middle door.*]

COUNT [*as he enters*]: What's the matter?
MARQUIS [*following him*]: What's all the noise?
FABRIZIO [*softly, so that the* BARON *may not hear*]: Signore,
   it's the Baron! He's trying to force open that door.
BARON [*outside*]: Open the door! Or I'll break it down!
MARQUIS: He's gone mad! [*to the* COUNT] Let's get out of
   this!
COUNT [*to* FABRIZIO]: Open the door. I've a few words to
   say to that gentleman.
FABRIZIO: Yes, but supposing. . . .
COUNT: That's all right. We are here.
MARQUIS [*aside*]: If there's any trouble, I'm off.

[FABRIZIO *opens the door and the* BARON *rushes in.*]

BARON: Where is she?
FABRIZIO: Who are you looking for, signore?

BARON: Where's Mirandolina?

FABRIZIO: I don't know.

MARQUIS [*aside*]: That's all right: it's not me he's after.

BARON: The little villain! Wait till I find her! [*He strides across the room and sees the* COUNT *and the* MARQUIS.]

COUNT [*to the* BARON]: What's the matter with you?

MARQUIS: We are your friends, Baron.

BARON [*aside*]: The devil! These two mustn't know!

FABRIZIO: What do you want with my mistress, signore?

BARON: That's no business of yours. When I give orders I expect them to be obeyed. That's what I pay for. And by heavens I'll see she learns that.

FABRIZIO: Illustrious signore, what you pay for is to be served in legitimate and honest ways, and that doesn't include expecting that an honourable woman should. . . .

BARON: What are you talking about? What d'you know about it? It's nothing to do with you! I know what I ordered that woman to do and. . . .

FABRIZIO: You ordered her to come to your room.

BARON: You get out of here or I'll break your neck!

FABRIZIO: Let's see you try.

MARQUIS [*to* FABRIZIO]: Quiet!

COUNT [*to* FABRIZIO]: Go away!

FABRIZIO [*angrily*]: But, gentlemen, I tell you he. . . .

BARON [*to* FABRIZIO]: Get out!

MARQUIS: Yes, go on, get out!

COUNT: Out with you, d'you hear?

[*All three of them advance on him to chase him out.*]

FABRIZIO [*aside, as he runs out*]: That suits me all right! [*Exit*]

BARON [*aside, to himself*]: The little devil. Making me wait in my room!

MARQUIS [*aside, to the* COUNT]: What the devil's the matter with him?

COUNT [*aside, to the* MARQUIS]: Can't you see? He's in love with Mirandolina.

BARON [*aside, to himself*]: Has she got this Fabrizio on a string as well? Perhaps talking to him about marriage?

COUNT [*aside, to himself*]: Now for my revenge. [*aloud, to the* BARON] Signor Baron, you should not laugh at the weaknesses of others, when you've such a fragile heart yourself.

BARON: What d'you mean by that?

COUNT: I know why you're so angry.

BARON [*to the* MARQUIS]: What's he talking about?

MARQUIS: My dear friend, I know nothing about it.

COUNT: I'm talking about you. Pretending you couldn't stand the sight of women! And then trying to steal Mirandolina from me!

BARON [*turning haughtily to the* MARQUIS]: Is it me he's talking about?

MARQUIS: *I'm* not saying anything!

COUNT: Never mind him. Look at me and deny it if you can. Or is it you're ashamed of behaving in such a way?

BARON: All I'm ashamed of is standing here and not telling you to your face you're a liar!

COUNT: A liar am I?

MARQUIS [*aside*]: This is getting worse!

BARON: What grounds have you for saying such a thing? [*to the* MARQUIS] The Count doesn't know what he's talking about!

MARQUIS: I don't want to be mixed up in this.

COUNT [*to the* BARON]: A liar am I? It's you who are the liar!

MARQUIS: I'm going.

[*He tries to go but the* BARON *holds him back forcibly.*]

BARON: Oh, no you're not.

COUNT: And I demand satisfaction.

BARON: With pleasure! [*to the* MARQUIS] Give me your sword!

MARQUIS: Calm yourselves, both of you. My dear Count, what does it matter to you if the Baron is in love with Mirandolina?

BARON: I? In love with her? It's a lie! Whoever says that's a liar!

MARQUIS: A liar? Me? No, no, it's not me who says that!

BARON: Who does, then?

COUNT: I say it. And I'll say it again. I'm not afraid of you.

BARON [*to the* MARQUIS]: Give me your sword!

MARQUIS: No.

BARON: Are you looking for trouble as well?

MARQUIS: I don't want trouble with anyone.

COUNT [*to the* BARON]: What's more, you're no gentleman!

BARON: By heaven, this is too much! [*He snatches the sword and scabbard from the* MARQUIS.]

MARQUIS [*to the* BARON]: How dare you!

BARON [*to the* MARQUIS]: And I'll give you satisfaction as well if you want it.

MARQUIS: There's no need to lose your temper! [*aside, vexatiously*] This is all most unpleasant!

COUNT [*drawing his sword and putting himself on guard*]: I demand satisfaction.

BARON [*trying unsuccessfully to pull the Marquis's sword out of its scabbard*]: I'll give it you!

MARQUIS: You don't know that sword. . . .

BARON [*struggling to force it out*]: Confound the damn thing!

MARQUIS: Baron, you'll never do it. . . .

COUNT: I'll not wait much longer!

BARON: There! [*He tugs out the sword and finds it has only half a blade.*] What the devil's this?

MARQUIS: You've broken my sword!

BARON: Where's the rest of it? [*He peers into the scabbard.*] There's nothing there!

MARQUIS: Yes, of course . . . I remember now . . . I broke it in my last duel.

BARON [*to the* COUNT]: Let me get a sword.

COUNT: By heavens, I'll see you don't get out of this!

BARON: All right! I'll face you with this! You're only worth half a sword!

MARQUIS: It's the finest Spanish steel!

COUNT: Enough of your boasting, you braggart!

BARON [*advancing on the* COUNT]: Yes, this bit of a blade's enough for you!

COUNT [*putting himself on the defensive*]: At you, then!

[MIRANDOLINA *and* FABRIZIO *enter*.]

FABRIZIO: Put up your swords, gentlemen!

MIRANDOLINA: Stop this nonsense at once!

BARON [*at the sight of* MIRANDOLINA]: Damn her!

MIRANDOLINA: Fighting with swords in my Inn!

MARQUIS: It's all your own fault.

MIRANDOLINA: My fault! How?

COUNT: This Signor Baron here. He's fallen in love with you.

BARON: That's not true! You're a liar!

MIRANDOLINA: The Baron in love with me? Oh, no, Count, you're mistaken. You're quite wrong, believe me.

COUNT: Oh, naturally, you can't admit to the fact. . . .

MARQUIS: But we know, we've seen. . . .

BARON [*advancing angrily on the* MARQUIS]: Who knows what? Who's seen what?

MARQUIS [*retreating*]: I mean. . . . What is, we know. . . . But what isn't, we've not seen!

MIRANDOLINA: The Baron has denied he is in love with me. He denies it to my face. By doing so, he wants to shame me, to show me how strong he is and how weak I am. Let me admit the truth. If he had fallen in love with me I should feel I had won a great victory. But how could one ever expect such a man as he to fall in love: a man who cannot bear the sight of women, who despises them, who thinks they are the lowest creatures in the world? Gentlemen, I'm a simple woman. I admire frankness and I detest insincerity. So I must be honest with you. Yes, I did try to make the Baron fall in love with me. But I failed. [*to the* BARON] That is true, isn't it, signore? I tried and tried, but I failed completely.

BARON [*aside*]: What the devil am I to say to that!

COUNT [*to* MIRANDOLINA]: You see! Now I've got him!

MARQUIS [*to* MIRANDOLINA]: He hasn't the courage to contradict you!

BARON [*angrily, to the* MARQUIS]: You don't know what you're talking about!

MARQUIS [*smoothly, to the* BARON]: Yes, that's all *you* can say to *me*, isn't it?

MIRANDOLINA: Oh, no, the Baron's not in love! He knows women's wiles. He can see through them all right. He's not one to be taken in by women's tears. Why, even when a woman faints, he only laughs.

BARON: Then, are the tears of *all* women . . . false? A woman who faints . . . is she always a liar?

MIRANDOLINA: What? Didn't you know that? Or are you pretending you didn't?

BARON: By all the powers in heaven! Such deceit as that would deserve a knife through the heart!

MIRANDOLINA: Come, Signor Baron, do not be angry simply because these gentlemen thought you were really in love with me.

COUNT: He is! Look at him! He can't hide it!

MARQUIS: Yes, you've only to look at his eyes.

BARON [*furiously, to the* MARQUIS]: No, I'm not!

MARQUIS: He always picks on *me*!

MIRANDOLINA: No, signore, he is not in love. I say it again. And to show you I mean it I'm ready to prove it to you.

BARON [*aside*]: I can't stand any more of this. [*to the* COUNT] Count, another time be prepared to find me provided with a sword.

[*He throws the half sword of the* MARQUIS *on to the ground.*]

MARQUIS [*picking it up*]: Take care! That hilt is valuable!

MIRANDOLINA: Before you go, Signor Baron, think of your reputation. These gentlemen believe you are in love. You must prove they are wrong.

BARON: There is no need. . . .

MIRANDOLINA: Oh, yes, signore, there is! And it won't take you a moment!

BARON [*aside*]: What's she up to now?

MIRANDOLINA: Signore, the surest sign of love is jealousy. If you don't feel jealous, you are not in love. [*to the others*] If the Baron was in love with me, he wouldn't be able to bear the thought that I was to belong to another. But now you'll see him accept that, and so you'll. . . .

BARON: Who are you going to belong to?

MIRANDOLINA: To the husband my father chose for me.

FABRIZIO [*to* MIRANDOLINA]: You ... you don't mean me?

MIRANDOLINA: Yes, dear Fabrizio. In the presence of these gentlemen I give you my hand in marriage.

BARON [*to himself, in a frenzy*]: That fellow? I'll never get over this!

COUNT [*aside*]: She can't be in love with the Baron then! [*to* MIRANDOLINA] Yes, marry him, and I promise you three hundred crowns.

MARQUIS: Yes, a bird in the hand is worth two in the bush. Marry him at once and I'll give you twelve crowns this very instant.

MIRANDOLINA: Thank you, signore. But I have no need of a dowry. I'm only a poor girl, without any of the graces and charm that would make me worthy of men of quality. But Fabrizio loves me and so here and now in your presence I take him as my husband.

BARON: All right, damn you, marry whom you please. You tricked me, so enjoy your triumph. You would like to see me grovelling at your feet, wouldn't you? You wretched woman, a dagger is what you deserve. And your heart cut out and shown as a warning to all women like you. Let me get out of your sight. I scorn and curse your female tricks, your tears, your lies. One thing you have taught me, to my bitter cost. It's not enough to despise women. No! One should flee from the very sight of them. As I do now. From you! [*Exit*]

COUNT: And he was just saying he wasn't in love!

MARQUIS: If he tells me another lie, I shall challenge him to a duel!

MIRANDOLINA: No more, please, gentlemen. He has gone, and if he doesn't come back I shall consider myself very fortunate to have got out of this so lightly. Poor man, I succeeded only too well in making him fall in love with me. I see now I was playing with fire. And I don't want it to happen again. Fabrizio! Come, my dear. Give me your hand.

FABRIZIO: My hand? Not so fast, signorina. You amuse

yourself like this, making men fall in love with you, and think I want to marry you?

MIRANDOLINA: Now, don't you start acting crazy! It was all a joke! A game! A bit of fun! Oh, it was silly of me, I know, but it will be different when I am married.

FABRIZIO: How will it be different?

[*The Baron's* SERVANT *enters.*]

SERVANT: Signorina, before we leave, I would like to say good-bye to you.

MIRANDOLINA: You are going then?

SERVANT: Yes. My master is having the horses put to the carriage. He is waiting for me to bring the luggage. We are going to Leghorn.

MIRANDOLINA: I am sorry if things haven't been. . . .

SERVANT [*much affected*]: I . . . I must not stay. Thank you. Thank you. Good-bye. [*Exit*]

MIRANDOLINA: Thank heaven he's gone. I am truly sorry for what has happened. Never again will I do such a thing.

COUNT: Mirandolina, whether you marry or whether you remain single, my feelings for you will never change.

MARQUIS: You may count always upon my protection.

MIRANDOLINA: Signori, now that I am marrying I shall not need your attentions, nor your presents, nor your protection. Until now I've been amusing myself. I have acted foolishly. I have hurt others and have been in danger of being hurt myself. That, signori, is now all ended. This is my husband.

FABRIZIO: Not quite so fast, signorina.

MIRANDOLINA: Now you're not making difficulties, are you? What d'you mean? There's nothing to prevent us, is there? Come, give me your hand.

FABRIZIO: I think we should first arrange the contract.

MIRANDOLINA: What contract? This is our contract — you give me your hand,* or you get back to where you came from.

* See footnote on p. 61.

FABRIZIO: If I do give you my hand – what then?

MIRANDOLINA: What then? Then, my dear, I am yours and yours alone. Do not doubt that. I shall love you always. You alone will be my protection, my consolation, my only love.

FABRIZIO: My dear, I do not ask for more.

[*He gives her his hand.*]

MIRANDOLINA [*aside*]: Now that's settled.

COUNT: Mirandolina, you are the most remarkable and extraordinary woman. There is nothing you cannot do.

MARQUIS: Yes, you're absolutely charming – quite out of the ordinary, my dear.

MIRANDOLINA: Your kindness, signori, encourages me to ask one last favour from you.

FABRIZIO [*aside*]: Now what is it she's after?

COUNT: You have but to ask.

MARQUIS: Speak.

MIRANDOLINA: I beg you to do me this favour. Find yourselves another Inn.

FABRIZIO [*aside*]: She really does love me!

COUNT: I understand. Yes, you are right, Mirandolina. I shall go. But wherever I may be, you will always have my admiration and respect.

MARQUIS: Tell me – did you happen to lose a little gold bottle?

MIRANDOLINA: Yes, signore.

MARQUIS: Here it is. I found it and I restore it to you. To please you, I also shall leave. But you may always, whatever the circumstances, count upon my protection.

MIRANDOLINA: Your kind words, signori, will always mean very much to me – within certain limits. For in changing my state to that of a married woman, I shall learn to change my ways. [*She turns to face the audience*] And you also may learn from what you have seen. Whenever you feel yourselves falling in love, and wonder whether you should yield or not, think of the infinite tricks of women – and remember Mirandolina!

The Superior Residence

LA CASA NOVA

The Superior Residence

THIS play, first performed in Venice in 1760, has been acclaimed by many critics as Goldoni's masterpiece, not because its character studies are more humorous than in his other plays, but because its plot is more deftly woven and its picture of life more natural.

Only in two other plays did Goldoni make the location their title. And here the new apartment itself does dominate the action. In his autobiography Goldoni tells how the idea for the play came to him.

I had changed my house and as I was always looking for subjects of comedy I found one in the embarrassments of my removal. I did not, however, derive the subject entirely from my own predicament, but the circumstances suggested the title, and my imagination did the rest.

And in the preface he wrote for the play when it was later published he did something quite unusual. Normally the most modest of men, he boasts that if he had written but this single comedy, it would have been sufficient to secure for him the reputation he had acquired through so many others. This play, like *Mirandolina,* contains in Cristofolo another perfect example of Goldoni's skill in creating old men.

But the most remarkable quality of the play is the skill with which it is constructed. Such skill usually, as with Feydeau, depends upon a superbly ingenious yet mechanical juggling with characters who remain puppets on strings. Goldoni achieves the ingenuity of a Feydeau plot and yet his characters remain intensely human.

The Players

ANZOLETTO, a Venetian
CECILIA, ANZOLETTO's wife
DOMENICA, ANZOLETTO's sister
CHECCA, a Venetian lady, married
ROSINA, CHECCA's young sister, unmarried
LORENZINO, a Venetian, cousin to CHECCA and
    ROSINA and in love with DOMENICA
CRISTOFOLO, Uncle of ANZOLETTO and DOMENICA
COUNT OTTAVIO, a friend of CECILIA: an Italian
    but a stranger to Venice
FABRIZIO, a friend of ANZOLETTO: an Italian but
    a stranger to Venice
LUCIETTA, DOMENICA's maidservant
OSWALDO, a Venetian building contractor
WORKMEN, (Three)
TONI, Servant to CHECCA and ROSINA
PROSDOCIMO, a Bailiff

*The action of the play takes place in Venice, in the first-
floor apartment of Anzoletto and in the second-floor
apartment of Checca.*

Act One

The reception room in the new residence of SIGNOR ANZO-
LETTO *which consists of an expensive apartment on the first
floor of a Venetian palazzo.*

[OSWALDO, *the contractor in charge of the alterations being
made to the apartment, enters, followed by three* WORKMEN.]

OSWALDO: Let's try and finish this room off, anyway. It's
supposed to be the reception room. Signor Anzoletto's
having the furniture brought over from his old house
today. So we'd better see what we can do. Onifrio, you
finish off those so-called decorations over there, will you?
And Prospero, you'd better get the locks on the doors.
Lauro, straighten out that door-post first for him, will you?
And try not to take all day about it.

[*The three men start working.* OSWALDO *is beginning to
make himself comfortable with a bottle of wine he has brought
with him, when* LUCIETTA *storms in.*]

LUCIETTA [*to* OSWALDO]: Now just you look here! What
are you starting your banging and knocking in here for?
Haven't you finished yet? Anybody else could have built
a house in the time you've taken to mess up this apartment!

OSWALDO: Easy on, Lucietta! There's no need to take on like
this. What's the idea?

LUCIETTA: What's the idea! I'll tell you what's the idea! The
idea is my master's new wife has decided she's moving in
here today. So how the devil d'you think I can get the place
swept and tidied up when you and your workmen start
kicking up more dust and dirt?

OSWALDO: It's not our fault, m'dear. It's that master of yours.
He doesn't know what he wants. Changes his mind every
day. Some friend of his tells him one thing needs altering;
somebody else tells him the opposite. Today we must do

this; tomorrow we must do that. First of all, three of the bedrooms had to have fireplaces. Then somebody tells him that's not healthy. So we had to bung 'em up. Then somebody else tells him that's all a lot of nonsense. So then it's, 'Open up this chimney again!' 'No, not that one, this one!' Next it's: 'Turn the room next to the kitchen into a dining-room.' Then that's altered because of the smoke from the kitchen. Next, the entrance hall must have a partition across it because it's too long. Then the partition has to come down again because it makes the hall too dark. One change after another! One expense after another! But when I ask him for some money – oh, that's quite a different matter! Then he begins wishing the place to the devil – *and* a certain lady who forced him into renting it!

LUCIETTA: You needn't think you can tell me anything I don't know! As if I didn't know it's that new wife of his behind it all. Oh, she doesn't half think herself somebody, that one! Do you know, no sooner had she married him than the master's old house wasn't good enough for her! It hadn't got a water-gate; the entrance hall was too small; it hadn't got three rooms leading into one another; all the decorations weren't modern enough. So now the master's having to pay one of the highest rents in Venice for this new apartment.

OSWALDO: Ah, well – I suppose the money will come out of the dowry she brought him.

LUCIETTA: Don't make me laugh! D'you know how much dowry she brought him? Nothing! Apart from a bit of old junk and all her lah-di-dah airs and graces. Mind you, my master's no fool by any means. But he will go doing things on the spur of the moment. And then he doesn't like facing up to the consequences. As for that wife of his – well, she's the last person he should have married. Oh, sure, she comes from quite a good family. That's the trouble. The way she's been brought up she should have married somebody with three or four thousand ducats a year. And, of course, my master did start throwing his money about after his father died. And now, poor man, he's not only got his young

sister to find a dowry for, but he's got this wife hung like a
stone around his neck. Yes, if you ask me, he's certainly got
good reason to swear every time you ask him for money.
And I'll tell you something else – but don't go repeating it –
I wouldn't like it thought I go telling everybody what
happens in this house: the master still owes a year's rent on
the old house. And that's not all. He hasn't paid the six
months' rent due in advance on this apartment yet. The
rent collector is calling every day and the master's told us
to say he's not at home. I don't know how it's all going to
end. What's more, I've got seven months' wages owing to
me. So – now you see how things are!

OSWALDO: Well, I'll be damned! If he hasn't been stringing
me along as well! D'you know, I've actually been paying
these men their wages out of my own pocket! Well, one
thing's certain, he won't put me off again with his fine
words! Gentleman he may be – but he'll pay me my money
or I'll know the reason why!

LUCIETTA: Don't you go and let on I've been saying anything. I'm not the gossiping sort – but this wretched
apartment has got me so fed-up, I might as well be dead.
I've never been so absolutely and completely bored in all
my life.

OSWALDO: Huh! That's one thing your master takes good
care I'm not! Anyway, what's wrong with this apartment?
He may not be able to afford it, but that doesn't mean to
say it's not what they call a very superior residence.

LUCIETTA: Oh, yes, it's superior all right – so superior you
never even see a dog passing here. At our old house I used
to get no end of fun just having a look out of the window
now and then. And the servants from the other houses
round about used to call and we'd have a talk and a bit of a
laugh. But as for this lot round here – you've no idea what
a stuck-up lot they are. Not one of them's even passed the
time of day with me yet. Not even when I've been out on
the balcony. Only this morning that little slut of a maid
over the street looked straight at me, and then slammed her
window in my face!

OSWALDO: Oh, I shouldn't worry over that sort of thing. You'll make friends round here in time, you'll see.

LUCIETTA: Not the kind I used to have at the old house.

OSWALDO: Aha! It's the men servants round by your old house you're missing, I bet.

LUCIETTA: Maybe – and maybe not.

OSWALDO: Don't they allow your gentlemen friends to call on you?

LUCIETTA: Certainly, but I'm not the sort of girl that invites her young men into the house. Anyway, it's not so much for myself that I'm sorry for in that respect. It's my young mistress I'm sorry for.

OSWALDO: Why? Isn't the Signorina Domenica happy about this 'superior residence' either?

LUCIETTA: Well, you won't tell a soul, I know, so I'll let you into a secret. Her young man lives exactly opposite our old house. So, of course back there she used to be able to see him quite often. But now we've moved here, it's been impossible for them to arrange a meeting.

OSWALDO: But won't her brother let her marry the young man?

LUCIETTA: And what d'you think Signor Anzoletto's got to give her in the way of a dowry?

OSWALDO: The old story again, eh?

LUCIETTA: Poor girl, I don't know what's to become of her, unless her uncle decides to help her.

OSWALDO: Old Cristofolo, you mean? Aye, he's certainly rich enough to help her – if he wanted to.

LUCIETTA: Yes, the trouble is the old man's fallen out with his nephew for getting married like this. So, what with her brother and her uncle at daggers drawn, the poor girl can't expect help from either of them.

OSWALDO: Sh! This sounds like Signor Anzoletto now!

LUCIETTA: You be sure you don't say anything – about what I've been telling you.

OSWALDO: Well, I like that, I must say –

LUCIETTA: Because don't think I'm not still annoyed I've not been able to clean this room up yet.

OSWALDO [*putting away his flask of wine*]: Mind I don't get annoyed – I haven't been able to get on with my work – listening to you and your chitter-chatter.

LUCIETTA [*starting to sweep the floor*]: Work! That's what you call it, is it?

[ANZOLETTO *enters*.]

ANZOLETTO [*fussily*]: Oh, dear, oh, dear, isn't this room finished yet? Now what's holding things up? Nothing has gone wrong, I hope?

OSWALDO: Everything'll be ready by tomorrow.

ANZOLETTO: Tomorrow! Tomorrow! That's all I've been hearing for the last three weeks. Everything will be ready tomorrow!

OSWALDO: Look, at least a dozen times you've told me to alter something. And then, as soon as I've done it, you've wanted it altered all over again. You listen to every Tom, Dick and Harry who thinks he knows how an apartment should be furnished. Well, if you go on trying to follow all the idiotic advice your friends give you, I may as well tell you here and now, this place won't be finished this time next year – never mind tomorrow!

ANZOLETTO: Yes, of course, you're quite right, my dear chap. Absolutely right. This time I'll not alter my mind. There – I've said so – and I'll stick to it. Now, you will hurry things, won't you, there's a good chap. My wife has decided to move in today from the old house. I suppose we'll just have to sleep in here for tonight.

OSWALDO: Oh, the bedroom's all ready.

ANZOLETTO: Oh, now really, that's too bad of you! What on earth will people think? To have the bedroom all ready but not the reception room!

OSWALDO: Let them think what they like. I can't do any more than I am doing.

ANZOLETTO: You could find some more workmen and get things done quicker.

OSWALDO: You let me have some money first.

ANZOLETTO [*stamping up and down*]: Money! It's always money!

That's all I've heard since he's been here. Can't the man forget about it just for one moment? He never stops! It's all he can think of! Money! Money! Money!

OSWALDO [*doggedly*]: No money – no more workmen.

ANZOLETTO [*changing his tactics and adopting a jocular tone*]: Suppose – just suppose – I haven't got any money!

OSWALDO: Then I *suppose* you'd see me and my men walking straight out of here.

ANZOLETTO [*peevishly*]: Oh, all right, very well – I'll find some by tomorrow. So please do not mention it again. Let it be understood that I do not wish to discuss the matter any further. Just do what you are told – and remember that you are dealing with a gentleman and a man of honour.

OSWALDO: Yes, signore. Until tomorrow, then,

ANZOLETTO: But take care you don't cause me too much expense.

[ANZOLETTO *goes over to the decorations on the back wall and starts examining them closely.*]

OSWALDO [*sarcastically*]: Oh, naturally, signore. [*He calls to one of the workmen*] You there, Onifrio. Go at once to my house and tell the three men there to leave what they're doing and to come here. [*Aside, as the workman goes*] And if he doesn't pay me tomorrow, I'll find ways of making him.

ANZOLETTO: Lucietta!

LUCIETTA: Yes, Illustrious?

ANZOLETTO: Go to the kitchen and give the cook some help if he needs it.

LUCIETTA [*surprised*]: You're dining here today, then?

ANZOLETTO: Yes, with my wife and a few friends. So you'd better warn my sister to make herself presentable as well.

LUCIETTA: But I don't think she's had all her dresses brought from the old house yet.

ANZOLETTO: Tell her I'll have the rest of her things brought over here right away.

LUCIETTA: That's not the only thing. All the table linen is still at the old house as well.

ANZOLETTO: Very well, very well! I'll have it all brought here.

LUCIETTA: How many guests have I to prepare for?

ANZOLETTO: Oh, just have the table laid for ten.

LUCIETTA: Ten! Oh, yes, of course, signore. I'll see that it's done, signore. [*Exit*]

[ANZOLETTO *goes back stage again and has another look at the decorations.*]

OSWALDO [*aside*]: There's no money for me, but plenty for this dinner of his. Well, we'll see what happens tomorrow.

ANZOLETTO [*coming forward*]: You know, I'm not quite sure whether I like these decorations after all.

OSWALDO: Well, I told you what *I* think of them. But you would listen to that artist friend of yours. They're costing you a tidy packet and they don't suit the room at all.

ANZOLETTO: Yes, I think you're right. You had better take them down again.

OSWALDO: Take them down! What the hell d'you think we're going to put in place of them? This room certainly won't be finished this evening if we start messing about with them again.

ANZOLETTO: Oh, well, I suppose we'd better leave them – for the time being.

OSWALDO: Of course, what you should have had is a large mirror here and plenty of gold braiding round the other walls.

ANZOLETTO [*enthusiastically*]: You're right, my dear fellow! Absolutely right! So let's get hold of some gold braiding and get it done right away, shall we?

OSWALDO: What d'you mean – right away? A job like that would take days!

ANZOLETTO: Oh, surely not. Not with these extra men you've sent for?

OSWALDO: What about the beading? I'd need at least a hundred feet of gold beading at five soldi a foot.

ANZOLETTO: Well, get it.

OSWALDO: All right – where's the money?

ANZOLETTO: Are you starting that all over again? I've told you I'll settle any accounts tomorrow.

OSWALDO: Then it'll have to wait till tomorrow. I haven't that much money either to pay out today.

ANZOLETTO: Oh, all right, it's getting late anyway. I suppose we'd better leave things as they are for today.

OSWALDO [aside, as he goes back to his work]: He's a proper case, this chap!

[FABRIZIO enters.]

FABRIZIO [affectedly]: May one enter?

ANZOLETTO: Come in! Please do come in, Signor Fabrizio!

FABRIZIO: My dear friend, haven't they finished the place for you yet?

ANZOLETTO: We are just trying to hasten them a little, my dear fellow. Well, what do you say? Does it please you?

FABRIZIO: To tell you the truth – I do not like it at all.

ANZOLETTO: You don't? But why ever not?

FABRIZIO: Oh, really, my dear fellow! Well, I mean to say, in the first place, you've made the most frightful blunder, you know, in putting the bedrooms on the north side. It's this room facing the south which should be a bedroom. You'll simply die, my dear chap, if you sleep facing the north!

ANZOLETTO: Oh, good heavens! Did you hear that, Signor Oswaldo?

OSWALDO: Now what is it?

ANZOLETTO: D'you want me to catch my death of cold? How would you like to sleep facing the north?

OSWALDO: You should have thought of that before.

ANZOLETTO: Well, thank heaven, we've thought of it now while there's still time to remedy it.

OSWALDO: What d'you mean – remedy it?

ANZOLETTO: Now surely it's not all that difficult to carry a bed from one room to another?

OSWALDO: What about these decorations?

FABRIZIO: My good man. If one has the men and the money one can do anything.

ANZOLETTO: Yes, of course, anything can be remedied when you've got the men and the money.

OSWALDO [*becoming angry*]: Well, I'll think of the men if you'll start thinking of the money!

ANZOLETTO: What way is that to speak? To hear you, any-body might think I refused you your money. Have you ever been short of money?

OSWALDO [*aside*]: Now I could show him up in front of his fine friend.

ANZOLETTO [*having turned to* FABRIZIO]: Did you hear? That's the way they speak to you nowadays. I've already given him well over a thousand ducats. And I've only just told him that tomorrow I intend settling any accounts that are still outstanding. [*to* OSWALDO] Well, and what will it *cost* to move a bed from one room to another?

FABRIZIO [*to* OSWALDO]: Come, sirrah, this is but a puddle in a storm. Do not forget that you are dealing with a gentleman and a man of honour.

OSWALDO [*aside and echoing in unison with Fabrizio*]: . . . and a man of honour! [*to his workmen*] Come along, lads, we've got another removal job on. We've to take one of the beds to bits and put it up again in here. [*to* ANZOLETTO] And there'll be no going back on this!

ANZOLETTO: You have my word for that.

OSWALDO [*aside, as he and the workmen go out*]: And tomorrow we'll talk about money. [*Exit*]

FABRIZIO: My dear Anzoletto, you have my sympathy. What boors these people are!

ANZOLETTO: I sometimes think they will drive me mad. I do nothing but pay out money – and yet never seem to see anything for it.

FABRIZIO: By the way, as I passed your kitchen I thought I saw your cook working there?

ANZOLETTO: Yes, I am dining here this evening.

FABRIZIO: With your wife?

ANZOLETTO: With my wife.

FABRIZIO: And – er – a few close relatives, I expect?

ANZOLETTO: Er – yes – and one or two friends.

FABRIZIO: Am I, alas, not numbered among your friends, then?

ANZOLETTO: On the contrary, my dear fellow, pray join us, if you wish.

FABRIZIO: The pleasure will be mine. I find your wife's company vastly entertaining. She has a charm and a wit, if I may say so, unusual in one so young and so beautiful. Her wit especially pleases me. It is so natural. So sparkling. So unrestrained.

ANZOLETTO: And sometimes so damned irritating!

FABRIZIO: You complain of her wit?

ANZOLETTO: Shall we talk of something else. I am most grateful to you for your suggestion about the rooms facing the north.

FABRIZIO: My dear fellow, I take great concern over your health. What's more – your dear wife might have suffered as well.

ANZOLETTO: My dear wife's so damned difficult to please, I am nigh past caring.

FABRIZIO [*looking beyond him through the open door*]: But – pray who is this lady?

ANZOLETTO: Lady? [*he turns to look*] Oh, that's my sister. I thought you knew her?

FABRIZIO: Not the little Signorina Domenica? But what a fine young lady she's become!

ANZOLETTO: Too fine – for my liking.

[DOMENICA *enters.*]

DOMENICA: May I come in?

ANZOLETTO: Of course you can come in. If you want to.

FABRIZIO [*with exaggerated courtesy*]: I am the Signorina Domenica's most humble and devoted servant!

DOMENICA: My respects to you, sir. [*to* ANZOLETTO, *ironically*] Thank you, brother, for the quite magnificent room you've given me.

ANZOLETTO: Now what's the matter? Isn't the room to your liking?

DOMENICA: I never thought that at my age I should find myself buried alive.

ANZOLETTO: Buried alive? What the devil are you talking about?

DOMENICA: It was most considerate of you to hide me away in a room looking out on to an enclosed courtyard where you'd never see a dog passing.

ANZOLETTO: Well, where d'you want me to put you?

DOMENICA: You can hide me under the stairs, under the roof, anywhere you like. But I'm not staying in that room!

ANZOLETTO: My dear sister, the apartment is not all that big, you know.

DOMENICA: Not all that big! You can stand there and say that, when there are four rooms on this side alone!

ANZOLETTO [*with forced patience*]: Oh, now be reasonable, my dear girl. These rooms are naturally for me and my wife.

DOMENICA: Of course! Everything's for the new wife! For her, there's a whole apartment! For her, there are four rooms all connected to each other! But for me, there's one tiny closet!

ANZOLETTO [*irritably*]: What are you talking about? What tiny closet? It's a fine room! Big! Bright! Airy! With two windows! What on earth are you complaining about?

DOMENICA: Yes, and if I look out of the two windows what do I see? Cats – rats – lizards – and a rubbish heap that turns my stomach!

FABRIZIO [*to* DOMENICA, *ingratiatingly*]: Ah! And what you would like to see – is a certain young man? Am I right?

DOMENICA [*icily*]: You, sir, would oblige me by minding your own business!

ANZOLETTO: If that's all that's troubling you, you can come in here and look out of the window as long as you like.

DOMENICA: If there's one place I'll never come – it's in here.

ANZOLETTO: There you are, then! How do you expect my wife to get to know you and to like you, if you behave so unsociably and ungraciously?

DOMENICA: Well, she needn't put on her airs and graces for me, either. They don't take me in. I know quite well she doesn't want anything to do with me. And I can manage quite well without seeing anything of her.

ANZOLETTO: And you've the damned impertinence to tell me so!

DOMENICA: I speak frankly, brother. *I* don't go saying behind your back what I wouldn't say to your face.

FABRIZIO: Ah! What a fine virtue is sincerity!

ANZOLETTO: But what has my wife done to you? What have you got against her?

DOMENICA: D'you think I enjoy having a sister-in-law running the house? I was the mistress of the house as long as our poor mother lived, and I have been ever since. But now her Excellency the Signora Cecilia is coming, she'll want to give the orders to the servants. She'll be the mistress here. I suppose I'll even have to ask her when I want a new pair of shoes.

FABRIZIO: May I say that I have found the Signora Cecilia to possess great tact and discretion. Moreover, a younger lady should, undoubtedly, defer to the wishes of a married lady.

DOMENICA: Can't you be quiet?

ANZOLETTO [*to* DOMENICA]: So! I should not have married my wife – just because you don't want a sister-in-law in the house!

DOMENICA: You should have arranged my marriage, first!

FABRIZIO [*to* ANZOLETTO]: Yes, your sister's right to a certain extent, my dear fellow.

DOMENICA [*to* FABRIZIO]: Whether I'm right or not, what's that to do with you?

ANZOLETTO [*to* DOMENICA]: If a suitable marriage could have been arranged for you, I would most certainly have arranged it.

DOMENICA: If? If? There's no 'if' about it! You had the opportunity and did nothing!

ANZOLETTO: What opportunity? D'you mean Lorenzino?

DOMENICA: Yes! Lorenzino! And you said 'No'!

ANZOLETTO: Yes – and I said 'No' because – because that young man's not good enough for you!

DOMENICA: Not good enough for *me*? For *you*, you mean!

Who d'you want me to marry, then? A count? A lord?
And what wonderful dowry will you be giving me? What
her Excellency your wife brought you? A lot of fine talk
and hot air?

ANZOLETTO [*shouting*]: The point is I'm able to do what I
want! I'm the master of the house. Nobody tells me what
I've to do!

DOMENICA: And no sister-in-law is going to tell me what
to do, either!

ANZOLETTO: Just what d'you think you can do about it?

DOMENICA: Just this. I can go and live with our uncle
Cristofolo.

ANZOLETTO: I warn you – if you so much as go anywhere
near that old fool – then I've finished with you! D'you hear?

FABRIZIO: Excuse me, old fellow, but don't you think that's
going a bit too far, what?

DOMENICA [*to* FABRIZIO]: Will you keep out of this! My
brother knows what he's talking about! Our uncle's a man
of good sense – and can't stand the sight of his nephew
here throwing his money away!

ANZOLETTO [*to* DOMENICA]: If you don't hold your tongue,
it'll be the worse for you!

FABRIZIO [*to* ANZOLETTO]: You know, I think if you gave
your sister a room with a good view, she'd be happy and
forget about all these other matters.

DOMENICA [*to* FABRIZIO]: Are you trying to be funny?

FABRIZIO: I speak, dear lady, for your own good. I, at least,
am trying to show some interest in your welfare.

DOMENICA: I can do without your interest, sir. I am well able
to look after myself. I do not intend to remain in that room.
And *that* – is *final*! [*Exit*]

FABRIZIO: Your sister is most certainly a young lady with
a mind of her own.

ANZOLETTO: Obstinate, you mean. As obstinate as the devil.

FABRIZIO: Still, your wife will no doubt calm her down and
make her see reason.

ANZOLETTO: My dear chap, my wife can be more obstinate
still.

FABRIZIO: Well, if that's the case, you'll just have to get your sister out of the house.

ANZOLETTO: Perhaps you can tell me how!

FABRIZIO: How much dowry *are* you able to give her?

ANZOLETTO: At the moment – not a thing.

FABRIZIO: But supposing your uncle was prepared to help her?

ANZOLETTO: Do not speak to me of my uncle! After the way he has treated me, I wouldn't ask him for a crust of bread if I were starving.

FABRIZIO: Shouldn't you make some allowances? He is an old man, after all.

ANZOLETTO: My wife would never allow it. He's offended her, as well.

FABRIZIO: Well, I suppose it's your own affair, but I think it's a little – inadvisable to allow your wife to come between you and a rich uncle!

ANZOLETTO: Look, old chap, I must go to the old house to arrange for the rest of the things to be brought here. Do me a favour and keep an eye on these workmen while I'm away. See that they bestir themselves, there's a good fellow.

FABRIZIO: Certainly, my dear Anzoletto, I will do that most willingly.

ANZOLETTO: To tell you the truth, my dear Fabrizio, though I've only been married for a couple of weeks, I try to avoid situations which might cause my wife to lose her temper a little. It's just a small precaution I've learnt to take. And if these two rooms are not finished by this evening, I fear I shall be having some not so sweet words from her.

FABRIZIO: You may rely on me, my dear chap.

ANZOLETTO: I knew I could. I am extremely grateful, all the same. We shall see you at dinner, then, this evening?

FABRIZIO: The pleasure will be mine!

ANZOLETTO: Until then! [*Exit*]

FABRIZIO: If the dinner is worth eating, that is! There goes a man, who has been trying his best to ruin himself for some time. Now he seems to have succeeded – by getting married. [*He goes to the door and calls*] Hey, you there!

[OSWALDO *enters.*]

OSWALDO: You called? -

FABRIZIO: Signor Anzoletto has had to go to the old house. He asked me to tell you to see that everything is finished by this evening. As a matter of fact, I shall be dining here myself this evening. So make sure that everything is ready, will you? [*Exit*]

OSWALDO [*alone*]: Yes, signore! You're the sort of friend who never misses an invitation to dinner if he can help it. [*Goes to the door and calls*] Come on, lads. Hurry up with that bed.

[*The three* WORKMEN *enter carrying the parts of a four poster bed.* LUCIETTA *enters opposite.*]

LUCIETTA: *Now* what's happening? Don't say you're starting all over again?

OSWALDO: Come to poke *your* nose in again, have you? [*to the workmen*] That's right, lads. Now, start putting the thing together again. Over here will do.

LUCIETTA: He's not really going to let his sister have this room, is he?

OSWALDO: If you must know, he's going to have this as his own bedroom.

LUCIETTA: Now what's made him do that?

OSWALDO: That Signor Fabrizio. Him that was trying to cadge an invitation to dinner. He told your master some nonsense about north and south.

LUCIETTA: North and south? [*A knocking is heard off stage*] Now who can that be? Run off my feet I am! What with answering the door, helping the cook in the kitchen, and trying to tidy up after you lot! I suppose I'd better see who it is. [*Exit*]

OSWALDO [*to the workmen who are erecting the posts of the bed*]: Always complaining! Like all these servants. They're never happy unless they're moaning about something.

LUCIETTA [*re-entering excitedly*]: Do you know who it is?

OSWALDO: No, you tell me.

LUCIETTA: It's the new wife!

OSWALDO: Fancy that, now.

LUCIETTA: Really, you should have seen the way she came in! You'd have died laughing! All those airs and graces!

OSWALDO: Is she by herself?

LUCIETTA: By herself! Not likely! She's got one of her lah-di-dah gentlemen friends with her. Some Count from Milan.

OSWALDO: Well, hadn't you better go and tell the Signorina Domenica?

LUCIETTA: Oh, she's locked herself up in her room. I've a good mind to do the same myself. But I suppose I'd better try and make myself polite to her. I've managed to avoid her, so far.

OSWALDO: D'you mean to say – she's your master's wife – and you've not spoken to her yet?

LUCIETTA: They've only been married a fortnight and he's been living at her place while I've been trying to clean up here after you.

OSWALDO: All right, you needn't start that again. [*to the workmen*] Come on, now, hurry yourselves and get this bed up.

[CECILIA *sweeps into the room followed by* COUNT OTTAVIO.]

LUCIETTA: Your servant, signora.

CECILIA: Ah, yes, who did you say you were?

LUCIETTA: Chambermaid, signora.

CECILIA: Has Signor Anzoletto engaged you for me?

LUCIETTA: No, signora, I have been here quite a time.

CECILIA: Is there a maid for his sister?

LUCIETTA: Yes, signora.

CECILIA: How many maids are there?

LUCIETTA: Only me, signora.

CECILIA: I see. Well, I shall be bringing my own maid, of course. Which room is this?

LUCIETTA: It was to be the reception room, but now it's going to be your bedroom, signora.

CECILIA: Now whose silly idea was that? [*to* OSWALDO] Yours?

OSWALDO: Mine? Certainly not!

CECILIA: A large room like this should be the reception room. Don't you agree, count?

OTTAVIO: Oh, indubitably, my dear lady.

CECILIA: What on earth put it into Signor Anzoletto's head to make such an alteration?

LUCIETTA: It's so he won't have to sleep in a room facing the north.

CECILIA: Facing the north? Somebody must have put the idea in his head. Was it this blockhead here?

OSWALDO [*getting angry*]: I did not suggest any such thing! And what's more – I am not a blockhead!

CECILIA: Don't raise your voice to me, my man!

OTTAVIO: Yes, a little more respect, please!

CECILIA: And put this bed back where you got it from. This room is to be the reception room.

OSWALDO: Is that an order – signora?

CECILIA: Count, would you deal with this person?

OTTAVIO [*to* OSWALDO]: The mistress of the house has expressed a desire that a certain thing be done. She wishes it to be done, moreover, without delay. Do you need further clarification?

OSWALDO [*to the workmen*]: All right, lads. Start taking that bed out again. [*Aside, as he goes out*] Signor Anzoletto's got a right one here, and no mistake.

[*The three workmen begin dismantling the bed, and take the parts out of the room at appropriate moments during the following.*]

CECILIA [*to* LUCIETTA]: A chair, if you please.

LUCIETTA: Yes, signora. [*She brings a chair to* CECILIA *who sits.*]

CECILIA [*after a pause*]: And must the Count remain standing? My girl, I shall not take kindly to it, if you have to be told such things.

LUCIETTA: I've always given satisfaction before.

CECILIA: And a good servant does not answer her mistress back.

[LUCIETTA *angrily fetches another chair and planks it beside* CECILIA.]

CECILIA: Pray, will you be seated, Count.
[*He sits beside her.*]
They are not very comfortable, these chairs, are they?

OTTAVIO: One does not use such chairs, dear lady.

CECILIA: I thought not. I shall have some little armchairs made. [*to* LUCIETTA] Tell me, you have a name, have you not?

LUCIETTA: Lucietta. At your service.

CECILIA: Well, Lucietta, can you tell me what my sister-in-law is doing?

LUCIETTA: She is quite well, signora.

CECILIA: Tell her I asked after her when you see her, will you?

LUCIETTA: Yes, signora.

CECILIA: Has she visited here yet?

LUCIETTA: Er – yes, signora.

CECILIA: Oh? When did she come?

LUCIETTA: This morning, signora.

CECILIA: She has returned to the old house?

LUCIETTA: No, signora.

CECILIA: What? Then where is she now?

LUCIETTA: She's here in her room.

CECILIA: She is here! And does not condescend to come to welcome me!
[LUCIETTA *remains silent.*] Well? Have you been struck dumb?

LUCIETTA: What d'you want me to say?

CECILIA: Count, please tell me – is that the way one's sister-in-law should treat one?

OTTAVIO: Not in our circles, dear lady.

CECILIA [*to* LUCIETTA]: There, you see! The Count, who is used to going about in society, says she is not behaving well. Go and inform my sister-in-law that if it is not too much trouble to her, I shall come and greet her in her room.

LUCIETTA: Yes, signora. [*Exit*]

CECILIA: It is quite a surprise to me, Count, that my sister-in-law is to live here. I had taken it for granted that she would live with her uncle.

OTTAVIO: It was foolish of Signor Anzoletto to have quarrelled with his uncle. Signor Cristofolo is not only very rich, he is also a gentleman.

CECILIA: I am sorry to say, Count, that I consider him to be nothing of the sort! In my opinion he is a bad-tempered, ill-mannered old blackguard! Do you know, he did everything to stop his nephew marrying me? Actually complained that I didn't bring his nephew a big enough dowry! And he with all his money! I'm quite astonished that you should call him a gentleman!

OTTAVIO: My dear lady! I did not know anything of all this! I withdraw what I said completely. The man's a complete boor.

CECILIA: He's a blackguard! A lout!

OTTAVIO: Whatever you say, dear lady.

CECILIA: But I ask you! Should a lady be scorned in such a way by – by such a person?

OTTAVIO: Ah, such a lady as yourself deserves to be treated like a queen! Would that I had but had the honour of knowing you before you became engaged to Signor Anzoletto!

CECILIA: Ah, my dear Count, that was fate.

OTTAVIO: Signor Anzoletto gives you no cause to complain?

CECILIA: No, only his uncle. But my husband loves me *and* he has the means to support me. So we have no need of his uncle. We are well rid of him. I shall be completely happy when we are rid of my sister-in-law.

[LUCIETTA *enters.*]

LUCIETTA: Signorina Domenica greets the Signora and says she prefers to come here to welcome you, since her room is not a reception room.

CECILIA: Were those her exact words?

LUCIETTA: I've told you what she said.

CECILIA: You see, Count, what she's implying?

OTTAVIO: Well, no, to tell the truth. Not exactly.

CECILIA: This impertinent young woman is as good as telling me that her room is not as fine as mine.

OTTAVIO: Ah, yes, I see what you mean, dear lady.

[*There is a sound of something being moved across the floor in the apartment above.*]

CECILIA: What is all that noise?

LUCIETTA: Oh, it's only the people in the apartment up above, signora.

CECILIA: But I shan't be able to put up with that sort of thing! Who are these people upstairs?

LUCIETTA: They're two ladies, signora. Sisters. Signora Checca – that's the married one – asked me to let her know when you arrived so that they might pay their respects to you. Oh, they're real ladies – signora.

CECILIA: In that case, when you see them you may say that I shall be pleased to receive them. That is the correct procedure, is it not, Count?

OTTAVIO: Perfectly, dear lady.

LUCIETTA: Wouldn't it be better if I said you hoped –

CECILIA: Simply do as you're told. I do not need lessons from scullery maids.

LUCIETTA: Who's a scullery maid?

CECILIA: That will be all! Get back to your work.

OTTAVIO: What can one expect, dear lady? Complete lack of breeding, you know.

LUCIETTA: Well, I certainly wouldn't come to you to learn good manners!

CECILIA: That's enough! The sooner you go the better! You may consider yourself dismissed.

LUCIETTA: Don't worry, I'm going! Nobody's going to speak to me like that!

[DOMENICA *enters as* LUCIETTA *opens the door.*]

DOMENICA: Is something the matter? Stay where you are, Lucietta.

LUCIETTA: She says I'm dismissed! But I've told her I was going, anyway.

DOMENICA: So, my dear sister-in-law, you've started causing trouble already?

CECILIA [*rising*]: That is no way to greet me!

DOMENICA: What has Lucietta done?

CECILIA: She was insolent to this gentleman.

OTTAVIO: Please, ladies! I assure you, such trifles are beneath me.

DOMENICA: I assume you have your own maid? Lucietta has been with me over a year and I am quite satisfied with her.

CECILIA: Oh, keep her, then. But see she doesn't cross my path.

LUCIETTA: You needn't worry about that!

DOMENICA: That's enough, Lucietta. Please go to your room.

[LUCIETTA *goes out with a toss of her head.*]

CECILIA: And now, sister-in-law, perhaps you will tell me – where is my husband?

DOMENICA: I haven't the slightest idea. My brother never tells me where he is going. He never tells me anything. I did not know he was intending to marry until three days before the marriage.

CECILIA: Indeed?

DOMENICA: But then why should he tell me anything. I never move from my room. Since my mother died I have become used to living as I do.

CECILIA: Well – for somebody who never goes into society you have an extremely fashionable hair-style.

DOMENICA: My maid attends to my hair.

CECILIA: That girl Lucietta?

DOMENICA: Yes. Lucietta.

CECILIA: But I had no idea she was so gifted. She must do mine as well.

DOMENICA: She will do nothing of the sort.

CECILIA: How dare you speak to me like that! That girl is paid by my husband and I shall certainly make use of her if I want to!

OTTAVIO: Ladies, please! One does not become angry over a maid.

DOMENICA: She's not going to order my maid about!

[ANZOLETTO *enters hastily*.]

DOMENICA: } Oh, brother, please tell –
CECILIA: } Just listen to this, husband! –

ANZOLETTO [*to* OTTAVIO, *interrupting them*]: My dear Count, a word with you, I beg you.

OTTAVIO: Your servant, signore.

[ANZOLETTO *leads* OTTAVIO *down stage. The two women follow them*.]

CECILIA: } Why don't you listen to me –
DOMENICA: } Will you please tell me, brother –

ANZOLETTO [*turning on both of them*]: Quiet, both of you! I want a word with the Count. Whatever it is, I'll attend to you in a moment.

[*The two women flounce away back stage*.]

OTTAVIO [*aside to* ANZOLETTO]: What's the matter, my dear fellow? You seem quite upset.

ANZOLETTO: Neither my wife nor my sister are to know about this! I can rely on you?

OTTAVIO: Of course, my dear Anzoletto. Whatever's troubling you?

ANZOLETTO: I have just been to my old house to collect some things. The landlord refuses to let me take them because I still owe him some rent.

OTTAVIO: Oh, I say, that's a bad business!

ANZOLETTO: I know that! The point is, can you help me? All I need is somebody to vouch for me.

OTTAVIO: Ah, now, one must consider such a situation from every point of view. I'll tell you what I think you –

ANZOLETTO: But it's urgent! There's no time to lose! All the table linen's still there and I'm entertaining people to dinner here this evening.

OTTAVIO [*aside*]: I don't know. I will do what I can. It is a difficult situation. [*aloud*] Signore, your most humble servant.

CECILIA: You are leaving, Count?

OTTAVIO: Alas, dear lady, I have some business to attend to.

CECILIA: But you will be dining with us?

OTTAVIO: Yes, of course – er – that is, I hope so.

ANZOLETTO [*aside*]: You are going to help me?

OTTAVIO [*aside*]: I'll see. I'll do what I can.

ANZOLETTO [*aside, accompanying him towards the door*]: But you must! I'm depending on you! I'll come with you!

DOMENICA [*to* ANZOLETTO]: Are you going out again already?

ANZOLETTO: Yes, yes! I shan't be long!

CECILIA: But husband!

ANZOLETTO: I said I'll be back soon! [*He goes out quickly after* OTTAVIO.]

CECILIA: There! Because of you my husband's started being rude to me . . .

DOMENICA: His rudeness was meant for me. He saw something was wrong and that Count of yours has told him it's my fault.

CECILIA: What d'you mean – that Count of mine?

DOMENICA: Oh, I'm sure I don't care whose Count he is.

CECILIA: And I'm sure I don't either. It's my husband I'm concerned about!

[LUCIETTA *enters*.]

LUCIETTA: Those two ladies from the apartment upstairs would like to see you.

DOMENICA: Who? Me?

LUCIETTA: Well, no – both of you, I expect.

CECILIA: Oh, no, they don't! Tell them to make up their minds who they think is mistress here. [*Exit*]

DOMENICA: Yes! Either her – or me! [*Exit*]

LUCIETTA: Well, if that's the way it is – I'll receive them myself!

A room in the Signora Checca's apartment.

[CHECCA *enters followed by* ROSINA.]

CHECCA: Well, what d'you make of that? Did you ever know such insolence! They ask us to come. Then when we're at their door, their servant says they can't see us. And she doesn't know why. I couldn't make out one word that girl was trying to say!

ROSINA: They ought to have given us some explanation. That servant was so pleasant when she asked us to come. You wouldn't think it was the same girl the way she muttered at us under her breath.

CHECCA: They're either complete boors and don't know any better – or they've a very high opinion of themselves.

ROSINA: Yet they seem to have plenty of friends.

CHECCA: Friends! Acquaintances, you mean! That sort of person doesn't have friends. The young woman's been married only a fortnight and she's already got one of those so-called gentlemen dancing attendance on her.

ROSINA: What about the young girl! D'you think she really is kept shut up, like a nun in a convent?

CHECCA: That's what our cousin Lorenzino told me. She wears a black cloak down to her heels when she does go out. But apparently she doesn't behave quite so circum- spectedly when she's on the balcony outside her room.

ROSINA: Didn't he tell you that was where they used to make love?

CHECCA: You know what these young girls are nowadays. Don't model yourself on them, sister. For myself, I can truthfully say that my husband was the first young man who ever spoke to me. You must always remember the precepts of our dear mother. And now that you live with me . . .

ROSINA: My dear sister, I have no need of your sermons. You should know that.

CHECCA: Why do you think these people downstairs didn't want to receive us?

ROSINA: Well, of course, they've only arrived today. Perhaps their apartment isn't finished yet. All the furniture may not have come.

CHECCA: Yes, you may be right. But still that wouldn't excuse their behaviour. Though to tell the truth, I must admit we were a little hasty ourselves. We could have waited till tomorrow. But I am so very curious to see this young woman.

ROSINA: I saw her when she arrived. To me she didn't seem anybody extraordinary.

CHECCA: They say she likes having her own way.

ROSINA: Yes, she looked as though she probably did.

CHECCA: But how will Signor Anzoletto be able to afford a wife like that?

ROSINA: He certainly won't on the dowry she brought him.

CHECCA: Yes, that's what Lorenzino said. She hardly brought Signor Anzoletto anything. And he's such a spendthrift himself. Simply throws his money away.

ROSINA: Yes, just think what that apartment must be costing him. Those men have been working on it for two months now.

CHECCA: And yet all the old junk that's been arriving! Did you see that old mirror with the black border?

ROSINA: Yes! Those things went out with the Ark!

CHECCA: And the big leather armchair?

ROSINA: That monstrosity! It must have belonged to his great-great-grandfather!

CHECCA: They squander money on painters, carpenters, upholsterers – yet they can't have one room furnished in good taste.

ROSINA: Yes, I must say I'd like to see it.

CHECCA: I've simply got to see it! Perhaps I could slip in one day when they're out.

ROSINA: What about Lorenzino? He did ask us to speak to the young girl for him?

CHECCA: Yes, that young man doesn't know what to do with himself. Now that he can't look at her all day from his window.

ROSINA: Then you will speak to Signorina Domenica?

CHECCA: Yes, to please him, I'll speak to her. Not that it will do any good.

ROSINA: Why not?

CHECCA: Well, what dowry d'you think that brother of hers will be able to give her?

ROSINA: But Lorenzino's so much in love with her!

CHECCA: Then he'll have to content himself with being in love. That young man's another spendthrift. It's not love that pays the bills, my dear sister.

ROSINA: Somebody's knocking.

CHECCA: Yes, and nobody's answering it.

ROSINA: I'll go and see who it is.

CHECCA: Don't let anybody see you on the balcony.

ROSINA: Oh, we're so high up here, who d'you think could see me? [Exit]

CHECCA [to herself]: Oh, I wish my husband would hurry his return to Venice. I must get him to arrange a good marriage for Rosina. The poor girl deserves a good husband.

ROSINA [entering]: Do you know who it is?

CHECCA: Who?

ROSINA: It's that servant from downstairs!

CHECCA: Did you pull the cord to open the door?

ROSINA: Yes.

CHECCA: Good. I'm glad she's come. Now we'll hear something.

ROSINA: Yes, servants always tell everything.

CHECCA: Leave it to me. I'll get her to tell me all she knows. But I know how to do it discreetly.

ROSINA: Here she is.

[LUCIETTA *enters*.]

CHECCA: Come in, my child.

LUCIETTA: Thank you, signora.

CHECCA [*to herself*]: What a lovely girl! [*to* LUCIETTA] What is it, my dear? Have your mistresses sent you?

LUCIETTA: The young one sent me, signora.

ROSINA: Signorina Domenica?

LUCIETTA: Yes, signorina. I expect you know I'm her maid, not the married one's. I've been with her quite a time and I'm very fond of her and I'd like to stay with her. But if I have to wait on that other one, I won't stay in that house another hour, even though I've nowhere to go.

CHECCA: That's right, my dear, you can tell me all about it. What is she like, the young married one?

LUCIETTA: I don't know what to say. I'm not one of those who talk, signora. If I can't say anything good, I don't say anything bad. Besides I've hardly seen her. But from the little I've seen, I don't believe there can possibly be, in the whole world, a more horrible woman than she is.

ROSINA [*aside*]: If she were one who talked, what would we hear!

CHECCA: Yes, but in what way? Is she a snob? A boor?

LUCIETTA: With her servants and with her sister-in-law, she's bad-tempered and rude. But she's not like that with everybody. There's a certain Count. . . .

CHECCA: Come, come, no more of that. [*She motions her to be quiet on account of her sister.*]

LUCIETTA: I understand.

CHECCA: Tell me, my dear, why did they treat us so ill-manneredly?

LUCIETTA: Oh, that wasn't my mistress's fault. It was that other one.

CHECCA: What? You mean, the young married one didn't want to see us?

LUCIETTA: I'll tell you . . . really, it's enough to make you die laughing! When she thought you were visiting her, she said yes. But when she found out you were visiting both of them, she got in such a temper and refused to see you!

ROSINA: What a thing to do!

CHECCA: How absurd!

LUCIETTA: So then my young mistress got annoyed as well.

CHECCA: Well!

ROSINA: Oh, my goodness, I *am* enjoying this!

LUCIETTA: So you see, it's my young mistress who's just sent me to beg your forgiveness, and to say that if it's convenient she'll come herself and pay her respects.

CHECCA: Oh, she mustn't put herself to that trouble. . . .

ROSINA [*softly, to* CHECCA]: Yes! Yes! Let her come!

LUCIETTA: Truly, signora, she is really very sorry.

CHECCA: That's enough. If she's merely being polite, tell her there is no need to disturb herself. We do not let such things upset us. However, if she really wishes to make herself pleasant, tell her we shall be pleased for her to visit us whenever she wishes.

LUCIETTA: Thank you, signora. My mistress really is the most kind-hearted young lady. But you will see that for yourself.

CHECCA: And I can see that you are very kind-hearted yourself, my dear. And that you are very fond of your mistress.

LUCIETTA: Oh, yes, indeed, signora. I couldn't do more for her if she were my own sister.

CHECCA: It is good to find a servant who speaks well of her mistress. Most usually find fault with something.

LUCIETTA: Oh, there's no danger of that with me. You'll never hear me speaking badly of her.

CHECCA: That is how it should be!

ROSINA: How old is your mistress?

LUCIETTA: She's quite young, signorina. I don't think she can be eighteen yet.

ROSINA: Isn't she in love with someone?

LUCIETTA: A little.

CHECCA: You know my cousin?

LUCIETTA: Who is that, signora?

CHECCA: Signor Lorenzino Bigoletti.

LUCIETTA: Good gracious, yes! I know him, of course!

CHECCA: Do you think she would like to meet him?

LUCIETTA: Wouldn't she just!

CHECCA: I believe it was because of him she didn't want to leave the other house?

LUCIETTA: Yes, it's really upset her, that has.

CHECCA: She often speaks of him?

LUCIETTA: Good heavens! All day long!

ROSINA: I do think it's rather hard on her. . . .

LUCIETTA: Yes, isn't it, signorina? If there's one thing I can't stand it's snobbishness.

CHECCA: But what will she do now?

LUCIETTA: Signor Lorenzino really is your cousin?

CHECCA: Certainly. He is the son of one of my aunts.

LUCIETTA: Then, don't you see, signora, *you* can help her!

CHECCA: How dare you suggest such a thing! Ladies do not involve themselves in intrigues. Of course, if she were seriously considering marriage with the young man, that would be quite another matter.

LUCIETTA: But she is, signora, she is! Only the poor girl hasn't any dowry. Her father was a grocer. Her uncle used to sell butter. Her brother's been able to live in such fine style on the money his father left him. But that'll soon be all gone. You know what they say: Easy come, easy go. There now, I'm boring you with my chatter. I'll go and tell my mistress she may come and visit you. Your servant, signore. [*Exit*]

CHECCA: What a chatterbox!

ROSINA: But she is very attached to her mistress.

CHECCA: The attachment of a servant.

ROSINA: Why did you say you didn't want to concern your-self over our cousin?

CHECCA: Because I most certainly don't want to become the talk of the neighbourhood.

ROSINA: I suppose you are right.

CHECCA: My dear sister, I know I am.

LORENZINO [*calling, off-stage*]: Hello? Anybody at home?

ROSINA: Oh, good gracious, here he is!

CHECCA: Come in! We're in here, Lorenzino.

LORENZINO [*entering*]: Most illustrious cousins, my deepest, my humblest respects to you both!

ROSINA: Oh, fie, cousin!

CHECCA: You are not usually so polite!

LORENZINO: I do my best.

ROSINA: Didn't you sleep well last night?

LORENZINO: No, very little.

ROSINA: Never mind, there'll be nothing to disturb you to-night, will there?

LORENZINO: Curses on this house!

CHECCA: Now why should you curse this house?

LORENZINO: Well, curses on that apartment downstairs then.

ROSINA: What! Even though your dearest one is there?

LORENZINO: I can't even find her balcony. For three hours I've been walking up and down out there, coughing like a madman to attract her attention. But there's not been a sign of her.

CHECCA: I could have told you that. Her room is at the back. It looks on to a courtyard where nobody passes.

LORENZINO: And you wonder why I curse this house! *And* that fool of a brother of hers. He pays sixty ducats more than he needs to – and then lodges his sister in some old cubby-hole. Anyway, how does he manage it? How is he going to pay the rent? With his wife's dowry?

CHECCA: You think Signor Anzoletto is in that sort of trouble?

LORENZINO: I know nothing. All I know is he's had that apartment for two months now and he hasn't paid the rent for the first month yet.

ROSINA: And you're well-off enough to get entangled with his sister?

LORENZINO: She has an uncle who will give her a dowry.

CHECCA: Yes, I've heard of this rich uncle of hers, but I thought he had fallen out with his nephew.

LORENZINO: But not with his niece.

CHECCA: My dear cousin, I think you should consider well before you do anything rash. *You* haven't money to throw away.

LORENZINO: With a dowry of two or three thousand ducats I could buy a position of office, and with the little bit I have I'd be able to live.

CHECCA: You certainly wouldn't be able to let your wife live in the style that Signor Anzoletto lets his.

LORENZINO: How d'you mean?

ROSINA: Oh, you should have seen her!

CHECCA: A crinoline, my dear, all flounced out from here to there!

ROSINA: The most extraordinary dress you could imagine!

CHECCA [*to* ROSINA]: Silk, embroidered with real gold by the look of it.

ROSINA: Frills all round it!

CHECCA: And her hair! Oh, the latest style, of course!

ROSINA: With diamonds even!

CHECCA: Murano glass, more likely!

ROSINA: Well, they certainly glittered and shone like anything.

CHECCA: So do cat's eyes!

LORENZINO: And the young girl? You've seen her?

CHECCA: Oh, we've seen her.

LORENZINO: What do you think of her?

CHECCA: Mmm . . . so-so.

ROSINA: She's not one of these beauties.

CHECCA: She's well-made.

ROSINA: But she's quite a good figure.

CHECCA: Oh, *I* wouldn't say so.

LORENZINO: Then you can't have seen her very well.

ROSINA: We aren't blind, you know!

LORENZINO: Well, where did you see her?

ROSINA: On her balcony.

LORENZINO: You mean – it *is* possible to see her on her balcony?

CHECCA: Our dining-room overlooks the courtyard, just opposite the balcony outside her room.

LORENZINO: My dear cousin, may I go into your dining-room?

CHECCA: Now don't start your comedy here!

LORENZINO: But you did promise me you'd speak to the Signorina Domenica for me. So why won't you let me have a look at her balcony?

CHECCA: Pardon me, young man, but you've got things the wrong way round. It's one thing for *me* to speak to her; it's quite another thing for you to make a fool of yourself on my balcony.

LORENZINO: But no one will see me. I promise I won't let anyone see me.

CHECCA: If you go on to the balcony, of course someone will see you!

LORENZINO: I'll just peep over. No one will see me.

CHECCA: Everybody opposite will see you.

LORENZINO: But I'll be hidden by the shutters. I'll only open them a little.

ROSINA: Please, sister! Let the poor boy go.

LORENZINO: Dear cousin! Just a little peep!

CHECCA: You certainly are in a bad way. Go on, then. But mind you take care and don't make yourself ridiculous.

[LORENZINO *goes out jumping with joy*.]

ROSINA: Checca dear! Let me go as well! I won't stay a moment.

CHECCA: What on earth for?

ROSINA: Only to have a little look.

CHECCA: Well! I like that! What *would* the neighbours think!

ROSINA: All right, if you don't want me to, I won't. But I only wanted to hear what the Signorina Domenica speaks like.

CHECCA: You can hear her speak when she comes here.

ROSINA: But we may have to wait ages for that.

CHECCA: What was that? Wasn't it somebody at the door?

ROSINA: Yes, I thought I heard something myself. [*She goes to the door and looks out.*] Oh! D'you know who I think it is?

Good heavens, yes! I do believe it's her! The Signorina
Domenica!

CHECCA: No!

ROSINA: There's somebody on the stairs speaking to our
servant. I didn't want to let myself be seen, so as not to
appear. . . .

CHECCA: Quite right. [*The* SERVANT *enters.*]

ROSINA: Here's Toni. Now we'll know.

SERVANT: Signora, the lady from downstairs wishes to see
you.

CHECCA: Is it the young girl, or the married one?

SERVANT: I couldn't say, signora. I don't know them.

ROSINA: Does she wear a crinoline?

SERVANT: No, signorina.

ROSINA: It's the young one.

CHECCA: Tell her we shall be happy to receive her.

SERVANT: Yes, signora. [*Exit*]

ROSINA: What about Lorenzino? He'll be waiting on the
balcony.

CHECCA: Let him wait then. He can't hear us from there.
We'll play a joke on him and not tell him.

ROSINA: Suppose he comes back in here?

CHECCA: Well, what if he does?

[DOMENICA *enters.*]

DOMENICA: Please excuse the liberty I am taking.

CHECCA: Not at all. We think it most courteous of you.

ROSINA: We so much wanted to welcome you as our neighbour.

DOMENICA: Thank you. As we are so near, perhaps you will
not mind if I come occasionally to call on you?

CHECCA: Why, of course. You must come whenever you
wish.

ROSINA: And we will come and call on you.

DOMENICA: On me? . . . Oh dear . . . I don't know how to
tell you. But I will. Yes, I will tell you. Everything.

CHECCA: Won't you sit down?

DOMENICA: Thank you.

ROSINA: Aren't you happy in your new apartment?

DOMENICA: Oh, the apartment's all right. It is simply that there are – well, some things about it I don't like.

ROSINA: For example . . . the view from your balcony?

DOMENICA: How could anybody like it? Nothing but an old courtyard!

CHECCA: And yet . . . perhaps it could be arranged that the view from your balcony did not displease you.

DOMENICA: No, signora. That's impossible.

ROSINA: For example . . . if you were on your balcony at this very moment – the view might not displease you.

DOMENICA: Oh, you mean the sun shines on the courtyard at this time of day? But I never look.

CHECCA: If you were there – at this very moment – you would see the sun shining full on to your balcony.

DOMENICA: Oh, I can't bear the sun full on me.

ROSINA: It depends on which sun you mean.

DOMENICA: You are making fun of me. Yes, I see you enjoy making jokes.

CHECCA: When you were on the balcony at your old house, was there not a sun whose rays you *could* bear to fall on you?

DOMENICA: I'm afraid it's no use trying to make me laugh.

ROSINA: Tell me, Signorina Domenica, hasn't Lucietta said anything to you?

DOMENICA: About what?

ROSINA: About a certain cousin of ours.

DOMENICA: No, she hasn't said anything.

CHECCA: But you do know our cousin?

DOMENICA: No, who is he?

CHECCA: Why, Lorenzino.

DOMENICA: Lorenzino Bigoletti?

CHECCA: Lorenzino Bigoletti.

DOMENICA: What? You really mean it? He's your cousin?

ROSINA: He is our cousin.

DOMENICA: Then . . . you know . . .

CHECCA: We know all.

DOMENICA: Oh, dear!

ROSINA: What a horrible time you must be having in that awful apartment down there.

DOMENICA: Terrible!

CHECCA: That horrible balcony!

DOMENICA: It's like being in hell!

ROSINA: And all you can see is a glimpse of the sky!

CHECCA: You might as well be in a prison cell.

DOMENICA: I might indeed! But now I begin to hope! That I may after all see him here as well sometimes.

CHECCA: Really?

DOMENICA: Who would have thought I should be so fortunate as to find two such understanding ladies as yourselves?

ROSINA: Cousins of Signor Lorenzino.

DOMENICA: It really is incredible.

CHECCA: Yes, wouldn't it be incredible if he should come in now and find you here?

DOMENICA: Oh, if only he would!

ROSINA: I have a feeling he may not be far away.

DOMENICA: You really think so!

CHECCA: Doesn't your heart tell you?

DOMENICA: My heart tells me that if he should come I would see him willingly.

ROSINA: And yet if you were at home you would be seeing him at this very moment.

DOMENICA: Where?

ROSINA: From the balcony of your room.

DOMENICA: But nobody can pass through that courtyard! It's enclosed on every side by warehouses.

CHECCA: I believe he's thinking of renting one of the warehouses.

DOMENICA: Oh, you're laughing at me again – and you're quite right to.

ROSINA: Seriously, would you really like to see him?

DOMENICA: With all my heart I would.

CHECCA: Signorina Rosina, have a look outside and see if there is anybody coming. I think there is somebody at the door.

DOMENICA: Oh, if only it were he!

ROSINA [*going to the door*]: We'll see. You never know who it might be.

SERVANT [*entering*]: Signora, the other lady from downstairs, the young married one, asks if she may, with your permission, also come to pay you her respects.

CHECCA: Most willingly. Ask her to come in. [*The* SERVANT *goes out.*]

DOMENICA: Oh, damn the woman!

ROSINA: It annoys you that she should come?

DOMENICA: That's putting it mildly. We simply can't agree. I bet anything she's only come just to annoy me.

CHECCA: But why?

DOMENICA: There isn't time to tell you all about it now. But I will later. [*to* ROSINA] Dear signorina, please do go and see if Signor Lorenzino may be coming.

ROSINA: But your sister-in-law will be here any moment.

DOMENICA: If only I could avoid her. Please, will you do me a favour?

CHECCA: Of course. You have only to ask.

DOMENICA: Since my sister-in-law is here, allow me to go through there.

CHECCA: Why through there?

DOMENICA: So I may leave through another door.

CHECCA: But all our rooms communicate with each other. There is no other way out.

DOMENICA: Then let me stay in your dining-room.

CHECCA: Really?

ROSINA: You poor girl! In the dining-room of all places!

DOMENICA: Would it be worse for me there?

ROSINA: Oh, no! You'd be all right there! Yes, indeed!

DOMENICA: Then let me go in there!

CHECCA: No, no, you will have to excuse me. I'll have no more of this nonsense. You'll just have to be patient with her this time.

DOMENICA [*to* ROSINA]: But you'll let Signor Lorenzino know, won't you?

ROSINA: I'll send someone to tell him at once.

CHECCA: No, no, wait! I'll send someone. [*She goes to the door.*] Where are you, Toni?

SERVANT [*entering*]: Yes, signora?

CHECCA: Is the lady from downstairs coming?

SERVANT: Yes, she's coming now, signora.

CHECCA [*drawing him to one side and speaking softly*]: Listen! Go to the dining-room and tell Signor Lorenzino he's to go at once. If he doesn't know the Signorina Domenica is here, don't say anything. If he does, tell him he's still to go, because Signorina Domenica's sister-in-law's coming and I don't want any trouble. You understand? Do your best.

SERVANT: Leave it to me. [*He goes out.*]

DOMENICA: You've sent him to look for him?

CHECCA: Yes, signorina.

DOMENICA: And what about my sister-in-law?

CHECCA: He won't come in as long as he knows she is here.

ROSINA [*aside*]: My sister's so sensible, she's probably told him to go.

CHECCA [*to* DOMENICA]: Does your sister-in-law know about Lorenzino?

DOMENICA: I don't think so. Unless my brother has told her.

[LORENZINO *enters.*]

LORENZINO [*indignantly*]: Thank you very much, cousin!

CHECCA: Go away at once!

LORENZINO: I've been standing in there in the cold, getting a crick in my neck while. . . .

CHECCA: Go away! D'you hear me!

ROSINA: D'you want to cause trouble?

DOMENICA: Where were you getting a crick in the neck?

LORENZINO: In there, in the dining-room. Waiting to see if you came out on your balcony. And you've been here all the time!

DOMENICA: Well! Thank you very much, Signora Checca! You've been most kind!

CHECCA: My dear child, can't you take a joke? That is all that was intended.

ROSINA: But your sister-in-law coming like this spoilt the joke, you see?

LORENZINO: Well, I'm not going, that's certain.

CHECCA: Go away, I tell you!

LORENZINO: I can't!

DOMENICA: Poor boy, he can't!

ROSINA: If he goes down the stairs now, he'll meet her.

CHECCA: They both want to drive me mad. A lot of help I'd be to them then. [to LORENZINO] Get back in there where you were.

LORENZINO: Yes, signora. But I beg you, allow me to say two words to her first. [to DOMENICA] Dear Domenica, if you love me, wait for me. [to ROSINA] Dear little cousin, help us also, I beg you. [to DOMENICA] My sweet darling!

DOMENICA [wiping her eyes]: You poor boy!

CHECCA: For heaven's sake, get out!

LORENZINO: I go! I go! [to DOMENICA] Bless you! [Exit]

DOMENICA [aside]: The darling! Oh, I'm not going now! My sister-in-law can say what she likes. I'm my old self again now!

ROSINA [to DOMENICA]: My goodness, but you two have certainly got it badly!

CHECCA: A great pity, if you ask me. Here she is, confound it.

DOMENICA: Make way for the princess!

ROSINA: You call her princess?

DOMENICA: What else would you call such a conceited prig?

ROSINA: Oh, Signorina Domenica!

[CECILIA enters.]

CECILIA: Signora, your most humble servant conveys to you her most respectful greetings!

CHECCA: Signora!

ROSINA: Signora!

CECILIA: My greetings to you, sister-in-law.

DOMENICA: Signora.

CHECCA: It is indeed most kind of you to favour us like this.

CECILIA: I have come to pay my respects in order that I may

gain the honour of your acquaintance and to thank you for already doing me the honour of inconveniencing yourselves by coming to see me and to beg that you will pardon me for having had to deprive myself of the pleasure of your gracious company.

DOMENICA [*aside to* ROSINA]: You'd think sugar wouldn't melt in her mouth!

CHECCA: My dear signora, pray do not overwhelm me with ceremony. I am accustomed to speaking plainly, so if there is anything I can do for you, you have only to ask. We are neighbours, so we ought to be good friends. You will find me most willing.

CECILIA [*making an exaggerated curtsey*]: Your kindness overwhelms me.

DOMENICA [*aside to* ROSINA]: She'll fall over if she's not careful.

ROSINA [*aside to* DOMENICA]: She does put it on a little, doesn't she?

CHECCA [*to* CECILIA]: Won't you sit down?

CECILIA: After you, please.

CHECCA: We'll all sit down then.

DOMENICA [*to herself as they sit*]: Yes, let's get this over with.

CECILIA: My dear sister-in-law, if you intended coming to pay your respects to these ladies, you might have let me know so that I could have accompanied you. But perhaps your intention was to make me appear lacking in good manners?

DOMENICA: My dear sister-in-law, I thought you were waiting until they had made up their minds who was the mistress.

CECILIA [*to* CHECCA]: You must excuse our little jokes. We are always teasing each other, my sister-in-law and I.

CHECCA: You must be very fond of one another.

DOMENICA: Oh, we are!

ROSINA: Yes, I can see you are.

CECILIA [*aside*]: If you only knew!

CHECCA [*to* CECILIA]: You are pleased with your new apartment?

CECILIA: Well, to tell the truth, it does not displease me. But, of course, I cannot forget my old house.

DOMENICA: Nor I, mine.

CECILIA: Oh, really now, when all's said and done, your house was only an old shack. I can assure you the house I was brought up in was very different. As a matter of fact, we often used to have a prince staying with us. There were four of us brothers and sisters, you know. And of course we each had our own suite of rooms. But I quite like it here. Oh, yes, indeed I do. Only when one's been accustomed to something better, if you understand . . . you do understand? . . .

CHECCA: Oh, I understand . . . perfectly.

DOMENICA [*to* ROSINA]: Now you see what I mean?

ROSINA [*aside to* DOMENICA]: I'm going to enjoy this!

CHECCA: What a beautiful dress you are wearing. You have good taste.

CECILIA: You think so? They're merely some old things I used to wear when I was a young girl.

ROSINA: You used to go about dressed like that when you were a girl?

CECILIA: Why not? Surely you know that the fashion nowadays is set by the young? Why, nowadays fashion no longer allows any distinction between a young girl and a married woman.

ROSINA: In our house it does!

DOMENICA: And between my sister-in-law and me, it seems.

CECILIA: My dear Signorina Domenica, if one wishes to appear well-dressed, one needs to have the means to be so.

DOMENICA: Yes, it's quite obvious I haven't the means, isn't it? But if I had I'd save it up for a dowry instead of wasting it on clothes and new apartments. Then people wouldn't say I'd married without a penny to my name! [*aside*] And you can make what you like of that!

CECILIA [*aside*]: The little wretch. I'll make her pay for that! [*to* CHECCA] How do you amuse yourselves? Do you go to the theatre? Do you entertain much?

CHECCA: When my husband is in Venice we go to the Opera

or to see a comedy once or twice a week. But as he is not here at the moment, we stay at home.

CECILIA: If you would care to use one of my boxes, do let me know and I will let you have the keys. I have a box at all the theatres, you know. And please do borrow my gondola, if you wish.

CHECCA: Thank you very much! But I really do not go anywhere when my husband is not here.

CECILIA: And when your husband is here, you always want him with you?

CHECCA: If he wishes.

CECILIA: But how embarrassing for the poor man. One should have a little pity on one's husband, I always think. Let him do what he wants and go where he wants, that's what I say. I mean to say – if one can't even go to the theatre without one's husband – well! what can one do!

CHECCA: Oh, I do not mind. If my husband cannot come with me, I had just as soon stay at home.

CECILIA [aside]: What a fool!

DOMENICA [aside to ROSINA]: Did you ever hear such cant and humbug?

ROSINA [aside to DOMENICA]: Yes, I do see what you mean now.

DOMENICA [aside to ROSINA]: Yet my brother doesn't seem to notice such things.

ROSINA [aside to DOMENICA]: If her husband puts up with it, good luck to her.

CECILIA: And at home here, what do you do? Play games?

CHECCA: Occasionally we amuse ourselves.

CECILIA: What do you play?

CHECCA: Cards. Snap and beggar-my-neighbour.

CECILIA: But how boring. We play bridge of course. You must come and join us one evening. You will find the company and the conversation quite distinguished. We are never less than fourteen to sixteen at table. Oh, yes, we have people in to dine nearly every evening. Four or five chickens, salted tongue, or some truffles, or some good fish.

Of course I have a wine cellar, which you will find is something quite, quite out of the ordinary.

ROSINA [*to* DOMENICA]: Divide all that by three!

DOMENICA [*to* ROSINA]: By five at least!

CHECCA: You enjoy yourself most fashionably.

CECILIA: What can you expect? It is how I was brought up.

ROSINA: Now that she is with you, the Signorina Domenica must be enjoying herself as well.

DOMENICA: Oh, yes, I enjoy myself. Confined to my room.

CECILIA: I'm sorry your room here doesn't provide what your room at your old house did.

DOMENICA: What d'you mean by that?

CECILIA: Oh, nothing! Did you think I don't know? That my husband hasn't told me everything?

DOMENICA: Well, what about it? Why shouldn't I want to get married?

CHECCA: Dear Signora Cecilia, if she *is* in love, she deserves our sympathy. After all, you have yourself, and so have I.

CECILIA: Being in love is one matter; being in love with a good-for-nothing wastrel is quite another matter. My husband has told me she is infatuated with some loathsome creature who has neither rank nor position. A certain Lorenzino Bigoletti. Some foppish little upstart with no money and no education. Can you really imagine that I, a person such as I am, could put up with a relation of that sort?

DOMENICA [*to* ROSINA]: Well! Did you hear that!

ROSINA [*aside to* DOMENICA]: If Lorenzino hears her, heaven help us!

CHECCA: Tell me, Signora Cecilia, are you acquainted with him? With this Lorenzino Bigoletti?

CECILIA: I most certainly am not. From what I have been told, he is completely undeserving of the hand of my husband's sister.

CHECCA: Well, I do not claim he is wealthy. But he is certainly a gentleman. He comes from a family whose reputation is quite irreproachable. Nor have any of *his* relatives ever worn a tradesman's apron.

CECILIA: What *are* you talking about, Signora Checca? I think my family is well enough known in this city.

CHECCA: Oh, did you think I was meaning you?

CECILIA: Who did you mean then?

CHECCA: Shall we let sleeping dogs lie?

CECILIA: Why are you getting so heated about this disgusting person?

CHECCA: In what way is he a disgusting person? If I am getting heated, as you put it, it is because he is a respectable young man who is as well-educated as you, and who, moreover, happens to be my cousin.

CECILIA [*rising*]: Your cousin?

ROSINA: Yes, signorà, he is our cousin. And he is a good young man and we don't like anybody saying such things about him.

DOMENICA [*aside*]: Bravo!

CECILIA: Now I see why you've been making up to me! Why you were in such a hurry to visit me! [*to* DOMENICA] This young man has found a fine go-between for you, sister-in-law!

CHECCA: Just what does that mean? Who do you think you are speaking to?

CECILIA: Not having met you before, I took you to be persons of some respectability. I am sorry to find myself mistaken. I bid you good day. [*to* DOMENICA] As for you, I can't order you to come home, but I'll have you told to by somebody who can. And you can get out of your head all idea of marrying this blackguard. Because I won't have it! And when I say I won't have a thing that's final! I happen to be somebody in this city and I have influence. Do you understand me? Good-bye. [*Exit*]

DOMENICA: Did you ever hear such a tongue!

ROSINA: But she must be quite mad!

CHECCA: I don't know how I contained myself. If she hadn't been in my house, she would never have got away with that!

[LORENZINO *bursts in.*]

LORENZINO: Cousin, for your sake, I've kept quiet till I was nearly bursting. But, by heavens, nobody's going to call me names like that!

ROSINA: You heard her then?

LORENZINO: I'm not deaf, am I?

DOMENICA: But it doesn't worry me, my dear.

CHECCA: Nevertheless, you will oblige me, Signorina Domenica, if you will kindly go home. Never before has there been such a scene in my house. And I do not want it ever to happen again.

LORENZINO: But it's not her fault!

CHECCA: And you get out of here as well.

LORENZINO: That's just what I'm going to do! To find this Signor Anzoletto and beat him to pulp!

DOMENICA [*loudly*]: Oh, what shall I do!

ROSINA [*to* LORENZINO]: Are you mad?

CHECCA: That's enough. Stop your nonsense and get out.

LORENZINO [*striding up and down furiously*]: Me, loathesome! Me, disgusting! Me, an upstart! Upstart herself! That's all she is! What's that husband of hers? What was his family? Grocers! Greasy-handed grocers!

DOMENICA: Oh, please – may I have a glass of water?

ROSINA: Of course! I'll get a glass at once. [*to herself, as she goes to the door*] Poor girl, she'll have me crying too. [*Exit*]

LORENZINO [*also going towards the door*]: Yes, I'll go out on the balcony and if I see her I'll tell her what I think of her!

DOMENICA: Don't!

CHECCA: Come back here!

DOMENICA: Please!

CHECCA: Listen to me!

LORENZINO: I'm warning you, cousin, you see what a state I'm in. Don't push me to something desperate.

DOMENICA: Please, Signora Checca, have pity on him!

CHECCA: But what is it you want me to do? Do you want me to expose myself to more insults? Do you want my husband to come home and find me quarrelling with my neighbours?

DOMENICA: But you're different. You're sensible and kind. Oh, please try and think of something.

ROSINA [*entering, carrying a glass of water*]: Here is some water.

DOMENICA: Thank you.

CHECCA [*to* DOMENICA]: But how can you marry without a dowry?

ROSINA: Do you want this water?

DOMENICA [*to* ROSINA]: Just a minute. [*to* CHECCA] If you would speak to my uncle, I'm sure he would help us.

LORENZINO [*to* DOMENICA]: Why don't you go and see him yourself?

ROSINA: Do you want this water?

DOMENICA [*to* ROSINA]: In a moment. [*to* LORENZINO] My brother won't let me go and I'm frightened of what he might do.

CHECCA: Very well, my dear. I know Signor Cristofolo. You would like me to ask him to come and see me, is that it?

DOMENICA: Oh, if you only would!

ROSINA: *Do* you want it or don't you?

DOMENICA [*distractedly*]: Want what? Oh, I am so sorry: I don't know what I'm doing. [*She takes the glass in her hand.*] Dear Signora Checca, that would be marvellous! Oh, it would be wonderful! [*As she speaks she begins to upset the water.*] Ask him to call. You speak to him. Then you can send for me as well.

CHECCA: My dear girl, you are spilling that water all over my dress!

DOMENICA [*gulping the water while speaking*]: Oh dear! I just don't know what I'm doing.

ROSINA [*to herself*]: She *is* in a bad way!

DOMENICA [*as above*]: Listen . . . his house is . . . on the other side of the Canal . . . on the Gaffaro . . . three bridges away . . . near San Pantaleone.

CHECCA: I know very well where he lives. He is a friend of my husband's. I will send a message asking him to call.

DOMENICA: Now – right away?

CHECCA: I shall send at once. And now you can thank me by getting back downstairs again.

DOMENICA: Of course, signora! I do thank you! And you, Signorina Rosina. Good-bye, Lorenzino. You will tell him everything, won't you? That I'm quite desperate? And you won't forget to ask him to call? Good-bye, dear Lorenzino. [*Exit*]

ROSINA [*to* LORENZINO]: Well, cousin, you've cooked your goose now!

LORENZINO [*to* CHECCA]: My dear cousin. . . .

CHECCA: You ought at least to offer to go yourself and ask Signor Cristofolo to call here.

LORENZINO: Good heavens, yes! I'll run all the way!

CHECCA: You know where he lives?

LORENZINO: Do I? What d'you think!

CHECCA: Off with you, then.

LORENZINO: Right away! [*He goes out running.*]

ROSINA: What a child he is!

CHECCA: What a nuisance.

ROSINA: Love can make a fool of anybody! [*Exit*]

CHECCA: Only if one's a fool to begin with! [*Exit*]

⊰ SCENE 2 ⊱

Anzoletto's new apartment, as in Act One.

[ANZOLETTO *enters.*]

ANZOLETTO [*to himself*]: All my property at the old house sequestrated! Everything seized until I find the money to pay all these debts. Nobody will lend me any money. Nobody will even act as guarantor. I'm smothered in debts and I've not one person to turn to. And now here are these workmen wanting their money. Not to mention a wife who thinks I can afford to buy her the whole world. If only I hadn't upset my uncle, I wouldn't be in this situation! He wouldn't lift his little finger to help me now, even if I were dying. And all because I got married. What on earth did I want to get married for! What a fool I was! What an absolute idiot! Yet who'd have thought you could regret it so soon? It's only a fortnight . . .

OSWALDO [*entering, with his workmen*]:Right, signore! I've come for the money.

ANZOLETTO:Didn't I tell you tomorrow?

OSWALDO:Yes, you told me tomorrow, but the men say now. [*aside*] Now I know the trouble he's in.

ANZOLETTO:But you've done nothing to this room. It's the same as it was before. You haven't even moved the bed in.

OSWALDO:The bed's not here because I was told not to move it.

ANZOLETTO [*furiously*]:Who the devil told you that?

OSWALDO:Her Excellency your wife did.

ANZOLETTO:Oh . . . well . . . as long as I know.

OSWALDO:So you'd best settle these bills now.

ANZOLETTO:I'll settle them tomorrow.

OSWALDO:These men won't wait.

ANZOLETTO:Won't they, by heavens! They will when I get my stick to them!

OSWALDO:There's no need to lose your temper. These men have carried out your orders. And they don't expect blows from your stick as their wages.

ANZOLETTO:All right, I'll pay you before this evening. Is that good enough for you?

OSWALDO:Very good. As long as you do.

ANZOLETTO:You have my word.

OSWALDO:Be sure you keep it. Because you don't get rid of us this evening if you don't. [*to the men*] Come on. [*They go out.*]

ANZOLETTO [*to himself*]:If I have them stuck here it will be the end. I can't even raise any money now on all my things at the old house.

PROSDOCIMO [*calling, off-stage*]:Anybody there?

ANZOLETTO:Who is it? What d'you want?

PROSDOCIMO [*entering*]:I am looking for Signor Anzoletto Argagni.

ANZOLETTO:I am he. What is it you want?

PROSDOCIMO: I pay my most humble respects to your Illustrious Excellency on behalf of my master the Count Semolini, who has asked me to inform your Illustrious Excellency that you owe two months' rent on this apartment, that he has already made six applications for payment – this being the seventh – that you agreed to pay the first quarter in advance, and that he requests you to pay this immediately, at once, and without further delay. Otherwise, he regrets that he will be obliged to take certain steps of which Your Excellency will be notified in due course.

ANZOLETTO: Illustrious signore, I find you most tedious.

PROSDOCIMO: It is too kind of your Illustrious Excellency to say so.

ANZOLETTO: Tell your master that I will have the matter attended to tomorrow.

PROSDOCIMO: If your Illustrious Excellency will pardon me, may I ask something? This 'tomorrow' of which Your Excellency speaks, how many times does it come in a month?

ANZOLETTO: Very funny! Come tomorrow, and you will be paid.

PROSDOCIMO: If your Illustrious Excellency will pardon me, does your Excellency remember how many times he has said to me: 'tomorrow'?

ANZOLETTO: You have my word you will be paid.

PROSDOCIMO: If your Illustrious Excellency will. . . .

ANZOLETTO: Will you and your Illustrious Excellency get to hell out of here!

PROSDOCIMO [*going towards the door*]: I am your Illustrious Excellency's most humble servant.

ANZOLETTO: At your service.

PROSDOCIMO [*as above*]: My salutations to your Excellency.

ANZOLETTO: Yours to command.

PROSDOCIMO: Your Excellency's most humble servant. [*Exit*]

ANZOLETTO [*to himself*]: That makes everything perfect! Never a dull moment! I only need my wife and my sister

to come in now. Yes, where can *they* be? Oh, well, they'll
come when they will. If only they wouldn't!

[LUCIETTA *enters*.]

LUCIETTA [*to herself*]: Oh, good heavens, he's back already!
ANZOLETTO: What d'you want?
LUCIETTA: When's all this moving going to finish? When
will the things be here?
ANZOLETTO: They're coming. Be patient and they'll be here.
LUCIETTA: It's dinner-time now!
ANZOLETTO: What's that to do with it?
LUCIETTA: Well, d'you want to sit down at table with no
table linen?

ANZOLETTO [*to himself*]: Here we go again. [*to* LUCIETTA]
Can't you manage somehow or other just for today?
LUCIETTA: I suppose I could use some hand towels.
ANZOLETTO: But you can't make table cloths out of hand
towels, can you?
LUCIETTA: They're all very worn and torn but I suppose
that doesn't matter.
ANZOLETTO: Well, can't you cut them up and make them
into table napkins?
LUCIETTA: Are you trying to make a fool of me as well?
Your wife's got to be pleased at all costs! That's it, isn't it?
Well, I'm sorry for my young mistress, but I can't do more
than I am doing. You just give me the seven months'
wages you owe me and try managing without me. [*Exit*]
ANZOLETTO [*to himself*]: What did I say? They're all at it! I
mention napkins and she flies into a temper and demands
her wages. Everybody's allowed to be sensitive and thin-
skinned except me! I've got to put up with being treated
any way they please! But everybody else – oh, no, *they* can't
put up with the least little thing!

[CECILIA *enters*.]

CECILIA: Husband, I've news for you.
ANZOLETTO: Now what's happened?

CECILIA: That sister of yours is a little liar!

[DOMENICA *enters*.]

DOMENICA: Brother, this wife of yours is an almighty snob!

CECILIA: Either she leaves this house or I do! [*Exit*]

DOMENICA: It's I who'll be leaving! And when you least expect it! [*Exit*]

ANZOLETTO: They're all at it! Of all the back-biting, beastly, vixenish. . . .

FABRIZIO [*entering*]: Here I am! In time for dinner!

ANZOLETTO: And to hell with you as well! [*Exit*]

FABRIZIO [*following him*]: Thank you. It is really most kind of you. Most kind. . . . [*Exit*]

Act Three

A room in Signora Checca's apartment.

CHECCA [*to herself*]: It's what I've always said, the least spark can set the whole house aflame. Some people just can't help making mountains out of molehills. My harmless curiosity about these people and their new apartment has caused all this trouble. Well, they won't find me bothering myself over them again, that's certain. All the same I can't help feeling sorry for my cousin. And for that poor girl as well.

ROSINA [*entering*]: Sister!

CHECCA: Now what is it?

ROSINA: That servant from downstairs, Lucietta, has been making signs from her balcony. I think she wants to speak to me.

CHECCA: Well?

ROSINA: Well, I've pulled the cord to open the door and told her to come up.

CHECCA: You shouldn't have! We're not having anything more to do with those people!

ROSINA: But you said Signorina Domenica could call again.

CHECCA: If her uncle comes, I will let her come up just that once. But never again, you understand. I want no more trouble with those people. Is that quite clear?

ROSINA: Why speak to me like this? It's nothing to do with me.

CHECCA: And I don't want any more familiarity from that servant.

ROSINA: But what can I do now? I've opened the door. I won't open it another time. Do you want me to send her away?

CHECCA: No, no. We'll hear what she wants.

ROSINA: I did hear some shouting. I am curious to know what it was about.

CHECCA: My dear sister, you must moderate this curiosity. What good is it to you to know what others do? If Lucietta is coming here merely to gossip, let us cut her short and not allow ourselves to listen to her.

ROSINA: Very well. I will do as you wish.

[LUCIETTA *enters*.]

LUCIETTA: Good evening, signore!

CHECCA: Good evening.

ROSINA: Good evening, Lucietta.

LUCIETTA: I've managed to escape for a moment. Nobody knows. I simply had to tell you. Things are happening down there!

ROSINA: Yes, go on!

CHECCA [*aside to* ROSINA]: Remember what I told you!

ROSINA [*aside to* CHECCA]: But what have I said now?

LUCIETTA: Have you something against me? What have I done?

CHECCA: I don't want any gossiping here.

LUCIETTA: I'm sorry, I only came to tell you . . . but if you don't want to hear. . . . [*she goes towards the door*].

CHECCA: Come here. What is it you want to tell me?

ROSINA [*aside*]: My sister's even more curious!

LUCIETTA: I only wanted to tell you in confidence what's just happened but if you think I've only come to gossip . . .

CHECCA: Come, come, if you've anything to confide in me. . . .

LUCIETTA: Such things have been happening, you'd never believe!

CHECCA: What things?

LUCIETTA: My master's desperate! He can't move in from the old house. They've put seals on all his things there. He can't even pay the rent for the new apartment. And the workmen are demanding their money. And I've seen nothing myself of my wages for the last seven months. Oh, things are in a bad way all right.

CHECCA: They are indeed!

ROSINA: This is terrible!

CHECCA: What has that fool of a wife of his got to say about it?

ROSINA: And his poor sister.

LUCIETTA: My mistress is crying. The new wife's raging like a fury.

CHECCA: Tell me: how has he got into debt like this?

LUCIETTA: Through trying to show off and by indulging the whims of that precious wife of his.

CHECCA: But he's been married only a fortnight. . . .

LUCIETTA: Oh, signora, you don't know the half of it. He was running after her for two years, ruining himself trying to please her.

ROSINA: Yet she brought him no dowry?

LUCIETTA: Absolutely nothing.

CHECCA: So that's the sort of fine lady she is, then?

LUCIETTA: She is that. Do you know, a servant who used to work in her parents' house told me she often had to pawn their gold bracelets to buy food for them.

ROSINA: This servant left them?

LUCIETTA: Yes, because they weren't even paying her. Oh, servants are not all like me, signora. I haven't been paid for seven months but I've not said a word.

ROSINA [*aside*]: Oh, yes, you're a pearl you are!

[SERVANT *enters*.]

SERVANT: Signora, somebody is asking for you.

CHECCA: Who is it?

SERVANT: It's an old man. Signor Lorenzino is with him.

ROSINA: It must be Signor Cristofolo.

LUCIETTA: My mistress's uncle?

CHECCA: Yes, that's who it must be. Now listen carefully. Go downstairs, take Signorina Domenica on one side, and tell her to come up here to me.

LUCIETTA: Yes, signora, I'll go at once.

CHECCA: But take great care nobody hears you.

LUCIETTA [*going towards the door*]: Leave it to me.

ROSINA: And don't tell anyone else either!

LUCIETTA [*as before*]: What a thing to say! As if I'd breathe a word!

CHECCA: Make sure you don't. This is something very important.

LUCIETTA: Well, really, signora. You're mistaken if you think I'm some sort of gossiping tittle-tattler. I know how to keep my mouth shut, when needed. Nobody will get a word out of me. [*Exit*]

CHECCA [*to the* SERVANT]: Ask this gentleman to come in. And tell Signor Lorenzino to wait outside.

SERVANT: Yes, signora. [*Exit*]

CHECCA [*to* ROSINA]: And you also, if you don't mind. While I am speaking to Signor Cristofolo, it will be best if you are not here.

ROSINA: But I'd so much like to listen!

CHECCA: I can see that. You're bursting with curiosity.

ROSINA: And I suppose you're not?

CHECCA: I listen only to what I ought to listen to.

ROSINA: Well, I certainly don't want to hear what I oughtn't to hear. [*Exit*]

[SIGNOR CRISTOFOLO *enters.*]

CRISTOFOLO: Pleasure to meet you again, signora.

CHECCA: And for me to meet you, Signor Cristofolo. Yes, indeed!

CRISTOFOLO: Now, now, none of that. No need for flatteries with me, dear lady.

CHECCA: Surely I may welcome you here?

CRISTOFOLO: You may. But there's no need for lah-di-dah compliments. Can't stand 'em. I'm a straightforward man. Say what I think. Always have done. As for all these modern compliments, you can have 'em, as far as I'm concerned.

CHECCA: As you wish. [*aside*] He's certainly one of the old school. [*aloud*] I hope I have not put you to any inconvenience?

CRISTOFOLO: Well, I'm here, aren't I? At your service, ma'am. Command me, and if I'm able, it'll be done.

CHECCA: Sit down then.

CRISTOFOLO: Certainly. How's your husband, Signor Fortunato? When d'you expect him back?

CHECCA: I received a letter from him only yesterday. He should be here by the end of the week.

CRISTOFOLO: Yes, he could arrive on Friday by the Bologna coach.

CHECCA: If you only knew how I miss him. I can't wait to see him again.

CRISTOFOLO: Ay, those who've got good husbands always want them with them, don't they, eh?

CHECCA: I seem lost without him. I have no desire to go anywhere or do anything.

CRISTOFOLO: Just as it should be. Respectable married ladies don't go gadding about without their husbands.

CHECCA [aside]: How on earth am I to begin?

CRISTOFOLO: Well then, Signora Checca, what can I do for you?

CHECCA: My dear signore, I beg that you will pardon me if you should consider I am taking a liberty, or that I am presuming upon our friendship.

CRISTOFOLO: There's no need to stand on ceremony with me. I'm a good friend of your husband's. Ask me whatever it is you want and don't beat about the bush.

CHECCA: Will you permit me to speak to you about a certain person?

CRISTOFOLO: Who?

CHECCA: A certain person.

CRISTOFOLO: So long as it's not my nephew, you can speak of whom you please.

CHECCA: Oh, I don't concern myself with your nephew's affairs!

CRISTOFOLO: Well, how was I to know? I know the young scoundrel's come to live below you here. It seemed quite likely you wanted to speak to me about him, and thought I mightn't come if I knew.

CHECCA: Oh, a gentleman such as yourself would never do that.

CRISTOFOLO: That's what you think. I've had more than I can stomach of that damn fool.

CHECCA: And his sister, poor child?

CRISTOFOLO: His sister's as big a fool as he is. When her mother died I offered to give her a home with me and she wouldn't come. Preferred to stay with her brother. Thought she'd have more freedom. Thought she'd have to go to bed too early at her old uncle's. No, that young scatter-brain deserves all she gets. She's made her bed, so let her lie on it.

CHECCA: But if you only knew what trouble the poor girl's in!

CRISTOFOLO: I know all about it. You think I don't, eh? Let me tell you there's nothing I don't know about those two. I know her brother's in debt up to his eyes. I know that in two years he's got through ten thousand ducats running after that precious wife of his. She's the one who's ruined him. Ever since he started going to that blasted house of hers he's never been the same. He had no time for me any more. Couldn't even come and see me. If he saw me in the street he'd go out of his way to avoid me. I wasn't well enough dressed for him. I didn't wear lace on my cuffs. Oh, I know it all. I even know what that trumped-up aristocrat of a strumpet of his says about me. I upset her stomach! I'm a disgrace to her! She couldn't bear to call me uncle! Let her wait till I call her my niece! That'll be the day! The little shrew! Scum! Riff-raff! That's all she is!

CHECCA [aside]: I'd have done better to have said nothing!

CRISTOFOLO: I beg your pardon. I get a little annoyed when I think of it. What was it you were wanting to say to me?

CHECCA: But my dear Signor Cristofolo, how is that poor young girl to blame for it all?

CRISTOFOLO: Look, my dear Signora Checca, suppose you put your cards on the table? What is it you want to see me about?

CHECCA: A certain matter.

CRISTOFOLO: Concerning yourself?

CHECCA: You could say so. It concerns a cousin of mine.

CRISTOFOLO: So long as it concerns you or one of your family, you've only to ask. As long as it's nothing to do with that nephew of mine.

CHECCA: And his sister?

CRISTOFOLO [*loudly and angrily*]: And her as well!

CHECCA [*aside*]: Oh, dear! [*aloud*] Well, as I was saying, I wanted to speak to you about my cousin.

CRISTOFOLO: Who is he?

CHECCA: He is the young man who went to call on you for me.

CRISTOFOLO: Oh, him!

CHECCA: You know him?

CRISTOFOLO: Never set eyes on him before.

CHECCA: He has not long been out of college.

CRISTOFOLO: Well he must know me. Found me in the Rialto, stopped me and brought me along here.

CHECCA: Oh, yes, he certainly knows you.

CRISTOFOLO: Well, what's he after? What's he want?

CHECCA: What did you think of him?

CRISTOFOLO: Seemed quite a respectable young fellow.

CHECCA: Oh, he is! He's a fine young man!

CRISTOFOLO: Yes, quite a pleasant young fellow. What's he do? Got a job?

CHECCA: He's looking for one.

CRISTOFOLO: Well, I've some influence. Friends, you know. Could be of use to him.

CHECCA: Oh, that would be wonderful!

CRISTOFOLO: Is this what you asked me to call for?

CHECCA: Yes, it was for this as well.

CRISTOFOLO: And for what else?

CHECCA: Well, I'll tell you. The young man wants to marry.

CRISTOFOLO: What is he? An infant prodigy? He's not stopped growing yet, and he wants to get married? He's got no job, yet he wants to raise a family? No, no! I don't think much of him then. He's gone down in my estimation.

CHECCA [*aside*]: Now I'm in a real pickle! [*aloud*] But supposing he finds a young lady with a good dowry?

CRISTOFOLO: They take some finding. . . .

CHECCA: And is able to buy himself a good position some-where?

CRISTOFOLO: In that case. . . .

CHECCA: In that case he wouldn't be doing badly.

CRISTOFOLO: In that case he'd have no need of me.

CHECCA: But that's just why he would have need of you.

CRISTOFOLO: Of me? I don't understand you.

CHECCA [aside]: This is where I put my foot in it!

CRISTOFOLO [aside]: She's got me so mixed up I don't know what the hell she's talking about.

CHECCA: Signor Cristofolo, don't you really think my cousin might be able to find a respectable young girl with a reasonable dowry?

CRISTOFOLO: Has he got any income of his own?

CHECCA: He has a little – and then if he obtained a good position. . . .

CRISTOFOLO: All right, signora, I'll agree with you. He's a presentable young fellow and he'll find a young lady.

CHECCA: Tell me, dear friend, if you yourself had a daughter, would you give her to him?

CRISTOFOLO: I'm not married; I've got no daughter; so there's no point in answering a damn silly question.

CHECCA: Then tell me, dear friend – your niece, would you give her to him?

CRISTOFOLO: Signora Checca, I'm not blind and I'm not deaf. I see what you're after. And I must say I'm surprised at you. I told you I didn't want to hear or to speak about those two. And so if there's nothing more I can do for you, I'll say good day! [He gets up.]

CHECCA: But listen. . . .

CRISTOFOLO: I don't want to hear any more!

CHECCA: I'm not saying any more. . . .

CRISTOFOLO: I don't want to hear or speak another word about those two.

CHECCA: Not even about your niece?

CRISTOFOLO: I have no niece!

[DOMENICA enters.]

DOMENICA: Oh, uncle!

CRISTOFOLO [*to* DOMENICA]: What d'you mean by this! [*to* CHECCA] What way's this to trick me?

CHECCA: Trick you? What way's that to speak? Anybody would think you were being robbed! Whether you like it or not, this young lady is your niece. She's been let down badly by her brother and she's very very miserable about it all. And when a young girl becomes desperate there's no knowing what she might do. When she has a rich uncle like you, he should feel honour-bound to find her a husband and help her to live in a manner commensurate with his own dignity. If you don't like hearing the truth, that's too bad. Out of kind-heartedness I have tried to help this poor child. As for you – you can do as you please!

CRISTOFOLO: Have you quite finished?

CHECCA: I'll finish when I want to! If I want to go on I could tell you a few more home-truths.

CRISTOFOLO: You needn't trouble. I've heard enough and I've understood enough. [*to* DOMENICA] Well, miss, what is it you expect from me?

DOMENICA: Dear uncle, I don't expect anything from you! Why should I? I'm only a poor girl who's had a lot of bad luck. By ruining his own life, my brother has also ruined mine.

CRISTOFOLO: Then why didn't you come and live with me?

DOMENICA: Because I acted foolishly. Because I let myself be influenced by my brother. Dear uncle, I ask your forgiveness!

CHECCA [*to* CRISTOFOLO]: Well? You must be made of stone if you're not moved by that.

CRISTOFOLO [*to* CHECCA]: Pity, signora, is a good thing, a fine thing. But you should keep it for those who deserve it. And not waste it on those who abuse it.

DOMENICA: Oh, what will become of me? If you don't help me I'll find myself without a roof over my head one of these days. I won't even have a pillow to lie on!

CRISTOFOLO: What are you talking about? Are you out of your mind? Hasn't your brother just rented this exclusive apartment downstairs? And paying sixty ducats more than he need for it?

DOMENICA: Yes, you are right to shame me so. The apartment is far beyond what he can afford. And he hasn't paid any of the rent yet. And tomorrow they're putting all our things out into the street!

CRISTOFOLO: So that's what it's come to, is it?

DOMENICA: And they've put seals on the furniture that is still in the other house! And I haven't even a dress to go out in!

CHECCA: Did you ever hear anything more pitiful?

CRISTOFOLO: What's that wife of your brother's got to say about all this?

DOMENICA: I've no idea, signore. I only know that on top of everything else I've to endure her wicked jibes and insults.

CRISTOFOLO: What's that? She's had the damn nerve to insult you?

CHECCA: I can vouch for that! She treats her most unkindly.

CRISTOFOLO [aside]: Blood's thicker than water, after all. I'm sorry for the girl. [aloud] Well, miss, what d'you think you can do about it?

DOMENICA: Whatever you wish, uncle. [She throws herself on her knees before him.] Here I am, kneeling to you. Please help me. [She remains kneeling with head bowed. CRISTOFOLO takes out his handkerchief and wipes his eyes.]

CHECCA [aside]: At last we're getting somewhere!

CRISTOFOLO: Get up, get up! You don't deserve it but I'll see if I can help you. Well? What were you thinking of doing?

DOMENICA: Oh, thank you, thank you! I'll do anything you say!

CHECCA: My dear Signor Cristofolo, she wants to get married. So why don't you help her to marry the young man?

CRISTOFOLO: Who is he?

CHECCA: He is my cousin.

CRISTOFOLO: Can he support her?

CHECCA: He has a little money of his own – enough to buy himself a position.

CRISTOFOLO: All right, but I'll have to have a talk with him first.

CHECCA: Would you like us to call him in?

CRISTOFOLO: Why, where is he?

CHECCA: Outside.

CRISTOFOLO: I see! He's outside, is he? He comes to fetch me here and now he's hiding outside waiting to be called in. So that's been your little game! Everything all arranged to trick me into doing what you want me to do! All right! I've heard enough. You'll get nothing from me. I don't want to hear another word about it! [Exit]

CHECCA: We'll see about that! He's not leaving here until he agrees to help you! [Exit]

[ROSINA enters.]

DOMENICA: Oh, poor me!

ROSINA: Don't give up hope, Signorina Domenica.

DOMENICA: But what can I do?

ROSINA: I heard everything you said and if you keep on at him I know you'll be all right. Throw yourself on your knees, weep, show him you're desperate. Lorenzino begs you. He's nearly dying, poor boy, because he can't do anything!

DOMENICA: Oh, poor Lorenzino! Yes! I'll do anything for him. I'll go and plead and plead with my uncle! I'll throw myself on the ground at his feet! [Exit]

ROSINA: That's more like it! When we women really want something we don't do things by halves! And tears are our best weapon! [Exit]

⊰ SCENE 2 ⊱

Anzoletto's new apartment, as in Act One.

[CECILIA, COUNT OTTAVIO *and* FABRIZIO.]

OTTAVIO: Come, signora, one must not abandon oneself to melancholy like this!

CECILIA: Oh, yes, Count! It's easy enough for those who are not in trouble to be full of polite consoling words! Have patience! Don't worry! But this time it's I who's got to have patience! [*She throws herself into a chair.*]

FABRIZIO: The proverb says: there's a remedy for everything except a broken neck.

CECILIA: Oh, what a fool I've been! What an idiot! I could have married into the best families in the town. I could have been covered with gold from head to foot. And here I am burdened with a man who wants to drag me down into the mud!

OTTAVIO: You will see things aren't as bad as they seem.

FABRIZIO: Yes, I am quite sure everything will be all right.

OTTAVIO: After all, a few debts! What are they?

CECILIA [*getting up and walking up and down*]: And yet I can almost pity that poor husband of mine. He lets his friends eat him out of house and home, yet when he's in trouble not one of them will help him.

FABRIZIO [*softly to the* COUNT]: That's one for you.

OTTAVIO [*softly to* FABRIZIO]: For you, you mean.

CECILIA: For this to happen to a woman like me! Brought up in luxury as I was! Waited on like a princess! Respected like a queen! [*She throws herself into another chair.*]

OTTAVIO: The Signora Cecilia will always be respected and waited upon.

CECILIA [*getting up and walking up and down*]: Ah, my dear Count, when you can no longer offer them a meal, few people will put themselves to the trouble of visiting you.

COUNT [*aside to* FABRIZIO]: It's you she means now.

FABRIZIO [*aside to the* COUNT]: Both of us, more likely.

CECILIA: But where the devil is Signor Anzoletto? Is he keeping out of the way and leaving me to face everything on my own? By heavens, I'll see they don't touch a thing of mine!

OTTAVIO: Signora, I would advise you to take out an insurance on your dowry.

CECILIA: How does one do that?

FABRIZIO: We will arrange it if you wish.

OTTAVIO: Yes, we will go and do what is necessary.

CECILIA: All right. You can at least do this little thing for me.

FABRIZIO: We will need to show the legal document concerning your dowry.

CECILIA: Is that necessary?

OTTAVIO: Certainly. One always has to produce the contract. Whatever the circumstances.

CECILIA: No, I don't want it to be said I helped to ruin my husband. And anyway, nobody in my family ever stooped to do such a thing, and I won't either.

FABRIZIO [aside to the COUNT]: Didn't you know she had no dowry?

OTTAVIO [aside to FABRIZIO]: I knew it better than you!

CECILIA: And where's my sister-in-law got to? Has she gone? Has she abandoned me as well? Where are they all? Why are they leaving me here all on my own? Are they trying to make me do something desperate?

OTTAVIO: But, signora, we are here!

FABRIZIO: We are both here! Whatever happens, we will not abandon you.

OTTAVIO: For heaven's sake, signora, take courage.

FABRIZIO: It's three hours past dinner-time. Don't you think you should eat something?

CECILIA: I've other things to think of than eating. The thought of food's enough to poison me.

OTTAVIO: Very well. Eat something a little later. When you feel like it.

FABRIZIO: But we will stay. We will not leave you. Not like all those others who came to dine with you and left as quick as they could when they heard how things were. Ah, no! We are true friends of the Signora Cecilia.

OTTAVIO: But dear lady, I urge you not to let your health suffer by not partaking of a little nourishment.

FABRIZIO: Would you like me to tell the cook to prepare a little chocolate?

CECILIA [getting up irritably]: I don't want anything! How could my husband treat me like this! Hiding everything from me! Pretending he was rolling in money! Making himself out to be what he wasn't! How dare he treat me like this! The lying villain! [*She throws herself into a chair.*]

COUNT: Do not distress yourself too much, signora.

FABRIZIO: Our presence perhaps is disturbing you?

[ANZOLETTO *enters.*]

ANZOLETTO [*aside*]: Oh, my poor wife!

CECILIA [*jumping to her feet and rushing furiously towards* ANZOLETTO]: Get out of here! Don't come anywhere near me!

ANZOLETTO [*holding out a knife to her*]: Take it! Go on! Take this knife and kill me!

CECILIA [*taking the knife and hurling it from her*]: You brainless – irresponsible – fool!

ANZOLETTO: Oh, my dear wife, you see what a state I'm in! Everybody is against me, but surely you will have pity on me. If I've got into debt, you know it was for your sake. . . .

CECILIA: What's that! You dare to say you've got into debt on my account! What have you ever spent on me? What jewels have you ever given me? What've you ever bought for me except a few dresses – and this cursed apartment on which you've not even paid any rent yet? Come on! Tell me! Just what have you spent on me? What debts have I made you make?

ANZOLETTO: None, none, you are quite right, my dear. I've done nothing for you. I've spent nothing on you. I've simply been throwing all my money into the canal just for the fun of it.

CECILIA: And don't you take that tone to me! Don't say another word, d'you hear?

ANZOLETTO: No, my dear, I won't say another word. [*to himself*] What's the use?

OTTAVIO [*aside to* FABRIZIO]: He'll need all the patience he's got, poor fellow.

FABRIZIO [*aside to* OTTAVIO]: He must know what she's like by now.

ANZOLETTO: Where is my sister?

CECILIA: How should I know? I've not set eyes on her for two hours.

ANZOLETTO: I only hope she hasn't gone there.

CECILIA: Gone where?

ANZOLETTO: To my uncle's.

CECILIA: If that's where she's gone, then she's shown some sense. And you'd better go as well.

ANZOLETTO: I? That's one thing I'll never do! Even if I have to go to prison.

CECILIA: Anybody in your position has to learn to swallow their pride.

COUNT: The signora is right you know!

CECILIA [to the COUNT]: Will you shut up and stop interfering in what doesn't concern you!

FABRIZIO: But we are your friends.

CECILIA: At times like this one finds out who one's real friends are. Deeds speak louder than words!

COUNT: If my presence disturbs you, that can soon be remedied. Signora, signore, your humble servant. [Exit]

FABRIZIO: Yes, indeed. Your most humble and devoted servant. [Exit]

CECILIA [to ANZOLETTO]: You see what sort of friends they are!

ANZOLETTO: Why say that to me? It was you brought them here.

CECILIA: Don't change the subject! So you're not going to ask your uncle to help you?

ANZOLETTO: Ask him? Not likely! Even if I'd the courage, I know what would happen. He'd only fly into a rage and call me all the names he can think of.

CECILIA: Perhaps I could speak to him?

ANZOLETTO: That wouldn't do any good.

CECILIA: Why wouldn't it?

ANZOLETTO: Because he can bear the sight of you – even less than he can of me.

CECILIA: Oh, I'd be able to calm him down.

ANZOLETTO: You calm him down! When you can't even calm yourself down!

CECILIA: At least I've enough sense to realize this isn't the time to lose one's head and get all heated.

ANZOLETTO: You can get heated with me all right. . . .

CECILIA: There you go again! As if things aren't bad enough without you keeping changing the subject, twisting everything so that everybody's to blame except you! Get out of my sight, you cruel beast!

ANZOLETTO: All right! I'll not say another word! Go on, then! Do what you like! Go and see him and come to what arrangements you please with him!

CECILIA: You come as well.

ANZOLETTO: Oh, no! Not me!

CECILIA: What a coward you are! Well, make your sister come with me.

ANZOLETTO: She may not want to.

CECILIA: She'll have to.

ANZOLETTO: Well, where is she? [*he calls*] Lucietta!

LUCIETTA [*from off-stage*]: Yes, signore?

ANZOLETTO: Come here!

LUCIETTA: Coming, signore.

CECILIA: It will be best if your sister does come with me because Signor Cristofolo does not know me. He's never seen me. And besides, she can do her bit as well. Leave it to me, I'll tell her what to say on the way.

[LUCIETTA *enters*.]

ANZOLETTO: Where is my sister?

LUCIETTA [*confused*]: I don't know. . . .

CECILIA: What d'you mean – you don't know?

LUCIETTA [*as above*]: No, really, I don't.

ANZOLETTO: Look! I want to know where she is!

LUCIETTA: All right, I'll tell you, signore. But don't say that it was me who told you.

ANZOLETTO: No, no, I won't say anything.

CECILIA: This is going to be interesting.

LUCIETTA: She's with the ladies in their apartment upstairs.

CECILIA: What's she gone there for?

ANZOLETTO: Has she gone to babble everything to them?

LUCIETTA: I'll tell you all, signore, but please don't say anything.

ANZOLETTO: Go on, I won't say a word.

LUCIETTA: Well! D'you know who's up there?

CECILIA: Ah! That lout Lorenzino!

LUCIETTA: That's right. But there's somebody else as well.

ANZOLETTO: Who?

LUCIETTA: Signor Cristofolo.

ANZOLETTO: My uncle?

CECILIA: His uncle is up there?

LUCIETTA: Yes, signora, but don't let on I told you!

CECILIA [to ANZOLETTO]: Quick! Come with me!

ANZOLETTO: Where?

CECILIA: Come with me, I tell you!

ANZOLETTO: I don't want to go up there.

CECILIA: Come along, you big baby. And you'll see what sort of a wife you've married. [She takes him by the arm and pulls him out with her.]

LUCIETTA: Now I've gone and done it! But why should I miss all the fun? I'm going up as well. [Exit]

⤜ SCENE 3 ⤛

A room in Signora Checca's apartment.

[CHECCA, DOMENICA, CRISTOFOLO and LORENZINO.]

CHECCA: Long life to you, Signor Cristofolo! A long life to your kind heart and your good nature. And may Heaven reward you for your goodness to this poor young girl.

DOMENICA: I shall never be able to repay his kindness to me.

LORENZINO: Nor I! Everything I value in this world, I shall owe to our dear uncle.

CRISTOFOLO [to LORENZINO]: Not so fast, young man. I'm not your uncle yet, remember.

CHECCA: Oh, come now! They'll be married tomorrow. And then you'll be his uncle.

DOMENICA: Oh, please don't frighten me!

LORENZINO: His word is enough for me. A man such as he doesn't go back on his word.

CHECCA: Perhaps it might be best to have it all down in black and white?

CRISTOFOLO: What I've said, I've said; and what I've said, I keep to. The girl's his. And I'll buy him a position. But before I sign the contract I want to know what's happened to all that her father left. [*to* DOMENICA] Your part of your father's estate should have come to you. If your brother's mortgaged it, we'll take him to court if necessary. I'll do all I can. I'll help you with my own money if I've got to. But I don't want to be taken for a fool.

CHECCA: I don't know enough about these things to give my opinion, but I'm sure you must be right.

DOMENICA: Oh dear, what a lot of things have to be done yet!

LORENZINO: Can't everything wait until after the marriage?

CRISTOFOLO: You're young; you know nothing. Leave it to me.

[ROSINA *enters.*]

ROSINA: Signora Checca, may I have a word with you?

CHECCA: Yes, I'll come, my dear. [*to the others*] Excuse me, please. [*She goes over to* ROSINA *and they talk in low voices.* CHECCA *makes gestures of astonishment.*]

DOMENICA: Uncle, where shall I live in the meantime?

CRISTOFOLO: You can come to me.

LORENZINO: May I come and see her?

CRISTOFOLO: You may – when I am there.

DOMENICA [*to herself*]: Oh dear, I'll be too scared to open my mouth in his house.

[CHECCA *and* ROSINA *finish talking softly to each other and* ROSINA *goes out again.*]

CHECCA [*to herself*]: What shall I do? I've succeeded so far, I might as well try and get them settled as well. I feel so sorry for her I couldn't say no. [*to* DOMENICA] Signorina Domenica, do me the kindness to go out to my sister for a little while, will you? I have a matter to discuss with Signor Cristofolo.

DOMENICA: Certainly. [*aside, to* CHECCA] Make him arrange everything now! [*to herself*] I'm sure she'll do it! [*Exit*]

CHECCA: Signor Lorenzino, will you do me a favour?

LORENZINO: Of course. At your service, signora.

CHECCA: Go to the post and see if there are any letters from my husband.

LORENZINO: You want me to go now?

CHECCA: Yes, run along. It's only round the corner. Go, and come back at once.

LORENZINO: But won't our uncle be going soon?

CHECCA: He won't have gone before you get back.

LORENZINO: I'll be back as quick as I can then. [*Exit running*]

CRISTOFOLO: Well, I'd better be on my way. I'm not as young as I used to be and I like having my meals at regular times. Because of all this I haven't had my dinner yet.

CHECCA: Dear Signor Cristofolo, since you have been so kind, will you bear with me a little longer? Will you do me a very great favour and listen to somebody who would like to say a few words to you?

CRISTOFOLO: Devil take it, if it's my nephew, I won't listen.

CHECCA: It is not your nephew.

CRISTOFOLO: Who is it then?

CHECCA: Now don't get into a temper. It's the young wife of your nephew.

CRISTOFOLO [*irritably*]: What does she want with me?

CHECCA: I'm afraid I don't know.

CRISTOFOLO: All right, damn it, I'll see her. But I won't be held responsible for what I say. If anybody gives me a pain in the neck, she does. So if I tell her what I think of her, don't complain I'm not behaving as I should in your house.

CHECCA: In that case, please behave entirely as if you were in your own house. Speak to her just as you please. [*Exit*]

CRISTOFOLO: So! This – lady, who says I upset her stomach, condescends to speak to me! Well, she'll get none of my money, if that's what she's after. A piece of my mind is what *she'll* get.

[CECILIA *enters*.]

CECILIA [*to herself*]: How I hate having to do this! But it's got to be done!

CRISTOFOLO [*to himself*]: Ay, ay! Battle-stations it is!

CECILIA: Your humble servant, signore.

CRISTOFOLO: Y' servant, signora.

CECILIA: Would you do me the honour of allowing me to pay you my respects.

CRISTOFOLO: Y' servant, signora.

CECILIA: Would you do me the great honour of allowing me to seat myself by you?

CRISTOFOLO [*jumping to his feet and moving away*]: Ay, sit, if you wish.

CECILIA: Why do you move away?

CRISTOFOLO: Because you don't like the smell of the bacon from my shop.

CECILIA: Dear sir, please do not make me drain my cup of misery to the dregs. Be kind enough to sit here.

CRISTOFOLO: No. You see, I don't want to upset your stomach.

CECILIA: Oh, my dear uncle. . . .

CRISTOFOLO [*turning as if bitten by a snake*]: Where d'you get this 'dear uncle' from?

CECILIA: Don't raise your voice; we mustn't make fools of ourselves here. I have not come here to make trouble. I have not come here to ask you for anything. I have come to humiliate myself in front of you. And even if you think such a gesture cannot be disinterested – and despite all the reasons you can have for disliking me – when a lady humiliates herself, pleads and begs for forgiveness, any gentleman would subdue his resentment and listen to her. I ask nothing from you – I deserve nothing – only that you listen to me. Will you show me that courtesy?

CRISTOFOLO: You can talk your head off, signora, for all I care. Go ahead. I can wait. [*to himself*] Then I can take her to pieces bit by bit.

CECILIA: I shan't beat about the bush because it's getting late. Besides, when one is in trouble, every minute is precious. I am your nephew's wife. Your nephew is your brother's son. In other words, you and I are closely related. I know you feel badly disposed towards my husband, and to me. And you've just cause to be. That's right, have a good look at me. I'm young, and I'm not ashamed to say that up till now I've behaved with all the foolishness of the young. It's been my misfortune never to have had anybody to give me good advice or to correct me. As a child I was spoilt and given everything I wanted. My husband, whom you know better than I, the poor man, has a kind and generous nature. And because of that, he has ruined himself. Without realizing what I was doing, I have kept asking more from him than he could afford. And it's true I have spoken badly about you. I have spoken very badly about you. But try to put yourself in my position. I was brought up to a certain way of life, to wear these foolish clothes, to behave in a way completely opposed to all your principles. And if my father wore the sort of clothes that you do, I would even have spoken badly of my own father. And now I am reaping the reward of the ignorant way in which I was brought up. I am finding it very hard to hold back my tears at the situation my poor husband is in. All our possessions impounded. Our furniture to be moved out into the street. My poor husband faced with arrest and imprisonment. Tomorrow morning we shall be on the street without food or home. Everybody mocking us. Everybody scorning and despising us. My husband become the laughing-stock of the town. And yet who is my husband? He is Signor Anzoletto Argagni. He is the nephew of Signor Cristofolo. And I am his niece. It is our own fault that we have ruined ourselves. But we have learnt from our mistakes. We have been taught our lesson and we would like to live better lives. And that we may do so, we ask the forgiveness of a compassionate uncle. We ask his pity and his help, and we ask it humbly and sincerely.

CRISTOFOLO [*to himself*]: What the devil can I say now!

CECILIA: And now that you have been so good as to listen to me, speak, say what you think of me, take your revenge. You have every right to.

CRISTOFOLO: If all you have said is true. . . .

CECILIA: Don't you believe we are in trouble, terrible trouble. . . .

CRISTOFOLO: I didn't say that. I said if it's really true that your husband and you are sorry and want to change your way of living, then, though I'm not obliged to do anything – what I've got I've earned through hard work – I've a good heart and I might be able to do something for you.

CECILIA: I'm not asking you to believe *me*. I'm a woman, I'm young. I know I've all these silly ideas now, but I could change. Listen – hear what my husband has to say. Take his word. And I will help him to keep it. Do you think I would be so unworthy as to try to ruin him a second time?

CRISTOFOLO [*to himself*]: She could twist anybody round her little finger! [*aloud*] Where is he, then, this good-for-nothing husband of yours?

CECILIA: Come in, husband. Providence is being kind to us.

CRISTOFOLO [*to himself*]: So he's here as well! This place is Liberty Hall.

[ANZOLETTO *enters.*]

ANZOLETTO: I hardly dare face you, uncle.

CRISTOFOLO: Get to the point. Make out a list of your debts. A transfer of your assets. A resolution to alter your ways. And I'll do what my heart tells me to – and which you don't deserve, you worthless young good-for-nothing.

ANZOLETTO: I promise, I swear, I will always do as you wish.

CRISTOFOLO: I will pay the rent you owe on this new apartment you've taken. But you will give notice that you're giving it up. It's not the sort of place for you.

CECILIA: Dear uncle, give us just one little room in your house.

CRISTOFOLO: There isn't one.

CECILIA: Dear uncle, please. Just while we find somewhere else to go.

CRISTOFOLO: Well, for no longer then, you cunning little minx. While you're in my house you'll both behave yourselves. And mark well, I'll have none of those friends of yours in my house either.

CECILIA: Believe me, I'm so disgusted with those people there's no danger of that.

[CHECCA *enters followed by* DOMENICA, ROSINA, LORENZINO *and* LUCIETTA.]

CHECCA: Well? Is everything arranged?

ANZOLETTO: Everything! Thanks be to heaven and to my dear uncle.

DOMENICA: And I will come and stay with you, uncle.

CECILIA: And I'm going to stay with him as well.

DOMENICA [*annoyed*]: You are?

CRISTOFOLO [*to himself*]: These two together would drive me mad. One'll be more than enough. [*to* CHECCA] Signora Checca, if I have done something for you, would you do me a kindness in return?

CHECCA: Of course. You have only to ask.

CRISTOFOLO: Would it inconvenience you if we arranged the marriage of my niece from your apartment?

CHECCA: But that would be wonderful!

LORENZINO [*jumping with joy*]: The wedding! The wedding!

DOMENICA [*jumping with joy*]: My wedding!

CHECCA: Let us do it now!

CRISTOFOLO: Now if you wish.

CHECCA [*to* DOMENICA *and* LORENZINO]: Take each other's hand.*

DOMENICA: Do you agree, uncle?

CRISTOFOLO: I'm agreeable. But what about your brother. Is he?

*See footnote on p. 61.

DOMENICA [*to* ANZOLETTO]: Are you pleased? Do you agree to our marriage?

ANZOLETTO: Of course. Whatever pleases my uncle will please me.

CHECCA: Good. Then give each other your hand.

LORENZINO: This is my wife.

DOMENICA: This is my husband. [*They take each other's hand.*]

ROSINA: I am so very happy for you, Signorina Domenica.

DOMENICA: Thank you.

CRISTOFOLO [*to* CECILIA *and* ANZOLETTO]: That leaves you two. You'd both better come home with me. And from now on, start showing some sense. Or it will be the worse for you.

ANZOLETTO: Dear wife, I owe all this to you.

CECILIA: I was the cause of your troubles, so it is only right that I should know how to put them right. I wanted a superior residence and it was my fault that you took this new apartment. Yet even from that has come good. For if we had not taken this superior residence, we should never have found the friendship of these two ladies. All this would never have happened. But it is not for us to sing the praises of The Superior Residence. [*She turns and addresses the audience*] Let us leave praise and blame to those who are qualified to give it, to those who have the right to give it – to all who, through us, may now feel their hearts full of kindness, gentleness, and love.

CURTAIN

MORE ABOUT PENGUINS
AND PELICANS

For further information about books available from
Penguins please write to Dept EP, Penguin Books Ltd,
Harmondsworth, Middlesex UB7 0DA.

In the U.S.A.: For a complete list of books available
from Penguins in the United States write to Dept CS,
Penguin Books, 625 Madison Avenue, New York, New
York 10022.

In Canada: For a complete list of books available from
Penguins in Canada write to Penguin Books Canada
Ltd, 2801 John Street, Markham, Ontario L3R 1B4.

In Australia: For a complete list of books available
from Penguins in Australia write to the Marketing
Department, Penguin Books Australia Ltd, P.O. Box
257, Ringwood, Victoria 3134.

In New Zealand: For a complete list of books available
from Penguins in New Zealand write to the Marketing
Department, Penguin Books (N.Z.) Ltd, P.O. Box 4019,
Auckland 10.

FIVE ITALIAN RENAISSANCE COMEDIES

MACHIAVELLI: The Mandragola
ARIOSTO: Lena
ARETINO: The Stablemaster
GL' INTRONATI: The Deceived
GUARINI: The Faithful Shepherd

Edited by Bruce Penman

From Machiavelli's sharp satire on a corrupt clergy to Guarini's pure pastoral, this collection represents the finest comedy to come out of the Italian Renaissance. Ariosto and Aretino bring us vivid and subtle portraits of life in the ducal states of Ferrara and Mantua, while 'The Deceived' illustrates perfectly the Italian genius for light comedy bordering on farce – it will be of special interest to English readers as an early treatment of the theme of *Twelfth Night*. All the plays in this volume are examples of the sophisticated wit and humour of the Renaissance, and in making us laugh they show us the world of amusing intrigue and interesting depravity beneath the glittering surface.

PENGUIN CLASSICS

'Penguin continue to pour out the jewels of the world's classics in translation . . . There are now nearly enough to keep a man happy on a desert island until the boat comes in' – Philip Howard in *The Times*

A selection